MISSION: OUTBREAK

Michael Gilwood

CACTUS RAIN
PUBLISHING

Arizona USA

MISSION: OUTBREAK

Published by Cactus Rain Publishing, LLC
San Tan Valley, Arizona, USA
www.CactusRainPublishing.com

ISBN 978-1-947646-07-0

Cover Design by Cactus Rain Publishing, LLC
Certified Proofreader Anita Beery, www.AnitaBeery.com

Published October 1, 2019
Published in the United States of America

MISSION: OUTBREAK

Michael Gilwood

DEDICATION

In 1968, from the back of a tan-coloured Volkswagen station wagon somewhere near Tunbridge Wells, I lay on my back and looked towards the stars. On this particular clear expressive evening, I asked my dad why the stars never shifted position when the car moved. He replied, "They are too far away. If I drove a little faster, they might change position."

"How fast?" I asked. That night I heard about the speed of light for the first time. I was looking at three stars in a row and they fascinated me. Shortly afterwards he bought me a telescope, allowing my imagination to see afar. I dedicate this book in his memory.

Peter John, may your lathe keep turning.

PROLOGUE

Just like planet Earth, their glaciers had come and gone. Gibbous landscapes, pocked and empty, meant the passing of another life cycle on their world. Above them, their changeless moons carried their secrets, silent and Omni-watchful.

Although these beings were not entirely humanlike, they were flesh and blood. Later, as they looked into and across the depths of space with conjecture, they speculated and told stories about someone like them: someone with intelligence; someone who could travel in that vast blackness; someone who would, one day, find them. They had dreamt for centuries what it was like—who and what was out there? What shape did they have? These inspiring and unanswered questions gave birth, with the help of sophistication and technology, to new ideas. As soon as they possessed the power, they began to seek fellowship among the stars. During their explorations, they encountered life in many forms and watched the workings of evolution on one thousand worlds. They saw how often the first sparks of intelligence flickered in the cosmic infinity. Our planet was like a shimmering lighthouse in the night.

An unknown time ago, a survey ship entered our solar system after a hundred-year voyage. The explorers swept past the frozen outer planets, paused briefly above Mars, and looked down on Earth. They saw a world teeming with life. For centuries to come, they studied, collected, and catalogued. They began to modify, and they tinkered with the destiny of many species on land and in the seas. There was so much to do in this universe of a hundred billion suns, so they set out once more into the abyss. They knew that they would never come this way again. There was no need: We, the servants they had left behind, would one day find them.

1. Anomaly

Cold temperatures floated above the ground like a hover-blanket. Early white tendrils of fog swirled between hardy trees agitating the frail, seasonal leaves of a terminated autumn. Thin crystals of ice began to form on parts of a riverbank like watery, mirrored stalagmites. The cloudless night enhanced and deepened the surrounding silvery-blackness of morning, making the stars unnaturally pointy and crisp.

Courageously and valiantly, Philip Wakefield embraced a down jacket and sneaked outside, traipsing the icy bracken. Stiff, cold fingers made it hard as he shakily unfolded the tripod for his Meade telescope. Watching the stars against his parents' wishes again, he silently turned towards the house and released a despondent frown. He didn't feel guilty; he just hated doing things behind their backs.

A precise hand adjusted the tripod. It clicked. *What more do they want?* he thought again. I already have one foot in med school. Philip had worked hard to please them, getting his application to Yale near the top of the pile on the dean's desk. *Wasn't that enough?* Burning thoughts became agitated words.

Throughout school, Philip's inspirations and incentives were physics and astronomy, not anatomy or physiology. He had become fascinated with telescopes when he was only six years old, and much of his youth had been spent collecting lenses of all shapes and sizes. These he had mounted in cardboard tubes, making instruments of ever-increasing power until he was familiar with the stars and planets, the nearer space stations and the entire landscape within thirty kilometres of his home. He had been lucky in his place of birth, among the mountains of Colorado. In almost every direction, the view was spectacular and inexhaustible.

He had spent hours exploring, in perfect safety, the peaks which every year took their toll of careless climbers. Though he had seen much, he had imagined even more. He liked to pretend that over each crest of rock, beyond the reach of his telescope, were magic kingdoms full of wonderful creatures. And so, for years he had speculated about visiting the places his lenses brought to him. Philip's sights were on becoming a deep-space specialist, and, even as a university student, he still had to secretly sneak off to the library or the back garden to read about astrophysics. He'd endured the pursuit of medicine only because of his parents' adamant determination to have him follow in their footsteps. They were both admired town doctors.

By the end of the twentieth century, the frantic search for other worlds had begun. They were worlds to conquer, worlds to populate, and worlds in which to begin again. This type of investigation required newer, more expensive orbiting telescopes that were capable of pinpointing, cataloguing and apprehending microwave transmissions in planetary systems from the farthest reaches. Now, almost a century later, planet Earth had sent out radio waves in all configurations, on all frequencies, in all directions, and in all languages without apparent success.

A hundred years to attain a better cartographical idea of what was out there wasn't what the scientists had in mind. Seventy thousand catalogued possibilities with the capability of sustaining carbon-based life didn't mean a link or a contact.

In 2080, the Charon Four space probe, like its predecessors, was to explore and survey the outer regions of the solar system. The probe had been equipped with the most sophisticated sensing apparatus and photographic technology. It was orbiting one thousand miles above Triton when a weak signal slowly began to appear on Houston's monitors like a stuttering noise. The engineers feared the worst. They thought a wire or a connector had come loose, but as the crystal-clear images of Triton's surface began emerging strip-by-strip on the visual display units, the noise transformed into a rhythmical and steady signal with pauses every four seconds. Eyes fixed on monitors. Hands waited for computer readouts. Undeniably, the noise was not theirs. The three-billion-mile-distant digital footprint was unlike anything they had ever heard.

A few days later, newspapers told the world that the probe had encountered something unusual. On page 90, a skimpy column mentioned the existence of an intercepted signal originating from the surface of the Neptunian moon and that NASA was attempting to cryptanalyze the transmission of unknown origin using the finest etymologists on the planet.

"Any ideas as to what it could be?" Philip could see the dismissal and intimidation in the other students when he asked the question. To him, the more the unexplained phenomena provoked and enticed his imagination, the more his fascination for this strange new visitor started to grow.

As the days passed, Philip had no idea that his life was about to take a turn for the worse. That Saturday, after a party at his best friend Mike's house, Philip's parents had arranged to come and pick him up. They never arrived. Two hours later, the phone rang. It was the police. His parents had been killed coming out of their driveway. Some drunken idiot had taken them from him.

Distraught, both Mike and Philip enrolled in the military as pilots. Philip's doctoring days had terminated. Military discipline would help ease the pain of losing his parents.

Three years after the discovery of the signal, thirty-five fact-hungry, diversely trained scientists eagerly began a two-year trip towards Neptune's ice-covered moon to get a closer look at whatever it was out there, three billion miles away.

At the age of twenty-five, Dr Norman Bell received the Nobel Prize in physics. His theories on space travel astounded even the most prominent minds. At the age of twenty-seven, he had become one of the wealthiest men on the planet.

Earth gasped, as the group of scientists led by Dr Bell descended onto a moon beyond the *liveable* barrier. If Triton could be reached and landed on, it proved that man could exist in temperatures far below what was previously imagined. Norman Bell's self-funded investigation brought fresh optimism into space exploration. Saturn's moon, Titan, with its temperatures barely reaching 100 kelvin, had a similar gravity to Earth. People began to settle there in 2057, but it was still too close to the sun.

3

The Triton signal gave the world's space agencies an excuse to take the step they had always been afraid to take. Never before had anyone ventured outside the liveable barrier, the human comfort zone, the difference between life and death. Scientists considered it ludicrous.

"A manned craft going farther than Saturn? My God, it's too cold! Apart from it being a waste of money, it would be suicide!" They said he was mad.

Triton was strategically perfect. Its distance, its gravity and its newly scientifically studied surface conditions made it the right choice for future human colonisation.

While investigating the source of the anomalous signal, the goal of the scientific team was to prepare Triton for future missions. This included atmosphere modification, constructions, out-world hydroponics, agriculture and phytobiology.

In February of that year, they set off after their preparation for the basin of Mangwe Cavus, a spacious valley on Triton's equator from where the signal had originated. Triton's severe temperature, but acceptable surface conditions, provided hope for the type of atmospheric reconstruction the scientists had in mind.

The scientists were divided into specialised groups for the mission. As one group erected living quarters and a communications centre, another analysed the surface and implanted oxygen modifiers.

The head team, led by Norman himself, went in search of the continuing signal that was now loud and clear. Philip had once heard a recording of it while he was undergoing his military training: something like a simultaneous high- and low-pitched drone with intervals.

A couple of days later, Norman told Houston that the anomalous signal had originated from a discarded, cigarette box-sized container. There were indications of inexplicable polymers at the site. After tests had been run, he called it a meta-material that could only have come from space. None of the scientists knew how it worked. More remarkable was the exact frequency of 80 gigahertz.

"It's the hardest, lightest material I've ever laid eyes on!" exclaimed Norman Bell on a long-distance interview from his three-billion-mile-away, gloomy outpost.

By May of that year, Philip, as was his custom to look in the newspaper, noticed there were no reports on the Triton mission where they were usually found. An admonishing silence gripped the scientific world. A month passed without a single word.

In early June, a public seminar was held in Geneva concerning the disappearance of Norman Bell and his crew. It was during the second day of the seminar when a NASA representative in constant communication with the Triton team reported they had discovered something, but didn't know what.

"There's a lot of commotion going on up there, that's why we haven't heard from them. Unfortunately, we cannot tell you more at this stage." An eruption of simultaneous voices shook the lectern.

"Ladies and gentlemen, please, please. We will keep you updated as soon as the news becomes available." The microphone fell to the refectory table alongside the lectern as the spokesperson scurried offstage. Then it happened. As the representative disappeared from view, a nearby reporter grabbed the fallen microphone, shouting, "They've found human remains!"

The world had been witness. It wasn't much, but it was enough. The newspapers filled with denials and hoaxes, but it didn't work for long as the truth slowly leaked out. By the end of June, Philip had learned that a construction team had discovered sixteen human remains in the Yasu Sulci Crater south of Mangwe Cavus. It happened when a group of scientists had commenced building a supply hangar, and, as a result, they decided to explore the crater further.

On June 29th, the Evening Standard website reported:
Human remains discovered on Triton, fact or fiction?

It had been more than a week since Norman Bell and his team of scientists dug up human remains on the eastern rim of Yasu Sulci Crater. The site, completely buried under rock and debris, revealed sixteen perfectly preserved biological entities in various stages of destruction. They ascertained that an asteroid striking the surface of Triton two hundred years ago had killed them.

Philip's tongue frantically bobbed about in his mouth as he read on.

"Norman Bell is at present searching for remnants and other significant artefacts."

They sent the right man to do the job; he's certainly crazy enough to pull this off, thought Philip.

In the forthcoming days, NASA confirmed that the "Human Town" was destroyed by a rampant asteroid and promptly blamed the asteroid for the deaths of the sixteen humans.

The Church emphatically denied all relation to the team of explorers. They stated their findings and beliefs were imaginary tales, and excommunicated them as being ungodly followers.

"They are a disgrace to the beliefs of our children." Pope Clement spent two hours a day, on every TV channel, convincing the world the wrongness of false beliefs. "The temptation of mankind comes in many forms," he said repetitively.

"God's voice will send us clear instructions when the time comes." When his wrinkled Tartuffian face didn't fill the screen, TV shows topped-up the spaces with animation artists who produced renderings of possible aliens for viewer comments. Nonetheless, special services were held in churches, mosques, and temples around the world. Prayers were offered to the lost souls recently discovered on the hostile moon.

In Britain, sixty-five-year-old Sir Thomas Grayson, the internationally famous best-selling science-fiction author and mathematician, not only told the British media that the discovery of human remains on another planet is the discovery of the millennium, he declared, "It is the beginning of an era."

The next day, Norman Bell dominated the front-page news again. His smiling face was discernible through the helmet of his thermal suit as he sat with a human form perched on a chair beside him. The biological entity was in perfect condition. It was perfectly preserved and intact. His scientific team was behind him. The headline read: Here's the Proof

These were not anthropoid; they were irrefutably human. In later years, specimen samples sent to Earth for examination revealed that not only were they similar, they were identical to us. The sixteen perfectly preserved bodies in a variety of battered stages had died around the time of General Custer's defeat. Where was humanity then? Norman Bell had also found a technology unlike our own. It shed light on a completely new avenue of science. It was unfamiliar and superbly advanced.

US Congress members were keen to display their forward thinking and their proactive engagement with space technology. They said their awareness of the benefits that the knowledge of these alien technologies might bring to the nation unsurpassed reimbursement. Whether or not external governments were peeved that they had no exclusive rights to the alien technology and the potential treasures that might be on Triton, their electorates made it abundantly clear that they were happy.

"At least another form of technologically capable intelligence exists," they said. But what really astonished them was that the remains appeared human in what had seemed up until then to be a vast, hostile, and empty universe.

The world had stirred; a reborn hope existed amongst the inhabitants of Earth. The existence of extraterrestrial life sent shivers down backs, intensifying the imagination and confidence of almost everyone.

Human phylogeny now had a different branch, a twisty-turn in the road they didn't know existed. Out there, in the infinite void of space, other sapiens roamed and examined planet Earth with particular interest. Earth had been a cynical observation table to a superior race, just as someone with a microscope studies creatures that multiply in a drop of water.

Scientific experts began to rework the impervious evolutionary beginnings on Earth, hoping this was a collision between mankind and technology. Disarray dominated the scientific world for years. Previous beliefs were hacked to pieces. Scientists had dissected the Earth and exhausted its scientific resources as if it had just awakened from a tremendous dream.

Every archaeological digging had been re-dug; every language on the planet had been broken down and re-studied. What had they missed? History was back in its beginning stages. They had used a technological scalpel on their own home while looking for answers. There were none, and that's why the *Excelsior* had to go.

Then came the agenda from above: the formalities, the stern smile. The orders were straightforward and simple: "Someone has to go out there."

Captain Philip Wakefield had been the most suitable for the job. It was the reason he was here in this hard, auto body-shaping chair, staring into the void, seventeen years later.

After serving seven years together in the military, ship commander Captains Philip Wakefield and Mike Branigan and their crew had spent four hard years training for this mission and a further six just to get to Mintaka, or in the case of Captain Mike, to get to Alnilam. Like Philip on the *Excelsior*, Mike now entered the outer orbit of Alnilam on-board the *Renaissance*. They had personally selected their crew for will and determination from more than two thousand aspiring possibilities. Now, their search for answers and more evidence had begun in the infinite Milky Way. What Norman Bell had discovered was merely a tiny piece of the puzzle. It was only the beginning. But this was a well-planned trip to Mintaka and Alnilam and the study of their planets.

Like Philip, Mike's loyalty and commitment was to search for extraterrestrial life forms and any category of higher technology that they could retrieve and eventually use to benefit the ever-mounting human need. The mission, named Outbreak, received top priority.

If humans did exist in the realms of space, and if they had existed in this domain for hundreds of years before then with the capability of space travel, they were out here somewhere. Philip would make sure to find them.

The identical spacecrafts *Excelsior* and *Renaissance* were finished in record time, taking only fourteen months to complete. Philip had been there to examine and test-run the *Excelsior* before they set off. A third spacecraft, a commercial freighter, transported one thousand scientists towards Alnitak to assist in the erection of Terron. Earth's most acclaimed scientists, awarded with the opportunity to participate, were rapidly building the metropolis as a command post in the Orion sector. Philip and his crew received regular updates concerning their progress. The scientists had reached their goal two years ahead of schedule.

Military activities on Earth had ceased, resulting in the rerouting of all available government funding to the multi-national construction of Terron, orbiting the last planet in the Alnitak system known astronomically as Cornopea.

Philip shuffled around on his commander's chair once more. *Damn*, he thought, *in those ten years, they'd figured out that the answers lay in Orion*. The information they'd pieced together before Norman Bell went crazy, walked out towards the Triton horizon and disappeared, led to Orion. Philip looked at the giant star Mintaka through the viewer. "What secrets are you hiding?" he whispered.

How many years were they going to devote to the search? How much money would they spend on this pursuit? It didn't really matter because they obviously knew where to look, and they wouldn't stop until they had either found what they were looking for or had satisfied themselves that there was nothing there.

The well-planned trip to Mintaka, a multiple star system one thousand light-years away, and the eventual study of its eight planets, also included Philip's best friend Captain Mike Branigan. Mike and his crew of four were now simultaneously entering the outer orbit of the large blue superstar, Alnilam, in the *Renaissance*.

Six years stuck in an oversized, sophisticated space vehicle without knowing what you are going to find does tend to work on one's mind. The academy psychologist warned them before they left. Philip, like the others, had altered personalities. It was unavoidable. Although they were scientists, they had no idea what was waiting for them. It inconspicuously played with their minds and their already overactive, tired imaginations. They spoke about their thoughts often during the journey while fantasising about the inhabitants of these worlds. What would they be like? Would they be friendly? Would they find what they came for?

Not even the Sentrywatcher computer, with her three septillion operations per second, could shed any light on their dilemma.

2. Sentrywatcher

Thought is provoked by uncertainty, just as their fears had amplified due to the exaggerated manifestations they had been pondering during the six-year journey. Braan, the farthest of the eight Mintakan planets, lethargically announced its arrival to the his crew on the radar as the blue circle breached the radar rim. Chemical engineer and ship's doctor, Baygorn Stanton, inched closer and said in an excited, yet unusual tone, "There she is."

Their ten-year wait could only make them, as always, silently speculate and swivel glances at each other. Philip watched as the sinister, digital ring representing an M-Class planet four times the size of Earth swung nearer to the centre of the monitor. By this time, the *Excelsior*, sensing their proximity, automatically began to reduce speed as the diminishing motor hum and an ever-dazzling display of lights acknowledged their approach. The Sentrywatcher computer came to life for the first time in six years.

A pulsating light pulled Philip to his senses. Two phosphorescent displays flicked on. Reams of numbers filled both screens in neat horizontal green and blue ranks. Information raced upwards and out of view as elementary quantities displayed themselves. The intricate scan process had begun.

"The elaborate on-board scanners will only begin their search for life forms once we have attained an acceptable altitude," said Baygorn, pressing a button. It was this unceasing analysis that would warn the crew of any change or any danger. Sentry-watcher would be their guide from now on.

"We will have to rely on her never-sleeping capability as she captures information received from the planet below," said flight engineer and weapons specialist Ramaan Davidson as he fiddled with a couple of buttons.

The images from the other cameras added nothing new. The long-hoped-for, long-feared encounter with the stars had, at last, happened. Ramaan remembered those first telescopic impressions he saw of Mintaka on Earth. He even drew representations of would-be surfaces. But there was one thing no electronic image or painting could possibly convey, and that was the overwhelming vastness of the nearing planet. He had never received such an impression when landing on a natural body like the moon or Mars during his training years before. Those were worlds he knew. He had read about them in books and had seen pictures of vehicles with people roaming the surface.

His large, muscular frame trembled, thinking of how small they actually were in comparison to what lay ahead. His judgment was wholly altered by the fact that this was a planet millions of times farther away than anywhere man had gone previously.

As Braan expanded onto the viewer, eager eyes scrutinised copious information oozing onto the video display unit.

"It's a bit hazy, try a higher magnification!" Ecstatically Lexia, analytical science and linguistics expert of the team, moved closer. It was no wonder that she felt a sense of insignificance and even depression as the planet of sculptured, ageless rock filled more and more of the external display. There was also a sense of danger here that was wholly novel to her experience. In every earlier landing she performed, she had known what to expect. There was always the possibility of accident, but never of surprise.

"Patience, Lexia, I'm working as fast as I can!" exclaimed Ramaan, giving her the eye.

Surface analysis had begun. The image was an immense landscape still too far away for them to capture the finer detail.

Philip, like all space commanders, was a cautious man. He had looked long and hard at the planetary surface while choosing the point of touchdown.

"Some of those interior sections are dotted with mountains and low hills. What we need is a flat area to land and begin our investigation. Sentrywatcher indicates there is a small variety of plant and insect life. It gets denser the farther inland we go. There are dozens of small islands scattered about on a frozen sea." Ramaan's eyes jiggled everywhere. Life forms showed as coloured blips on their display. Philip walked to Ramaan's side.

"Our hand-held communicators, Sonysubishi C-12, will constantly transmit and receive information, including photographic and surface analysis, to and from Sentrywatcher via the pod."

Lexia, overhearing everything and missing nothing, walked to the main console. "How does Sentrywatcher distinguish between intelligent and non-intelligent life?" Lexia's gaze hooked on to the intricate video display unit while extracting the still-ambiguous clarity of the terrain. She fixated her eyes on stationary coloured blips.

Baygorn smiled at her. "Sentrywatcher's scanner is carbon- and silicon-sensitive. She also has to familiarise herself with whatever we will find down there. At this stage, we know as much as she does. What Sentrywatcher momentarily calls intelligent is a carbon-based object with the ability of vertical movement. Unfortunately, she hasn't yet fathomed out the difference between friendly and non-friendly. We have to give her time to do her calculations and collect more information."

Philip continued to look at the display. "Okay, let's land ourselves and set up camp there on that flat area, not too close to those blips." As Lexia painstakingly studied the reading, Ramaan, with equally trained meticulousness, typed in the coordinates. Sentrywatcher acknowledged with a beep.

Ramaan continued with the analysis. "There's plenty of oxygen and a number of trace elements. There is carbon and iron in large quantities. Surface temperature is presently six below, sunrise is imminent. Sentrywatcher has identified two unknown elements. Look at that spectrum!"

"That's one of the many reasons why we're here, Ramaan." Baygorn took a reading and fed the results into Sentrywatcher.

"In 2084, Dr Robert Holsworth invented the Higg's Ion-Engine, enabling us to travel many times the speed of light. The Higg's Ion-Engine gathers the fuel necessary for the journey from space itself." As he often did, Baygorn was thinking aloud. "It's just a Tachyon gatherer. Robert referred to it as a TGC engine. I actually met him once at a convention in Cambridge." Baygorn twiddled a knob. "A very interesting, cold type, he was explaining the effects of gravity at high speed between martinis. Thanks to his TGC, we were able to travel just under a thousand light-years in a little over six years."

A blue light pulsated on the console. "Almost there!" Philip's solid statement attracted the attention of everyone.

The hum of the main engines weakened.

Lexia's excited voice leaped from the cockpit. "Engines One and Four have been cut!" The reducing mechanical drone vibrated through the *Excelsior*, and they perceptibly felt the change in gravity.

As defence specialist and strategy analyst, Alana Norton drove the vehicle into the pod, and the main communications screen blinked on, making the rest of them jump.

"Hello, Philip, this is Commander Jones from Terron. How are you holding out up there? I won't take up too much time, as I know you are about to leave the *Excelsior*. I thought you would like to know that Captain Branigan began his descent towards Pleniton six hours ago. I would like to take the opportunity to wish you all the best of luck before your departure. This is the biggest event since Norman Bell landed on Triton in the eighties. All eyes and ears are on you." The screen flickered and went off. The crew looked at each other.

"If anyone wants to say anything before we leave, now's the time." Equally confused, Philip looked at remorseless and solemn faces. Alana smiled. In all her bewilderment, she was thinking that one thousand scientists on Earth would have cheerfully mortgaged their souls for this opportunity. Now they could only watch over the TV screens, biting their lips and thinking how much better they could do the job. They were probably fighting amongst themselves, but there was no alternative. The inexorable laws of celestial mechanics had decreed that the *Excelsior* and her five occupants were to be the first to ever make contact with the Mintakan planets.

Philip broke the tension. "Okay, let's keep those heads screwed on straight and those thoughts clear, got it? No time for goof-ups. The pod's auto-mapper is going to start charting the surface the moment we unhook ourselves from the *Excelsior*. As soon as we land, Sentrywatcher and the pod will continue talking with each other. This information will be accessible on your C-12, so keep it handy." Alana climbed into the pod. The other three were safely strapped in, so Philip initiated their disentanglement from their temporary home, the *Excelsior*.

Some decisions would be delegated to Terron. While they were away, the *Excelsior* would be virtually helpless in her lone orbit, but Mintaka was a prize worth any risk, short of a suicide mission. For the first time in our history, an element of total uncertainty had entered human affairs. Uncertainty was one thing that neither scientists nor politicians tolerated well. If that was the price of resolving it, the *Excelsior*, like the *Renaissance* and her crew, would be expendable.

There was a creak followed by a heavy thunk sound and a crunch as the latches and couplers released them. It made Philip's stomach go into his mouth. Seconds later, a pithy scraping sounded before weightlessness made whatever they had forgotten to put away lift itself into the air.

Eagerly glimpsing through inadequate portholes, the crew saw Braan's sparse, silvery ethereal rings. The dull green-blue colour radiating from the surface of Braan made them feel insecure. They had practised for this moment so many times in the simulator, but this time was for real. There are phobias and things that not even the most sophisticated simulator can predict or teach.

Ramaan looked towards the viewer. "There's an icy lake next to the hilly area where we're headed. Dawn is close but it's still quite dark down there."

Baygorn unhooked his safety harness and squinted into the visual scanner. "This information would have already been sent off to Terron for their study and perusal. Whatever we look at, they look at, and a week from now, those on Earth will be watching it as well."

Jim, their commander, had told them before they left that they would have daily updates. It was their own TV programme where they would televise their progress for those interested in it.

A control panel blinked on and warned them of turbulence as they entered the thermosphere. A yellow pulsing console light abruptly flicked on. Mintaka, from their plummeting perspective, had scarcely risen above the horizon. It formed a twilight barrier revealing thin wispy noctilucent clouds laying in their path like a luminous blanket of oranges and reds. "Hold on, this might get a bit bumpy!" Passing through, the pod jerked and shuddered like a plastic toy.

At the time of their separation, the single moon was not visible. It was on the other side of Braan. An hour later, the *Excelsior* was photographing and surveying it as the satellite came into view from behind the planet. They studied the results that appeared on the viewer. It was nothing like their own moon, with its population of 80,000. It was inhospitable and uninviting.

As the pod gently lowered towards Braan, Philip's thoughts were with Captain Mike Branigan. Their synchronized landings were separated by only a handful of hours.

The landing area was sandy. It made their arrival tricky. Excitement bulged from their frames as the pod made a gentle thump on the soft surface one hundred metres from the edge of an icy lake.

Braan was as silent as a tomb which, perhaps, it was. There were no radio signals on any frequency, no vibrations suggesting activity the seismographs could detect. It was ominously quiet. One might have expected that even an asteroid would be noisier.

What did we expect? Philip wondered. A welcome committee? He was unsure whether he was disappointed or relieved.

Ramaan immediately began scanning the surface composition and said, "Most of our Periodic Table is here. Even several trace elements are in abundance. Radiation levels are low. Gravity is at G.91. It looks okay."

Their orders were to wait two hours, then to go out and explore. They spent the wait time monitoring their probing instruments or simply looking at the landscape out of the observation ports. Is this world alive? they asked themselves, over and over again. Is it dead? Or is it merely sleeping?

The early-morning sky was navy-blue. Absorbing this out-world beauty, Baygorn and Alana began to finger through the star maps. Betelgeuse and Saiph, Orion's principal stars, were on opposite ends of the horizon. Baygorn and Alana smiled at each other before turning their attention to Mintaka's pea-sized, miniature red globe peeking above the horizon.

Lexia was deep in thought. She was glancing at strange formations of thin clouds in the distance. She mumbled something about them being far higher than the ones on Earth before commenting on their distinctive autumnal look. The crescent moon was lowering behind the high-altitude clouds. Their cirrus form and wispy extremities were dimly illuminated in an ominous brownish-red. It was a signal that the sun of this planet had awoken from slumber. *This is actually an alien dawn*, she thought.

As Mintaka lazily initiated the climb into the amethyst sky, the mountains' slow morning cold shadows began caressing the pod. It was a barren-looking orb, tinted faintly yellow, like crumbly parchment. Ramaan performed an atmosphere check.

"Minus five degrees. Oxygen levels are quite high. Argon is a little over 1 percent. Nitrogen is at 30 percent. It's a bit like Earth 200 million years ago. It should be okay." Turning, Ramaan's smiling face confirmed the okay.

There was a silent commotion. Philip could feel it. He felt the electricity alive in everyone, even himself. The body movements, the occasional twisting lip, the upping of a brow. He sensed the nervousness in them all; it was a day-dreamy, almost uncontrollable urge.

"Let's get those suits on. It's time."

Baygorn moved to zip up the rest of the crew. He made doubly sure there were no leaks. It seemed like an eternity. Lexia helped him put on his suit.

Philip and his crew walked to the back of the pod where the armoured vehicle was waiting. They climbed in. With a gloved hand, Alana pressed a switch, and the side of the pod opened outwards like a budding flower, allowing the first wisps of Braan air to enter. Silently rolling out the pod, Alana drove them outside.

Philip could sense them smiling underneath their visors. He turned his vision and thoughts to the outside. His training—he remembered it well. Part of it consisted of previous landings on other worlds. What they did when they stepped out for the first time. What were their first words? The first man on Mars, way back in 2028, announced,"Eagle 2 has hit the sand, Houston."

Then there were the Europa and Titan settlements a couple of decades later: "Houston, the *Discoverer* has touched down safely." My God, how far we'd come! Never before had Philip felt so strongly his kinship with that long-dead Egyptologist. Not since Howard Carter had first peeked into the tomb of Tutankhamen could any man have known a moment such as this, yet the comparison was almost laughably ludicrous.

About a hundred metres from the pod, Alana suddenly stopped the vehicle, jerking Philip to his senses. He inhaled deeply and was astonished by a peculiar, but familiar odour. Puzzled, he inhaled again, this time concentrating on the smell. There was no doubt about it, it was vanilla. His mind raced into overdrive, searching for an explanation. He only flared his nostrils and made a comment about the temperature.

"Could be the plant life," said Baygorn, noticing Philip twitching his nose and fully anxious to analyse something, anything. To the right of them, maybe fifty metres away through the porthole, were patches of deep-green vegetation. Baygorn took last-minute measurements from the vehicle's control panel, and when all the protocol checks were completed, he gave Philip the "okay" sign.

Philip secured his visor and thermal panel on the suit, walked towards the opened entrance and climbed out. As boot gently caressed sand, he reached downwards, not speaking, and touched his knees. He realised that this was a moment for History, not to be spoiled by unnecessary small talk, and continued on his unvoiced inspection.

Alana climbed out and pointed. "Is that a cycad? How odd, a bit prehistoric." Baygorn moved towards the plant. Alana, Ramaan, and Lexia climbed down onto the surface. There was nothing particularly exotic or alien about the scene: In fact, it bore a considerable resemblance to an early-morning desert landscape. Philip felt a vague sense of disappointment. After all this effort, there should have been some dramatic, even transcendental revelation.

Then Ramaan saw it. "Hey, Baygorn, look over there!"

Baygorn swung around, first looking at Ramaan, and then followed his hand. "What on God's Earth is that?"

"Not so fast, Baygorn. Look at it again!" Alana's trembling voice opened the door of question. From maybe ten metres away, they could see the plant begin to move and shift.

"What in the—Did you see that?" Baygorn gained pace and reached the plant before the rest of them.

Quickly, Philip caught up and held him back, propping his shoulder. "Take it easy, this is an alien planet with alien habits. We must expect anything, it doesn't matter how strange."

The plant, about six feet tall, was dipping its tentacles into the icy lake laying at its roots. Philip thought briefly of a hungry Texan oil rig. Up and down, up and down, and in goes a tentacle. They followed the tentacle. Baygorn bent down.

"Not too close, Baygorn!" Alana came up behind him. She was watching the plant carefully.

"Look at this! The end of the tentacle has teeth. On the sides near the teeth, there are two sharp-looking claws. It seems to be drilling into the ice, and then sucking up food."

Baygorn bent down. "No wait, it is putting whatever it sucks up into a hole. Probably, it's a mouth."

Ramaan scanned the horizon with binoculars. "There are quite a few of these things around. They're all doing the same as this one."

Baygorn, now fearless, moved closer to get a look at the mouth. "It looks like the underside of a mushroom. These gills have more teeth." The mouth was chewing something. With well-trained hands, Baygorn took out a scalpel from his side bag. "Think it'll let me take a sample?"

"You can try," said Lexia.

The mouth was on what appeared to be the front, so Baygorn crept behind. The tentacle didn't stop fidgeting. From their distance, they couldn't see what it was doing. As Baygorn reached the rear of the creeper plant, it sensed his intention and immediately turned to face him.

Ramaan noticed the bewildered expression on Baygorn's face as he backed away. "Where's its eyes? I don't see any eyes. How did it know?"

Slowly, the creeper regained confidence and returned to its haven of ice. Undefeated, with scalpel in hand, Baygorn quickly moved closer to the creeper, swipe-cutting at a small strand from a stationary tentacle. As living tissue fell to the ground, the creeper turned, faced him and barked before returning to its icy meal.

While Baygorn strolled towards the vehicle with the sample placed in the container, the rest of them scanned the horizon with mystified interest. The terrain was slightly reddish and dotted with low hills. A speckled abundance of shrubbery reminded Philip and Ramaan of desert cassia or desert broom. It appeared in hugging clusters; hundreds of them, as far as the eye could see.

Lexia was busy looking up at the slowly intensifying morning. The waxing moon grew brighter as it escaped clouds near the horizon and entered a patch of clear dull sky.

Climbing back into the vehicle, Alana carefully drove them towards a dip between two hills, away from the small lake where they had landed. On the other side, and taking them completely by surprise, were four immensely tall vertical columns resembling giant cigar pylons.

Ramaan studied his C-12 as Baygorn raised his binoculars. "They are over five hundred metres high." Baygorn handed Ramaan the binoculars. "Take a look."

"Is that an entrance at the bottom? That seems to be a lookout point at the top, too." For his entire professional career, Ramaan had always looked upon the universe as an arena for the titanic forces. He had never believed that life actually played an important role in the scheme of things. But now there was proof that life not only existed outside the solar system, it had scaled heights far beyond anything that man had achieved, or could hope to reach, for centuries to come. Ramaan handed Philip the binoculars.

"Hmm, we are definitely not alone here. There must be enough material for decades of research on this frozen carcass of a world."

Alana, overhearing Philip's comment, registered no carbon-based life signs in the vicinity. With the help of Sentrywatcher, Alana steered the vehicle in the direction of Mintaka towards a rectangular object Sentrywatcher had picked up in their vicinity.

Steering towards it, an enormous yellowish bunker came into view from behind a small hill. Alana thought it looked like a derelict aeroplane hangar, only this one was much larger, and it took them almost ten minutes to reach at full speed. The vehicle's top speed was thirty kilometres per hour with the batteries fully charged. The neglected bunker, eroded by time and desert wind, from their proximity appeared ghostly. Its fading colour was evidence of the lack of upkeep. They drove around its discoloured form searching for an entrance. There was none. They couldn't find a door or a way in, so in the end they continued on their way in the direction of Mintaka.

Twenty minutes later, they dipped downwards and arrived at a small plain with a clump of trees; an icy oasis about ten metres side to side. One of the trees remarkably resembled a willow. The longer, slightly yellowed, hairy branches that had been trapped in the iced soup were helpless. From closer inspection, they could see that the ice had begun to melt in places. Baygorn got out of the vehicle to take a sample of the water. Here, they noticed there were more of the creeper plants, but these were dormant and motionless.

Inquisitively, Alana moved closer to one of the creepers and started studying it more closely. "I don't see any eyes." Her voice was alarmed. Alana began to comment on strange lumps on what she called the head. She probed and prodded the indigenous life form until a piece came off in her gloved hand. It was soft, slightly squishy, and there were no bones. She squeezed the boneless effigy, and it started to twitch as the nerve cells died out. At precisely that moment, another creeper suddenly, without warning, woke from its peaceful siesta and started advancing towards her.

She jumped back a step with her ion pistol at the ready. No one knew what to do. "Do we attack or defend?" Captivated, everyone watched as the creeper edged forward. The tentacles were frantically waving about, yet it still posed no threat. It was moving too slowly.

"What now?" asked Alana, and still moving backwards.

Ramaan pushed between her and the plant, and shot it near the middle. It fell down onto the cold, dry, sandy surface with a thud that awoke another plant from idle slumber. It unfolded itself as a flower would and started advancing towards both Ramaan and Alana with increased stride.

The clenching, menacing claws at the end of the tentacles made a clicking sound as the two-metre-high creeper attempted in vain to gain ground between itself and its aggressor.

"Now you've done it. It looks pissed," said Baygorn watching its movements. "There's a kind of extra-sensorial communication between them."

The creeper was moving on what appeared to be an elastic, rubbery root, slithering yet maintaining perfect balance as it shuffled. Its perpendicular mouth opened in a peculiar way, producing odd canine sounds. Alana fired her weapon at it. The thing died instantly.

Baygorn knelt down and began to examine the remains. His eagerness turned sour. "They don't have internal organs. There's no skeleton. Damn, it's all muscle tissue!"

It is in man's nature to meddle and destroy. If these plants had landed on Earth and then shot someone, what would we have done? Here the crew was on an alien world, a world that seemed increasingly absurd to them. In reality, they were the trespassers here, even if the life forms were plant-like. Here they didn't know the rules. Alana suddenly let out a perceptible shriek of alert, and everyone quickly turned and followed her hand.

"Look, over there!" They looked towards the hills, alive with dozens of zombie trees. Sentrywatcher had completely mapped the surface.

Philip and the others quickly entered the vehicle and contacted Sentrywatcher to receive the new coordinates of another hangar she'd found ten kilometres away from their present location. Pressing the expanded view, Philip scrutinised the map. He looked outwards along the axis of the world and could see strangely shaped continents separated by sporadic seas and hundreds of lakes. There were strange mountains at the south pole.

Baygorn showed interest in what Philip was looking at. "It's highly unlikely that our perceptive, slow-moving friends will be able to follow us."

Lexia interrupted him. "Hey, remember one of the blips we saw on the video display earlier up in the *Excelsior?* It's gone. If I'm reading my C-12 correct, it's moved."

Baygorn stared at his C-12, and uttered a grunt. Philip did the same. It was true. A blue blip, a carbon-based life form, had simply disappeared and reappeared in another sector of the map.

Baygorn looked at Philip blankly. "That's impossible; it's nine hundred kilometres away!"

Philip looked once more toward the C-12, and scratched his head. "But how? It doesn't make any sense."

A hangar appeared for their waiting imagination. It appeared smaller than the first one they had encountered and unmistakably had a different colour. Two white, closed, stage-like doors denominated an entrance, so they drove up and parked the vehicle directly in front.

Curiously, Ramaan got out first to study the doors. "It's a kind of plastic, stuff's incredibly hard."

Baygorn walked over to help Ramaan force them open. They stepped inside. On the other side of the door, the air was warm. The rise in temperature was obvious as steam formed on Philip's visor. He checked his C-12, and determined it to have breathable air. He took off his helmet and breathed deeply, filling his lungs. Baygorn calculated the hangar was more than a kilometre in length, and at least six hundred metres wide. Coming from inside the hangar was the faint hum of a motor. It echoed and vibrated with a constant din. Philip trained his ears and followed the sound about a hundred metres down a passage.

They felt the intense heat coming from the piece of equipment from more than a metre away. No one knew what it was. It resembled a boiler, functioning and humming: a round grey machine three metres high with red flashing lights. There were pipes and cables leading upwards towards the ceiling almost thirty metres above. At chest height, buttons and levers were labelled in a strange language.

Lexia moved closer. "Looks like Archaic Latin. I've never seen anything like this before."

On both sides, many cupboards and closets lined a wall. One of the cupboards had reams of an ultra-thin, extremely tough paper written in the same lettering, like letterheads. A variety of battered books written in Latin adorned a shelf. A case of odd metallic connectors lay forgotten underneath an overturned box. Powered upright slit lights were everywhere, providing their illumination.

In a cupboard to the left of the humming machine, Baygorn came across a yellow octagonal sphere the size of an apple. On closer inspection, there was a variety of coloured spherical objects. He superficially toyed with them, feeling their weight.

A proximity alarm sounded on their C-12. "We have company."

Alana excitedly ran back down the passage and disappeared through the entrance doors. She reappeared seconds later. "They've found us!" They quickly followed her back to the doorway and peered out. The nearby, arid landscape had come alive with writhing, barking creepers, all making their way towards the hangar like a forest in a gale-force wind. Alana, Philip and Baygorn went to the vehicle.

"What do you want me to do?" asked Lexia nervously.

Ramaan didn't reply to her urgent request. He was studying the spherical shapes with anticipation and desire. "They don't seem to have any surface features," he said as he gently rubbed his fingers on the exterior of the blue octagonal design. That was when he disappeared.

Lexia screamed. Her eyes widened. "Shit, where'd he go?"

Philip, Alana, and Baygorn ran to her, and the four of them anxiously looked around and at each other.

"Lexia, what happened? Where's Ramaan?" Philip and Alana were looking behind boxes and in cupboards.

"I was asking him what I should do, you know, talking. I saw him rub one of those blue spheres with his fingers. He was mumbling something, and then suddenly, poof, he vanished before my eyes. I know it sounds weird!"

"Calm down, Lexia, calm down! He has his communicator."

Getting over the shock of what had happened, their occasional glimpses one to the other looked for reassurance.

An irritating silence hovered as they waited for Ramaan to jump out from somewhere.

"Hey, you're not going to believe where I am!" The four of them jumped as Ramaan's voice blurted out of the C-12.

"These spheres are transportation devices of some kind. When I rubbed my fingers on that blue sphere, I ended up here. It's an immense complex." Ramaan sounded excited. "There's a bluish light in the distance, and I can hear faint grinding sounds. There's cupboards here as well, with the same spheres inside."

"Ramaan, listen, these creepers are getting too damn close! I'm sending Lexia across to you." Lexia's look drilled into Philip. She was afraid, but when Alana told her the threat was only fifty metres away and could break down the door, she falsely smiled and rubbed her fingers in more or less the same manner as Ramaan had. Everybody watched her. Lexia vanished in an instant. They waited, what seemed an eternity. Ten seconds later, Ramaan's gruff voice confirmed the arrival of Lexia.

"She's here. I got her."

The three of them turned around after hearing a tremendous crash. "Move it, they're here!" shouted Alana, rubbing the sphere. A nearby door fell to the ground. It was followed by the dull sound of breaking and clattering as the creepers entered the hangar in an attempt to gain access to their human prey. Philip saw a tentacle come around a corner as he disappeared.

Coming to, Philip sensed a simultaneous breathlessness and relief as Ramaan came into view. He felt numb, yet he wasn't numb. There were no lights or flashes. The nearest he could come to describing it was that it felt like thousands of ants crawling over his body. Ramaan took him by the shoulder.

Philip saw Lexia laughing. "You okay, Philip?"

"Bloody idiot, you gave us quite a scare back there!" Philip straightened himself. Alana helped Baygorn.

Ramaan's look intensified. "Now that the worst is over, check your C-12s."

Lexia, hearing Ramaan's request, pressed the position icon. "How's that possible? We're ten kilometres from the vehicle!" The rest anxiously did the same.

They were in another hangar, only this one was much larger than the one they had left. Philip looked down once more at the C-12 and gaped. Breaking through the thoughts of their find, the sounds and sights Ramaan had previously told them about hazily appeared in Philip's mind. As he focused in on a constant humming, Ramaan intentionally rubbed a yellow sphere.

"Wonder where this one goes," he said as he vanished. Moments later, he reappeared, holding a blue sphere with his suit torn and left arm bleeding.

Lexia ran to him. "What happened? Why in God's name do you do that?"

Ramaan was panting furiously. "The yellow ones take us to the woodlands we just escaped from. It was crawling with those plants. They are hostile! One of them jabbed me in the arm."

As Baygorn dressed the wound on Ramaan's arm, Philip's eyes went rummaging down the long passageway while listening to a humming motor a long way off. He glared into the infinite aisle, as the dimly illuminated corridor became a pinprick. Without waiting for the rest, he started to walk. Well-spaced, identical, unmarked doorways loitered on both sides, making a zigzag pattern. About two or three hundred metres down the corridor, he noticed a faint flashing light.

Philip brushed away thoughts of the flashing light for a second and thought, *it's too far away. Whatever it represented would have to remain a mystery for now.* Maybe he could get to it later. He tuned in once again to the humming and began to walk down the passageway to find whatever it was.

The mechanical unit, or so it seemed, looked like an oversized air conditioning unit. The writing on the front panel was in what appeared to be Chinese.

Alana returned. She had been searching through some of the doors a short way farther down the corridor. "They're storage areas. What do you think that is?" she asked, pointing at the machine. The last couple of her words reverberated down the infinite aisle.

Baygorn moved closer and said, "You know, this might very well be the first hangar we came across in the vehicle. I haven't noticed any doors. It certainly fits the description."

The blue light that Ramaan had described earlier was on the other side of the hangar. Philip could see it. No, now looking attentively, he could see many of them suspended on the ceiling, concentrating their irresistibly powerful violet light in a circular pattern downwards onto the ground level. Making their way towards it, they saw each door was a replica of the next. There were no names, markers or numbers, they were just doors.

Leading off from the long corridor were dozens of shorter perpendicular aisles that eventually led onto another six parallel, one-kilometre passageways. They, too, had the same unmarked doors. As there were no physical markings identifying what lay beyond and behind, they randomly opened some of them.

Reaching the first door instinctively made Alana draw her weapon, as no one knew what was inside. There was a plastic table with some papers on top. They could see it had been untouched and forgotten. Dust wafted through the air as Philip fingered the papers for the first time in incalculable years. The lettering on some of them was different from what they had seen so far. Black time-smeared ink had altered its colour to an unsavoury yellowy-brown.

Lexia, who loved languages, came to lend a hand. She was fluent in nine languages, including Khoisan and Sanskrit. "Let me have a look," she said.

Behind the table was another unmarked door. A workbench lay in the centre, and just behind it, shelving held a couple of time-ebbed books and accommodated small, neatly placed electronic boards. Everything was covered in an overly generous layer of dust.

"Well, obviously no one's been around here for a couple of years," thought Philip aloud.

"At least a hundred," broke in Baygorn, fingering the dust thickness. "Never seen dirt like this, not even in my Aunt Betty's place."

Ramaan stormed into the room. Seeing Philip was busy, he crept off, muttering about going to look for the hangar's power source. Ramaan returned a few minutes later and told them that he had found a solar energy converter. "That's not all I've found," he said impatiently.

"What do you mean?" Philip and Baygorn moved closer to Ramaan, but it was not easy for him to explain, even to himself.

"Come see for yourselves."

Calling for Alana and Lexia, Philip and Baygorn followed Ramaan for a short while before he disappeared into a room with cables leading to the roof.

Baygorn caught sight of an indigenous beetle scuffling across the floor and bent down to pick it up. "Looks hungry. My, my, take a look at this." Baygorn held it closer.

"It's definitely not the builder here. Crikey, it's got a good set of gnashers on it." Carefully, Baygorn set it down and watched it scuffle under a box.

The enormous generator-converter housed nearby was behind yet another unmarked door. Thousands of cables guided by metallic posts ran their course up to the ceiling before disappearing into the immense void of the hangar to their ultimate connections. It reconverted light from a weak Mintaka back into a usable power source during the day; but once night had fallen, the residual power stored in a giant battery lingering alongside the generator continued to power the hangar. The generator gently hummed.

His gloved hand shook excitedly as Ramaan pointed to a button on the side of the generator. "There, there it is. Take a look at that." The button on the side was marked "On/Off" in English.

"What the devil?" Philip retorted.

Ramaan smiled. "I told you that I'd found something else."

There were more controls described in English, a black intensity control and a black sensitivity lever. The words "Williams Star Converter" were neatly imprinted on the front just above the simple control panel.

"Anyone heard of Williams?" Philip got blank looks.

They entered and searched more doors, finding, as expected, that each room was different. Most of them had green electric plugs mounted on the wall near the desk. Some were tiny outlets almost like theirs; others looked heavy-duty and came with a toggle switch underneath.

Other rooms had elaborate mechanical pieces stored on shelves: small tubes, a pump maybe, and varying sizes of electronic boards unlike any they had seen before with squared components. Each respective laboratory was properly equipped for its respective research and development for a different part of something, but what was that something? They picked up whatever they could, mostly paperwork from the laboratories they visited and handed it to Lexia to study.

However, as they neared the open area with the suspended ceiling lights, the increasing luminosity became overbearing. It wasn't quite ultraviolet; it was an annoying intense blue that played havoc with their eyes. They could barely make out through the murky haze that it was an assembly plant. It was a dusty accumulation of hundreds of mechanical and electronic spare parts lying categorized in their respective boxes. Some of the components were by now already familiar to them. Twenty similar benches, all covered with an assortment of jumble, neatly filled the gigantic area. In the middle of the dazzle in the centre of the benches, a single, longer table stood out from the rest. Two assembled projects caked with time stood there upright, completed and forgotten.

The identical robots didn't appear to have been switched on. Maybe someone hadn't had time to. Measuring a little over two metres, they both had a very distinctive human likeness. The oversized feet and round faces, the five-digit hands all formed a part of these mechanical wonders. Even bulges appeared in the right places.

Philip walked to them with interest. "A robot is a continuation of the species that makes them. Our robots on Earth look like us; they perform tasks that we would normally do. In my opinion, whoever made these guys are in every way similar to us."

Lexia broke in. "Maybe those coloured blips on the scanner were robots and not life forms." In a way, although they never spoke about it, they hoped she was right. Even after intense preparation and extensive training, a robot sounded like a much better adversary.

"Lexia, that depends on their composition and intelligence. You know, some robots may take offence to your remark," added

Baygorn before moving over. "Okay, so each laboratory or unmarked door here in the hangar makes and manufactures its separate and individual piece for their slotting-in later. I can only presume all this takes place here on these tables. Then they stopped. Something must have happened here about a hundred years ago, something really bad." Baygorn briefly thought of a war or an outbreak, but then dismissed the idea, as there were no bodies anywhere.

"And this intense light, it's been on for a hundred years. No one even bothered to switch it off. Really odd. I'd say it could be a germ-free environment or an open-air clean room."

They could speculate about the use of the robots and to whom they served, but the most curious question that no one had an answer for was why their makers were familiar with English. Returning their guessing thoughts back to the situation at hand, Alana began to study the spheres.

"Blue means here, and the yellow means being scoffed by plants at the nursery."

"You got that one right, Alana. Tell me, where do you think the others go?" added Ramaan. "Speaking of nursery, when are we going to fetch the vehicle?"

As Ramaan finished his sentence, Lexia came in from another room holding more papers. "Looks like these robots are harvesters. You know, farming and stuff."

Following Philip, they made their way back to the entrance, where Ramaan rubbed a yellow sphere. He reappeared less than a minute later. "All clear. They've gone, but we've got quite some cleaning up to do." Some of the supplies they'd left behind had been damaged. Broken cupboards and upturned boxes were strewn everywhere, like the aftermath of a hurricane. Alana snuck off to the vehicle and returned with a blue-ray rifle. She set up the rifle on a tripod, walked up to the damaged doorframe and peered outside towards a dune about two hundred metres away. Both doors lay buckled on the outside in the sand. A single receding creeper about to reach the summit turned and looked in her direction. Alana pulled the trigger. A powerful beam of silver-blue energy left the front end and struck the creeper before it could warn the others. It disappeared in a brief puff of smoke.

Once more out in the fresh air, they noticed that the tiny red orb of Mintaka had now risen well above the horizon. As the temperature began to rise, they drove back to the pod to take water samples from the frozen lake before boarding the ship.

Due to the lack of light earlier, Ramaan hadn't noticed an island in the middle of the lake, about a kilometre or so away, so he called Philip to take a look. No one had ever seen a frozen alien lake before. Not until then did it dawn on him, or did Philip fully realize, what was happening. The ice was breaking up. It froze at night and thawed during the day like on Earth, but he tried to think of a reason for such a dramatic reality check. It was nothing like this alien world; this wasn't Earth.

"That looks like a building on the crest of the island's central ridge." Ramaan pointed to the island as Alana joined them.

Philip raised his binoculars. "Not just an ordinary building, more like an observatory. It's not quite the Jodrell Bank type, but there is a small parabolic dish." Ramaan and Philip exchanged glances and walked to the pod to remove an inflatable dingy from the back section. He pulled out the rubber cap, and the dingy began to unfold itself on the ground as the bottle of compressed air did its job. Ramaan picked it up, placed it on the verge of the lake, and Alana climbed in with him.

Alana always went into unknown situations. Not only was she the best of them in self-protection, she also knew what had to be done in extreme circumstances like if something jumped out from behind a door with two heads or dropped from the ceiling covered in hair. It had been a part of her training. She was ready for anything. Alana reached in her pocket to pull out her portable weather monitor. It dropped on the bottom of the raft, making a short clacking sound in the calm morning. Alana picked it up a few seconds later. The monitor told her that the temperature was minus 2 degrees centigrade and that a soft wind was blowing across the watery ice at eight kilometres per hour.

The raft drifted towards the island, but there were sections of the water still frozen, making their advance randomly difficult.

"It's quite thin; I think I can break it with the oar." Ramaan inserted a marine scanner. In the lake, something spun for a brief moment in the morning glare and splashed back into the water. It was like a small starfish with tubular arms breaking the surface, and at first sight, it was impossible to tell whether it was an animal or a machine. Then it flopped over and lay half awash, bobbing up and down in the gentle aftermath of the slow waves as if it were glad to see them.

"It's quite active down there." Ramaan made an adjustment to the monitor just as an odd mustard-coloured ball fish came to the surface and swam past the scanner. It pecked at the raft, then disappeared from view. Ramaan put his camera down as the raft reached the shore of the small island with a gentle bump.

They jumped out, leaving the raft on a suitable flat area, and clambered up a small rocky embankment leading to the observatory. A dirt footpath led to a door with a window alongside. Above the door and mounted on the wall were two antennae. One of them was the parabolic dish Philip had seen earlier. As they neared the door, Ramaan noticed the other was of a different technology. The antenna was U-shaped and covered with tiny metallic insect-like feelers. Alana opened the door with weapon at the ready and sneaked in.

Inside was a receiving station. Winking lights of all shades of green and red sparkled and twinkled against a darkened wall. Below them, something hummed.

Ramaan commented, "It could be another power generator." Their eyes adjusted to the gloom. Wall-to-wall shelves made from the same plastic polymer they'd found in the hangars held up a variety of interesting equipment. One looked like a radio receiver.

A round dial placed to the left in between buttons and knobs curiously bobbed from left to right. A faint, living crackle from a speaker below the front panel immediately told Ramaan it was still on. Whoever had switched it on had left it that way. Burning with curiosity, Ramaan walked over and began to study it. None of its markings made any sense, so he began fiddling with boyish fingers and played with its variety of knobs and buttons. No radio signals on any frequency, only static that may have been caused by the sun's increasing heat. It was almost ominously too quiet; one might have expected that even an asteroid would be noisier.

Alana, scuffling about in the semi-darkness, grabbed his attention with her footfalls and made him shake out of his delusion. Ramaan turned and faced her. "Hey, come check this out." Alana tiptoed over. "What do you make of it? It looks like a radio receiver, and it's been switched on. Someone's been here—probably recently too!" Alana said something about the undisturbed dust and looked around to verify that she hadn't missed anything. To the right, two dusty stacked books were laying one on top of the other. Ramaan picked them up and placed them into his side bag.

3. Footprints

On the floor, imprinted against the deep layer of dust to one side of the receiver, were footprints of someone or something that had recently been there. Whoever he was, he had opened the door like Ramaan and Alana, looked at something, used the receiver, and then walked out. This being, whoever he was, resembled or had most definitely a human similarity.

"Boots. Look—incredible—they're fresh as well!" Ramaan bent down and examined the footmark. Alana backed off slightly and retraced her steps towards the door. It was the only time that Ramaan had ever seen her scared, but this was the reality for which she had trained so hard.

Ramaan raised his head. "I know this is scary, God knows who or what made this impression. Your guess is as good as mine. Pull yourself together, Alana, we are relying on your instincts." Ramaan took some photo images.

Her instincts said that they should leave—now!

With sufficient data, they returned to the rubber craft and rejoined the rest of the group. Ramaan gave the reading material to Lexia to study.

"You say the radio was left on?" Philip curiously looked at Ramaan.

"Yeah, not only was it still crackling, the footprints we found led up to it. Here, take a look." Ramaan showed Philip the images he had taken in the observatory.

Flicking through the pictures, Philip turned and faced Alana. "What do you think?"

Feeling relieved that they were all together again, she managed a grin.

"Back on Earth, I was trained to look at and deal with hairy slimy monsters with three eyes or things that might jump out from behind a cupboard or inhabit captain's quarters in the form of God-knows-what; never thought they would actually be human."

"Yes, you did. Remember Norman Bell and Triton? Anyway, it's better this way, don't you think? You don't really want to see gooey and hairy things, do you?" Alana's grin turned to a smile.

"That's better. Remember, and I am talking to everyone, we are here for each other; never forget that. We didn't spend ten years of our lives only to be afraid about what we might find hiding around a corner. Look, we know there is a life form around here somewhere. If they are intelligent, and I think they are, they already know we are here. That means they already know more about us than we know about them. The hangars and the observatory can only make me think that robots didn't build them and that the prints you saw were made by flesh and blood."

Philip glanced at the images once more. "The sooner we can make contact with these, whoever they are, the better. Maybe they can tell us what happened here."

Baygorn burst in. "If it wasn't for our seemingly inadequate technology, we'd already know what we were up against."

"Baygorn, they are humanoid, and so far, we've only seen what they have built. More importantly, and a topic we have to discuss, is whether or not they are friendly. I personally don't think they'll harm us. Well, at least I hope not. If we are of a lower intelligence, I think they are as curious about us as we are about them. What are your opinions?"

Lexia stood up. "Maybe we can assist them in some way. You know, exchange our technology for theirs. What do you think they eat? I hope they are not carnivorous."

"Somehow I doubt it. Anyway, let's make contact first. There always exists a possibility to further our relationship. The most important fact here is we have to find out what happened a hundred years ago."

An hour later, back in front of the hangar, they stepped over the two broken doors. Alana went in first.

Shelf supports were everywhere. Ramaan, the strongest and the fastest of them and possibly the most daring, bent down and picked up a green sphere. "Someone's gotta do this."

"Keep that C-12 on. The moment you get there, wherever you get to, you let us know." Lexia's hand crept into Ramaan's, showing concern.

"Don't worry, Lex," he said gently before he disappeared. A few seconds later, his clear, whispery voice came over the communicator.

He cleared his throat. "It could be a nursery or some kind of garden city. It's enormous and it smells wonderful. I can't see anyone. My God, there must be hundreds of plants here, thousands. I can hear sounds of insects coming from the vegetation."

Philip and the rest joined him. Ramaan was right; it was gigantic. Every conceivable species of plant was here. Some they recognised. Row upon neat row, categorized by type and variety, stretched as far as the eye could see.

Philip knelt down behind Ramaan. "Christ, this is more than just a nursery."

Alana crept over and lightly tapped Philip on the shoulder. "Take a look at your C-12," said Alana's whispery voice.

Philip unhooked it from his belt, held the device at arm's length and returned a look of utter surprise. "My goodness, it can't be!" The grey liquid-crystal display flashed nine hundred kilometres from their terrain vehicle.

Alana went on. "It's the same spot where we saw that blip when it changed position as we landed." They were inside another hangar even bigger than the first.

"Fantastic, it must be fifty metres to the roof at least." Philip's voice was cut short as a faint rustling coming from the insides of the undergrowth turned all their heads at once. Something shifted around, making a constant rustle. Shuffle, scrape, rustle. Ramaan, crouching to Philip's right, added, "Like I said, there's something alive in there."

Ramaan reached for his sidearm. As the weapon came out of the holster, a funny little stumpy robot silently brushed Philip's trouser leg. He backed off, totally awestruck and in fright, while watching it continue hot on the trail of something scuffling through the stems.

"Wow, luckily I'm too big for it," he thought aloud. Its two front paws were making a metallic click-clack as it briskly zigzagged through plants in pursuit of the crawling victim. The word "Stawker" had been neatly engraved on the badly scratched head. The Stawker only measured half a metre in height, and in the distance Philip saw another one nimbly roaming the undergrowth, dashing and zipping between plants. They showed signs of wear and tear with many scratches and dents, possibly previous battle scars.

To the one side of the garden, they saw a white alcove. Keeping low, they furtively edged toward it. The door was open. There were no walls or cubicles dividing the room into partitions, yet its rectangular dimensions were clearly suballocated into different tasks. Square glass windows filled the sides and roof like a typical greenhouse. Plenty of light revealed many simple gizmos.

Philip bounded inside. Lexia saw a thermometer hanging on the far wall with markings written in the same numerical language they had seen before. She lifted her hand and delicately put it in her side pocket. Philip was rubbing herbs between his fingers when suddenly increasing chattering reached their ears from the other side of the vegetation. Baygorn had a worried look.

Alana turned towards Philip. "Are you armed?"

Philip whispered, "Always," the equally down-toned answer.

"There are people on the other side of the shrubbery." Philip was speaking so low that she could hardly make out what he'd said. They dropped to all fours and sneaked past the plant life to take a closer look. About sixty metres away, two people stood facing one another discussing something in an unknown tongue.

"Lexia, can you make out what they are saying?" She turned her head and focused her ears.

"Sounds a bit like Mandarin, a Korean dialect maybe."

Alana crawled over. "Well," she whispered, "they look very much like us, a little shorter maybe, but we are physically the same." They stared at their first live representation of an alien with complete interest.

Suddenly, Lexia yelped. "Ouch, something's just bit me!" Her face turned sour.

Alana had an upright finger on her lips. "Keep it down, Lexia."

Baygorn rushed over and immediately lifted up her trouser leg and revealed two tiny bites. A small beetle scuttled around on the ground in a vague attempt at escaping the already lowering, heavy foot of Ramaan.

Baygorn looked at Ramaan. "Get my virometer out of the case, hurry." The voice was faintly irritated.

Baygorn took a tissue sample from Lexia's leg and placed it onto a slide. Seconds later as the results appeared on a tiny screen, Baygorn sighed.

Ramaan connected with his worry. "What's up, what's it say?"

"Nothing." Baygorn felt incapable. All he could do was administer a cream and hope.

"At least this should calm the swelling until I know more about what it is we are dealing with. Why don't the three of you go on? I'll take Lexia back to the terrain vehicle with me and look after her there where my supplies are at hand." The last piece he mumbled.

Ramaan lifted his binoculars and looked around. "I don't think we're going to find Lexia's cure here." The three of them looked at each other, picked up the last of the coloured spheres and simultaneously placed their fingers on them.

Philip went first. Goosebumps charged the full length of his body. The feeling of pins and needles quickly devoured his lungs and heart. He had a distinctive taste of wood in his mouth. Ants ran through his hair, between his toes, behind his eyes and down his back. Itchy flashes of light accompanied the voracious insatiable nest as Philip melted away. A second later, they were 1,200 kilometres from the terrain vehicle.

They were inside yet another giant warehouse. Here there were more voices, a lot more voices. Ramaan raised his binoculars. These voices were dressed in red. One of them had an apple-green band around his waist. He was standing alongside a large table containing something that Ramaan was trying to get a look at. Without warning or sound, the individual swivelled in their direction and said something. Ramaan ducked down like a dart. The words continued. The man in red then turned his whole body towards them. He was greeting them. Philip faced Ramaan and Alana.

"This is it." They were so nervous that no one could say anything. No words evolved when words should have shot out;

nothing. Forcing his will and desire, Philip swallowed and stood up. Alana and Ramaan pulled up to Philip's side, tightly holding his arms.

"Do you speak our language; can you understand me?"

"Yes, we have been studying you since your arrival here. My name is Shar and we are the Peblinus." Shar was five feet tall and had a distinctive Asian look about him. They inched nearer.

"It is an honour to meet you, Shar." They shook hands.

"My name is Philip. This is Alana and Ramaan. We are scientists. We have come here to gather information about this planet, its life forms and cultures, its riches and composition, and then we will move on to the next planet in this system we call Phot. We come from Earth, the third planet of a G7 star in the Centauri region."

"We know why you have come. Here, you'll need a flask of Amostalina for your woman." Shar gave them a small phial of white liquid for Lexia and smiled.

"Almost 20,000 of your years ago, we lived in peace in your solar system on the planet you call Mars. Everything was perfect. Everything was as it should have been until the war between the Gorinos, the Dark Ones, and us began. At the same time, a terrible disease struck Mars. It drifted quietly and almost destroyed us. As a result, we separated and fled to different parts of the galaxy to escape the impending doom that encircled us. We have our Platnios outside to warn us of intruders. It was them who told us of your arrival."

"Those plant creatures, you call them Platnios?" Philip's confidence suddenly came back with a rush. He felt at ease.

Shar sensed it and smiled again. "They are territorial. If you don't provoke them, they won't hurt you." Ramaan felt an urge to roll up his sleeve and show Shar his arm.

"They are genetically made to serve and obey us." Shar moved forward and gave them a book written in their language. Philip was sure the gift would help Lexia with her translations. Ramaan meanwhile was taking photographs of interest and sending the results to Sentrywatcher.

"How is it that you are familiar with the English language?" asked Philip.

"It is our second language and the mother tongue of our descendants. Come, I will show you and your crew our hangar and what we are doing here." Everywhere Peblinus were watching them.

"Would you mind if I had a look around on my own?" asked Philip.

"You may go where you please." His eyes thinned and acknowledged with a toothy, white smile. Taking Ramaan and Alana by the arm, the three of them disappeared towards the middle of the hangar and out of sight. Questions were rattling around in Philip's mind. Their descendants, who were the Dark Ones, came from the same solar system. Walking in the opposite direction, Philip heard snippets of their strange language, which to him and Lexia had mentioned, sounded like clicking Mandarin. Even the writing on crates and papers looked like Chinese. Although the hangar was enormous like the other two they'd seen, this one had a strange shape. The corners were rounded and the roof slightly inclined. From the top of an observation ladder, the three sections in the hangar, one at each end and another in the middle, each looked like geodesic domes from the outside. Shelves were everywhere in partitioned laboratories. Military personnel brushed past.

"Jeez, what type of research could they be doing here?" Philip thought aloud. He walked down a short corridor until he reached a table full of odd mechanical parts.

A thin Peblinus walked over with unsteady legs. "Hello, do you vant some help?" The accent was terrible, and he was sniffing like he had a cold.

"No thanks, I'm fine here. All okay here."

"Here not good, here we have ploblem with other type of people." The face grinned. "We need your ghelp. Will you ghelp us?"

Philip briefly wondered why they would need their help. These Peblinus should be more than capable of sorting out their own dilemmas. Philip made a quick glance towards a table with weapons on it before letting him continue.

"They have two legs like us. Vely intelligent and vely dangerous. They live in vertical columns dotted throughout the hills. Maybe you see them when you coming here. They hunt us and we cannot stop them!"

"Why do they hunt you?" asked Philip. Then he began to think that wherever they went, there would never be peace, not even out here. Where there is a man, there is a problem. "With your technology, you should be able to defend yourselves with ease." Philip looked once more towards a variety of weapons on a table. A technician was making some adjustments.

"But it more complicated than it sound. They called Bods. They want to destroy us and gain control of Blaan. They are thieves, dirty rotten thieves." His accentuating voice almost breached soprano level. Inside and biting his lip, Philip almost laughed. Philip was sure he had noticed a grin.

"They use different technology to ours, vely effective. They vely much like you—vely tall." His hand reached upwards in a futile description and the black, marbled eyes inflated themselves to abnormal proportions. There was a definite tinge of fear thrown in.

"They live in columns in this sector because they are closer to us." The Peblinus laid out a map on the table and they began studying an area with two of these vertical columns.

"Wait a minute; of course! We passed them when we came here, long tall towers with an entrance at the bottom." He smiled.

Shar's voice turned Philip's head. "I see Chan has been filling you in with our dilemma. Can you help us?"

"I'm sure we can work something out. Where do these Bods come from?"

"Our remote past. They have pursued us across the limits of the galaxy to this system! We're not certain, but it is possible the Bods are the reminiscent result of interbreeding between our ancestors."

Toying with what he had said, Philip left Chan and regrouped with the rest. Outside in the cold air, a deep-red sunset waited. As Mintaka's tiny orb lay to rest on the horizon, the darkness came so fast and was so intense, that Bellatrix produced a shadow on the terrain. It was as if someone had turned out the light with a switch.

Shar tramped over. "Philip, where's your transport?"

"It's parked outside one of the other hangars."

"Better bring it here where you will need it—just sit inside and use the sphere."

Philip walked to Ramaan and Alana. "I'm going to fetch the terrain vehicle and give Lexia's anti-toxin to Baygorn. Appears we have a date with the Bods."

"Who?" asked Alana.

"Bods, hill dwellers. The Peblinus are having problems with them. They've asked us to help. Remember those four columns we passed on our way? Turns out they're Bod homes. There are more not too far away. Later, we're going to pay them a visit."

Philip rubbed the sphere and vanished.

"How's she doing?"

Baygorn was pleased to see Philip arrive. "She's developed a bit of a fever, but at least she's stable."

"We've met our first inhabitants. They call themselves Peblinus; friendly, too. The one in charge gave me this for Lexia." Philip handed over the Amostalina.

"Is this what I think it is?"

"Yes, keep me posted if there's any change in her condition." Philip climbed into the vehicle and disappeared.

"How is she?" asked Ramaan. Alana climbed into the vehicle.

"Bit of a fever still. Baygorn will notify us of any changes."

Shar pointed in the direction of the two towers and they set off. The terrain was dark and almost flat, enabling the vehicle to move smoothly and quietly. Alana switched on the infrared. Their objective was about twenty kilometres from the Peblinus hangar.

"Why don't these Peblinus clean up their own mess? Why us?" asked Ramaan.

"Ramaan, right now, we are in the middle of nowhere in search of an armoured enemy that lives in a five-hundred-metre vertical home with a hunger for Peblinus. You know as much as I do."

Alana interrupted. "Quiet you two, listen!" Alana slowed, stopped and turned up the sensitivity of the audio tracker.

"Over there, in that hilly area!"

Philip bent nearer, reached to the dashboard and turned on the interior lamp. "It sounds hollow, almost like growling."

Alana switched on and quickly directed their halogen spot lamp towards the outland in the direction of the sound.

"Over there, look!" Alana's hand directed their eyes.

Philip turned on his infrared headgear. He could hear the distant lashing of their roots even without the audio tracker. They were moving faster than during the day, and their barking was imminently closing in on them.

"Definitely hostile intentions. How fast are they moving?"

"Four kilometres per hour," said Alana, looking at Sentrywatcher's information.

"They'll be on top of us in no time. They seem excited about something, maybe it's dinnertime."

Alana prepared two infrared-sensitive blue-ray rifles. "Anything that moves out there is toast." Alana fiddled with the remote control pad and typed in a couple of commands. "Shar said these things were their early-warning beacons. Why are they out here?"

Ramaan smiled. "In amongst all that muscle there's probably a brain somewhere. You could be right; maybe they are just hungry and fancy something different for a change. Have you ever eaten jam sandwiches for a year, and then suddenly got a whiff of a good steak?"

"You said these Platnios get their orders from the Peblinus. Where's the connection—" she stopped herself mid-sentence.

"One hundred metres!" Alana's hand reached down and touched an icon on the screen.

The ebony terrain came alive with spiky, silvery-blue gasps of light. Silver needles came to an abrupt end, producing puffs of wispy smoke. Philip stood up in the vehicle and watched their lashing and struggle. The engagement lasted two minutes.

Alana picked up her infrared binoculars and searched the horizon. "Maybe they're still mad at us for what happened earlier?"

Ramaan checked the horizon with the infrared. "All clear."

Alana picked up the still-smoking rifles and placed them onto the rack.

Philip looked at Ramaan. "I don't think these plants have memories. It must be ESP, mass communication."

Baygorn's voice erupted through the C-12. "Philip, I administered the anti-toxin half an hour ago. It's working, her temperature's dropping."

Philip was happy with the news. "Excellent, we'll collect you in the gold zone. Is she okay to travel?"

"She's fine." Lexia's happy tone sharply came over the speaker.

Philip's face returned a calm note.

"We'll be there before you!" Lexia said.

"See you both in ten minutes. Go and introduce yourselves to Shar."

"I've been looking forward to meeting these Peblinus. We've been talking about them." Alana stopped and turned the vehicle around.

Shar was waiting outside the hangar. "Can you explain what just happened? A disturbance—no, a major disturbance—has reached our ears from the Platnios. Someone has attacked them! Do you know anything about it?"

Alana walked up to him. Shar's face was red with anger.

"How well do you know your Platnios?"

Shar backed away from Alana's acidic, but calm tone. She didn't feel like laying it on too thick, they had just met. What ticked off Alana the most was his accusation.

"Was it you who sent them? We had an earlier encounter; did you hear about that, too?"

"Of course not! And no, I didn't."

Alana bit her tongue. All the evidence so far showed that he was lying, and his acting skill was better than hers.

"Where we come from we call it self-defence," she uttered, but the appearance of Lexia and Baygorn made Alana give off a smile.

"You're looking perky. Nice to see you up and about."

"Same here. I still have a bit of a headache."

"Lexia, have you met Shar?" asked Philip.

"No, not yet. Where is he?"

Shar, overhearing snippets of their conversation, walked away and went back to what he was doing.

Lexia smiled. "Leave him alone, I'll catch up with him later."

"Has Ramaan briefed you both on what's been going on?"

"Yes, some."

"Good, we'll fill you in with the rest, on the way." Shar was pretending not to notice them, but his wandering, sly eyes were watching and listening over his shoulder. *That man knows more than what he's letting on*, thought Ramaan, helping Lexia onto the vehicle.

"What the heck, let's be on our way."

The night was still and the stars were unnaturally pointed and crisp. It was a moonless night, and not even their lights of 4,000 watts were able to cut through the uncharted ebony of nothing. The outside temperature had descended to minus 10, and they had to rely on their digital compass to guide them in the darkness. Their audio tracker revealed many strange nocturnal sounds. Some were not far away.

"At least this time they're staying their distance. Still a lot of sporadic groups of creepers out there."

Alana glanced towards the radar then twisted her head to the surroundings.

"Now you know what happens if you don't behave yourselves." Alana put her foot down, but the terrain became bumpy in places, so she reduced speed again.

"God, there's nothing out here. It's so dark, it's scary. Hey, Ramaan, where did you say we were going?" Baygorn looked at the radar. All before him was total darkness; not a glimmer of light was reflected back from the beam.

"And that?" asked Lexia while watching two small circular objects making their way onto the radar.

Alana swung round. "Presume that's where we are heading."

Ramaan noticed her curiosity. "Apparently Bods live there. Remember those tall, cigar-shaped buildings we saw this morning when we started out? Well, that's what those are. Our Peblinus friends are having some problems that they want us to sort out."

"Hey, Ramaan, I thought they'd been briefed!" Philip said.

"Very briefly."

They reached the base of the first column ten minutes later. The other structure was a little more than two hundred metres away. Alana parked the vehicle. During the day, the almost-black hillside would have appeared small against the enormity of the column. The brightest star was Saiph. Its glimmering lustre, brighter than Venus, added an eerie gloom to the dreary surroundings. The hillside seemed to move and shimmer, making delusional phantoms. On the horizon, the Horsehead Nebula was beginning to set.

Nervously, Baygorn felt someone was watching them. "It's like two huge chimneys stacked up one on top of the other!"

Alana was looking at the results on her C-12. "Good, there's no one at home. Let's go in."

The outside of the chimney was made of a hard substance which Ramaan was rubbing. "It's that same plastic from the hangars again. The stuff seems to be everywhere." The door at the base measured two metres and opened easily when Philip pushed it. It made a long creak, like a thick old oak door in a horror movie. At first, Philip could see absolutely nothing. It was as if he had suddenly been struck blind. His dark adaptation, his physiological alteration of the eye's response to light in low-light environments, hadn't produced enough rhodopsin.

Philip blinked twice and stood motionless in the total darkness. "Uggh, it smells like a damp cellar," Philip whispered. His footstep, trampling dirt or small pebbles, echoed far above. Inside it was humid, still, daunting and insanely dark.

Ramaan activated a hand lamp. His finger disturbed a surface. "Looks like no one cleans around here, there's dust everywhere."

"Is that your professional masculine impression, or are we trying to be scientific?" Ramaan mumbled something. Alana smiled through the gloom of her lamp, went on ahead of the rest and switched on her communicator.

"There's a crude elevator and some stairs. I would assume they go to the top." Alana swivelled her head and moved towards the steps.

Ramaan stared downwards at the base of the elevator. "There are footprints here, too. Someone's been here, all right."

"That's much better." Alana sarcastically wiped the lamp on his face. The place was like the inside of an infinite lighthouse.

The light from Philip's lamp didn't reach the roof. Lifting the lantern, Philip bathed the interminable coil of steps in a silvery beam and created wobbly shadows. Their breathing became heavy from looking up and thinking what might be up there. Alana began to climb the stairwell. There was no banister, so they went up in single file, keeping as close as possible to the outside wall. It took them ten minutes to reach a small room to the left about two hundred metres up. Disordered, strewn papers were everywhere. To one side, there was another book. Alana shone her lamp on the wall and noticed graffiti.

Amongst the coloured pencil-drawn art, something of meaning caught Philip's eye. Three rough horizontal lines about ten centimetres long, with a funny face drooping in the middle and over the top, made Philip move closer. Philip sensed and felt it had been drawn by a nostalgic hand. Not a particularly good representation, it did make its point, though. The humorous face with a big plump nose placed in the centre on the top line actually had a smile on it. Drawn vertically, evenly spaced subdivisions within the lines represented bricks. Five fingers to each side of the face held on to the top line, dramatizing a wall. It simulated a human form. The artist had signed it, "Kilroy was here."

"Looks like these bad guys are more human than our good guys," Philip said. The room only contained rubbish, but they sifted through it all the same. Close to the one wall, Philip found a page of a book written in English; next to it, a one-armed, dirty forgotten doll. Its once-pink outer clothing had turned brown. Philip picked it up. "How in God's name did this get here?"

"And that?" asked Alana.

Philip dropped the doll and bent towards a battered human mandible.

Baygorn turned his lantern.

Lexia's face turned up with worry. "Damn, one hell of a blow to the face. Look at it, it's practically destroyed! It's been here for a very long time."

Baygorn examined it some more before they returned to the central shaft. Small windowless apertures offered cold brisk air every ten metres. From one of them, they could make out the lights from the Peblinus hangar in the distance. The occasional echoes of chitchat and footsteps ping-ponged up and down the colossal central column like an immense echo chamber. The wind was making an eerie whistle. Finally reaching the top landing, they came across two rooms without doors. In the first, Philip found three books. They were battered, but readable. The first, *Gardening and Cycads: a Must for Every Gardener*, was in good condition. The other, *Home Improvements and Roof Repairs*, had a number of pages missing. The third, written in ancient Latin, had a picture of a loaf of bread on the cover—a recipe book, maybe.

Lexia grabbed it from Philip's hands and started flipping the pages. "Wow, who said Latin was dead?"

They strolled to the big, glaring window aperture they'd seen from the bottom to view the other column.

Alana pulled Philip back. "Don't move; I've just seen someone scurry out of sight on the other column."

Philip sneaked his head around the window frame. There was a light. A few of them. Somebody was at home and they had seen the intruders' hand lamps.

Lexia continued to study the room, worried she might find other human remains. "How could they erect these buildings to such heights; and out of plastic? How do they live and survive? The nearest thing we've seen so far regarding food was in the Peblinus hangar."

In the other room, Baygorn augmented the sensitivity of his infrared and started ferreting around on the floor. Suddenly he stood up as if he'd received an electric discharge. "Look at this —this is no ray gun, it's a dart gun! There're tranquilizer darts scattered on the floor. The Bods probably made these towers high enough so they could observe the Peblinus from a safe distance. They probably kill the Peblinus for food because they don't have an alternative." Lexia was trembling. She was still thinking about the mandible.

Some distant and frantic voices were echoing up the tower's central shaft. They were getting closer.

Philip crouched low and raised his weapon. "Natural causes, maybe. Let's not judge till we're sure. We're gonna find out real soon, though. Put those weapons on Stun," he added, moving deeper into the room.

4. Second Contact

It happened in the blink of an eye. The form entered the room, sparsely giving them time to react. Alana stunned him in the leg only centimetres away from her. He dropped like a stone and hit the floor with a loud, painful thump.

Ramaan pushed between Philip and the door. "Wait, more will be on the way!" he shouted. The second one slowly walked inside. He was unaltered by Ramaan's closeness and blankly looked at his pointed weapon before staring at his unconscious companion on the floor. All their lights were on him. He sighed. His intelligence allowed him to understand what was going on. He raised a hand behind him as more were coming up the steps.

"Stay back!" Rigid words exited a firm mouth whilst simultaneously preventing the pushing, ranting figures behind him from entering. Five of them stopped dead in their tracks. They examined Philip and the others with their unusual and powerful lanterns while nervously looking at them up and down. The beams occasionally scraped their faces. It seemed like minutes before an air of tranquillity loomed in the room.

Lexia, noticing his prudent stance, stepped forward and began to communicate with him. He backed off slightly, but the figure had gentle eyes, and he appeared dazed by their presence.

"We are not here to hurt you. We are here to help. Your friend here on the floor is not dead, we only stunned him."

Philip came next to Lexia. "What is your name?" Philip asked.

He was restless and jumpy. His eyes opened in a crazed gaze as the mouth began to crease open. "W-we are Bods, who are you?" The words shuddered outwards.

Philip could see that the brave and valiant soul before him was startled and scared. Alana lowered her weapon and slipped it back into her holster. The other five Bods behind the leading man began nattering amongst themselves. Scooting, one of them disappeared in the elevator back down to ground level.

Philip immediately began to think he had gone to warn others and watched as the devouring black void ate his deteriorating lantern beam. "We represent an investigation team from Earth," Philip said, now out in front. Faces looked at him and at one another.

"Where is Earth? I've never heard of it." He paused. "Is it close by?"

"No," Philip said, "it's on the outer edge of the galaxy." A note of surprise covered the man's face. "To be exact," said Philip, "it's one thousand light-years' distance from here." Questions formed, and a faint smile appeared in a dying-to-ask way.

Alana moved forward. "Do you live in these towers?" Lexia was more worried about the broken mandible. Philip could hear her ask him to ask about the mandible in the next room.

The Bod, now calmer, started to regain confidence. "No, these are our lookout posts. Here, we study the Peblinus. Have you met them?"

"Yes, they sent us here to look for you. They told us quite a bit about you."

The Bod looked to the floor. "Those hangars you saw where the Peblinus live were once ours." A perceptible smile left his confident lips, and he knelt down to see to his sleeping colleague. Placing his fingers on his companion's throat, he felt for a pulse. He stopped and looked at Philip.

"We settled here 20,000 of your years ago. We were a race in peace until they showed up a hundred years ago." Philip rapidly turned and looked at Ramaan and Alana.

"They took us completely by surprise! They came in huge numbers and wiped us out almost to extinction. We used this planet only for research and development, and we weren't equipped to deal with them. We constantly watch them from these towers." He paused. "They have their Platnios guarding all entry points to their facilities and have begun to leak into the outer areas as well."

"Yes, we've met them too," added Alana with confidence.

"Our lives are a real misery with those things out there. They've eaten more than fifty of my men in the last six months, and they seem to be getting smarter." The Bod issued an order to one of his clan and waved his hand. The scampering form disappeared.

"We managed to construct two hangars with the last of our resources. At least the Peblinus have left us with those."

"Where do you come from?" asked Philip.

"We originated from a solar system of nine planets. Our planet was the third of that system which received its light from a type G2V star. I can't tell you a lot about it. What I will say is, approximately 12,000 years ago, the last one of us left the third planet because our two civilizations were going in separate directions. It was chaos and getting worse. Our mentalities and requirements were different."

Philip asked the others, "How many G2V stars are there in the galaxy with nine planets?"

Ramaan glared a moment. "Alpha Centauri is G2V, but it has four planets. Apart from Alpha and our sun, I don't know of any."

"That's it then. If this race came from Earth and the Peblinus from Mars, what image comes to mind?"

Lexia broke in. "Well, Mars had vegetation that dated back 20,000 years. You remember, they discovered the traces in 2068. The important ancient constructions on Earth also date back almost 12,000 years. Maybe it was an invasion. Maybe the Peblinus invaded Earth 12,000 years ago, but luckily, the Bods had already started to leave in search of this place eight thousand years before by then. God, this is exciting!"

Their collective commotion and enthusiasm didn't go unnoticed by the Bod. Philip, the calmest of the group, thought the others were going to have a nervous breakdown; but as the team began to relax once more, the Bod continued.

"Before we left that world, we constructed for their kind various buildings and artefacts that we scattered in many different parts on the planet. Using the culture of each island, we constructed the buildings and memorials to the specifications of each race. Our immortal sign of goodwill and thank-you remained behind for all to see. Maybe they're still there."

Alana was speechless and dumbstruck all at once. Philip turned his attention to Ramaan and Baygorn. "Do you think he is referring to the continents by saying islands?"

"Possibly." Ramaan was wearing a cynical grin.

"Then the variety of buildings he is referring to can only be the major ancient structures we know of today. Incredible. They must have been built by the Bods. Considering we had always speculated they were of alien origin—my God, now we know for sure," said Philip before he continued. "There are structures in Mexico and Peru that date as far back as that."

"And our Pyramids?" broke in Ramaan. "They, too, must have been constructed around that time, not 5,000 years ago as we've all been led to believe. Those blasted bureaucrats must've known all along. Cheapskates. Oh, how this is all starting to make so much sense!"

Bods were anxiously starting to appear out of nowhere. "What's a human?" one asked.

"Let me see," said another, pushing in.

Philip studied them as more appeared on the scene and towards their host. "What if I was to tell you, there is a big possibility that your third planet and our home world are the same? The only difference, of course, is that we are separated by twenty millennia." The Bod was listening intently to Philip's words.

"Before we jump to any conclusions, tell us more about these constructions you left behind."

"I would love to, but I am afraid I don't know anything else. What I will say is, on one of our recent visits to the third world, we brought back books and personal things. They are our memories and our strength. It's what keeps us alive spiritually." The Bod reached into a shoulder bag and retrieved a *Time* magazine. The date was July 2091. Philip could feel the hairs on the back of his neck begin to stand up as the familiar cover, the one he'd read and held seven years before, slowly touched his hands.

The smiling, creased face of Wally Banks was stupidly portrayed on the front cover. Wally was president of the amalgamated Amerussian States. Only six years before, he had funded the longest road in history, stretching across the northern Pacific Ocean, joining the two empires. It hurt to see him again, especially way out here. On the two painful occasions Philip had met him, he'd always thought Wally was the most callous person ever conceived. Global nations worshipped him, though, saying he was something of a god. Philip jerked away from what he held in his hands and returned it to the Bod with a thump. It was true: There were human roots on this uncharted planet, living representations of Norman Bell's frozen discovery. The unconscious Bod lying on the floor groaned.

Alana helped him up. "Sorry about that, I thought you were going to kill us."

"It's okay; I thought you were Peblinus, glad you're not." They exchanged smiles as the Bod rubbed his head.

"Everyone calls me Randolph," said their host. His hand shot out and Philip took it firmly, introducing himself. The man was probably about thirty-five. He had strong hands and a well-cared-for smile.

"We may be less in number, but we're stronger than before," he said, leading them towards the elevator.

"Instead of researching flora and fauna, we've been forced to study armaments and defence. Our progress here has been surprising, especially during this last year." Randolph waved his hands about in a rhythmical way. During their descent, Randolph told them he was an area director.

"Each sector of twenty columns has one like me." More Bods came to greet them at the base. Once in complete darkness, an array of lights had been erected outside the entrance of the column.

Baygorn walked to Philip. "You know, they even walk and dress like us."

Randolph ushered Philip towards a waiting vehicle. "You know, Philip, there is one sphere the Peblinus weren't able to take," said Randolph. "The red sphere; they're unique. We discovered them by accident and began to make red spheres because they allow us to go anywhere we want to. The Peblinus continuously blame us for the deaths of their own kind. They say we eat them! I mean, can you imagine us eating the Peblinus?" Now that Philip had met him, it did sound absurd.

Excited Bods walked over to touch the humans or to see their evolutionary differences. Not even 20,000 years could produce any. There were none. At the base of the second column, Randolph pushed a disguised, rusty lever. Shortly afterwards, a whirring was followed by a sharp click. It was an entranceway to a lower level. Randolph walked inside and beckoned them to follow. Philip, Ramaan and the others followed Randolph down one floor via a flight of dusty stairs. Philip's eyes widened as he reached the bottom. Although there was no physical difference between them, there was a grand difference in their technologies. It almost became too staggering for the humans to absorb. Their brains could've gone into overload at the mere thought of unravelling possibilities. Bod engineers and technicians were manipulating holographic images. They were images of terrain landscapes, hills and exact positions of Peblinus hideouts. It was in real time.

"Look," said Lexia. "That must be the pod. There are the first four columns we saw and the other two hangars."

"Yes, we saw you when you landed," added Randolph excitedly. "Been following you ever since. The Peblinus don't know about this place. These white areas are groups of Platnios. Watch what they do." Their eyes fixated on twenty or more white patches, all near to and roaming about Peblinus outposts. They were patrolling back and forth, learning and gathering information.

The startlingly clear 3-D image of the Peblinus hangar enshrouded by intense dark was a large, well-defined square. To the one side, a single Peblinus, a red blip, had ventured outside to gather some plant life or maybe just have a pee. Without him knowing it, the Platnios had surrounded him. They watched as the white patch moved closer, closer and closer, then launched its attack with total surprise and precision. Within minutes, the red blip had completely disappeared from view.

"As you can see, Philip, that wasn't us. Don't worry about it; it happens all the time, at least twice per day. They still think it's us. They are such fools. You say the Peblinus sent you here because they think we are a menace. Well, I think you've seen your answer." Randolph thanked and bade farewell to his engineers. Outside, Philip and the others climbed into a vehicle and headed in the opposite direction, away from the Peblinus.

The two Bod hangars were constructed in a deep valley. Ramaan calculated they were about twenty kilometres from the columns, taking them ten minutes to reach.

Over the hill, Alana saw it first: an artificial, sunken flat mountain, far bigger than any of the others they had seen before. Randolph entered a guarded tunnel and parked the vehicle under cover on an overly lit patio.

Anxiety struck Philip and his team once more as extremely luminous, warm lights revealed more tables and gadgets close to the entrance. "You know, Randolph, I think it would take our scientists decades to go through all this, and it looks like we haven't even scratched the surface yet." Philip didn't know what he was going to see inside. No one did, but they shivered at the thought.

In one near section, Baygorn noticed some ultraviolet lights. "Hey, they look familiar to you?" Ramaan nodded. Alana grunted. Randolph led them to a table full of armaments. One particular example, which he showed them and seemed particularly proud of, he called a Multi-Frequency Gamma Gun.

"We call them GF rifles. It's changed the face of the war. We came up with the concept about a year ago, and now we are all using them. Just last month, we sent one thousand examples to Retolox and Traxon."

"What is it?" asked Alana, wanting to touch. Ramaan was just as intrigued.

"The GF rifle discharge is variable, making the ion-gamma pulse capable of vaporizing a large variety of materials."

"This is certainly a fresh idea. Can I see it from a little closer?"

"Here's one each." Randolph handed Philip and the others a GF. It was comfortable and weighed no more than two kilograms. It weighed less than half of their own blue-rays. Alana enthusiastically picked it up and toyed with it.

"That's the adjustment control," said Randolph, pointing to a knob. Alana's brief assessment was cut in two as a Bod suddenly came screaming into the hangar. He was out of breath and could hardly talk.

"Randolph, sir, Lionel has just been eaten by a Platnios, and there's a column of well-armed Peblinus heading our way!"

Randolph explained that the Peblinus aren't bad, "They are just greedy. The Platnios, on the other hand, relentlessly slaughter anything in their way. If there was a way to defeat the Peblinus without harming them, we should strongly consider it."

Alana left to speak to one of the weapons specialists in the area they had just left. She returned shortly after with some flashing control panels.

"There is a way," she said. "Apparently the Peblinus use a high quantity of iron in their weapons design. Your specialist has shown me how to set the GF to vaporise iron without causing harm to the Peblinus." She handed Philip and Ramaan a panel and plugged it into the rifle with a short lead. Baygorn and Lexia watched with interest.

"This one's yours," she said to Philip as she programmed the gun, unplugging the cable. Their first confrontation they would face with diligence and conscience. They followed Randolph and some of his men into the dark night of Braan where ten heavily armed Peblinus and a slouchy lieutenant waited under an illuminated area on the patio. They, too, had infrared.

"One side, Humans, our battle is not with you!"

Ramaan and Alana stood in plain view. "What's your grudge? What harm have they done to the Peblinus?" Philip and the others stood up. Eager eyes scrutinised them from head to toe.

"They're a dirty race and a menace. We've come to clean them," said the lieutenant sternly without blinking an eye.

"You cleaned them a hundred years ago," said Baygorn, flashing his lantern in the face of the lieutenant. "Wasn't that enough? Why don't you leave them in peace?"

"They're a nuisance. They kill us for no reason. This planet is ours; we claimed it then, and we claim it now."

"This planet isn't yours!" snapped Philip. "And the Bods aren't responsible for the deaths of your people, either; it's your Platnios! You have to grow with a planet for thousands of generations. You have to learn its secrets. Even then, it's not really yours. You will always be boarders wherever you go."

Clearly, the man didn't like the response and made a gesture. One of the other Peblinus slowly started lowering his hand towards his sidearm.

Alana and Ramaan opened fire instantly, disintegrating five plasma rifles. Baygorn and Philip followed suit, and in less than two seconds, eleven rifleless owners looked about, bewildered and stunned. They scooted into the night like scared rabbits.

"You were right. They do have greed written all over their faces." Philip directed the comment towards Randolph standing five metres behind him. As Alana went inside, she programmed auto targeting blue-rays and left them outside to clean up the Platnios during the dark hours.

"How many Peblinus live on Braan?" asked Philip, walking next to Randolph.

"About 80,000. Braan is too extreme. Luckily, they aren't adapted to the cold like we are. Some of the other planets are infested with them, though. On Ganus, the fifth planet, they have installed themselves into gigantic cities and underground bunkers."

Philip seemed concerned. "Randolph, I have to go back there. I have to find out, go and pay the Peblinus another visit. I have an itch I need scratching."

Randolph's look turned worried. "You be careful with them, Philip. They're sneaky and full of surprises. Do you want some of my men to go with you?"

"No, I think we'll be okay. Anyway, Shar won't take too kindly to your guys being there. It's us he wants to see. Better you stay low for a while." Philip called the others, and they headed back to Shar's hangar with Randolph's words rattling around in his head. "Be careful of them, they're sneaky."

Like an irate, frustrated general, Shar haphazardly traipsed around outside issuing orders. Philip could see the reluctance of the Peblinus. Was that hatred so plainly evident on the men's faces?

He turned and faced Philip as he jumped out. "Glad to see you're back, good. Did you find those Bod towers? Did you go in? Did you meet them?"

Ramaan pushed Philip gently back and continued, "Of course, they were pretty hard to miss! What's it between you and the Bods anyway? Did we miss something here? And all those troops; something about cleaning, being a menace. Do you really think Bods eat Peblinus? My goodness, man!" Ramaan slammed his hand hard against the roof of the vehicle. Shar moved closer, changing the tone of his voice. Two of his men pulled up alongside him with rifles at the ready.

"Now you listen here, Earth people. Don't get mixed up in our affairs. Don't even try it! I sent you to do a job and order you to comply. Meddlers, if you cannot fulfil this simple task, I will make sure you perish alongside them! Do I make myself clear?"

Small gobs of spit exited from his mouth. *This wasn't the Shar we met*, Philip thought. He was enraged, rabid; but why? Philip stared at his contorting visage and his forced, false smile and pursed his lips. They all did, as he seemed irritated with their presence.

"Go on, do what I say. Carry out your orders! What are you waiting for?" Shar stomped off and continued shouting at anyone in hearing distance. Within his fading voice, Alana made out the words "stupid humans." She looked at Philip and Ramaan.

"I know, Alana. It's time to leave before this whole thing gets out of hand." Without further word, they climbed back into the vehicle and returned to Randolph.

"That didn't take long. How'd it go?"

"Not that good, I'm afraid. There is a possibility we have to prepare ourselves for the worst, I think. Under the orders of Shar, those Peblinus are capable of anything! He'll probably march in here and soon, with all he has."

Randolph didn't show signs of distress and seemed unperturbed by the pitch of Philip's voice. Philip actually thought he'd seen a thin smirk come out from beneath those turned-up lips. Teeth appeared. It was a smirk.

"Philip, the Peblinus are greedy and want everything. It is in their nature, and they won't stop till they get it. So, we are going to let them come and try to take what they think is theirs." The smile disappeared and hardened again.

"Have no fear when Randolph is near. We've been studying this Shar for some time. A hundred years ago, we didn't stand a chance. They could've wiped us out. Luckily, they didn't. Now, if he plans anything, don't worry, we'll be waiting for him. Come, I have something to show you."

They followed Randolph to a table. "We call them stealth bombs. It is a fully programmable multi-missile. We have six ready to use."

Alana came over and studied it, emitting a smile. "It's a bit like our zip bomb. Once it's armed, the zip acts entirely on its own. Eight hundred self-targeting, explosive missiles get released into the air once sufficient enemy targets are in reach."

Randolph, amazed by Alana's brutal veracity, began studying ideal geographical locations with her, figuring out where to place them.

Philip grabbed Alana by the shoulder. "Can I see you for a moment, outside?"

Standing outside the front entrance, Philip began waving his arms in the air. "What's going on here, Alana—I mean, look at this place, what's happening to us?" Alana blankly stared at Ramaan and the others now nearing before hooking up again with Philip's drilling glare.

"We represent Earth! We didn't come here to fight other people's battles. Where's the science in that?"

Lexia broke in. "True, Philip, but this place isn't quite what we thought it would be, either. Our investigations so far have turned up a genetic plant that apparently thinks. Even you've had a run-in with them. Why do we have weapons in the first place? Going back, our training was actually useless. All this talk of stealth bombs and zips goes completely against our policy of why we are really here."

"Defence, Lexia, we have them for our defence. I agree, Lexia, with you, but we had absolutely no idea of what we would find once we'd landed. What do you want to do then, stand around and watch innocent people get eaten by plants or destroyed by a race calling themselves Peblinus that so happen to speak English?" added Baygorn.

Philip turned up his face. "I want everyone's opinion here. What's going through that brain of yours, Ramaan?"

"Everyone has a point. We met the Peblinus, we studied them. We met the Bods and we studied them too. Hey, that's being scientific! Forget the intentions for a while. Forget the zips and stealth bombs and stuff. I mean, and I am trying to be scientific here, Philip. Like Baygorn says, do we want to sit back, or do we want to be able to work with a clear conscience? It's not about taking sides or choosing who we want to be with. It's about protecting our heritage, and I think our heritage just asked us to help them defeat an enemy that happens to speak English."

Philip gave a long sigh. "And you, Alana?"

"If Norman Bell were here, or could see us now, he'd probably have a heart attack. Deep down inside we knew this would happen. No, not the skirmishes and stuff, I'm talking about the likenesses between our species. I have to agree with Ramaan about our heritage. We protect that and we protect ourselves. Come on, Philip, you understand what I'm saying, don't you? Look what we have so far: four hangars, two robots, spheres that can transport people and objects over a long distance in the blink of an eye. From my point of view, we arrived in the nick of time to rescue this race of people from certain peril."

Philip sighed again. "We're going to have to report this to HQ. Jim's going to want to know."

Baygorn interrupted. "Stop. Jim trusts your judgment, Philip. If we wait, we die. You said it yourself, remember? Shar's going to ride in here with his cavalry and—"

"All right, all right." Philip knew Baygorn was right.

"One condition, Alana: You programme those zips two different ways. Listen carefully, I don't want to provoke an interstellar incident here. We have to play our cards right. What are our possibilities? Our position is, we have one enemy, possibly another—two programmes. Yes, one to destroy only the Platnios, the other for the Peblinus and the Platnios—just to be on the safe side. Put the shape and size of those things onto that keypad of yours, Alana, and do what you do best. If all hell breaks loose, and only if it does, you wait for my command to activate the second programme. I want no buts and no ifs!"

"Consider it done, Philip." Inside, Randolph was patiently waiting.

Alana walked past him and immediately began to programme the zips. An hour later, with help, she had strategically placed ten zip bombs outside the hangar, two on each side, two in the rear, and the remaining four faced the Peblinus encampment.

Another hour had passed when a small group of Peblinus militia roamed to the hangar and asked if Philip and his crew knew where the previous column of soldiers had gone.

Alana, hearing the remark, smiled and walked over. "Of course we know where they are."

"Well?" asked the official through gritted teeth.

"They ran off like scared animals back towards your hangar. Do you want to end up like them? Do you want to know what it's like to be scared?" Bitterly, Alana lowered her tone. Quietly, the Peblinus officer looked towards his men as ten armed Bod guards pulled up next to Alana and pointed their rifles at the Peblinus.

"Well," Alana said with sarcasm.

Mouths opened. "We'll be back," said the Peblinus official, stumbling back a pace and almost falling over his own two feet. They scooted off into the night.

"You know it's people like you that start wars," said Philip, directing his glare towards Alana.

Alana's grin disappeared. "What can I say? I hate greed," she said. "They sweat greed, they talk greed, and above all they are just plain rude. I couldn't help it, I guess."

A short while later, Randolph's right-hand man, alias the Stomper, announced over his communicator that the radar had picked up mass movement coming from the nearby Peblinus hangar.

"They are everywhere, sir. They started appearing five minutes ago. Seem to be flanking, too, and getting closer."

Randolph handed Philip his portable radar. "Have a look. They didn't waste any time."

Philip saw the two hangars were clearly marked like boxes. One was green and the other was red. The Bod hangar, the green one, was slowly being surrounded by a soup of red pixel-sized dots gently swaying while slothfully making its way in their direction like an army of red ants. Suddenly without warning the menacing cloud of red stopped.

Randolph breathed deeply. "Look, they must be waiting for the advance order. Fools to think we can't see them!" It was some time later when the blotch of red pixels began to move again.

Ramaan commented, "An irregular stain making its way over plasma, like a spider from one box to another."

Stomper walked over. "They're only two kilometres away. If I know Shar, it won't be long now."

Stomper was so thin that when he turned sideways, Philip could hardly see him. Stomper, noticing his glare, said, "I am like this on purpose. It makes me a hard target for them." The man went beyond anorexic, but his firm voice made up for his size.

Suddenly, there was a distant ping as a projectile hit the hangar on the roof. Then there was another. The calmness of the night was changing. Philip was sure he could hear the Peblinus army shouting. He brushed away his thoughts. Less than a kilometre from their hangar and completely encircling them, Shar and his army stopped. There was a brief silence, that respectful minute of silence before they started firing on them. At first, it sounded like someone throwing rocks. Seconds later, it turned into a hailstorm. In less than a minute, thirty Bods had been injured or killed.

Annoyed, Philip grabbed the radio. "Shar, stop your carnage or we will return fire!"

Shar's familiar, cynical voice retorted over the speaker. It was sickly, and it made Philip's skin crawl to hear him again. Philip shivered. "I told you to carry out your orders, you stupid human! Why didn't you listen to me in the beginning? Now we are coming to kill all of you. Tell me where you are, and I'll come for you myself. I'll make it nice and quick, I promise."

He laughed, so Philip rammed his fist into the radio and irately looked at Alana. "Are those zips armed?"

Alana waved the control panel in the air and with a cynical smile, raised an eyebrow. "Nice to have the same itch once in a while, isn't it? Press here and your question shall be answered."

Philip bolted to her side. The control panel had one flashing yellow light. As if invisible wires were attached to the light, the moment Philip's finger pressed the pulsating blink, multiple bangs rocketed into the newly lit night sky.

The zip bomb rocketed upwards and split up into hundreds of tiny projectiles, all targeting their victims. "Intelligent bullets" was another name for them. They released their miniature mortal cargo of death on top of the oncoming army. In less than a minute, it was all over. Bods on the outside had described it as a massive meteor shower as missiles homed in on their Peblinus and Platnios targets. The scene must have been unforgettable for them. The uneasiness had a sudden emptiness. It hit Philip like a vacuum. Randolph's men put down the odd occasional Peblinus who lingered too near like a rabid dog.

Randolph told them to come inside the hangar and started fiddling with his remote control. "The stealth is armed," he said. "There will be no escape from its deadly law. Stealth micro-missiles seek out their prey for a distance of up to ten kilometres." Randolph pressed a button.

Five gruelling minutes passed as Peblinus died near and far. They fell down, dotting the arid landscape with blood and gore as bullets ripped through them. Decapitated Platnios waited for the cleanup team as other Platnios, too, waited for the opportunity to feed on their own dead. They ate anything.

Scavenger birds began to appear out of nowhere. Their grotesque forms were here for the gorge of the century. Philip watched them through his infrared binoculars fighting over scraps. Before Randolph had time to arm the second stealth, a message shot out of the radio like birdshot. It was the distraught voice of Shar.

"Stop please, humans. Please stop. I am sorry. You were right and I was wrong. I wish to negotiate."

Alana grabbed the mike. "We warned you, now look at what you've gone and done. Who is Mister Stupid now?" Philip always loved Alana's emphasis on certain words. The radio clicked and fell silent.

Twenty minutes before Mintaka was due to rise, Philip and his team climbed back into the vehicle and drove to the Peblinus hangar. It was time to pick up the remaining pieces with Shar. Randolph and two guards sat at the back. Randolph leaned forward, "You know, this is the first positive move we've seen in a hundred years." Uninterested by his input, Lexia stared at the cold, reddening sky revealing odd, vague clouds before tilting her head down towards the many silhouetted, strewn bodies.

Philip glanced at Randolph. "This is such a waste."

A man was sprawled on the grass, flat on his back, unmoving. Philip jumped out the vehicle, scrambled to his feet and went to contemplate the remains. The man lay straggled in the middle of nowhere. There was just enough light to see that his face was gone. Jesus. Gone, as if it had been torn off. His hair and ragged ribbons of his scalp bristled over the white bone of his forehead. The skull peered up at Philip.

Baygorn pulled up to his side. Suppressing nausea, Baygorn examined the man's hideous wound. The morning light was not quite bright enough, so he used a flashlight to inspect the edges of the injury and to peer into the skull. The centre of the dead man's face was blown away clear to the bone. The skin, flesh and cartilage were gone, ripped away by the impact of the stealth bullet. It was as if a torture artist had designed a frame of healthy skin to set off the gruesome exhibition of bone on display.

"Horrible, isn't it?" Randolph, using his flashlight to illuminate the corpse, released an authentic tone of pity. "Despite all these innocent losses and this ridiculous waste of life, this is the first."

"Don't tell me it's the first positive move you've seen in a hundred years!" Philip's razor-sharp tone made Randolph step back before getting in the vehicle.

When the Peblinus hangar came into view, a basic laser turret much like their own blue-ray aimed and fired at the vehicle. A shower of sparks rained down as the burst hit the vehicle on the front. Their own weapon system automatically came alive with a whirr, and the two turrets disappeared in puffs of silvery smoke.

Shar was standing away from the hangar waiting as the vehicle pulled up. Two Peblinus elite were lingering not far away from him, becoming shadows of his shadow. Randolph called on his communicator for the backup unit waiting over the hill. They arrived scant seconds later and placed Shar under arrest. The rest of the Bod recon squad moved into the hangar. Two rough-looking, filing cabinet-sized gorillas picked up Shar by the scruff and lifted him up with his feet dangling in mid-air.

"Wait! Before you take him away, I want to ask him something." The two tremendously large squad members released their grip on Shar, and his feet fell with a dry thump.

Philip looked into Shar's sorry face. "What made you attack Braan all those years ago? What drove you to such insanity? What could have been the reason for killing so many Bods?"

Shar lowered his head and spoke with softness. "We call it tellurium. It is not only vital to our existence, it's our main source of income. We use it to make machinery, vehicles, and use its semi-conductive qualities for the manufacture of electronic components. We thought the Bods were going to steal it from us, so we exterminated the majority of them when we arrived."

Philip felt an urge to throttle him.

Alana came over and pushed Philip to one side. "I've known worms with a greater pride than you! You're so callous, so empty." Alana raised her chin with a look of pure fury and smacked him across the face with her hand. "I am sure there was enough for everyone. You exterminated them like animals, like you just exterminated your own troops!"

Philip and the others shook hands with Randolph and bid him farewell. His first contacts had been emotional and successful.

They returned to their waiting pod and made the preparations for the next phase of their journey.

It took the *Excelsior* a week to reach orbit around the bleak, volcanic yellow planet Phot. Philip and Alana were watching as its sterile sphere unhurriedly reached the centre of the visual display unit. She reached up and disconnected the main motors. As the *Excelsior's* gravity began to diminish and alter, the door leading to the laboratory opened. Lexia failed to see why or how it was inhabited or by what, yet the scanner revealed a few blips.

"Maybe they are trees," said Lexia with anticipation.

Ramaan expressed, "Definitely not trees, Lexia." He momentarily discredited Lexia's distinguishing abilities.

"Then what are they?"

The gigantic, floating grey volcanic rock with vast shadows and pits was nothing more than a corroded, suffocating surface, yet apparently it wasn't entirely dead and barren.

The duration of their interplanetary trip allowed the team to rest. It gave them the time to get back into gear. Rejuvenate. This, of course, varied from person to person.

During the trip Alana had been experimenting with the GF rifle. She was tweaking and fine-tuning it. Getting to know it better. She called it a personal relationship.

Lexia was making progress in the Bod and Peblinus languages, although she sometimes complained about their complexity as frequent screams often echoed down the passageway.

Baygorn studied the plant samples they'd brought back from Braan, and Ramaan had been working on bettering the remote control and programming unit that Randolph had given him.

Philip sat on his commander's chair running scans while staring out at the compellingly dead, nearing orb of Phot. He watched as a star disappeared from sight behind its planetary curvature.

This time as they neared, the two moons, Diamees and Plosnu, were in plain sight. The *Excelsior* examined them. Its life-sensing beams roamed and probed the surface of the moons, meticulously looking down cracks and under rocks. The interrogating tendrils barely touching, scarcely illuminating the surface, peeked into the depths endeavouring to find life, to find something, anything.

They did their job by finding nothing where there was nothing to find in the first place. Only desolateness had evolved on these pieces of floating rock. Moving at fifty thousand kilometres per hour, Diamees was irregularly shaped and reddish-brown, with meteorite pocks caused by previous bombardments, owing to its magnetic composition.

Due to an incredible impact an unknown time ago, a large chunk of it had been broken off, fractured. They called it Diamees B. They watched as the lonely chunk drifted close to the moon, forming a binary orbit. Sentrywatcher showed curiosity about the light curve.

On Phot, an eruption occurred every ten minutes. The atmosphere consisted of large quantities of oxygen and sulphur dioxide together, forming a volatile cocktail. As the *Excelsior* neared, Ramaan glimpsed at immensely tall trees dominating parts of the Photian surface, scrabbling for oxygen the best they could. This time, they were going to land themselves at night in an area called Alfonsus 9. It was the only area with a surface composition hard enough to withstand the weight of the pod. The ground, although volcanic, was treacherous, and they had to choose their landing site with precision.

Sentrywatcher picked up a life sign twenty kilometres from Alfonsus 9.

"Could be Peblinus," added Philip, squinting at red dots on the scanner. Lexia pulled up next to him and frowned.

Alana flicked a switch on the console. "Okay. Buckle up, people. Ten seconds for separation."

Lexia felt like a prisoner awaiting sentence. Her executioner's chair waited without answer or consolation. Baygorn's contemplating eyes were shut.

During their descent into the fiery yellow atmosphere, tiny fragments of rock, micrometeorites, collided against the hull of the pod. It slowed them as the already blackening acidic air made Sentrywatcher believe that they were near an eruption. Conventionally, they couldn't see by visual means, so they used the radar's penetrating eye for guidance. They landed the pod on the rim of the huge crater an hour later. Their first impressions were that the setting was practically like that of Earth's moon.

The crater was a gigantic impact puncture hundreds of metres across. An object the size of a house had collided here an eternity ago and had left behind this deformed and vacant, lifeless hole. At this stage of the trip, the routine checks they made were vital. They missed nothing.

Before leaving the safety of the pod, Baygorn analysed the surface and air composition. Ramaan searched for energy sources and constructions. Alana looked for intelligent life forms or movement, anything that contained carbon or silicon. Lexia listened for any radio signals that could prove the existence of intelligent life, while Philip revised all the findings and took the planet's temperature. It was his duty. They had to continue with this until there were no doubts as to where they were going. There had to be no loopholes, no mistakes. There were no radio signals, on any frequency; and no vibrations that the seismographs could pick up, apart from volcanic or the micro-tremors undoubtedly caused by the volcanic surface and the sun's increasing heat. There were no electrical currents, and the radioactivity was insignificant. It was almost ominously quiet; one might have expected that even an asteroid would be noisier. Philip asked himself, what did we expect, a committee of welcome? He was not sure whether to be disappointed or relieved. The initiative, at any rate, was up to him. Only when Philip was convinced could they put on their space suits and make the proper preparations to leave the pod.

Alana suddenly jerked up from behind her scanner. "I found something, Sentrywatcher was right." Her voice trembled.

Baygorn looked at her viewer. "What do you think it is?"

"Well, now that we are closer, it's not Bod or Peblinus; they are farther away. I'm not sure what it is. All I can say is, it's moving."

"Life forms normally move, Alana. What's the problem with that?"

She steered her head. "It's liquid, that's the problem. It's liquid and it's moving fast."

"Liquid, how odd," commented Ramaan in a not-so-natural tongue.

Alana reviewed the results again. "Got something else!" Her tone made everyone jump. "Looks like a bunker, deep underground."

A blinking light attracted Ramaan's attention. "Yeah, I see it too! Wait a minute; I have energy readings coming from that same area. Take a look at this; it's a big one, almost three kilometres long!" The recent map extracted from both Sentry-watcher and the pod revealed a volcanic area about twenty kilometres from their position, right next to the bunker.

Philip turned and faced the others. "I have no idea what it could be; suggestions, anyone?" He waited ten full seconds, but only received blank looks.

"Thought so. Let's get those suits on and let's go find out."

Leaving the tranquillity and luminance of the pod, the surface immediately became obsidian. Philip could feel heat coming off the recently cooled lava surface through the floor of the vehicle. Sporadic steaming fumaroles of noxious gas, constantly squirting with a hiss and a thrust, alleviated the pressures below from the angry magma. Alana stopped the engine for a moment, so Philip, complete with breathing apparatus, could climb out and get his first view of this totally alien landscape. As his vision lethargically adjusted in the absolute darkness, he noticed surface haze, then introductory outlines of dull grey mountains. Philip switched on his lamp. Ice had accumulated close by on a rocky ledge, ridiculing the magma not far below.

Averting this, he looked into the night sky, endeavouring to glimpse upon a familiar constellation or star group. He saw none. Not even their own sun was visible. It should have been close to Alpha Centauri, but it wasn't there. Its insignificant orb was too dim and too far away. The only evidence of where he was were the red and yellow flames raging near, far and farther in the distance. Noxious quantities of sulphur dioxide swam in tendrils between the rocks as ochre fingers probed the surface erratically, slithering and pausing before being driven by geothermal currents. This was hell without a doubt. Philip climbed back into the vehicle to continue their journey.

An odd occasional ground rumble accompanied them on their slow stride. A notepad fell to the floor next to Alana, disorienting the vehicle and their minds. It was an overpowering sensation crowding in on them as they drove themselves towards the bunker. Death had visited this primordial inferno many times.

If I were a painter, thought Philip, *I would've painted a black canvas with blotches of yellow and red.*

The absence of light, animal life, bacteria, water or anything with an occasional rumbling sound has a tendency to distort the sturdiest of imaginations; let alone having a liquid life form for a host. As intriguing and baffling as it all sounded, they moved over ancient lava flows. Then their fears began to pounce in on them like an invisible shroud. Not even the most experienced psychologists could predict solitude similar to this. They could only dissimulate their terror on this hostile world. If they lost it here, they would be in a world of hurt. No one said anything. Their faces were as gloomy as the outside, and it was only when they neared the location of the bunker when Lexia broke their depression. Her hopeful, shaking hand pointed outwards. "Look, that might be an entrance!"

Crimson light doused the entire area. To Baygorn, it was a wafting sea of purple mist against a rock face.

Sentrywatcher bleeped. Ramaan looked at the scan of a volcano not far away. "Talk about the dragon's lair!" he said, frowning.

Alana parked next to a post on the jagged surface. The nightly silence strained their apparatus to such a limit that the search for anything diminished. The only audible sounds were substratum rumblings every now and then.

The entrance was a vertical round hole, three metres in diameter, which from closer inspection became a rocky yellowed doorframe embedded on the side of a small incline of a hill. Alana poked at the sulphur encrusted on the walls. Moving to one side, Ramaan went in first. The cavern led downwards and culminated into a long, wide flight of steep, rock-carven, ash-covered steps. There was light at the bottom. The rest of them followed in single file and moved downwards, guided by the wall, towards the light. Perspective had a new meaning, and they found it increasingly difficult not to lose it.

"Got energy readings going off the scale!" said Ramaan through the visor, peering at his scanner. The light grew brighter.

Baygorn took an atmosphere check. "Seems to be plenty of artificial oxygen down here."

"It can only be artificial. Where's it coming from, and why all the way out here?" Philip asked. Soon after they'd reached the bottom, Ramaan took off his headgear. A slow draught stirred at his hair. He sniffed the air. "I can feel a lot of heat coming from the other end of the corridor. It smells a bit bad, slightly sour, though, not too difficult. Reminds me of rotten eggs."

The others followed suit and took off their masks before squinting down a straight passageway that extended to the imagination. Every ten metres or so, on both sides, two powerful vertical arm-sized strip lights separated an unmarked door.

"Do those things look familiar?" Baygorn twisted towards Alana.

"Yep, we also know why my scanner showed us energy usage. Look at the size of this place. It makes dinky toys out of the bunkers. Also seems like this plastic stuff is everywhere."

Baygorn walked to a door. Taking off a glove, he felt the round protruding plastic knob. "No keyholes; they're identical to those on Braan. Obviously the same builders." Baygorn lifted out a portable drill from his bag and took a sample. Curly swarf fell into a flask. Closing the jar, he placed his hand on the knob and slowly opened the noiseless door. Alana drew her weapon.

Inside was a laboratory. One wall was lined with shelving and cupboards and contained dozens of dusty books and jars. A hammer and other hand tools, containers, small machines with keyboards that appeared to have been made for five fingers were strewn on the left of a table in the middle of the room.

On the right were scientific instruments, conventional domestic utensils, including knives and plates, which, apart from their size, would not have attracted a second glance on any terrestrial table. Another table towards the back had three empty chemical sample jars. Two were smashed. Many browned papers and charts lay on the floor, as the adhesive that supported them on the wall had long ago decomposed. Glass beakers and corked test tubes were on another tabletop, bearing rings of anonymous, long-evaporated liquids.

"Where's the oxygen coming from?" Alana asked.

Lexia moved towards a bench. "Probably from that ventilation shaft up there. It gets fresher the nearer you get to it."

Briefly peering up, Alana unzipped her C-12 and lifted it to waist height.

"Our life form is four hundred metres straight down that corridor. No wait, make that beings." Alana paused a second. "There's quite a few of them. Definitely not silicon or carbon. Things are very active too!"

Philip noticed the shiver in her voice.

"What do you think they were studying here?" asked Lexia, as she raised her eyes from the bench to a shelf. Dust flew in all directions at the smallest of touches.

Alana replied, "Whatever it was, Lexia, it was important."

Lexia continued stirring. "Such a diversity of languages. Has anyone tried tearing this paper? I'll have it analysed; maybe there is a way for Sentrywatcher to de-atomise it." Lexia continued rummaging, with the hope of discovering something else.

Michael Gilwood

The ventilator shaft attached to the roof of the laboratory by metal pegs had a definite oxygen tinge flowing from its interior. Without a doubt, it was the source of their oxygen, but from very close, right underneath, it turned somewhat stale. Ramaan curiously pulled up a rickety chair and balanced himself on the back. Peeking inside the grid-less shaft, he commented on the sound of distant drips resonating from its interior.

"It sounds like a cave in there, and it's definitely an air duct. Bit crude though, just an effective communicator to all the rooms down here." The light from the room gave him little assistance so Ramaan, now squinting, reached forward up to his thighs and forced the dull obsidian insides into focus. He imagined he could see a light far down in the distance.

"There's droppings scattered about the interior. The dripping seems nearer now. Smells a bit like a drain," he said as he ventured farther into the ventilator shaft with his xenon-ion flashlight. The length of the shaft disappeared from view.

"I can't see anything else. My voice is distorting itself when I talk; must run the full length of the corridor." His voice bounced down the enormous length of the ventilator and reappeared with a phantasmagorical echoic shift in pitch. Ramaan climbed down and brushed himself off.

Some of the jars placed on shelves below the ventilator contained colourful powders. Baygorn was trying to read the label on one of them that had a jelly-like substance. He unscrewed the lid, took out a spatula sample and placed it on a slide.

A grunt ripped through the lab. "Damn knows what this is. So many things, so many mysteries."

They returned to the passageway, and Alana opened the second door and walked in. It was a storage room.

Scuttle, shuffle.

"What was that?" Lexia's face twisted in response to a sound she'd heard. It was a scuttling noise and it made everyone turn and prick up their ears. It seemed to reverberate down the passageway behind and in front of them.

"It sounded like it came from the ventilation shaft as well!" Lexia moved to the middle of the group of huddling bodies.

Philip's eyes drilled in to Alana. "Lexia, it's probably the construction. You know, frequent ground tremors and all are probably dislodging parts of it." As Alana stared at rubble lying in the passageway, she was not convinced. It didn't sound like a brick falling or a stone coming adrift or a crack forming. It sounded more like tiny feet, the scuffling sound a hamster makes in a cage, or a tiny foot sliding down the stairs.

Leaving the storage room, Ramaan bent down. "Look, there are more of those droppings I saw earlier in that vent. What's this?" Next to the soiled patch, he picked up and handed Baygorn a bone.

"It's a human toe! What's a bloody toe doing down here on the floor?" Everybody steered their heads and looked at one another. The toe was totally clean. Suddenly, there was another foot-scurry of something not too far away. Philip and the others found it difficult to pinpoint the source because it seemed to come from all directions.

Nothing showed up on Alana's scanner. "Maybe it's too small."

"This place echoes too much, damn thing could be anywhere!" Baygorn readied his firearm and looked around. Ramaan did the same and hovered behind Lexia and Philip.

"Obviously something knows we're here." Lexia's quivering voice moved her alongside Ramaan, gripping his arm. Moving ahead, Alana opened the next door. It was a sleeping quarter with four beds and a couple of cupboards. It had a striking resemblance to any bedroom Philip had ever seen. Inside a cupboard, Alana found a single shoe with the sole lying limply alongside.

"God, this place was abandoned a long time ago. Whatever went wrong here, we missed the party."

Philip was thinking of the hangars and thought it had something to do with them. Alana directed herself towards the next door. As she pushed it open, a large rat had picked up their scent and scuttled past her leg. The thing was almost as big as a cat and stood there eyeballing her with forgotten hunger. It seemed just as stunned as she was. It sniffed the stale air.

"Christ! Of all the things!" Suddenly, it sprang forward like a jack-in-the-box, teeth flaring, and ran desperately towards her.

Weapon already drawn, she vaporised it without hesitation. Omni-directional squeaks simultaneously echoed through the bunker as other rats sensed the loss of their companion.

Identical to those on Braan, evenly spaced vertical strip lamps bathed the corners in coherent light and revealed the immensity of the bunker. Philip looked once more back to the stairs then down into the void of the corridor.

5. The Library

Lexia was so nervous that at times she felt she didn't always fit into their recon team. She was a scientist—no, not just any scientist, she was top-of-the-class material, multi-faceted and by far the cleverest person anyone could hope to meet. At least being with the others, she was well protected, especially with Alana.

With a jolt, Alana opened the next door and went in. Philip and Lexia followed closely behind her. Ramaan and Baygorn stayed in the passageway to keep watch. At first, the room was completely dark. With the aid of Philip's flashlight, Alana's stare noticed an aisle, a subdivision. It was a wall. As Alana moved towards the segment, her presence in the room excited a hidden sensor for tiny light emitters. The light level gently rose to reveal hidden wonders where she had triggered the sensor. It was not only a wall, it was a shelf; a wealth of information unlike anything she had ever seen.

"My God, come see this. Come see what I found!" The room extended more than twenty metres at a 90-degree angle to the passage. The vent here was undisturbed and intact.

"Hey, Lexia, come look at this." Lexia quickly walked over, hearing Alana's excited tone. As Lexia directed herself towards an unlit area, the light in that area began to rise to welcome her arrival.

"It's a library. Look at all of this. There are thousands of books here, alphabetically placed, too." Before her, shelf upon shelf of dusty history had been unmoved for countless decades. Books reached the ceiling. The aisle also had books on both sides. Philip walked to the aisle to see Lexia take one from its place.

"Before I came on this voyage," she said, "I thought I knew the general dimensions of the relationship between my own knowledge and the knowledge of mankind. But what is staggering about this mission is how very small the entire range of human knowledge might be compared to what could be known. Just think, the sum of everything all human beings know or have ever known might be nothing more than an infinitesimal fraction of the *Encyclopaedia Galactica*."

"It's frightening," Philip interrupted enthusiastically.

"And thrilling at the same time," said Lexia. "Sometimes when I'm in a bookstore or a library, I am overwhelmed by all the things that I don't know. Then I am seized by a powerful desire to read all of the blurbs, one by one. Imagine what it would be like to be in the true library, the one that combined the knowledge of all the species in the universe. The very thought makes me woozy."

"Hold on to those horses, this might just be it. There are lots of maths and cognitive sciences here. Many of them are in English. I wonder if the Bods know about this place."

A hardcover book caught Philip's eye. "What's this—I don't believe it!" Philip lowered to a book spine, catching a glimpse of familiarity.

"It can't be, no!" Philip grinned as he yanked it out. He looked at the cover, the spine, the back cover. Before Philip opened it, he wanted to smell the paper. He wanted to be the first man in generations to lift incalculable value from a shelf.

"My God, Tutankhamen was nothing in comparison to this," he whispered, "a fairy tale." As he opened the book, dust flew in all directions. It was a book on Neptune. He held it up and began to laugh.

Alana turned. "What did you find?"

Philip tilted it and showed her the book.

She gave a long sigh, turned back to her book and lowered her voice. "The impossible here shall become the possible." The face lowered and the smile disappeared before silently going back to what she was doing.

Philip ran his nose over the rim before opening it. He suddenly began to think of all the newspaper cuttings he'd collected years ago. Was Norman's team still alive? On Earth, nobody had heard a word about him or his scientific crew for more than a decade. Their use had expired.

Excitedly, Philip opened the book. Once more, there was Neptune's unliveable icy surface. He turned a couple of pages.

His tongue did the Twist. On page 91, Triton's familiar dreary, grey orb filled the page. The Bods called Triton "Tretolon," just as they had called Neptune "Neptunth." He had recognised the book by the similarity. In the Tretolon section, photos of Yasu Sulci with its expedition of sixteen Bod explorers were all happily rummaging over the surface before the disaster.

"God, I have to get this back to the pod," he whispered again before stopping himself. "Why? Triton was old news, just as the scientists were." He caught sight of a book on Earth. The book was called *Terrus*. A bibliophile had bound it in green leather with gold calligraphy on the front. Its lightweight, inherent beauty stunned Philip as he raised it between his two flat hands and smelt its ancientness. It crackled and popped beneath his fingers as he slowly exposed the contents. Part of it broke off and gently fell to the floor. The first page was a dedication, with a brief index underneath. The printing had yellowed from its once-black state.

The book, written in perfect English, began with Earth during the Goranic Age, twelve thousand years before.

"Maybe they mixed up the planets, this can't really be Earth," said Philip, but the planet was without a doubt theirs. Philip sneezed as some dust reached his nostrils. He comprehended what he held. It was probably the most valuable book ever seen by the human species. It went beyond price.

Ecstatically, Philip read on. The book was about the human race in its early stages. Clearly, it was a branch of history that no one had researched, seen, or heard of before.

"So those speculations were actually true," said Philip, turning to somewhere in the middle. The chapter was headed: "The Abandoned Constructions on Terrus during the Goranic Age." Thinking back to Randolph, Philip turned more pages. Plans, geometric designs and locations, everything was here. It revealed unknown archaeological sites and undiscovered constructions no one had yet dug up and analysed. On page 89 were the Egyptian Pyramids. It showed when, how, and by whom they were built—the hidden treasures, the subterranean corridors, the chambers, all of it.

"Oh—damn! What a book. What a treasure." No archaeological find even came close to this.

Other solar systems, too, had their individual sections as encyclopaedias filled dusty shelves. Another one of the fascinating volumes Alana found mentioned a possible link between the Peblinus, Bods and the Gorinos, and the people of Earth.

"Maybe we all have a common denominator," she said. It was certainly a feasible thought.

Philip began to feel fuzzy looking at all the rows and columns. "There are so many language variations and dialects! Not even in my wildest dreams could I have imagined this!"

Baygorn busily looked up and down and continued, "With all this back on Earth we wouldn't have anything left to find. It's all here."

About an hour later, Alana huffed and walked back into the passageway towards the next door. "I can get back to this later. Right now, I'm moving on to what is next."

Inside were thirty upright aquariums on heavy stands completely filling the floor space. Each closed, heavily reinforced tank had been sealed with an equally heavy lid. Cables leading from each two-metre-wide tank rose to the ceiling and eventually ran their course off towards a central control panel in the far corner. The glass of each aquarium had a thickness of about four inches. Two were broken. Crystalline chunks were scattered on the floor, smashed and in ruins, like the aftermath of a fallen building.

The occupants of the remaining twenty-eight aquariums looked like living mercury balls of varying sizes. Whatever they were, to break an aquarium of these dimensions, they would have to be very strong and powerful. The others joined Alana. Ramaan went and examined the control panel while Philip moved to have a look at these strange creatures. As he placed his hand on the glass, the ball immediately stuck itself to the inside of the tank and began imitating the shape of his hand and its every move. When he left it to go and look at another ball, it became furious and started bashing itself against the glass sides with tremendous force.

Philip turned towards the noise and said, "They're studying our movements."

Alana came over and examined them the best she could from outside the tank. "So that's why they didn't show on our scanner, they're Hafnium-based!" On a single table to the left of the control panel, an electronic machine, possibly some kind of high-tech computer equipment, was still operational. Its physical appearance was far smaller than anything Philip had seen before. Logos and strange symbols lined the screen. It was operating in absolute silence. Philip called Lexia and asked her to translate the symbols.

"All this stuff is connected," she said. "It must have something to do with the process of the tellurium and the volcanic terrain. Leave it with me; I'll see what I can figure out."

The mercurious balls definitely possessed an intelligence of some kind. When Philip and Alana walked next to the tanks, they imitated them by mocking their movements. On the far side of the wall, a large, round metallic tube like a chimney disappeared vertically underground. Small wisps of sulphurous smoke rose from its interior into the already tangy air.

"Philip, I've found something." Lexia waved a hand. Alana and the others moved closer to hear.

"Remember what Shar said about the tellurium? We know the Peblinus need large quantities of it for their everyday needs. Well, these metallic balls go into that tube you found via a transport trolley, the tubes leading from each aquarium. Tellurium is a volcanic residue and these creatures are diggers. Our mercurious tank dwellers burrow into the volcanic magma as their way of attracting tellurium due to their hafnium structure. When they return, they are heavily coated with the precious mineral. They apparently return to an emanated signal coming from a transducer fitted to the lid of each aquarium. All the Peblinus had to do was to remove the tellurium from them, which, as it turned out, was an easier chore than anticipated because as the ball began to cool, the pure tellurium fell off in small flakes."

Philip sat in a chair. "Interesting. Seems like our Peblinus don't like to work, but want to reap the benefits at all costs. These mercurious balls are slaves like the Bods were. Seems logical."

Alana gave off a giggle. "Look, this one's forming the shape of my hand." The metallic form laxly transformed itself like jelly to the shape of her hand on the other side of the tank.

Lexia interrupted. "There's more. It appears the Peblinus stumbled upon the life form by accident when they were exploring the volcanic underground tunnels. By then, of course, it had killed two of their scientists, including their discoverer. When they did eventually manage to capture it, they found it was coated with traces of their precious substance."

Philip stood up. "Just remember, there are two of them loose down here somewhere."

"What are we going to do if we see them?" asked Lexia.

"It depends, Lexia; we only know a little about them. So far they don't seem aggressive."

They were returning to the library to continue with their research when suddenly a screech reverberated along the immensity of the ventilator shaft. It was a long and distorted, drawn-out echo that threw itself at them as it exited the grid. Something had just died, and it had the rats in a frenzied panic. One shot by Baygorn's leg without even bothering to look up. The screech faded.

"What the hell was that? Crap, it sounded close!" Baygorn raised an eyebrow. Without showing any fear, Philip opened the book of Neptune again.

"I'll be damned; the Peblinus have a base on Titania. Ramaan, didn't we send a probe to that Uranian moon back in the fifties?"

"Yes, Captain Stolings was his name."

"Now I know why it just vanished." Another shriek dragged his eyes from the book. Closing it gently, Philip placed the book on a table.

"Damn, there it is again." The galvanising sound of pain dissipated down the corridor and into the nothingness.

Alana shot into the passageway with her pistol in hand. "It's down there all right," she said, looking at her motion detector. Random, infrequent rats scuffled about, ensuring their own survival. Farther down the passageway, the team came across a chemical storage room. Next to the door, a single reinforced fastened window revealed some bottles neatly stacked against a far wall. A metallic shelf forming an aisle contained hundreds of labelled jars of varying sizes and colours. Some were broken on the ground.

Next to the door, as if it had once tried to gain entrance to the storage area, a dead Platnios lay on the floor outside the door in eternal rest. Its reduced size was due to the evaporation of body fluids. Volcanic heat and time both had contributed their wrath to the fossilised mass now lying painlessly on the floor. What would a Platnios be doing out here so far from home? Baygorn could see it had died a long time ago. As he moved it to one side, it crumbled into small dusty pieces.

Something moving on the inside of the storage area caught their attention. A young and playful Photian rat had stumbled upon something crawling on the floor. It was a bug. The bug was vainly attempting to escape the ever-nearing furry mass. It seemed happy in its apathetic world. They watched the young rat have fun with its newly found toy and encircled it with persistence.

"It's only an insect," Lexia said as the bug frantically ran for its life. As they were watching the spectacle, a mercurious ball the size of an orange suddenly enwrapped the rat. It leapt on top of the defenceless rodent, engulfing and digesting it. The rat disappeared. They heard the penetrating death screech bounce and resonate once more down the passageway. The bug, however, had recovered and continued on its wobbly path before disappearing beneath a cupboard. They were awestruck by the sight.

Between the storage room and the passageway, a metal grill or a vent became the new target for the metallic ball now rolling itself in that direction. It appeared on their side of the wall like a steak mincer. The strands flowed back into the form of the orange-sized globule it once was a mere five metres from their retreating bodies.

Ramaan turned and fired a shot at the thing with his GF rifle, but the ray bounced off it like a stone hitting a windscreen. "Some good that was!"

"Quick, try a different frequency!" shouted Alana as Ramaan hurriedly fiddled with the buttons and fired again. The metallic ball, obviously annoyed and unscathed, moved onwards, having them perfectly lined up in its sights. Ramaan changed frequency again as the small ball started to gain velocity. Alana tried with her blue-ray, but as she pulled the trigger, the bolt of silver fire bounced off like light on a mirror and destroyed part of the ceiling. The ball was by now moving at the same speed as they were. Ramaan, after a last-second adjustment, pulled the trigger and hit the ball directly in the middle. It disappeared in a gust of red, disseminated smoke.

They stopped, caught their breath and returned to the storage room to force the door. It gave way. On the far end, a door led into a changing area. Inside, protective clothing hung on the walls in various stages of disintegration. Rags that were once clothes fell apart at the mere touch. Strewn pieces were in random piles alongside boots and gloves. Dust-covered plastic benches waited for someone to sit on them. It would never happen again.

Baygorn began sifting through debris. "Like everywhere we've seen so far, whatever happened, took place a long time ago." Most of the bottles and jars in the central aisle area contained unknown compounds. Lexia could only translate a few of them.

As Baygorn and Lexia bent down to read the contents of a bottle with a white powder, another rodent shrieked.

"Damn, that sounded close. It could be in the next room."

"No," said Alana looking at her motion detector. "It's down the passageway!"

"How far?" Philip's quavering concern made Lexia move closer.

"Thirty metres." Philip, Ramaan, and Alana went into the passageway to look. There, way in the distance, a mercurious ball was stationary in the middle of the walkway. Philip could feel it studying them. Invisible eyes tore into them and listened with invisible ears to everything they said. It toyed with them, sliding from left to right, preparing its attack. A blue-ray Alana had placed in the passageway was delivering its full charge with absolutely no effect.

Without warning, the ball advanced and picked up speed, knocking over the blue-ray like a toy in a child's bedroom. From twenty metres, they could see this specimen was much bigger than the previous one in the storage area. Ramaan and Alana fired simultaneously, disintegrating the thrusting beast only ten metres away. They shuddered, exchanging glances. What if the GF had failed or if they'd set it wrongly? It was a close one.

Security became an issue. After the narrowness of the incident, they decided not to venture farther down. Instead, they returned to the vehicle with their findings.

Rushing up the stairs and out into the harsh atmosphere, condensation began to accumulate on Philip's visor. Through the steamy murk, he could make out the first wisps of a volcanic dawn.

"Anywhere was better than down there. Hell, what were those things? Why all the aggression?" he thought aloud.

It was cold even through his suit, so Philip turned up the temperature. Mintaka was due to rise at any moment, and he didn't want to miss it. It wasn't every day that he got the opportunity to watch an alien sunrise. The dirty, grey horizon began to blink out stars like someone with a light switch as the first deep red rays peeked and edged their way over the terrain.

As Mintaka's radiation excited the high-altitude volcanic particles, eerie, waving borealis tendrils swam over the horizon.

"Isn't it spectacular?" Lexia stared out at the blood-red landscape.

During their absence, Sentrywatcher had completely mapped Phot and its two moons. Together, Alana and Ramaan studied the planet's surface while Baygorn seemed more interested in the two moons. Lexia sat next to Philip, absorbing the striking contrasts and ranges of colours brought by the spectacle of dawn. Once Mintaka had risen, only then could the true variety of reds become discernible.

After studying the cartography of Phot, they planned their route to a city Sentrywatcher called Niobe and departed the bunker.

"God, I hope we never have to return here," said Lexia with a critical tongue.

Alana turned away from the steering wheel. "Don't worry, Lex, I'm sure Head Command will get someone out here to do the

the dirty work, you needn't worry." They passed a cluster of inactive volcanoes with faint wispy puffs rising in streams. Passing behind a low ledge, they turned towards mist lurking near some rocks. It was a sulphurous fog bank coming up from an icy lake. It looked uninviting. Sparse, acid-browned flora encircled the extremities. Some species had fallen over, due to erosive winds. Rocks eroded in strange patterns coiled their way into natural caves.

Baygorn put his hand on Alana's shoulder. "Hey, slow down, I want a sample of that."

Alana stopped the vehicle, Baygorn climbed out with a sample flask and began to siphon some liquid. A few lights came on and the results appeared on a small liquid-crystal screen. It was water polluted with sulphur, making the liquid completely undrinkable and unsuitable for life. The pH levels indicated that it was almost pure acid.

"Wow, not even the volcanoes on Earth produce water this acidic."

Alana and Ramaan jumped out of the vehicle. On the far side of the lake, there were large nests hanging by thin threads from a tree. Insects were flying in and out. With the aid of their binoculars, Alana commented on their unfriendly wasp-like characteristics.

To Baygorn, the sulphur-adapted flora was unclassifiable and resembled nothing he'd seen before. "Stuff's like straw. How something can survive out here in these conditions beats me," he said, climbing back into the vehicle. He was glad to sit down again and immediately began to wonder about his own survival.

Their thermal suits made it difficult to walk on the surface. Although they were light, they were uncomfortable and the visor had limited vision. Ramaan always compared them to wearing horse blinkers and also claimed, every time he got undressed, that he seemed thinner.

Sentrywatcher's map indicated that Niobe was a city populated by Peblinus.

Philip wondered what their reception was going to be like. "If it's anything like Braan, we should approach with caution." They wandered the bewildering hallways of the bunker for more than three hours; but thinking about it, they would have been hopelessly lost without their personal navigators. Even though they still had no thorough plan for the search, the hour trip to Niobe brought to light new speculations from each of them as to where they were going, and above all, what they would encounter.

Niobe was an enormous complex of four well-spaced hangars placed in a square format. A three-metre wall surrounded the city, and in the centre of the four hangars, a slanting, heptagonal obelisk about sixty metres high dominated a central plaza. The level of oxygen was higher here.

At the one end of the city close to a hill, Baygorn pointed out activity: loaded trucks with rock samples, machinery, and people on foot. Philip watched them speed off and disappear into one of the far hangars. He assumed they were excavating tellurium. Although he'd never seen an operation like this before, he just knew it couldn't have been anything else. They drove to the front entrance and were greeted by a lieutenant dressed in red. He approached the vehicle and lowered his gloomy face to the round window. Tap, tap.

Alana reached over Philip and asked, "Who's in charge?"

The slightly magnified face took one look at her and gasped. "My, my, look who we have here." The accent was high-pitched, Asiatic. "I got word flom High Command, if you showed up we were to give you whatever you needed. You are vely good people."

Baygorn chuckled.

"What are you excavating?" asked Philip, looking into the face.

"Tellurium," responded the guard. Philip knew this was going to be his answer.

"Can we take a look around? There seems to be an awful lot of activity going on around here. Where are those trucks going?"

"They are bringing people up from the mine. Some of our mine workers exposed an ancient alcove in the old dig site. They say there's something horrible down there. We're clearing out the stocks and personnel just in case." The guard opened the gate and gave them directions to the site.

Niobe wasn't just a city, it was a mass concentration of Peblinus all there for one purpose: to mine tellurium. Like man, they, too, had dreams. Philip stared agape, watching as they chaotically walked or ran everywhere. It was pandemonium. Peblinus were flocking towards a hillside close to the last hangar. Their vehicle chugged along, and some miners followed them from behind.

The hillside was artificially carved and vertical, having been levelled and flattened before becoming the mine entrance. According to Sentrywatcher, the site wasn't volcanic; the nearest activity was more than sixty kilometres away. Alana parked the vehicle next to a group of workers. One of them, taking interest in this strange new vehicle with five oddly dressed strangers, made him turn his head, swing the rest of his body and walk over.

Alana climbed out. "How far down does it go?" she asked, looking at his attire.

He curiously studied her. "A little more than two kilometres, the entrance was built at an incline of twenty degrees. At the base, in the gallery, other exploratory tunnels lead off on both sides. One of our technicians accidentally broke into an aperture apparently of alien origin, and they won't go back in there until it's safe," replied the Peblinus worker.

A Peblinus officer walked towards them. "Ah, you must be the humans the front guard told us about. After monitoring your transmissions, we've been expecting you. I am Colonel Rarts." Philip climbed out of the vehicle and they shook hands.

"Thanks to you, as Shar went into custody, he confessed to everything about what happened on Braan. Anyway, like our lieutenant explained at the front gate, if there is anything you need, you only have to ask."

Philip moved closer. "The gate guard mentioned something about an alien alcove. He said there might be something horrible down there. Give us ten men and we'll go and find out what's going on."

The colonel flicked his fingers, making a sound like the splintering of wood on a fire. Philip wondered if he had done the right thing by offering their help. Alana returned from the vehicle with motion trackers and weapons. With a quick pace, a lower-ranking officer arrived. Colonel Rarts issued him a hushed order, making him run off again. Five minutes later, ten fine-looking, young and inquisitive Peblinus soldiers came in single file. Alana studied the ten fearless men and divided them into their rank and age before beginning their long descent into the tunnel.

Their simple plan was to enter into the cavity and slowly make their way to the reactor and switch it back on. The mine entrance was two doors split in the middle. They opened like a slow auditorium curtain when Colonel Rarts gave the order. Halogen lights hanging from the ceiling efficiently revealed the way ahead. Philip looked down into the slope. The tunnel had boxes and crates on both sides and disappeared into his imagination, into purgatory.

There was not a soul to be seen anywhere, just lots of disarray and an occasional machine left running. The miners had left in a hurry. The sloping shaft was easy to walk down, and there was a warm thermal draught coming from the bottom. At eighteen hundred metres, they set up first camp. Philip left Lexia and Baygorn with three Peblinus guards. Daylight was still perceptible from the surface as a tiny pinprick in the distance.

Farther down, one of the Peblinus became claustrophobic. Philip gave him a shot to calm his nerves. "Some warrior you are, panicking like that. If anyone should be shaky, it should be me. What's your problem?" The man's teeth chattered like in an Arctic winter. He looked at Philip without replying. *This guy knows more than he's letting on*, thought Philip.

At a little more than two kilometres, Ramaan saw a body lying on the ground perched against a wall of the shaft. He walked to it, yet it seemed flattened, inexpressive and out of perspective. "What the blazes is this? It's just a pile of clothes put there to resemble someone." The clothes contained no blood or bones, only skin and rag.

"Like it's been sucked dry. Jesus, it's just a sack."

Philip turned away from an eye lying on the ground. He looked at the seven Peblinus soldiers staring back up the shaft, away from him.

Michael Gilwood

"Any ideas as to what might have done this?" They were jittery silent. Down they went. At the base of the tunnel, the gigantic tunnelling machine lay dormant. Next to it were the five operators—five flattened sacks of skin and clothes. Philip asked a nearby soldier, "Do you know what's in there?" The man looked down a dark side tunnel. "I'm not sure. No one knows. No one has ever lived to tell the story." Quickly turning his head again, he looked back once more into the side shaft. "It comes from in there, in the mine. Yesterday one of the workers accidentally discovered a hidden chamber leading onto the tellurium excavation site. When he ran out, he accidentally switched off the lights. That was when all this started." With an electric jolt, he looked back into the side tunnel. "I might as well tell you. Our Kappa crew saw it first, those five excavator operators you just saw lying next to the digger. Yesterday, they were still digging. One of them radioed the surface and told Colonel Rarts that one of the workers had found a big chunk of tellurium and had yanked it off. He said the worker was hysterical and that he was running about like a mad man, shouting 'I am rich!' He then said the worker saw a red blob squirming about in the depths of the mine." A shaky hand pointed back into the dark side shaft. "That's all I know," said the Peblinus soldier.

"How far in does the unlit shaft go?" asked Ramaan.

"It goes down deep, almost six kilometres. The mining engineers normally construct these tunnels to the limit."

"Do you have a map of the mine?"

"Yes," he said, pulling out a massive layout of the excavated area. He was right, it was extensive: dozens of side tunnels both long and short. Ramaan noticed that some of them led nowhere.

Another soldier walked over and pointed to a location on the map showing up as a little cubicle about two kilometres inside. "It's a tellurium reactor. You can only switch it on if you first lift a lever." The Peblinus continued to draw a makeshift lever on a piece of paper.

"You press the red button next to it for two seconds before the lights will come on." A circle appeared on the rough sketch. Philip reported their position to both Lexia and Baygorn.

6. The Mine Shaft

Constant steam exited the tunnel in fat clouds. Haphazardly strewn tools lay in the hot sulphurous air. A closed toolbox lay next to a smaller, handheld machine. There were no signs of struggling or suffering. No, it had been quick, very quick. Whatever it was, pure fear had struck this place. Fear like a lightning bolt, and as a result, death had come.

Philip and Ramaan walked closer to the steamy, rough entrance and nervously peeked in. It was hotter than out there in the safety of the light. Maybe ten degrees higher. My God, it was so dark and so terrifying in there!

The soldiers were reluctant to enter, so Philip left four of the shaky ones in the tunnel with a weapon. Ramaan turned on his infrared headgear and peered into the labyrinth. Three hundred metres separated him from the first corner. It seemed like a mile. Twenty metres inside, they came across two empty human sacks. One dryly crinkled as Alana lifted an arm with her foot.

Philip remorsefully looked away and said, "Whatever does this, damn, it doesn't leave any footprints or tracks. But it could've only come from this direction." There were no side tunnels between the entrance and the first corner, so they continued until reaching a curve leading to the right. There were cables leading everywhere, to and from the waiting lights. Philip's infrared stopped working as one of the sensor wires had come loose. Ramaan said he would fix it once they returned to the *Excelsior*.

By the time they had reached the corner, the low plasticized ceiling had disappeared and transformed itself into a solid perpetual platform twenty metres above them. The rest of the tunnels from that point onwards were ceilingless. From where Philip was, it was an endless drawing of walls. They were immersed in a rocky garden labyrinth, and it stretched for kilometres.

Ramaan reached into his side bag and produced small data-capturing capsule pods that could be placed on the walls every hundred metres or so. They would form a network of images of the tunnels and would relay them back to their portable computers, enabling them to see, showing them their way back if they were to get lost. "We will be able to track our enemy from here," he said, looking at the amazing digital image he received just from one capsule.

The image reminded Philip of a Dungeons and Dragons game with six tiny white dots. The invisible became the visible.

In front of them was an infrared view of this mind-boggling underground city of which they had to traverse to get to the generator. Nozzles of steam infrequently appeared from the unfinished walls and constantly played havoc with their infrared.

The number of hidden caverns was incalculable. Ramaan placed a second mapper pod on the wall and produced a better three-dimensional image than before.

In one of the side tunnels, they discovered an opened crate full of explosives and ammunition that someone had tried to empty in a hurry. His lifeless body lay beside it. The look on his empty, flaccid face still emanated fear.

Suddenly, a scream echoed and bounced off from in front of them. Its blood-curdling recoil cloned itself along the walls and reappeared as an unrecognisable shift in pitch. One of the Peblinus left the group seemingly in fear. Philip's unheard holler towards him disappeared into the labyrinth. He ran off and vanished into the myriad of tunnels. While placing another capsule on the wall, Ramaan looked at the laptop and watched the Peblinus disappear from view.

Eight hundred metres from the generator, the man who'd previously left the group came running back, breathless. "I found him. It was Morogan, the electrical engineer. His body was thrown over a rock."

Suddenly, Ramaan started picking up another white dot on his radar moving in front of them at tremendous speed. It was moving directly towards them. "What the devil!" he gritted. "I've got something closing in on us, fast. Christ, it really knows these tunnels! What is it?"

The entity approached until it reached a corner about twenty metres away. It stopped out of view, then retreated some. At first, it inched back and then travelled various metres before it came to a standstill. Then slowly it moved towards the corner again to make itself visible to them. Scared and pinned against a wall, Philip and his team were incapable of movement. The thing had no definite shape. Its analogous snail form measured more than a metre in height and gently slithered from side to side about five centimetres above the ground. It was waiting for their next move.

"We don't move until it does, and for Christ's sake, nobody fire!" gritted Philip. Twenty short, unforgettable metres separated them from the thing. Ramaan was glued to his laptop in search of more formless creatures. None came. The five minutes that followed were eternal while the creature ogled them. It didn't have eyes, but Philip could feel they were being examined one by one. He felt it enter his mind and suck his thoughts, and for the first time in his life, he was really scared.

Like a dart and without notice, it fled and vanished into the innumerable tunnels once more to hide in the eternal shadows of the mine shaft. Ramaan followed it with the laptop until the blip left the screen.

Philip had a picture in his mind that he couldn't shake. He was imagining coming to the end of one of these long underground tunnels, walking through an aperture and then being blinded by the light of the sun. How good it seemed. He was imagining being an intelligent creature living in this maze of dim light and tunnels and then, by chance, stumbling onto something that would irrevocably change his entire concept of the universe.

The Peblinus were shaking like dry leaves.

"You know what that thing was, don't you? Come on; tell me, damn it!"

"Not only do we know what it is, we know why it attacks us," responded the Peblinus.

"It is called a Magnopod. It uses the tellurium for its own needs. Four years ago, we started mining for the precious mineral and encountered it dormant. At first, we thought it was a rock that moved. Later, we discovered layers of tellurium and abundant supplies in the lower caverns in the shape of balls. We sold them to a trader, only to find out later that they were its eggs. That was when the Magnopod woke from slumber and started wiping us out one by one. We sent in our best troops and they never returned. Two years ago, the creatures killed forty of our elite squad. They didn't stand a chance! I can still hear their screams coming through the radio. Two years have passed without a single incident, until yesterday."

The soldier was trembling and shaking. "We do not know anything that can kill it. We've tried everything!"

"How many eggs did they sell?" asked Alana.

"Four hundred. They made an instant fortune. A day or two later, the trader was found murdered, and the merchandise had mysteriously disappeared without a trace."

The generator room was bigger than Philip had imagined. The nearing soldier knew exactly what he had to do. He reached over, threw the lever and pressed the button. The lights came on without hesitation.

"Thank the stars," said Alana, gleefully taking off her infrared goggles. "I was beginning to cook in there."

One of the soldiers left the group to show them an egg of a Magnopod. "Here's one," he said, lifting it with both hands to his chest.

The egg was the size of a tennis ball and weighed an astonishing eighty kilograms. The soldier was ecstatic. "In this cavern alone," he said, "there are more than two thousand eggs. We can all live like kings for the rest of our lives. Each one is worth a fortune. It is pure tellurium. We could have saved many lives if we had extracted the tellurium in the normal manner, but with a couple of these in our pockets, we wouldn't have to worry ourselves about doing the dirty wor—"

In less than a blink, the egg fell to the floor with a hard thump.

They had witnessed his last words. The Magnopod appeared out of nowhere and placed itself on top of him like a giant flyswatter. It remained stationary for one or two seconds. All Philip could see was a jiggling hand and the confused face of the soldier. His lips were moving, but no sound came. Suddenly, the embraced shuffling stillness forced on the soldier by the Magnopod followed a ghastly crunching sound that turned up everyone's hairs and tightened their stomachs. Philip and the others watched as the life of the Peblinus, to whom they were listening to only scant seconds before, drained from him like a deflating balloon.

Why in God's name did it kill him? thought Philip.

Then he heard it. It was a husky, low-pitched voice that lucidly modulated itself into his brain. It was unmistakable. Philip looked at everyone to see who was speaking, but they were staring at the horrendous spectacle at their feet. The voice continued like an anechoic deadness before abruptly discontinuing like the offing of a light switch. Simultaneously, the Magnopod stopped hovering aboveground and settled itself down ever so gently before twisting and swivelling in Philip's direction. It was watching him just as Philip stared at its incarnate, humongous shell form. Then the same warping voice became his thoughts. Philip was thinking with its voice. It sounded like it had dust in its throat and was trying to clear it. At first, Philip didn't know how to react. He couldn't believe what he was hearing, yet the message was clear, and it appeared that only he could hear it.

"He lied," said the Magnopod, a mere three metres away. The rock shook and trembled and seemed to have little finger feelers on the side that made it move. A bit of dust lifted into the air.

"He was going to sell them on the next freighter. With the lights operational, it made his work easier. We rid this planet of greed. We mean you no harm. Go in peace and relay my message. Tell them they are welcome to mine what they need, but they must not touch the eggs. If they touch the eggs, we will devour them all." The message came through loud and clear. Everyone around Philip was shaking. Like a static discharge, the Magnopod zipped down a passage and out of sight.

Alana and Ramaan were motionless. The soldiers eased up a little while the remains of the other looked emptily up at them.

One of the Peblinus soldiers had urinated in his trousers and left behind a rippling puddle. *Why had it chosen me?* wondered Philip. He faced the rest of the group. "Let's go! It's time to leave."

Alana and Ramaan collected their gear and started back. Ramaan, with the laptop, watched the Magnopod follow them from twenty metres behind, all the way to the exit, until it finally returned to do whatever it does. His observations were sometimes confirmed by a distant scuffle that made him look back.

Philip jumped out of the entrance and shouted to the other Peblinus waiting in the main shaft. "Assemble your stuff, we're leaving!" Without even looking at them, Philip stomped off and immediately began the ascent to collect the others.

"What happened down there?" The glee turned sour when Lexia saw the worry and noticed the missing Peblinus. Philip didn't know what to say or how to say it. He didn't say a word until they reached the surface.

Colonel Rarts wedged his way through the opening doors with a smile. "Did you turn the lights on?"

"Yes, we did." Philip placed the cups of his hands on his knees and took long gasps of air.

Colonel Rarts looked around. "Wait, there's a soldier missing. What happened? Where is he?"

Philip paused a breath. "He's dead. No one told us what we were to expect down there. We went down there risking our lives! You must've known. My God, man, you must've known what was down there." Philip then told them, "The thing spoke to me."

Colonel Rarts rotated his head towards him. Everyone did.

"What! It spoke to you?"

"Yes, it told me to warn you. You can mine the tellurium, but don't touch the eggs. If you go in there with wrong intentions, you will all be devoured if you so much as think about it."

Colonel Rarts didn't know what to say. Philip, on the other hand, had the intention of returning to the pod craft before it got too dark, but they could assume that duty tomorrow and continue their journey on to Haradan. They had done enough running around, so that evening they spent the time they had and rested before going back to the *Excelsior.*

7. Haradan

From a distance of a million kilometres, Haradan was an emerald. Its unscathed landscape, free of roaming shadows from its distant moons, was flat. From above, they could make out no surface features or seas. It was just a gigantic green cloud-covered planet, nothing more. Plaam, the nearest of its three moons floating four million kilometres away, had a gigantic meteorite impact crater directly in its centre that occupied half of its mass. Its remote silhouette would never reach the planet.

On Haradan, the busy, penetrating eye of Sentrywatcher revealed ample levels of oxygen and a wide variety of plant life on its two-degree surface. As Sentrywatcher peeled the atmosphere away farther, marine life in diverse stages of evolution became evident in sporadic seas placed between gigantic landmasses covering about 80 percent of the surface. The luminescent green cloud layer hovered high above the surface, and it was only when they approached that they could see this gem as it really was. Humidity levels were off the scale and gave birth to immense rain forests, with trees reaching over two hundred metres in height.

Ramaan localised a suitable landing place on the outskirts of an immense rain forest. "Looks hard enough," he said entering a command with a bleep. He had that look in his eyes—they all did. It was fear. The fear they never spoke about; yet, its existence would never abandon their minds, especially after their experience in the mine shaft. The dread they had before setting off onto another world and finding out what was down there.

A little over an hour later, they landed on a hard, rocky surface on the outskirts of an immense forest two kilometres from a deep sea. The audio scanner was going crazy. There was evidence of both crawling and flying animals. This bizarre jungle seemed endless, and certainly alive. The scrabbling insects, odd animal cries and flutterings reminded Baygorn of a midday Amazon jungle in summer during a full lunar cycle.

During their routine analysis of Haradan, Lexia read about a race that lived there. They called themselves the Haak.

Baygorn added, "Due to the height of the cloud layer covering the planet, it made it impossible for us to see the surface when we entered the atmosphere. No wonder there's so much vegetation."

Alana smiled and zipped up her suit. The outside was warm and very damp. Soil squished beneath their feet. Philip lifted his visor. It smelt like a fresh, humid, autumn early morning. Small patches of light battling their way through ruptured clouds lit up the jungle in small areas. The bits of sky they saw were a dull green, whereas the landscape was a light- and dark-green combination and stretched all the way into the distance. Even the haze and fog drifting in between a variety of trees and shrubs seemed green. No one had been here to tend or care for the jungle, and it was an out-of-hand wild.

"I could get used to this." Baygorn loved dense gardens and vegetation on Earth, so they all knew he was at home here.

"You know what the difference is?" His hands waved about in an exhibition of frenzy. "Here it's all new. Here you turn a leaf and voila, you don't know what you're going to find underneath." Baygorn's chemical background and inner instinct were ready to explode. "It's an entomologist's dream."

They walked back to the pod, ready to probe deeper into this world. Sentrywatcher by now would have mapped the surface.

"Okay, Alana, let's have a look. See what we have out there."

She twiddled with a panel. "The screen is full of blips; we've got lots of movement going on. Plenty of carbon-based. Could be the Haak that Lexia told us about, or maybe it's Peblinus." The early-morning sun broke through the clouds, bathing the vehicle in a light-green shimmer. Baygorn moved a hand towards the sunlight entering the porthole and turned it like on a grill. He commented on it being vaguely warm.

Philip turned away from the screen towards Lexia. "What can you tell us about the Haak?"

"Not much. I read they are a sympathetic, giving culture and shouldn't cause us any problems." Ramaan asked Alana the location of the blips.

"There's a crater with a large concentration of blips. The city must be there." As a hand pointed at the screen, Ramaan plotted the course for the journey. Hydraulic motors whirled and hissed, and a strand of sunlight hit Philip in the eyes as they rolled out to begin their drive towards the unknown city of the Haak. In the listless light offered from Mintaka, there, between the trees and dense vegetation, was a bunker. It was identical to the one they had encountered on Phot. Their sensors revealed the same length of passageways as well as the same chemical composition on the doors and walls. Another hangar inhabited by Peblinus was probably not too far away from where they were going. Sentrywatcher confirmed it.

"If they are Peblinus, it can't be tellurium. Sentrywatcher says the nearest volcanic activity is more than one thousand kilometres away." Their scanners didn't reveal life in the hangar, so they broke up and went in two groups.

The bunker was one giant laboratory, with partitioned rooms all studying the same thing. The only difference was that here it was a bacterial substance and not tellurium. All the rooms were analytical laboratories for different chemical substances. One, Lexia said, was a sediment room. The next was fermentation.

In the frothing section, Baygorn moved over and started ferreting through papers and manuals. Suddenly, as if he'd received an electric shock, he jolted upright and released a long howl. Papers brushed against his other hand. "Amorfilium? That's impossible! This stuff's a legend. Its existence was only a rumour. Jeez, that was ages ago." Baygorn let out a wide smile.

"A legend on Earth is no legend here." Baygorn looked at everyone.

"That's not all," said Alana, running into the room.

"I've found another library. Come see it for yourselves." With the aid of the Bod and Peblinus technology, the Haak had developed an alien bacterium that apparently originated from the mountains. The indigenous vegetation only grew in a cold climate, taking decades to reach maturity.

Lexia flipped pages in a manual. "They definitely made progress, but the funny part is the journal entries stop six months ago. There's nothing else, only blank pages. How weird." Lexia picked up another file. "They call it Sporna. The Haak have lived in the city of Sporna for hundreds of years, countless generations. They built Sporna on the rim of Arno Crater not far from here. It says they chose the area because of the protection the crater offered. They could see the enemy approach from great distances. It says here the crater is more than twenty kilometres in diameter and over two kilometres deep."

Farther down, the rest of the subterranean passage had caved in, so they turned back to return to the surface and plan their route to Sporna.

"According to the map, we can go the beach route or the forest."

Baygorn ecstatically tapped Philip on the shoulder. "Did someone mention forest? Come on, it'll be more interesting. Might take us a bit longer, but I'm sure it'll be worth it."

Alana turned up the audio scanner's volume. "Sounds busy in there; are you sure?" The drag of the wheels over dirt or gravel was recognisable. "This must've been a road at some point, it's still quite clear. Distinguish any of those sounds?"

Baygorn was attentively quiet. He stretched his ears, searched his knowledge and strained his imagination. He didn't answer; he only wiped his smiling mouth with a hand and continued to observe their route through the porthole.

An hour later, the voice of Lexia snatched the attention of everyone. "Look. That must be the crater!" Lexia's hand pointed through trees into a gigantic clearing. Sporna on the other side was breathtaking. Even from their distance of almost thirty kilometres, it was futuristic and superbly alien.

"Looks like these Haak were brilliant architects as well," said Alana, evading the last of the trees. Five or six kilometres nearer and reaching the crater rim, some patrolling haze rising from the crater bottom had materialised and had eroded parts of the scene, leaving only the tops of the tallest buildings of the city. Two perpetually watching grey towers, like twin fingers, pointed from above the floating mist, guarding Sporna from any possible infringement or roaming horror. Sentrywatcher sent Alana a clear route, so they circled the crater.

Nearing Sporna, smaller architectural replicas encircled the bases of the enormous skyscrapers like progeny. Nearer still, the mist dissipated close to the entrance. Alana's audio scanner went surprisingly quiet and revealed nothing. This slice of world was in complete slumber. Not a sound. It was as if it wasn't even switched on. The only way she was sure of its working state was an odd occasional crackle emission.

"It's just suddenly stopped. I have a bad feeling about this."

There were parked vehicles, and a couple of open or broken windows exposing their interiors. There was a blowing wind, and rubbish was scattered here and there. Nothing seemed to be out of place, no signs of foul play.

Alana checked her life scanner. "Those blips we saw earlier are Peblinus, they're up north. I'm not even picking up a cricket here. Damn, this place is deserted. Skyscrapers from hell, if you ask me."

Outside, a constant breeze ate its chilly way into their minds, seemingly appearing from behind bushes into every part of their bodies and into their imaginations. The sheer absence of movement or life amplified their fears, deafening and solemn. Feeling the wind against their faces, the ghostly silhouettes of the skyscrapers sent an exhilarating chill down their spines. They arrived moments later at the edge of the town. At last they could seek the answers to the lifetime of questions, unencumbered by someone else's arbitrary schedule.

They walked around and looked at the two octagonal towering buildings. They were covered in black glass, efficiently reflecting the frail light from Mintaka, in whatever posture it was during the daytime, into the surrounding buildings, providing both warmth and light. Was this triumphant architecture, or was it just an everyday construction? A yellow metallic division, magnificently sculptured on top of the black surface, separated each floor. The other numerous smaller buildings, placed like quartz crystals, had the same dark, absorbing material coating their exterior walls.

In the centre of the two giant buildings was Arno Square: so named by Lexia. Arno Square, a once-breathtaking garden, lay forgotten. Shrubs and plants had gone wild, invading streetlamps and roof structures. It was in semi-ruin. Weeds had grown to never-before heights. Interlacing vines were destroying and defacing where they could. Flowers in their brilliant yellows flourished in the cold atmosphere.

Leading off from the central square, myriads of intertwining mathematically situated streets attached themselves to all the buildings. A variety of glass sculptures and statues formed exquisite, eye-catching art.

To one side of Arno Square, next to a park, a single-floored construction, different in design from the rest, led off from one of the side streets to a dead end.

Philip pointed towards the out-of-place building. "Well I'll be; that looks like my old tax office. I'll go take a peek in there while you lot go find what you can. Keep that radio active at all times."

The building had no handle, only an electronic device that resembled a thumb reader. *What the hell?* Philip thought. He put his right thumb down on the plastic pad and a quiet relay clicked somewhere inside the house, immediately opening the door.

A feminine voice shot out of a speaker to his left as he walked in the front door. "Bienvenido," said the voice. It was definitely a government building, all right. The sickly, oily aroma of paperwork and sweat still adhered to and roamed down the passageways. Philip searched five dusty rooms. Where was everyone? Books and papers were still in the same original neat and unaltered position they had been in since the disappearance of the Haak. He gathered whatever official procedures he found to be of interest, which wasn't much, and left to unite with his colleagues in Arno Square.

Alana was waiting for Philip. "Where are the others?"

"They've gone into Wilson Tower." He followed her hand. "Ramaan found the identity plaque as he went in. They should be on the second floor. I spoke to Lexia a moment ago."

Wilson Tower had a glass and marble statue in the entrance hallway, a magnificent wavy sculpture of interchanging material weaving its compounds and colours into a striking piece of art. On either side were two enormous flights of stairs leading to an open octagonal first floor. Ramaan was ferreting out on the second floor, trying to switch on a computer he'd found.

"Where's the switch? I don't see the switch."

Suddenly, a short bleep emanated from the innards of the undersized box, and the screen pulsed to life. The operating system, to call it something, was vaguely similar in appearance to their own. On the left-hand side of the monitor were strange-boxed symbols and icons with adjoining unknown words just underneath.

"It's astounding. It's in ancient Latin," said Lexia depressing the small keypad a couple of times. The computer suddenly came alive. Its velocity was remarkable. Ramaan curiously opened it up, only to determine that it didn't have electronic boards or connectors like the ones he knew. All the connections seemed to be made by a single optical cable. It weighed less than two kilograms. The power source was a tiny rectangular block mounted on the side. Ramaan knew this because as he took it out to have a closer look, the computer switched off. The data was stored in a toughened cylinder containing a white pasty gel. Two visible fibrous wires were in its centre.

"It's called a petadrive, and there are no moving parts in it," said Lexia, going through a manual she'd found in a drawer. "It's an all-organic molecular processor. Probably more advanced than our Nano-scale quantum processors. It says the computer produces pure random bits and employs quantum entanglement and superpositions to do trillions of calculations at once. I would guess at least fifty yottaflops." Ramaan ran his hands through his thick hair in shock as Lexia began doing maths on a small piece of paper.

"Ninety petabytes per cubic millimetre of white liquid. It's more than I thought," she said. Philip found it interesting because petabyte technology was still in its initial planning stages on Earth, and here they were at ninety already. Next to the computer on the desk lay small yellow cubes.

Ramaan curiously picked one up. "It doesn't weigh anything. I can see through it," he said, while holding it to his eye.

"The cubes go into the side of the computer in a special hole." Lexia took the computer from Ramaan and showed him the small square slot. "You can put it in any way you want," she said. "No A or B side. In our own technology, the laser light is stable. The disk spins at a high velocity, enabling the laser to extract the information and send this data to be processed. The manual here says the cube in this case is stationary, and a compilation of six tiny lasers built into the computer rapidly scan it and records or extracts the data. It's the reverse of our own technology," she said.

Ramaan switched off the machine and left it on top of one of the tables for retrieval later. Rubbish bins and paperwork were in their correct places. Nothing had been disturbed and nothing had been broken.

"It's like everyone just left for holidays." Philip ran his finger over a table. Eight elevators inhabited the main aisle of the reception area, with a vacated long desk close by.

"Creepy when there's no one to greet you. It seems odd. Where do thousands of people disappear to?" Alana peered behind the desk to make sure no one was hiding there.

Lexia started studying the still-illuminated, multicoloured lift buttons. "This one goes to the top floor."

Alana and Ramaan were strategically placing motion detectors on some of the desks and other office paraphernalia.

"If there are any Haak here," said Ramaan, "we'll know of their presence long before they know of ours."

The elevator was large enough to accommodate eight people. Inside, the same glassy substance they saw in the lobby entrance covered the ornamented side walls. On the ceiling, a dull green light excreted an eerie beauty onto a full-length mirror at the back of the elevator carriage.

Lexia pressed the top-floor button. The metallic doors silently closed. Moving steadily, it took two minutes to reach the top. A speaker announced their destination with the same woman's voice as earlier.

As the doors opened, two small intertwining human-like glass statues silently glared at the ceiling on both sides of the passageway. The corridor was long and lit in a green gloom, casting shadows from the statues at the elevator. Orderly ranked tables had numerous computers on their worktops. An abundance of yellow data cubes was stacked on another table. Ramaan took a couple of cubes.

They walked to the exterior windows to get a better view. In front, the enormous crater filled their awe beyond words. To the right, as the slow veer of the crater rim continued, tendrils of formless haze drifted upwards in all directions. To the left, robotic machines were working far off in the distance. Philip guessed that someone had forgotten to switch them off.

Alana lifted her binoculars. "They are mechanoids. Damn, they're big!" She watched them slowly, methodically reach down with their gigantic hand grabbers and pick up broken rock before placing it into a metallic basket. Close by, another robot was picking up and driving the basket to some unknown destination.

The view, in whichever way they looked, was staggering. They stood there for ten minutes, spellbound by the spectacle. Mintaka was once again beginning to lower and settle.

Breaking away from the others, Lexia discovered a terminal on one of the workbenches. "Before the Haak disappeared, wherever they went, I have ascertained that they were producing amorfilium and ditrium."

Baygorn's ears tweaked upwards. "So all that blabber I read about is true." Baygorn ecstatically moved forward. "Apparently, amorfilium comes from a plant with similarities to maize. Ditrium comes from its roots." Baygorn's exhilaration was heard by everyone. "I thought I'd read it wrong. Amorfilium is a legend! The stuff not only prolongs life, it reduces the possibility of disease by almost 100 percent. If this race cannot die, then where the hell are they?" Suddenly, the proximity alarm on the second floor sounded.

With the speed of a true expert, Ramaan peered down at his laptop. "Hey, it's close to where I left that computer." He ran for the elevator with Alana on his heels. At the base, Alana dashed out with her gun in hand and rushed forward, towards the area where the alarm had been triggered. The floor was open-plan with not much space to hide. There, crouching on the floor behind a filing cabinet, was a young boy. He was a grubby specimen. Alana guessed him to be about twelve. As Ramaan's substantial frame appeared out of nowhere with arms grabbing forward like a hungry octopus, in the eyes of a boy, Ramaan must have appeared like a monster. He screamed in fear and ran for dear life. Alana, more agile and with quicker reflexes, grabbed him by the scruff. The boy fought with all his might. Alana evaded flying arms. With a smile, she began caressing his hair and began talking in a gentle tone to calm him.

Lexia dashed out of the elevator and ran over. "Shh, don't be afraid. We won't hurt you." Arms were still flying.

"What's your name?" asked Alana. The boy's snivelling eyes widened still further in fear. He emitted an even higher-pitched bellow.

"He doesn't understand you, Alana," interrupted Lexia, now asking the boy his name in her rusty version of the Haak language.

The boy stopped his frenzy, looked toward Lexia and smiled. A dirty rack of teeth explained his diet. He jumped up excitedly from behind the cabinet, leaving Alana with a betwixt stare.

"My name is Bobby." The sullied face creased under layers of dirt.

"Where are the others?" Lexia's smile disappeared. "The other people who lived here, where are they?"

Bobby jumped up at her and held her firmly in a child-like grip. "Thank you for coming for me," he said, as tears began making clean spots on the grimy face. He held on tighter.

"Where are the others?" put in Lexia again in a sturdier tone. Letting go of Lexia's body, Bobby's smile disappeared, and he looked to one side before starting to play with a rubbish bin.

"It was the spider things." The boy's face changed almost to that of fear.

"They came one night and they were all captured or killed by the spider things," said the boy, grabbing Lexia's arm again. Lexia didn't know what to say. She translated the boy's words the best that she could and looked at Ramaan and Philip standing close by before continuing.

"What spider things? How long ago did this happen?"

"Maybe half a birthday," he replied, holding on for dear life.

Ramaan turned and looked at Philip and Alana. "Well, at least that explains the sudden stop in the entries in the underground bunker six months ago," said Lexia to Ramaan, bending nearer while trying to understand what Bobby had just said.

"They came one night and killed everyone. They didn't find me because I was in a storage area on the twentieth floor. I was inside when they attacked the city. Every day since then, they come every night, to kill whatever they see moving about in the darkness." At that point, he let go. "I have a friend who was with me when it happened. He still hides in the storage area. His name is Gahm. He is twenty."

"Show me the storage area," added Lexia in a playful tone. Alana moved closer.

"Bobby here says that Gahm claims to have killed one of the spider things." Lexia walked over and filled the others in with the details. Lexia, lowering her hand, took Bobby's and they all climbed back into the elevator.

The storage area occupied most of the twentieth floor. There were lots of doors down a small passage, and discarded rubbish was strewn everywhere. Extending their vision and opening some doors, they could see it was stacked with every type of tinned consumable imaginable.

On the floor, Gahm passed the time by reading a book he had found. "Hey, are you for real?"

Lexia walked up to him. "Hey, I hope so. We're here to help you, both of you."

Baygorn picked up a pack of biscuits.

This area probably contains enough food for fifty people for ten years, thought Philip as his gaze examined the shelves. They all sat down on the floor.

Lexia looked sternly at Gahm. "Bobby says this happened about six months ago."

Gahm's face tightened. "Yes, it was just any ordinary night when they came. That night we were hungry. Bobby and I were here raiding the larder at the time. When we'd finished and left to go home, there was no one about. Even the security guard we would normally sneak past to get in here wasn't outside. It was just as it is now. We didn't know what to do, so we came back here to the storage room. We've been here ever since."

Ramaan and Philip, catching snippets of what was going on, leaned nearer. "Tell us about these spider things Bobby mentioned."

Michael Gilwood

"They are taller than you and me. They have big wavy tentacles and they place their victims in a giant mouth," said Gahm waving his hands and contorting his own mouth.

"They move slowly and growl when they eat. I once saw one capture and kill one of our colonists. It was snarling like a wild animal. The thing placed pieces of him into its mouth." Gahm's mouth uttered a sound. "Those tentacles have teeth as well!"

Lexia explained the details of what Gahm had said. In an eerie, unexpected kind of way, the thing what Gahm had just described started to ring a familiar bell. It couldn't be. They encountered a dead one on Phot, but how in hell's name did they manage to get here? They couldn't be Platnios, could they?

Alana's face soured. "Remember what Shar said about them being genetically made to serve and obey? It's a wild guess, but maybe the Peblinus sent them here to kill the Haak."

"Possible, but it still doesn't explain how they got here." Baygorn scratched his head.

"That wasn't bad, try this: After their creation, they performed their duties, watching and learning. They probably know all there is to know. Heck, we all saw one eat a Peblinus, remember? Now imagine they have learnt all the weaknesses and habits of the Peblinus. Reprisal shall descend toward its creator disguised as a meat-eating Platnios."

Ramaan chuckled. "That's very interesting."

Baygorn interrupted. "What would an invertebrate, organ-less plant, or spider thing, or whatever you want to call them, do with this accumulation of information? What could it possibly want? Let's try and think like a Platnios for a moment."

Ramaan raised a hand. "Planting ideas again, are we?"

"Oh, be quiet. Did we find a brain? No, we didn't, look. Of course it has one hidden somewhere over that mushroom mouth that apparently has a taste for Haak or anyone else that gets in its way."

Alana butted in. "In one hundred years, do you honestly think they've accomplished space travel? It must be one hell of a brain. Imagine having a weed for a captain." Lexia smirked.

Philip interrupted. "Come on, both of you, that's enough! We still don't even know if they are Platnios. We're only speculating.

If these things come out at night as Bobby and Gahm have said, then let's give them a little welcoming party."

Alana and Ramaan disappeared down some steps. Gahm beckoned to Lexia. "He wants to show us his invention on the twenty-second floor."

Gahm smiled. "I plastered one to the wall one night, right there." A hand pointed. Gahm proceeded to show them the crude catapult system and the long, rusted kitchen knife.

"It works with movement," he said, smiling. Philip looked down at the crude trip wire.

"They come back every night, never during the day. The light affects them and they die. We hear them in the lower levels, rummaging and scavenging about. We hide here in the storeroom until morning. Seems they go to the Peblinus city of Thornz for the hunt about ten kilometres away. I don't know where they come from, but they certainly know how to multiply."

Philip's C-12 vibrated. "Yes, Ramaan."

"All done, six zips and ten blue-rays should give them quite a headache." Alana and Ramaan told Philip they'd placed them all around the main square and entrance hall to Wilson Tower. As Philip's C-12 flicked off, his attention averted to the already dissipating light from Mintaka. Their side of Haradan was preparing itself for night. Ramaan and Alana returned to the second floor, and Philip, Baygorn, and Lexia went back to the top floor. Through her binoculars, in the distance beyond the mechanoids, Lexia noticed two strange craft.

"Odd we didn't see them before." Lexia twiddled with the magnification, noticing movement in and around the two craft.

"Weird, what strange-looking craft they are. Yeah, they're Platnios all right, no mistake. Hundreds of them. My God, they are fighting amongst themselves." Gahm pointed a finger at the other side of Arno Crater. On the rim, way up and distant through the haze, there was another gigantic hangar. Philip recognised the architecture.

"That's Thornz. When the spider things first came, our people fought with them. Now the spider things fight with them at Thornz. Every night I see flames and explosions. It's getting worse, too."

Ramaan and Alana stepped out of the lift to join Philip. "We should be quite safe in here now," said Alana, pulling up alongside. Thornz, like the two hidden Platnios ships, was hard to see, even from up where they were. Dense mist constantly patrolled the outer regions of the crater, making the unobserved sporadically invisible; but as the crimsoned orb of Mintaka shifted nearer the horizon, the temperatures began to fall and the mist had begun the arduous process of dissipation. Their vision began to open up. From their distance, Thornz seemed void of all life, but the two Platnios ships weren't. They were busily preparing themselves for war with the Peblinus. Philip had an advantage—no one knew they were there.

As the grain of rice-sized Mintaka made its ultimate gasp for air over the distant hillside towards dusk, Bobby walked towards Lexia. Ramaan thought he wanted to say something for them to hear, but it wasn't until he noticed something odd in him that it put Alana on full alert. They seemed different. They had wrinkled faces. Bobby's childlike voice stammered. Gahm couldn't form any sentence; only a raspy chatter. Bobby bent down and placed his hands over his face. Gahm followed. Ramaan and Philip hurriedly walked to Gahm. Lexia wasn't far behind.

"Look!" Lexia's worried tone made Alana come running. His eyebrows had changed into thick hairy bushes. It was like watching a high-speed reproduction of a budding flower. Next, his ears disappeared, sucked into his once-human head. Bony hands changed into long, sharp and threatening claws. Both of them collapsed on the floor like bricks falling from mid-air.

Baygorn moved closer. Philip put his hands high in the air. "Wait, Baygorn, don't touch them! I need to see this." Philip remembered a film from the twentieth-century archives about a werewolf in London. He was a nice young man who changed into a hideous beast during full moon and went around massacring innocent people in their homes. It was happening here too. They watched and felt sorry for them as they screamed while the vile transformation took place.

In less than two minutes, they had seen their first representation of the spider Platnios. Bobby's and Gahm's ordeal was quickly over. The Platnios, disguised in their human form, had arrived here to the wonderful, peaceful Haakian city and were accepted as guests into their homes during the day. That same night, the camouflaged Platnios transformed themselves back into their original, horrendous state and killed the inhabitants of this once-beautiful and tranquil city.

Alana vaporised them with her blue-ray as they began shuffling towards her with flapping tentacles. "Thank God they die easily." Baygorn was trembling at the sight. Downing her weapon, Alana quickly looked at them. "Comments, anyone?"

Lexia reached a consensus about the two young boys. *What a mindless waste! How could such a creature do that?* she thought.

Philip spoke. "This awful incident answers many questions, Lexia. Regarding what we were talking about before, it looks like they haven't only achieved space travel; it seems they have attained the gift of metamorphosis as well."

Alana watched as Platnios poured out of their two distant spacecraft to head towards Thornz. Sporna was the detour and Philip's element of surprise.

Ramaan snuck himself next to Alana and raised his infrared. "Christ, there must be thousands of them down there!" Alana reached down, pressed a button on a small pad and armed the zips and blue-rays. A red flicker shone between her fingers. By the time they arrived to the ground floor, Thornz was already ablaze with activity. The Platnios had realised the threat from them and veered away from Sporna, and headed directly to Thornz.

It was obvious the Peblinus had been at war with the Platnios for some time. Philip could also plainly see evidence of a losing Peblinus. Although Platnios were easy to kill, they bred like bacteria, slowly depleting the Peblinus ammunition and the population of Thornz, until one day they would simply run out. It was a survival of the greater number.

But not all of them had gone directly to Thornz; some of them had made a diversion towards Sporna. Two hours after nightfall, their blue-rays and zips had killed a large number of Platnios before they managed to reach Thornz, but they were not enough. Platnios continued to pour out of the two spacecraft like a tap.

Unexpectedly and without warning, Phillip and his crews' communicators came to life with the angry voice of a Peblinus emptying his lungs. "Who goes there? Identify yourselves."

Ramaan pressed the talk button. "We are explorers from Earth. We are visiting all the planets in this sys—" Ramaan was cut off by a facetious and angry tone.

"Oh, it's you! We've been hearing about you. Shar's officials on Braan have already notified me about your interfering meddle. Thanks to you, one of our finest officers was incarcerated, and for that I now warn you: If you come into our territory or interfere with our business, we will destroy you!"

"But we are no harm to you; we are only trying to help." Ramaan intentionally softened his voice, to no avail.

"You'll be infinitely sorry, you hear me? Infinitely sorry!" the receiver gave a click.

Alana went outside with Ramaan by her side. Two blue-rays lit up the area in silvery bursts. Ramaan turned towards her. "Stupid idiots. Hey, it's obvious that our only allies around here are the Bods. If we help them, they can be stronger and a more formidable foe to these Peblinus."

Ramaan, deep in thought, was sucking his teeth. The night stilled. Irritated, Ramaan faced Philip. "Obviously these Peblinus don't know where to look. It's so easy to blame someone else. I've got an idea. While these Platnios are low in numbers, let's go pay those two spacecraft a visit."

"What do you have in mind, Ramaan?" asked Philip, taking an interest.

"Before they breed again, while their numbers are low, it should be easier for us. We can place a couple of charges and —boom! These Peblinus need our help and they don't even know it."

"It's going to be risky." Philip scratched his head. "But I like it." Philip turned and acknowledged to a nudging Alana. She placed her blue-ray on automatic outside the entrance to the Wilson Tower and climbed into the vehicle. Ramaan inserted two blue-rays on the roof of their vehicle.

They knew Thornz was in trouble. Although the Peblinus didn't admit it, the population of Thornz was rapidly approaching the endangered species list, making the nightly Platnios attacks easier each time.

Platnios replenished their numbers during the day and released vast numbers nightly, all with one aim. Soon they would overcome this ignorant race; it was only a question of time. Their method of reproduction was as intriguing as it was mysterious.

The vehicle sped off, leaving behind a trail of dust. Before reaching the two Platnios spaceships, they came across one of the mechanoids they'd seen before from the top of Wilson Tower. It was the same one Alana had seen. Its old, powerful stepper motors were struggling to lift debris and planetary residue. It churned as massive bearings, now worn, groaned and creaked as the gigantic arm lifted boulders and ore material twice the size of their vehicle. Lights were attached on the top and the mechanoids' gargantuan forms created roving shadows on the landscape. A continuous, eerie silver fog drifted, coating the windscreen. The ground gently rumbled as they carefully crossed its path and into the beyond. Their roof laser dealt with stray Platnios along the way as bolts of energy, faultless in their aim, vaporising targets both near and far. Platnios disappeared in a puff of smoke.

Drawing nearer, the two Platnios spacecraft appeared menacingly stagnant. A wisp of haze floated around and enshrouded each one, making the scene even more perplexing and awe-inspiring. They resembled two slices of melon, husk down. Outside, they were almost lifeless. Philip and Ramaan agreed that they never would have expected to have been able to creep up on them like this. Alana vaporised the few guards who were stationed outside.

With his radar only revealing distant movement, Ramaan and Alana made their move. "Looks like most of the Platnios are at Thornz. This place is defenceless and empty," said Alana as she set up two blue-rays outside, while the rest of them studied the absurd hideousness of the Platnios spacecraft. They knew that their timing had to be perfect. They couldn't wait till morning for Mintaka to rise; by that time it might be too late.

Locating an entrance, Baygorn entered first. He made comments on its structure, while extracting a sample from the walls. "It's soft. Damn, it reminds me of soapstone. How does this thing manage to fly?" The inside was so cold and dark that their sophisticated infrared had trouble discerning the walls and ceiling. The air was filled with a rancid wafting odour. It seemed to glide around everywhere, secreted as tears on the wall.

They walked precariously, as the floors were slippery with an obnoxious slime. The interior of the craft ascended and descended asymmetrically into various levels. Uneven, bumpy passages went in all directions, and they didn't know where to start. All they knew was that they were looking for an entity with the capability of reproducing Platnios at an astronomical rate.

Fifty metres ahead they came across a hole in the floor. It was about two metres in diameter and had a gooey substance dripping down over the edges. They could hear a distant dripping of water. Closer to the hole, a sudden scuffle made them shiver, and then a shifting of a large bodily mass transpired into an unearthly groan reverberating throughout the chamber. It must've echoed throughout the entire spacecraft. Without a doubt, it was definitely coming from the depths of the hole in front of them.

They knelt and peered in. The thing making the noise was at least six metres tall. The huge Platnios, now sensing their inquisitiveness, raised its head upwards, glared at them and moaned again. It grumbled, shifted and shuffled about in its nauseating, slimy frame. Surrounding it in its pitiful environment, thousands of twitching eggs were preparing to step out into the night in search of their new enemy, in search of them.

"Looks like we don't have too much time, those things are about to hatch," said Lexia's perturbed voice, watching an egg crack and break.

Alana dropped a tritium charge into the hole. "Fifteen minutes!" Leaving the spacecraft, they ran like the wind to the vehicle and drove hastily back to Wilson Tower. From the top floor, the explosion occurred exactly as Alana had predicted. From the safety of Sporna, they watched as the two spacecraft dissolved from view in a burst of powerful white flash.

The next morning all that remained were two giant, spooky scorch marks.

Philip turned and to Alana. "What weaponry do we have left?"

"Ten blue-rays, two GF rifles and nine zips. Oh, and a stealth bomb I borrowed from Randolph."

"One of us has to return to the pod. There are more zips in the back section."

"Let me go," said Baygorn. "The journey will take at least two hours. I'll be back before they miss me."

"On two conditions: You keep that radio open at all times, and don't stop for anything."

As Baygorn shot off into the morning light, their frequent communications nurtured their uneasiness. He was alone. If something happened to him, they'd be powerless to assist. By this time, both Peblinus and Platnios, creator and servant, were engaged in their war chores. The Platnios had metamorphosed into a human form, causing the Peblinus to often shoot their own. They still didn't know why all this was happening. To them, it seemed more feasible to blame the barbaric Earthlings. Thornz was blazing with numerous battles between the remaining Platnios and the unhurried, dwindling number of Peblinus. Ramaan, through his binoculars, had estimated there were about five thousand Peblinus inside Thornz.

As they looked towards the horizon, the radio hissed, coming alive with the gruff voice of a Peblinus official. "Humans, we want to talk!"

"Must be related to Shar, he's offensive and rude." Aggravated, Ramaan, making an attempt at maintaining his composure, pressed Talk. "What do you want? How can we be of service?"

The received tone was as equally distasteful. "You must surrender, Humans. If not, you will perish!"

Alana crept besides Ramaan and whispered, "Buy us a couple of hours, enough time for Baygorn to get back. Come on, I know you can do it."

Ramaan gave off a thin smile. "We'll think about it, give us a couple of hours." Ramaan's spontaneous answer made the rest of them bite their lips. There was a silent pause as they waited.

"I give you three hours, not a minute more!" replied the official.

Alana quickly grabbed the communicator. "Baygorn, where are you?"

"Twenty kilometres from the pod," Baygorn responded. The sound of whirring electric engines came clearly over the speaker. "Don't stop to admire the scenery. Move it, we have little time!" They had three hours to prepare themselves for outright war against five thousand Peblinus.

Baygorn arrived at the pod, slamming on the brakes. He opened the rear section and started removing the remains of their arsenal onto the armoured vehicle. He counted eight zips, ten blue-rays, twenty ion pistols, and a GF rifle. Thanks to Randolph, another well-hidden stealth bomb was in the food section. It was a welcome sight. Slamming the boot and returning like a swift to the vehicle, he started to make his way once more for Wilson Tower.

"I see you got my message in good time," said Alana, patting him on the shoulder.

"You mean luckily I had the reserve power on the vehicle charged," said Baygorn, handing over the GF. They had fifty minutes left, and began mounting the remaining weapons in calculated positions. If their strategy worked, the Peblinus wouldn't stand a chance. The Stealth looked like an oversized briefcase, no patterns of pulsating lights belied its working state, no humming mechanical parts told the enemy it was armed or close by. Stealth status silently relayed its status back to a remote control panel in Alana's hands.

A short while later, the radio erupted with the gruff voice again. "Well, have you made up your minds? Are you ready to surrender?" They were such sardonic, mocking words that Philip could imagine his sarcastic lips. "We'll destroy you if you don't!"

Ramaan scratched his head. "But we are only five, you are five thousand! We are explorers; you have nothing against us. Why should we surrender? Give us one bloody good reason!" He snapped the last couple of words.

Five seconds passed.

"You are a pest, people from Earth. Prepare to die!"

"Just one moment, what's your name?" Ramaan stuck the last word in. "I'm going to report you to your superiors and nail your sorry subordinate butt to the wall. If I don't know your name, I can't do it!"

The fading deprecatory voice of the Peblinus official lingered long enough for them to hear his last words, "Stupid humans!" The hiss of the radio returned.

All of their weapons were either programmable on site or via the remote control panel that Alana held. Her eager eyes glancing at jiggling, dancing lights and data displays on the remote revealed the status of each of their deadly, active bombs. From their position behind a small incline, their infrared scopes and sensors didn't detect any movement on or around the premises. As far as they could tell, Arno Square was lifeless, with the exception of the five of them.

A couple of minutes later, a blast of energy came from the direction of Thornz and destroyed one of their blue-rays. Camouflaged Peblinus had managed to get close enough without exciting their detectors. On closer inspection, the ground was alive with lethargic, snaking bodies crawling their way towards them.

"There they are. Let them get a little closer."

While two minutes passed, Alana reconfigured and made a couple of adjustments to the weapons and pressed a button on her remote. The sky lit up like an impressive meteor shower. Explosive bullets rained down on their targets, taking less than five minutes to kill more than half the Peblinus. Like on Braan, there was so much senseless destruction and so much pain. Philip was sure that not even the presumptuous Peblinus was so talkative. He knew he was watching.

Still they came, wave after wave, column after column. Alana activated the blue-rays and GF rifle to clean up the last few. Ramaan said they had suddenly retreated towards the direction of their hangar. He grabbed the microphone and pushed Talk. There was no reply, only crackle.

"That's odd," said Lexia. Baygorn returned to the top floor and radioed down minutes later.

"Damn, there's lots of activity going on out there. It's a major battle! It looks like the last of the Peblinus is fighting for his life."

They gathered their supplies and headed for Thornz. The enlarging form grew to immense familiar dimensions. Platnios were everywhere.

"There must be another nest on the other side of Thornz! Damn crafty. They probably waited for us to do their dirty work." Alana set up as many blue-rays as she could while Ramaan popped off a couple of strays. "At least Peblinus have two legs and we can talk to them. You ever tried talking to a tree?" Ramaan's humour went unnoticed as he pulled the trigger again.

Gathering the remaining Peblinus, Lexia and Baygorn huddled behind the defence line while Alana and Ramaan vaporised those who came too near. The more Platnios they killed, the more that appeared from over the hill.

Without delay, Ramaan climbed into the vehicle with Alana and shot off. Alana punched the map function on her C-12, with the vehicle showing as a red pixel in the centre. Surrounding hills, ditches, dongas, and valleys showed up as yellow topographic geometrical lines. Plants and trees were white. Platnios showed up as white masses, and there was a large concentration of them not far away. Alana had found what she was looking for. It was a well-hidden white clump in a valley.

"That's the only place where they could hide a spacecraft of those proportions. Sneaky little devils; they've concealed it well." Alana put her foot down and accelerated.

Ramaan scanned the area with binoculars. "Must be around here somewhere. This is definitely the place." The blue-ray increased in intensity.

"Over there, look!" Alana pulled over and they drew up as near as possible to the Platnios spaceship. The blue-ray on the back was beginning to overheat.

"Five minutes!" she said, wearing a stern look. She opened the door of the vehicle, holding the tritium bomb. Ramaan jumped into the driving seat.

"You keep that engine revving! I'll throw it as close as I can." Ramaan had never seen her mouth open so wide. She was off in a flash like a jackrabbit in amongst flashes of firing. It had happened so fast that Ramaan only had time to nod. In less than a minute, Alana jumped back into the vehicle, and Ramaan's foot fell flat on the accelerator.

As the device went off, all life in a radius of three kilometres ceased to exist. Alana sensed the intense heat wave on her neck like a summer sun. The Peblinus were now under their control, safely behind a makeshift defence barrier.

Philip was already interrogating them when Ramaan drove up. "Apparently, they'd received their orders from Head Command on Ganus. The orders were: Five humans are killing Peblinus. Shoot to kill on sight."

Alana jumped out of the vehicle and walked towards the small gathering of Peblinus. "But it was the Platnios that attacked you. You saw it with your own eyes."

The short Peblinus worker stepped back. "You provoked us, the same as you did on Braan!" The trembling man moved farther back after hearing Alana's bitter tone. He stammered, "They say if you land or attempt to land on Ganus, you will be destroyed."

Alana moved closer to the gathering of Peblinus. "Oh, really? Tell me, does anyone know where these spider creatures come from?" The reaction was blank looks back and forth like in a tennis match. "They are your Platnios, your own creation. You made them, and now they are coming back for you. They are the ones destroying you, not us. Can't you see?" Alana furiously stepped back.

Philip took over. "They have evolved into a superior killing machine, and they've learned all your defects and weaknesses. They won't stop at anything until they achieve their objective of wiping you off the face of the planet." Faces turned. "I wouldn't be shocked if the Platnios are en route to Ganus right now to finish you off. If I were you, I'd get ahold of your Head Command on Ganus and enlighten them."

"I can't," retorted the shocked and trembling Peblinus. "The only one with the authority to do that is dead! We don't have the access codes for the transmitter."

Ramaan walked to the vehicle and picked up his computer. "Let's see what we can do. It's important that you get a message to the headquarters on Ganus as fast as possible, make them understand what's going on. Lexia, I need you here."

The five-digit code Ramaan needed to unlock the transmitter and the alphanumeric keypad from one to nine (Ichi to Kyuu in the Peblinus language) did not seem much of a task. He hooked

117

it onto the computer and asked Lexia to decipher the code. It took her less than ten seconds. In a blink of an eye, the radio burst into life, giving a beep acknowledging its working status.

Philip took the microphone. "This is Haradan calling Ganus. Can anyone hear me? Can anyone acknowledge this radio transmission?" There was no reply. There was silence. Only a dismal hiss merging with the odd occasional murmur from Mintaka that made them fear the worst. Two billion lives were dependent on their one simple transmission, and all they received was a deathly, overbearing silence. Was Ganus still there?

A Peblinus walked over. "Ganus is the single largest settlement of our race in this system. If it's wiped out, we'll never recover."

"You're damn right. If these things eat two billion, you can't imagine how they'd spread!" said Alana, trying to conceal her anger.

"We have no option but to go there ourselves, and right away," Philip gave a blue-ray to one of the Peblinus.

"Are you mad?" said Alana. "We could turn our backs and get shot!"

"We need their full confidence as they need ours, just remember."

Philip looked towards the worker as the vehicle began its journey back to the pod. "It's imperative you reach Ganus on the radio and inform them of the situation."

Evolution is a macabre journey with organisms relentlessly cannibalizing one another in the pursuit of survival. Without doubt, the human race had remained at the top of the food chain for 40,000 years. Not any more—they had competition.

8. Ganus

Flight time between planets accentuated their psychological uncertainty, thus was the power of imagination. Usually they faked confidence and passed time by studying languages and the samples they had taken from previous planets. Enduring mental exercises that not even the wildest nightmare could have prepared them for. They rarely spoke during this period. Each planet so far had been a different hell, and they'd left the last one with a heavy conscience.

Ganus would take them seven days to reach. On this journey weapons became their priority. They would have to assemble more before they arrived on Ganus. In the meantime, Ramaan made an urgent petition to the next freighter that was due to reach them in a few days.

As the largest planet in the system crept up on the radar, its immense blue realm thirteen times that of Earth didn't resemble anything they had seen so far. Its vastness and dense polar caps reminded Philip of the Earthly composition he'd left behind more than six years before. Then it hit upon him like a sledgehammer: This isn't Earth. You're more than one thousand light-years away from home. This godforsaken disguise was misery and demise. It was another hell waiting to be trampled. Was Mike Branigan going through the same as them? Did they share similarities? Crowning it all, they were putting themselves at great risk just by landing there. The Peblinus hadn't been very receptive so far, and for some reason, had been blinded by lies. Philip had always said that self-defence didn't always mean unnecessary bloodshed. It is self-preservation, and they had to preserve their well-being at whatever cost. It sounded so human to say that their motives, as always, were peaceful and friendly. Well, they were until now.

Philip turned towards his silent crew. Truthfully, they were coming here to see what they could take, and, obviously, someone wasn't going to like it. What would they do if another race suddenly appeared from space with an appetite for their technology?

Approaching orbit, insistent attempts at contacting the Peblinus came up empty. Ganus was definitely there, they could see it, but the stifling silence accentuated their uneasiness, along with the incessant gamma glitches and thutling sounds emanating from Mintaka. As Sentrywatcher scanned and studied the surface of the planet, a flickering orange light averted their attention to one of its moons.

Lexia leaned towards the scanner and studied the recent maps. It was Abnarak, the fifth moon. The surface details of Abnarak appeared on the main viewer, and their mouths widened at the sight of an immense infestation of Platnios.

These were not ordinary Platnios like the ones they had encountered so far. Even at a fleeting glance, they could see the differences. Sentrywatcher zoomed in. There were hundreds of dense groups nervously fidgeting and fighting among themselves on the surface. They were more agile, and darker. They had formed themselves into ranks and strategic patterns. Where in hell were the Peblinus?

From the pod, Ramaan locked on to the Peblinus headquarters and landed the pod directly in front of the front door. As the undercarriage met the surface of the landing pad, armed Peblinus rushed from the building, onto the platform, and surrounded them. They wanted to play all their cards.

Guns of all shapes and sizes pointed at the pod, combined with a stern voice through a megaphone, made them get out with their hands over their heads. They didn't have time to breathe.

Lexia was trying to hear what they were muttering. "Idiots. Ignoramuses. They insist on calling us stupid humans! Apparently, we're under arrest until their commander-in-chief wakes up, something about a meeting. I know, I know it sounds absurd. That's what I heard." The guard mumbled something and shoved them towards a holding room.

Ramaan banged his fist on the door. The door clinked shut. Inside, it stank like rotten cheese and stale piss. "If Lexia's right, a planet's future and two billion people are at stake and relying on a man in bed." Lexia held one of the cell bars.

"That's about it in a nutshell."

A guard sat on a chair watching them, irritatingly thumping a crowd stick on the wall. It was almost metronomic and rhythmical. He wore a violet waistband on top of the customary red robe stating his rank. The cell was a three-by-three-metre cubicle. They waited as the overpowering drifting urine smell and the uncontrollable tap, tap, tap started to get into their minds.

Alana broke first. "Hey, guard! Can you understand me?" The guard turned his head slightly in her direction and continued tapping. Someone's clothes lay untidily stacked on the floor in the corner. The brawny guard rose to his feet, still banging his stick, with Alana in his sight when a man's voice erupted from his wireless. He placed the stick into his belt and mumbled something Lexia couldn't catch.

The guard turned. "That was the commander. He won't be coming himself; he has dispatched an officer to come for you. He should be here at any moment." His accent was terrible.

Alana couldn't wait. "Lexia, tell him we need to speak to him now; it's an emergency!" The man continued to bang the crowd stick on the wall.

"Be quiet! You shut up in there! I told you, an officer will be here soon." The stench was like an unscratchable itch.

Philip had an urge to change his clothes. "It's time we don't have," he said angrily. "The sooner we can get out of here—"

Philip was interrupted as a senior officer ran into the cell area, shouting at the brawny guard and telling him to open the cell and let them out. "At once!"

The guard immediately took out a wad of keys and opened the squeaky entranceway. As the door clinked open, he said, "Maybe we meet again soon. I will keep it ready for you."

"Don't get your bloody hopes up," said Baygorn, cracking his knuckles.

"Come with me, please," said the officer, giving the guard a dirty look and pushing him to one side. They briskly followed him onto the outside landing area where they saw the pod, immobile and still heavily guarded.

"It's important we speak to the commander," said Alana.

"He knows about the situation. He is waiting for you at headquarters to discuss what happened on Haradan."

"Haradan? But we're not here to discuss Haradan!" Philip broke in. "There was nothing we could have done for them on Haradan!"

They walked down a garden path past shrubs towards a glass building. Baygorn inquisitively wanted to stop. Philip pulled him away and they went in.

"We have urgent information for your commander!" shouted Philip. A door at the end of a corridor creaked open and a large, vibrating frame wobbled out. He walked in their direction and took Philip's hand. The commander in chief lived well; they could see this from the hallway.

"Sorry about the cell and the smell." The tone was sarcastic. "Hope the cell guard wasn't too rough on you. Anyway, you must be the humans I have been hearing about." The man released Philip's hand.

"Although the receiver is switched off, the transmissions I get are recorded on an antiquated machine. I listened to them a few hours ago. Tell me what happened up there on Haradan, I want to hear it coming from you." They sat down and Philip explained what had happened from the moment they'd landed. The fat man listened intently, occasionally averting eye contact. Ramaan broke into the conversation.

"We have located a huge mass of Platnios on the fifth moon of this planet. Our scanners indicate they are almost ready to attack."

A man walked into the room. "We stopped receiving signals from Haradan two hours ago. They might have a problem with their transmitter."

Ramaan butted in. "There's was no problem with that transmitter! I checked it myself before we left. Have you tried contacting Braan?"

"There's been no reply from Braan for quite a while now, two days at least." All of them stared at one another.

"It's so obvious." The fat man asked Philip to repeat what he'd just said.

"Don't you see it? Ganus is next in line." Philip explained that the Platnios army was probably waiting for the right moment to strike. Thank the stars their freighter would be entering the atmosphere of Ganus tomorrow morning to offload their weapons for the remainder of the trip. They all hoped it wouldn't be too late. Alana and Baygorn returned to the pod, angrily dismissing the guards, and offloaded the rest of their supplies into an office.

"My God, look at this place. They don't have anything, it's just a desk and two chairs," murmured Baygorn staring at a couple of flattened boxes. The office was small and untidy. They lived and survived like the next man without worry.

Many hours still separated them from the next morning. All they could do was wait, hopeful to be mesmerized by the sunrise.

Alana noticed Baygorn's concern. "Stop it. Worry is infectious, you know. When the freighter enters the atmosphere tomorrow, it will search for the pod's homing beacon and steer itself towards us. Once it's landed, the weapon transfer is only ten minutes, so put a smile on that face." Alana's words did little to appease Baygorn. His brain was active.

The Platnios bred and evolved quicker the closer they got to Mintaka. Braan was a much colder world. They had less motivation there. They succumbed more easily to the Peblinus. Here on this hotter world, things were different. Sentrywatcher had sent them front-row images. She had calculated by the density of Platnios that they had been amassing for a lengthy period, planning and preparing. The only way to destroy them was to engage the Platnios on their temporary home ground. If they came here, it would be over in a matter of days, even hours.

On the edge of the town, from behind a side building, Baygorn came across a full view of the landscape. "I take back what I said. What a fabulous sight, this place is stunning."

Ganus was beautiful and had similar conditions to Earth. Fresh air rushed into Baygorn's nose and mouth. He took a deep breath, filling his lungs. The windy, warm air smelt good. From where he was, he saw immense swaying trees and the beginning of a mountain range that reached well into the cloud layer. As the remaining minutes of light dwindled, each of the team members gazed intently at the magnificent alien landscape that stretched out into the distance.

For Lexia the dominant feeling was one of elation. Cautious by nature with her expectations, until this moment of the expedition she had not allowed herself the intense pleasure of believing that she would ever again see her parents. Sporadic video transmissions to them letting them know she was all right weren't enough. Her mind was now flooded by the bucolic beauty, and she imagined in detail the joy of her reunion with her father. It would be wonderful, Lexia said to herself expectantly. By the time she turned around and faced the others she was having difficulty containing her jubilation.

Baygorn was sure it rained occasionally, as he saw menacing black clouds. He suddenly felt homesick and thought, *What in God's name am I doing here?* Hazy and distant lightning bolts accompanied faint rumblings of reverberating thunder. Even the Peblinus here seemed more passive.

"I have contact!" shouted Ramaan, staring down at his C-12. Philip turned on his C-12, glaring at the most eerie picture. Two large groups of Platnios, two unimaginable, colossal gatherings of death and destruction, were waiting for the perfect opportunity. It looked like they only had hours. As the results came clearer, one group consisted of no less than 300 million fully developed, battle-ready Platnios.

"To destroy the Platnios on their home ground we'll need a very special weapon."

"You're talking about Grionic warheads, aren't you?" Baygorn gasped at the thought.

"It's the only way we can effectively destroy them way out there, Baygorn. This is a safe distance."

"They discovered the Grionic weapon ten years ago. Wasn't it some Harvard University professor? I read about it once in a *Harvard Weekly Science Review*. We were still undergoing training for this mission when he made the discovery," said Baygorn.

"Correct, by the time Professor Thomas Noodle stumbled upon mass disintegration, he'd been studying atom technology for more than twenty years. It was a real breakthrough. It's an uncontrolled chain reaction where one atom destroys another. These two dead atoms then move on and destroy another two, and so on up the ladder. Whatever material it encounters, it disintegrates, living or dead. As far as I know, it's never been tested in the real world, so this is the perfect opportunity."

Each of their two pods came equipped with five Grionic warheads. They could only be used under special permission, using launch codes obtained from the Association of Planets based on Terron. Ramaan didn't waste any time and rigged up the interstellar antenna.

Philip grabbed the mike.

"Hello, Philip," said the commander. "How are things going over there?"

"Not so good, Jim. We need permission to use the Grionic technology." Philip waited a few seconds for the reply.

"I'll have to get back to you on that one."

"No can do, Jim," said Philip. "Time is something we don't have. We need those launch codes right now."

"What's the problem then?"

"Jim, I am talking about two billion lives!"

Jim grunted and sent them the authorisation patch. The codes followed soon after. "Remember, this is the first time they're being tested. We need to see the results. Where are your targets?"

"If a word be worth one shekel, silence is worth two."

Jim caught on and the radio clicked off. Alana and Ramaan lifted out two heavy Grionic canisters from the back of the vehicle and made the final preparations for the morning's arrival on the launch pads.

"How do they trigger?" Lexia asked.

Alana replied, "On impact. They're not going to make an explosion like you are hoping. Grionic warheads simply release their charge of anti-matter directly onto the surface. The chain reaction begins from there. I'm sure it's quite painless."

However, waiting for the freighter wasn't painless. It simply meant they had a couple of nerve-racking hours to themselves. Philip sneaked off from the group to look around and see a bit of Ganus for himself. It was peaceful out there. It was so perfectly quiet. The coming night left a dark blue tinge in the sky. Bizarre birds, he was sure, sang in tall trees marking the beginning of a dense wooded area fifty metres from him. A pathway led somewhere. If he had just woken up here, he never would have thought that tomorrow could be his last. He would have woken up ignorant and blissful. He thought, *Why don't I have the wings of a bird?*

With the same brightness as Venus, Abnarak, suspended almost directly overhead, scrutinised them with its malignant shimmer and silence.

But as the birds continued with their anthem of flavourful, exquisite warbling that drifted unknowingly between the buildings, the Peblinus had caught wind of what was going on. Many of them began to enter the subterranean refuges with their belongings. As there were no mining facilities on Ganus, each resident had his domain given to him free of charge. All he had to do was to work the lands and provide food. The two billion Peblinus living on Ganus lived in concentrated areas on each of the three continents. Each continent was connected by a sea port and had a principal city, just as each city had duplicate subterranean refuges.

Philip fixed on their current position on the map. They were placed right in the middle. They were the tasty ham between the two slices of bread.

Baygorn, observing his concentration, approached. "Philip, remember that sample I took from the Platnios spaceship on Haradan?"

"Of course I do, why?" snapped Philip, coming out of his dream.

"I've had it analysed. Those Platnios ships are made of bone. Mostly Peblinus DNA. I found what could be our dear Haak there, as well, all mixed in with a large variety of other species. Conclusion: Platnios build their spacecraft from the remains of the ones they slaughter. They must be reproducing on Abnarak on a massive scale."

What Baygorn had speculated was a gruesome tale, but Philip was sure that the Platnios had not only been studying the Peblinus and other races for decades, their methodology had probably been carefully planning this massacre for decades. Their only weapon was quantity and a voracious nature to go with it. Only they knew when it was going to occur.

A Peblinus approached, breaking his thoughts. He invited them to join him at once around the dinner table. "The commander and his staff are expecting you immediately."

It sounded perfect. They could finally meet the rest of the high command and maybe punch the lights out of that prison guard. Baygorn and Philip trotted back and joined the others. The dining table was antiquated, reminding Philip of a pre-modern Middle Ages. It was long and rectangular, made from heavy wood. The Peblinus sat on both sides, all lifting metallic cups. Some were chanting, happy. It was a jolly sight. They had no concern for the impending doom that could arrive at any moment. Ramaan, sitting next to Alana, looked around in disbelief.

As Philip sat down next to Lexia, Ramaan stood up and turned his sturdy frame towards the commander, who was laughing and joking. "Excuse me, Commander, please enlighten us: What were your opinions of the Bods when you met them? What did you think of them?" The commander's face turned a bit sour at the interruption. That was how it started.

"Pleasant. I once met a few of them on Braan. They are a very intelligent species and very likeable. What was your judgment?"

"We are the best of friends. Between all of our races, there is a profound similarity that goes way back. We have been searching for a connection. After meeting and getting to know the Bods as we have, we feel that the Bod nation is the true intelligence in this system." The commander stopped chattering to the man next to him and stood up. A grapefruit silence fell into the room.

Ramaan continued. "Tell us what happened a hundred years ago. Tell us what the Peblinus did to the Bods. Tell us about the massacre and murder. You must've been aware that Peblinus troops exploited them almost to extinction because you thought they were going to steal the tellurium."

"No, as a matter of fact, I was not aware of this incident. I will look into it, though." The commander turned his head and continued talking with the man beside him.

127

Michael Gilwood

"You'll look into it? Come on, how can a nation such as yours conceal a scandal such as this, and then blatantly deny any knowledge of its occurrence?" blurted Alana, now standing up. "The Bods told us that a hundred years ago the Peblinus landed on Braan and killed most of them. You stole their technology, their hangars, and their pride. You bled them almost to extinction!"

The commander banged his chubby hand on the table. "Such contempt! If this is the purpose of your visit, I must bid you farewell this instant!"

Philip stood up. "Now hang on just a minute, Commander. What they're saying is true." He took a deep breath and lowered his voice. "We are not here to offend anyone, Commander. You do know that if we leave, you will be destroyed by the results of your own creation. We came here to warn you. You have been warned. You see, part of our investigation relies on searching for the truth. The Platnios want to finish what you started a century ago. It's payback time, my friend, and let's hope to Christopher they don't come soon!" Philip and the others walked out, leaving the commander agape and looking at the others.

Dawn came with a marble-sized Mintaka rising above the horizon. Alana informed Philip that the freighter pod was entering the atmosphere and should land in a little over an hour. They made the final preparations while each of them took it in turn to have breakfast.

When the pod arrived with its only occupant, he stepped out, smiled and stretched his legs. "Arggh, that's better. Hello, I'm Stephen Quaid," he said, regaining his posture and touching his knees.

"You must be Philip." They shook hands. "It took forever to get here. Take whatever you need, and I'll be off. They called me a week ago to stop off on Telus-Three with provisions. Then, for some reason, they cancelled it. Suppose they had similar problems."

They offloaded everything on-board, and as fast as he had come, Stephen disappeared into the morning sky and out of sight.

Ten minutes later, the first of the Grionic missiles waited on its launch pad. Philip handed over the launch codes to Ramaan. Alana was programming the trajectory. Using Sentrywatcher's scanner, Baygorn and Lexia were studying Abnarak for movement. So far, there was none.

9. The Platnios

It was about seven in the morning when the first shadow of a building caressed the vehicle. Two fiery streaks left the launch pads and zoomed upwards into the clear, violet sky. Sentrywatcher would track the Grionic missiles' progress every step of the way until their eventual detonation on Abnarak. The *Excelsior* was patient in the front row, constantly sending images back to Terron. If everything went well, the impact would take place in about five hours. Alana had programmed the second missile to impact on Abnarak on the dark side, just in case the Platnios had some device to prevent the missiles from landing. Lexia continuously scanned Abnarak for any changes in behaviour, but it was as worryingly tranquil as it was before. Between all of them, they erected a formidable wall of defences, combining the new batch of weapons with their remaining stocks.

Alana programmed the blue-rays, strategically placing them on walls or high ground, pointing towards valleys and vacant space on all points of the compass. For up to seven kilometres, the forest-surrounded city and its flattened splendour gave them an ample, perfect view. All entrances to buildings protected by blue-rays brought comfort to all of them.

A general alarm sounded for all civilians to come into the city for protection during the skirmish. Philip had never seen a mass concentration like this before. It was an endless sea of heads appearing out of nowhere. More than four million Peblinus scuttled into the city and disappeared into the underground bunkers to banish the cold and dark. Each one of these people had hypothesised the coming happenings, but they had put aside their nightmares of fire and war and insanity. Some came on their strange wind vehicles, while others drove electric machines with small, mounted stumpy wings like flaps. Down they clambered in the hundreds, down and down. Millions of clueless, confused Peblinus went into hiding from an enemy they didn't know or perceive.

The tunnels stretched for dozens of kilometres under the city. They consisted of three levels accessible only by a metal ladder. At each entrance to the bunker, a guard tower added extra protection. The underground tunnels could sustain life for up to six months, each one capable of housing more than half a million Peblinus. The normal, everyday Peblinus here on Ganus was a shy person; they avoided confrontation. The few times Philip or Lexia tried to communicate with them, they backed away without saying a word, so they never forced the issue.

"Just look at them," said Baygorn, "two billion people without defences. The scuffle wouldn't have lasted even a day." Some of the elite guards would use their ion and plasma technology. They seemed capable enough to handle them.

"We got an impact warning!" shouted Alana, watching Sentrywatcher's transmitted image on the C-12. The first missile landed directly in the middle of the two infestations. The visual images they received were fascinating, because the detonation didn't cause a physical explosion. Instead, as it struck the landscape of Abnarak, the rocky surface began to melt away like an ice cube on a hot summer's day. All matter, living or dead, would become part of this rapidly forming, giant drop of water. By the time the second missile hit, Abnarak had almost transformed; but before the missiles had completed their task, twenty Platnios warships had reached orbit around Abnarak. They were debating their flight path. In part, their plan had worked.

Lexia was observing them with the scrupulous eyes of Sentrywatcher. Suddenly she stood up. "Here they come!"

The maths was easy. Ramaan calculated that each warcraft carried about 100,000 Platnios. The good news was that they didn't know Philip and his crew were here, but Philip wasn't sure if they could defeat twenty of these enormous freighters with their limited firepower. Philip certainly wasn't sure of the quality of the commander's manpower. The Peblinus were completely untrained for any type of military manoeuvre, and all Ramaan could do was to show them how to point and shoot. Many of these Peblinus would die. They knew it, yet it was up to them to prevent it. Ramaan and Alana showed them strategic positions. Philip gave them powerful weapons, but they had limited time.

The twenty warcraft could arrive at any moment. Baygorn constantly monitored and relayed their distance and speed. One of the Peblinus gave them a map of the central continent. They called it Astmad. Philip unwound it on the floor as the C-12 continued reporting their progress.

A Peblinus, staring at the map, moved closer. "It's possible they could land there and there," he said, pointing with a long plastic ruler, revealing fourteen possible points of descent.

"The remaining Platnios will probably land on the other side of Ganus. Those maps are not available, but we did manage to warn them. They are aware of the situation."

Alana did the last of her routine checks and sent the elite guards to their posts. Philip waited. The city was more or less ready.

When the first of what seemed to be a decelerating meteorite broke the stillness of the daytime sky, landing a great distance from them in the east, another two simultaneously landed still farther away to the south. Another came, and another. The sixth landed about three kilometres away. Philip watched through binoculars. The nearest one balanced itself on the sand like a sinister crescent-formed ship out of water. Another one arrived.

"Look," said Alana, "it's that same design we saw on Haradan." In less than a minute, tens of thousands of expelled Platnios squirmed and writhed their way towards the city like an expanding ripple on a pond. They poured out of their spacecraft. Philip could hear them, a subdued and faint rustling bark, far off and incessant like the creasing of paper. Blue-rays situated on higher buildings began releasing their silvery needles. Platnios began dropping in the hundreds. The Peblinus elite on ground level started firing the moment the Platnios came into range.

Alana was thinking more about the enemy craft than the Platnios. She placed a tritium warhead on the end of a grenade launcher and set it to explode on impact. Two minutes later, a temporary sun lit up the horizon, and Philip felt the heat on his face. The warship, along with thousands of crazed Platnios, simply disappeared.

The orbiting *Excelsior* sent them the panoramic view. Mostly them, but other cities, too, were slowly being surrounded like an anxious, enwrapping hand around an ice cream cone, ensuring their devouring. Hundreds of thousands of spiders crawling and edging their way along the web towards the prey could only but make Philip stand there, agape and unable to speak. They seemed to be appearing out of nowhere. Another craft landed on the other side of the city. Alana vaporised it before the Platnios disembarked.

Zip bombs placed on the outskirts of the city were almost depleted. Blue-rays were beginning to heat up to unaccustomed levels. This was what Philip feared: The first space freighters were the suicide squad. If they were able to break the Peblinus defences, it would be good on their part. Now came the attack.

Near where the last spacecraft landed, another two thudded onto the surface, making the ground distantly rumble and shudder. Alana reloaded her grenade launcher as quickly as she could and disintegrated them both. Ramaan said these two craft had disgorged different species of Platnios. They were a faster version, more supple and slightly smaller than the others, moving with incredible agility towards the encampment. The firing continued.

"Hey, the ones on Haradan couldn't come out during the day. Do you think they are a new strain?" asked Lexia.

"At least they seem to die as easily as the others," said Ramaan, putting another GF rifle in place. The blue-rays outside the perimeter wall began glowing red, and Ramaan urgently needed to rest them before they burnt themselves out. Six GF rifles, depleted of their charge, grinned helplessly at the advancing wall of Platnios. That was when it happened. Three more melon craft thudded in front and behind them. Astounded and in shock with more than 300,000 Platnios advancing towards a defenceless, tired and worn-out Ganus city, Philip gaped in awe, as he knew there was nothing he could do.

10. The Bods' Return

Unexpectedly, a fuzzy human form materialised directly in the middle of the city next to the fountain. At first, Philip thought it was a hologram fizzling into view, but it was a man, many men. Philip recognised the diplomatic Bod by his clothing. Holding a sphere, he took shape and looked around. Ten heavily armed elite and five military, all holding spheres, surrounded him. One of them passed the diplomatic Bod a megaphone. It squeaked.

"I have a message for the head council of Ganus," he said. A hopeful silence gripped the terrain in amongst the distant rumbling of advancing Platnios. The chubby head council member wobbled onto a parted platform alongside the diplomatic Bod.

"What do you want, Bod?" asked the Peblinus commander.

"Still have your sense of humour and eating well, I see. This place will never change. Well, let's see what you think of my sense of humour, Commander. I'm here for two reasons. Recent intercepted radio transmissions originating from the orbiting Earth spacecraft have brought us here to save you from your stupidity and constant greed. We feel it wouldn't be right for the Peblinus to fall while you waddle your way down to your safe vault for protection. Secondly, thanks to these transmissions, a fact that had been kept from us has come into the limelight. It concerns Braan and the slaughtering of the Bods one century ago. Also the technologies you stole and now use, thanks to us. If you surrender yourself and return the stolen technologies, you'll live, because it is in our power to preserve your pitiful lives against this oncoming threat that approaches your cities." The Bod's hand pointed out onto the horizon. Eyes followed.

"If you do not, you'll die like the thieves you are. I represent the head council for Retolox and the newly appointed Braan. We have more than two billion Bods on Retolox requesting that your feeble race of bandits return what is rightfully ours. We, in return, will grant you this one planet to flourish and maintain yourselves without interference. I felt it duly correct to have this visit before you exterminate yourselves completely." The Bod swung around and looked in their direction.

"I must add, I fail to see why these Earth beings insist on helping you."

Ramaan cupped his hands over his mouth, but he couldn't contain himself. "We're not going to watch two billion lives get wiped out just because a few are guilty. On Braan, Shar promised us that he would return the stolen technology to the Bods. Shar gave us his word!" Later they realised that this was the case; Shar hadn't backed down on his decision to return the stolen technology. His reward for trying to do so was imprisonment in a high-level security prison on an unknown location.

The trembling head council waved a hand. "How do we end this reign of violence and terror preventing peace between us? My goodness," he continued, "there is really no one at home, is there? We want all the technology pertaining to the Bod race for the past hundred years, and our hangars. Before that time isn't my concern. If only you'd asked in the beginning instead of pillaging, we wouldn't be here now. We're the makers and the shapers of this slice of the galaxy. Most of what you have is ours. I'm not voracious; just realistic."

"Then I'm afraid you leave us with no choice." The commander's head drooped. "Take whatever you want, including all the investigations we have done using those technologies. Mind telling me how?"

"We'll simply repossess every means of data storage, every machine, mechanical or electric, every electronic device, and lastly, every land vehicle possessed by you using our design. Consider our constructions on this planet as a loan. We will then leave you in peace to do your own research," said the diplomatic Bod.

"All other Peblinus in this sector will be sent here to join you on this planet. We will watch your every move and, in a way, will be your guardian angels." The diplomatic Bod raised his arm and clicked his fingers.

Michael Gilwood

The high council member did a U-turn and shook hands with the Bod. They walked together in an orderly fashion towards the main building. Suddenly more than one thousand Bods appeared on the outskirts of the city and opened fire on the advancing wall of barking Platnios. It was over in a matter of minutes.

The head council appeared from the main building after signing the treaty with the Bod diplomat. Alana pushed in to have a word. "General, oh General, excuse me, please. May I ask you something?" Two muscular bodyguards rapidly intervened, putting more distance between her and the diplomat.

"Down, boys, I just want a word with the general."

"It's okay, she's one of the Earth people. How may I be of service?"

"Do you know Randolph, Randolph from Braan? He is the area director we met."

"I don't talk to area directors," said the general, "That's a job for zone captains. On Braan we have two hundred area directors and twenty zone captains."

Alana moved a bit closer. "We came from Earth to investigate this planetary system. Unfortunately, that was when we stumbled upon this giant mix-up of cultures. If it is possible, we'd like to know more of our background coming from you."

"Quite frankly, I don't have the time, but I will gladly pass you to one of our zone captains to give you all the information you need." The general pointed a hand and flicked a finger.

"I must apologise, right now I have an urgent meeting on Retolox and must attend it. Goodbye." Using a red sphere, the general disappeared along with the rest of his underdogs, except one stayed behind.

The zone captain was a thin, big-jawboned man. He walked closer. "Hello, I'm Arbuk. I know the area director you spoke about with the general. For centuries, we have been sending out search parties and probes to all parts of the galaxy in search of answers, much like you're doing now." Arbuk gave off warmth as he spoke.

"Our Bod nation began to flourish more than 20,000 years ago. Before that is a bit misty. At first, we exterminated the weak newborn in an endeavour to breed a stronger race. We trained

136

every one of us in the most modern way possible. I am sure you do the same where you come from." Arbuk beckoned them to follow and went on, saying, "Since then, we have strived for survival: surviving wars and the Peblinus. But now we are at the peak of our knowledge and are at last ready to venture into the outer regions of the known galaxy, and hopefully into the next. We particularly have our eyes on Andromeda. It's a vast and unexplored region."

Ramaan was doing mental mathematics. "Andromeda is more than two million light-years away. How is that possible?" Maybe he would share his inner secrets over a martini as well.

Arbuk did mention that their surreptitious success was their engineering department. Their fusion-ion reactor was so powerful that it could almost destroy an entire planet. This fusion-ion reaction was responsible for their travel velocity.

"Under normal circumstances, a journey to Andromeda would take us four thousand years," he said, followed with a cough.

"But it's this fusion-ion technology that enables us to reach our objective in only eight years. We have already sent five hundred terra-farmers to investigate and begin settling there in a special craft."

"What made you come to Mintaka?" enquired Baygorn.

"At the time, it was the most peaceful part of the galaxy. The Spica and Fomalhaut regions, yours including, were at war involving the Gorinos. We conducted our studies and enhanced our abilities using the tranquillity of the Mintaka system. Later as we separated on different planets, the Peblinus took advantage of our lower numbers and annihilated the majority of us. But with your efforts, we have rejoined and regrouped ourselves, forming the Bod Nation we once were."

"The Gorinos, we've heard about them. Didn't they fight the Peblinus on Mars?" asked Alana.

"We call them the Dark Ones. Mars at one stage belonged to them. They claimed it almost 100,000 years ago with the expectations of settling down. Mars at the time was a flourishing planet; a bustling civilisation like yours is now. Then the Peblinus arrived with their incurable diseases and pillage. It was an invasion with the intention of keeping Mars for themselves. The

Gorinos, seeing what was going on, subsequently chased them all over the galaxy until they reached here to continue their thieving habits. I am afraid to say some of them, on leaving Mars, also fled to Earth."

Philip asked Arbuk if the Bods were the ones responsible for the major ancient constructions on Earth. "We found evidence in subterranean bunkers explaining in great detail that the Bods were the ones responsible for the construction of the Pyramids and other structures in many parts of our planet. That they assisted with the aid of wondrous machines from the stars and taught talented men the gifts of invention."

"Oh, I see you found one of our bunkers. Our secrets are hidden in them. But returning to your question, of course we are."

Philip saw the birth of a most wonderful smile as Arbuk continued to speak. "We constructed them, as well as many others, as farewell gifts to the ancient human. Many of these gifts are now underwater, hidden by time and its relentlessness. Stimulating their still-naïve minds, we introduced writing and showed them how to draw. Their petroglyphs are evidence of this. We left behind many of our cultures and traditions, so they could be utilised by them. All this, as well as our habits and behaviours, paved the way for your future. The late Cro-Magnon allowed us to use their home planet as a trampoline in our existence. Earth at the time was perfect. Its atmospheric and climatic conditions were ideal for us." They followed Arbuk away from the bustle.

"In the following eight thousand years, the post Cro-Magnon developed themselves into a more intelligent species, to eventually become what you call the Homo Superior. We defended the early Cro-Magnon when we were there against the Homo Neanderthal. They were a cruel and vile species. To them, the man who possessed fire had the possession of life itself.

"We could see the difference between the two. The post Cro-Magnon were using primitive tools to create, thus showing their culture. Our reasoning was, what they lacked in civility, they showed in promise. We assisted them and paved their way by defeating these creatures called the Neanderthal. When they built greed into your DNA, our individual interests began to collide. We evacuated Earth in search of another world. Some of us came to this system. I honestly believe if it wasn't for our intervention and DNA restructuring, the Neanderthal would have won the war. Defeating the Cro-Magnon would have created a different future for the sapiens."

"Then what was the Goranic period?" asked Baygorn.

"That is just before the time of our departure. When the Peblinus invaded Mars, your extravagant blue planet at the time was home and host to a wide variety of species inaugurating their dark, obtrusive beginnings. They came from various sections of the galaxy. At one time, the Gorinos, hence the Goranic period, fled from the rampaging Peblinus. Many of them ended up on Earth. Mars was uninhabitable by that time. The virus the Peblinus brought not only destroyed lives, it rampaged through the Martian vegetation as well, leaving it as dead as it is today. The other planets throughout your solar system were useless. They were either too cold, too hot, or too gaseous, so Earth at that time received many visitors. Every species in the galaxy flocked towards that paradise, including the Gorinos and the Peblinus." Arbuk smiled again.

"In the land you call Egypt, to the southwest of the capital, there is a small community called Gebel Qatrani. We hid artefacts five hundred metres below the sand before the humans began their hostility and skirmishing for treasures and power. It is our complete knowledge accumulated at that time. We hid it deep enough so an advanced human being with technology could later discover it. There you'll find all you need to know about our cultures and ages going as far back as 80,000 years. We also reveal our methods used in the construction of ancient structures. Some of them I'm sure you haven't discovered yet.

"Sapiens began his pillage of the weak and submissive more than two thousand years ago. Your kind is not ready to receive our more advanced technology. You are too savage and too primitive a race to be immersed in the wealth of extra-galactic space travel. Those riches come with time, and I am afraid to add, that won't be for at least five hundred years."

Alana's face dropped in disapproval. "Arbuk, apart from that being the most fascinating story, we must tell you, we've come a long way since then. You are referring to the capitalistic crappy world we left behind almost fifty years ago. Things have changed and drastically. What about our role in this little interstellar family reunion, for example? If it wasn't for us, where would you be now?"

"You are partly right. We were at the point of changing our tactical strategy when you arrived. We had grown tired; it was only a matter of time. Your arrival merely speeded up the process, that's all."

"No, I am not referring to that. I'm speaking about if these Platnios had eaten two billion Peblinus and increased their arsenal of ships? Where do you think they would've come next?" Arbuk bit his tongue.

"Whether you like it or not, Arbuk, we have lent you a big helping hand. Anyway, if that didn't work, I was going to mention the bit about re-establishing the link."

Arbuk gave a smile. "In many ways you are probably correct; you know you are. I was only testing you," said Arbuk, looking downwards. "That is why I am willing to share our secrets with you." The head lifted up again. Arbuk then told Philip that his people were grateful for his intervention. He also touched lightly on the topic of their own imperfections.

Ramaan moved closer. "And these spheres, they're fascinating."

"The four planetary spheres are a unified matrix of six elements forming an alloy with astounding properties. Their attometric structure responds to the person touching it. To help you understand, it works kind of like a receiver/transmitter principal. It is actually very simple. The fifth sphere is the red. They discovered it by accident on Braan a hundred years ago. One of our scientists working with an extremely rare seventh element called nastelonium, only found on Haradan, incorporated it into the matrix.

"Records say that the scientist was thinking of an overdue meeting. Suddenly he appeared in the middle of the meeting floor. Of course, everyone stared at him, thinking he'd gone mad. On rethinking of the laboratory whence he came, the scientist reappeared in the laboratory. That's how it started. Later on, we enhanced this seventh element, sort of tuned it up if you will. Now we can project people, even objects, on an interplanetary scale, as you all saw demonstrated earlier with the general.

"Our home planet in this system is Retolox, and if I am not mistaken, it's your next stop. I've been told to accompany you there as an observer and guide. I think you will find Retolox of great interest. For the first time you will see us in our natural environment. You do know, of course, we have many pleasures."

Alana's ears pricked up, trying to catch any stray words. Arbuk, noticing Alana's suppressed expression, opened a box and showed her a red sphere.

Before departing, Arbuk explained in detail where they had to land. "It's the only continent with a lake in the middle. Once you see it from orbit, head straight for it. I'll contact you once I have you on the sensors. I'll send you detailed landing instructions once you reach orbit. I'll see you in a couple of days."

Retolox was the size of Neptune. From their distance, nine huge landmasses intertwined themselves with spirally oceans. Arbuk had referred to the continent as Babonia for their landing. From their perspective, it looked a bit like a skewed, sliced egg, slightly oval. A big formless lake gutted the middle, the yolk. Alana stationed the *Excelsior* directly overhead in a geo-synchronous orbit.

From the descending pod, Baygorn watched the *Excelsior* melt from view and turned his attention towards Retolox. Arbuk was due to contact them at any time, so they made their way directly towards the lake, so he could see them. The lake increased in size until it became an ocean. The receiver's light flicked on.

"Okay, I got you, I can see you. To the left of the lake there is a long chain of mountains, head for the top. The smallest one, Mount Gibbun, has a large dome just to the left. That's where we are. We call it Arkos. You should be seeing it by now." The communication briefly went dead as they entered the atmosphere.

Breaking through, the receiver erupted with his voice. "The dome protects us from meteorites and undesirables that seek shelter or food. It vaporises anything, so listen carefully. The entrance is near the summit of Mount Gibbun."

Exiting high-altitude cumulus clouds that had engulfed the pod, they had their first view of the city of Arkos. The force shield was a pulsating green dome and extended over the city, with the exception of a small yellow circle close to the mountain peak. Dense vegetation extended almost all the way to the summit of Mount Gibbun.

"When you see the yellow circle, fly to it and wait until it turns blue."

The tiny ring grew until completely filling their front view. Below it, a most fascinating city awaited their arrival. It was a much bigger version of Manhattan, with recreational facilities and positively the most glamorous architecture. There were three rivers. As the yellow rim fluttered bright blue, they lowered, drifting past the rim of the force shield, and entered into Arkos air space. Some of the buildings were hundreds of metres high. Large multi-shaped parks, giving it that confident human touch, had idle futuristic murals, yet they were luxuriously positioned on each corner like centurions.

"Okay, your landing site is directly in front of you. It's the large rectangular building with a red flashing light on top. Can you see it?"

Alana pressed Talk. "Yes, we can."

She lowered the pod to about two hundred metres from the ground. There were vehicles, tiny people and majestically carved structures.

"What engineering!" Philip said ecstatically.

Going lower, crowns of tall trees whisked past. Beyond any doubt, the Bods were advanced enough to venture into the far regions. The team lapped up the entire spectacle and settled their pod onto a landing strip indicated by Arbuk.

Arbuk, still holding a communicator, waited as they climbed out. "Hello again," he sniffed. "I have a little surprise for you."

They left the pod, taking deep breaths of air and feeling the warmth. It smelt like the insides of a greenhouse on a cool spring day. He led them along one side of the landing area to an elongated single-floor glass building with a carved door. The reception hall allowed the sharp reddish-silver light of noon to enter through a clerestory window. It poured onto a floor worked in green-blue and eggshell tiles simulating a bayou, with water plants here and there, and a splash of exotic colour to indicate bird or animal. The outside wall bragged a red flashing sign: Fresh Coffee.

11. Ancient Cultures

Arbuk flicked his fingers to someone behind a counter. Philip and the others stood and looked at each other, totally speechless. Arbuk noticed their numbness and smiled. "Yes, amongst other things, we also have hot chocolate and wine. They were some of the many cultures and customs we left behind on Earth." The man brought five steaming cups of coffee. They could smell it from metres away. They were big cups; different flowery designs adorned the sides. As cup met surface, forgotten memories reached Philip's nose. It had been six long years since he'd had coffee. It hadn't been allowed on the trip. Caffeine was a diuretic and alkaloid. He still remembered Jim's words: "Sorry, Philip, you'll have to live without it." Philip's nostrils widened. There was a brief ten-second silence.

"You mentioned earlier, you have other things." Ramaan lowered his nearly empty cup.

"Well, apart from consumables, we introduced a wide variety of bird and insect life onto Earth about 20,000 years ago. Two of them you commonly know as the wagtail and the sparrow. They originally came from the system of Pollux."

They drank and listened. They were in heaven. Philip thought he'd not heard Arbuk's last words because the bar he was in, wasn't any ordinary bar. It was an alien bar filled with all types of interstellar liquors, wines and paraphernalia. They absorbed their surroundings: odd pictures, bizarre plants in pots, sculptured marble shelves with green lights over each bottle, illuminating its contents.

Alana asked Lexia if she could read what was in the bottles.

"Maybe I can help," offered Arbuk. "It's mostly a collection of liquors we've taken from a wide variety of planets in these systems. Some are local."

Alana pointed at a blue bottle. "That looks almost phallic. What's in there?"

Arbuk picked up on her anxiety following her hand. "It's Flagovac. It comes from the Bellatrix system. It tastes like a strong root whiskey, except it comes from distilled animal remains and wood." Alana looked away.

"Anything non-animal?" Ramaan seemed agitated.

"What about an insect-based vodka?"

Ramaan twisted his face away saying, "That's disgusting."

"What! Reporfin takes twenty years to mature. It comes from beetles."

Alana continued. "Let me rephrase our likes. Do you have anything with good old-fashioned alcohol in it?"

"Alana, drinking around here goes a lot further than just feeling the effect, or having a headache the next morning. Take this, for example. We call it Spician spice rice. It's a really hot aperitif that cleans your stomach. It also possesses an intense aphrodisiacal after-effect."

Going through the glass containers on the shelves, they calculated there must have been more than eight hundred different bottles of every conceivable shape, colour and size.

Arbuk caught their attention. "You know, we return to Earth every now and then. We don't attract attention, no one suspects us. We can dress and think like you. Hell, we can even talk like you," he said in an American accent.

"It's good to keep an eye on things every now and then to see how you are progressing and coming along; but I must say, I still find humans volatile. Sometimes your kind sees our spaceships. I cannot comprehend why your officials prefer to keep everything hushed and out of the public eye. Instead, they put it in a specialized gazette published under government auspices, something you call Project Blue Book, or the Advanced Aviation Threat Identification Program. Many of your countries have their own blue book. I just don't see the logic of keeping us tucked away like that."

Their mouths opened. "Arbuk," said Philip, "for decades, we were told that the UFO phenomenon was a hoax. We were told that our governments had no official interest in the study of aliens or UFOs. Statements to the contrary, official-sounding people cautioned, were probably the musings of crackpots in tinfoil hats.

The first recorded sightings go back to the late eighteenth century. In the late twentieth century, Major Keyhoe said, 'For the past 175 years, before the founding of the United States, planet Earth has been under systematic close-range examination by observers from another planet.' Are you saying that the frequent UFO sightings we see in many parts of our world are the Bods?"

"Yes, often they are us, but from time to time the Gorinos fly through Earth space as well. This will obviously explain the diversity of what you call UFOs. Ours are rounded or triangular, whereas the Gorinos' interstellar spacecraft are more cigar-shaped. We were never the best of friends. That was another reason why we had to leave in a hurry. We tolerated one another without harm coming to each other. Anyway, I think that is all behind us now. The Gorinos won't hurt anyone, they're just curious about the up-and-coming human technology. They are also very protective. What's theirs is theirs, and they will fight to the death for it."

"I'm sure there is something we can still teach you." Alana's look drilled into Arbuk.

"I am sure there is," he said, returning a smile. "Anyway, welcome to Arkos. You'll need this to travel around." He gave them each a map of the city in the form of a palm-sized computer and a neat wad of Arkosian Erons.

"If you need more, just let me know. I've provided you with sleeping quarters on the twentieth floor in the Charring Manor Hotel. It's not that bad; I think you'll like it. One more thing: Your vehicle won't be allowed in here because it gives off too many pollutants. You can drive my car during your stay."

The red car he referred to came equipped with a visual windscreen sensor system and communication equipment to converse to and from the central headquarters of Arkos. It looked like a Lexus.

Arkos was one of nine identical domed cities that dotted the surface of Retolox. Each one was home to about 300 million Bods.

"The nine cities are connected by tunnels and an underground train service. We have a commercial freighter service, too." Arbuk told them it had been this way for three hundred years.

"The force shield has never failed us during this time. More than nine hundred meteorites have been vaporised, any one of them capable of destroying part of the city. If you look outside, you'll see the landscape is moderately pitted."

"Haven't you ever lived outside the dome? Don't you find it a bit crowded in here?" asked Lexia.

"Not really. Centuries ago we lived in buildings and natural caves; there are a lot of them out there. That was before the barrier was too dangerous. There are more than a million hill-dwellers still. Cretins are worse than the meteors! We've lost so many people over the past fifty years that no one wants to go out there anymore." Arbuk banged a heel on the wall.

"They still try and attack us from time to time. A month ago, they blew up one of the underground train tunnels. They keep on trying, they keep on dying. Luckily, they can't penetrate the boundaries of the dome. If they did, I'd hate to think. Arkos is free of violence and crime. It is historical talk. Only business and technology rule within these walls."

Arbuk began to smile again. "The vehicle will take you straight to the hotel. I'll see you later."

The Bods were in every way like them. The way they dressed, the way they walked, the manner in which they held hands walking down the street. They even had a sense of humour. It gave them the impression of an Earth in a not-too-distant future, a planet in symbiosis. Was this harmony, or was it this way because they didn't know otherwise? A couple of the pyramid-shaped buildings in the distance plainly revealed their ancestral connection.

Their Charring Manor Hotel was built near to Arkos headquarters, so they didn't have to travel too far. Probably close by for important guests. Inquisitively, they looked around. In comparison to other constructions, the hotel with its fifty floors appeared small. It was neatly tucked between other immense buildings of similar design. Jet craft swooped overhead to and from somewhere. *They could be taxis*, Philip thought. On the outside of the hotel, a blinking, intense, red sign dominated available air space, "Rooms for Rent." On the ground level of another building not far away, they noticed an L-shaped chimney bending upwards, the extremity alive with smoke residues excreted from the life within. Rubbish bins and carton boxes lined an alley.

Baygorn stopped dead. "If you woke up and saw that, what would jump into mind except for downtown New York?" He looked at the others. "You remember throwing stones at streetlights to darken the alleys so no one can see you, don't you? My God. You want proof? Look at that, it's right there!"

The lobby receptionist with a toothy smile came to greet them at the brilliantly lit desk area.

"Ah, welcome, my friends," he said with a slight lisp. "Arbuk has instructed us to give you precisely what you require. Here are your keys. You're in room 2041." Philip looked down at the register at the other names of guests in the hotel. Most were written in undecipherable Bod.

"Excuse me, what do you use to write with here?"

"We use laser inscribers, they are very practical and cheap. Here, take five of them. Each one has the name of the hotel engraved on the side."

Lexia tapped Philip on the shoulder. "There's a tavern down here. Maybe they have beer or whiskey." Her hand excitedly pointed towards a lit area down a couple of steps. "After we unpack our stuff, let's come down and grab a swig of something."

Baygorn overheard. "With what, insect-flavoured beer, cactus whiskey? Who fancies a swig of scorpion-soda? That should put hairs on that chest of yours, Lexia."

"Ha-ha, very funny, Baygorn. A few days of relaxing down here will do us the world of good, so if you don't mind."

As they entered the twentieth floor and made their way towards number 41, making a faint click, the door automatically opened as they neared. On the inside, there were five framed pictures placed at eye height on the left. The right of each different nature scene culminated in another coloured door. A well-defined yellow light shone over each door, illuminating a number. On the inside of each identical room, apart from being dim, they had a nice blend of greens and reds that decorated the walls, complementing two antique-looking wall lamps hanging above the beds. The double bed was neatly positioned in the middle of the wall with a wardrobe on each side. They selected their respective rooms and unpacked their stuff. Each bedroom came with its separate bathroom, of course, with someone's good taste in pictures hanging to the right.

Half an hour later, they returned downstairs to the lobby area where Arbuk was patiently waiting for them.

"I trust you've settled down all right. Philip, something very delicate has come up. I'm afraid I'm going to need your help."

12. Assassination

"In Arkos, we haven't had a case of murder for more than a hundred years. Here, crime does not exist. Alana told me that it might be possible that you can still teach us something. Well, I am afraid that time has arrived. I need your help."

"What's happened?" Philip asked.

"The Arkosian general you met on Ganus, he's been assassinated! Couldn't have come at a worse time," replied Arbuk. "Election time is around the corner. I need your help to find the assassin."

"Don't you have your own policing services?"

"Of course we do; at the moment they are busy on other chores. This is the procreation time of year and everyone's out of action. Our police prefer chasing after other more charming attributes. Truth is, these emergencies don't exist, haven't existed for so long that no one knows what to do anymore."

"Well, why not?" They had nothing better to do. Baygorn was the expert in forensics, so Philip gave him the responsibility of the investigation.

Lying out on the metallic table in the Bod depository was the mutilated body of General Flambers.

Baygorn reached over. "Yeah, it's him, all right. The last time we saw him alive he had just signed an agreement with the Peblinus head member." The general had been shot. Philip didn't want to guess how many times from the neck down to the stomach area.

"He didn't stand a chance," said Alana, looking at the mangled mess.

"Where did it happen?" added Philip.

"In his private living quarters on Eleventh Avenue; apparently he was going to bed. Ten bodyguards were downstairs when it happened. They ran in after hearing the shots and found him dead on the floor next to the bed. Parts of him scattered all over the room. Nothing was missing; nothing else had been disturbed, only what you see on this metal table."

"Might've been a Peblinus activist," broke in Baygorn, looking into the rib cage of the dead body.

"Quite possible," said Arbuk. "They are normally arrested on sight if they approach the city. By our knowledge, there are none within the walls of Arkos. Of course, I am not saying there are no Peblinus; they live here passively. They have lived that way with us now for generations."

Lexia stepped next to Baygorn. "Whoever he was, he seemed pretty pissed at the general."

"What about those red spheres? Could someone have used one to get into the general's quarters and then disappear? Are they all accounted for?"

"It's possible, not out of the city though. You need special authorisation; otherwise, the force field prevents it. Nothing penetrates the force field."

"Good to hear. So he's still here, then."

"Precisely," said Arbuk with a concerned look.

"The next commercial freighter arrives in twelve hours, and I cannot stop him if he decides to leave the city boundaries, which he'll probably do."

"Do you know what firearm was used?"

"From the calibre and marks on the bullets we took out of the walls, it could only have been a holocaust multi-shooter: forty rounds in two seconds. It also explains why the guards had no time to reach him, poor man. There was plenty of gunfire, but unfortunately no witnesses. No one saw a thing. No vehicles, and our external cameras didn't reveal anything either. Only the tremendous noise of the gun going off. His bedroom where this happened is the only area without cameras. He didn't allow them in his abode. The killer must've known this. Well thought-out, you'll see in a moment," said Arbuk, leading the way to the waiting transport.

Their vehicle came to a halt outside the enigmatic, splendidly lit building on Eleventh Avenue. At first glance, the electrified fence that separated them from the general's house seemed impenetrable. People were scuffling everywhere, while security guards searched in, around and everywhere on the over-elegant grounds surrounding the property for clues.

"Some protection it served in the end," said Baygorn.

"Look at this place. It makes Fort Knox look like a matchbox toy! This guy really knew what he was doing."

Arbuk flicked his fingers and the security fizzled off. Then he beckoned the guards to go inside, where they waited for him in formation along the hallway. Each of them was respectfully dressed in their official apparel.

One at a time, Baygorn asked them questions. Some easy, some hard, but they all had a perfect alibi. Each one's story substantiated and corroborated the next man's tale, all except one. An hour later, Philip only had one doubt. Gregori Dadju was a strong, fearful man and had served the general well over the past six years.

Arbuk looked at his record. "He has predecessors of Peblinus origin. His mother, a simple Bod worker, met a Peblinus trade warrior forty years ago while they were still allowed into the city. She died ten years ago. His father's death remains a mystery to this day. Needless to say, they fell in love."

"And Gregori appeared a short while later. For this, you believe he might be guilty," said Alana, breaking in. "There must be dozens of Gregoris lurking in the city. We can't hold him responsible based on those accusations."

"True, but none of them were as close to the general like Gregori was. He was his second officer. He knew the security system well, and he must have known about the cameras being absent in his bedroom."

Baygorn spoke, "That still doesn't mean anything. Gregori served the general just like the rest of them. I would suppose all his employees are heavily screened before they begin their service. Maybe they missed something?"

"I doubt it," said Arbuk. "The tests are comprehensive."

"That's it then. You have your proof, and it's purely circumstantial evidence."

There existed within Arkos submissive movements of Peblinus that lived in their respective areas, so Arbuk paid one of them a visit. With the aid of their portable computers, they learned that the most densely Peblinus-populated area appeared in Club Avenue.

"Look at this. Guess they like to stick together, same as on Earth," Philip said, as more than six thousand individual names ran up the monitor screen, revealing their Peblinus nationality. Club Avenue's 10,000 neat matchbox homes were serene and silent. Everyday vehicles parked in the front of each soundless house accentuated the nocturnal-bird life. There was nothing, not a shout or murmur; not even a stray dog. It seemed unnatural. Ramaan checked for any Peblinus that might have flights booked on the next freighter. The list was short; only one man.

"So, you want to go to Rigel, do you? Well, it's not Gregori, but he might know something. According to this, he's staying at number 812. He came to Arkos a month ago." Armed only with a bare thread of information, they directed themselves towards the house.

"Says here he has a strong influence within the Peblinus community as a big-shot business kook. You never know; he could've committed the act for money." The only thing they were sure of was, if he didn't do it, he might know who did.

They stormed into the tiny home. Alana went first. Her infrared tracker told her there was someone sitting directly ahead. He was immobile. They ran into the roomy dining room, and there sitting on a chair was a man, or rather what was left of him. The upper half of his skull was lying on the other side of the room beneath a chair with his brains splattered all over the wall. Conveniently placed next to him was a letter. Baygorn grabbed it. It read:

"I am sorry for the trouble I have caused. It was not my intention to kill the general. He forced me to do it; he was reaching for a gun himself and would have certainly killed me. I had no alternative, but to save myself. I merely went to see him and ask if he could change the pact he had made for the Peblinus a few days ago on Ganus. The signing of the space treaty was wrong; the Bods are amassing the Peblinus on Ganus to die. I was enraged and unable to contain my fury.

"Once I had pulled the trigger, it was too late. Wounding the general was impossible, as the gun I used was a holocaust forty shooter. You will find it in the dresser. I gained access to his apartment with a red sphere I borrowed from a friend."

Then it was signed: Donial Fribers.

"What do you think, Baygorn?" Philip asked as he placed the letter down by his side. Clueless and silent, he scratched his head and breathed in deeply.

"It's too straightforward," he said with a snap. "Can't be. We found him too easily. This Donial chap certainly had motive. or so he says in his letter, but I don't think he was capable of doing the actual murder. He didn't have a killer's face."

Baygorn turned and faced the other direction. "He probably thought he did and blamed himself, poor bugger. Someone else is implicated in this, and big time!" Baygorn did another spin.

"Lexia, check the handwriting on this letter and reference it against anything you can find: a family member, a friend. You'll probably find that it's not his writing at all. Philip, find out where he worked and if he knew Gregori." Lexia ferreted around and came over with some papers.

"What do you make of this?" She handed Baygorn an un-posted letter.

"It's to his brother." The writing was different. What they were looking at was the handwriting of the authentic assassin; it could only be. Their investigations led them nowhere, as the sample from Gregori didn't match, either. There was absolutely no connection whatsoever between Gregori and Donial. As far as Baygorn could tell, they had never met. Unfortunately, Gregori had been involved thanks to his genetic background, nothing more. Arbuk said he would send him an official letter of apology later during the week.

Donial Fribers had worked as a sheet steel worker in the Bloch Foundry on Surplus Hill, and there was no tie whatsoever between him and the general. Most importantly of all, why would he supposedly do it and later commit suicide? This whole thing was starting to get messy.

"He could've been framed," suggested Ramaan. They scraped together whatever information they could and decided to pay Bloch Foundry a visit the next morning.

Bloch Foundry had been constructed on the edge of the city close to the dome. Its enormous Himalayan shape, with random ups and downs, took up one entire side of Arkos. A seemingly infinite five-metre security fence surrounded Bloch Foundry, obscuring the lower half from view. The visible part boasted twenty chimneys, six high ovens and a couple of ventilation chimneys. It was obviously a good job for those who knew how, or the unfortunate Donial, who knew too much.

Finding the front entrance, they parked the vehicle and got out. A strong pungent sulphur smell loomed in the air, leaving a tinge of bad eggs. The closed front gate, complete with a dirty guardhouse, showed no signs of life.

The foundry seemed as dead as the crispy ivy-like creeper plants still clinging to the walls. Curiously turning their heads, they saw that not only the wall, but both sides of the road was a floral cemetery. Random pointing crackly, blackened fingers whistled as long-ago suffocated branches shook in the wind like phantoms. A man strolling on the interior noticed their vehicle close to the gate and walked towards them.

Ramaan greeted him. "Excuse me, good morning. Can we speak to someone in charge, please?"

The security guard seemed to be in shock at the sight before him. Without a word, he turned, half-waddled away, and then dashed off like a bullet down a long walkway towards an office. Seconds later, the security guard reappeared in the shadow of a well-dressed office administrator. Nearing the fence, Philip noticed the worried looks on their faces.

"Can I help you?" asked the supervisor.

Arbuk handed him a photograph of Donial. "Do you know this man? I believe he worked for you. We want to look at his service record. We are investigating his death. It seems he blew his head off for no reason at all."

The supervisor told the guard to open the gate and then pointed Arbuk to the third door of a storage building. As Philip followed the hand, the supervisor was already speaking over his communicator. It was not a large office, but it was quite spy-proof and undetectably so.

An anorexic woman named Henetta sat at a desk waiting for Arbuk and the others to arrive. Her proud finger pointed at the gold lettering on her scratched black name tag, and she smiled. "Mr Blunt told me that you are looking for information concerning one of our employees."

Arbuk moved forward. "Yes, his name is, or was, Donial Fribers. We were wondering if you could tell us something useful about the chap."

Henetta got out of her high-backed chair and languidly walked towards a filing cabinet. "Hmm. Friar, Fribbs, ah, here we are, Fribers." With a bony hand, she handed over a yellow file to Arbuk.

Arbuk went through its contents with attention. Medical records, attendance reports; it was all there. Even his temperamental makeup had been subjected to great scrutiny. Bloch Foundry hired private detectives to check on all its employees, as they only admitted clean employees, and Fribers, of course, was no exception. The personal section contained two pages of unmentionable information that probably not even Donial himself knew about. Apart from showing off at the pool table where he won quite a bit of extra cash, Donial spent a lot of his free time drinking and flirting.

Arbuk gave the woman a receipt for the file, and the six of them returned to the vehicle.

"Well, he was medically sound," said Baygorn, "only two days missed in his three years of service. Not bad, seems normal to me. It says here on Friday evenings he went to Surrey's Bar."

They headed to the bar. According to Arbuk, Surrey's was just another typical down-the-road pub with well-sat-on chairs. The long bar area was filled to overflow levels. There were the occasional dents and scratches on the tables, but the abnormal quantity of exotic brands behind the counter did manage to capture Philip's eye. It was unlike any bar he had ever seen.

This came neatly bound together with a cheap waitress. "Allo, what'll it be, then?"

"Nothing today, thank you," said Arbuk, waving her away. People were whispering at other tables. They were staring at Philip and the others.

"Maybe it's our uniforms," said Alana, looking towards a couple.

As they proceeded with the investigation and flipped through papers and evidence, Baygorn discovered that the bar owner, a certain Ralph somebody, was Peblinus and had purchased the place only a month before.

"Hey, look. Before this place, he had been head guard for our defunct general. It seems he was fired for impudence three months earlier; could've been a grudge."

Arbuk was a fully qualified police officer. Later he told them that he had served five years of active service here before acquiring transfer to zone captain.

"Do you know they don't even include homicide in the exams anymore? I had to study these things after-hours and out of curiosity. Our police research rape, counterfeiting and robberies. That is as high up the ladder they go."

"So why aren't you off procreating like the others?" asked Alana.

"Because I'm not a police officer anymore," he said, then smiled. "Zone captains have stricter responsibilities. We are required to perform more inhibited tasks."

Arbuk pointed at a man sitting at a table, "There he is."

Ralph was a man of the people, by self-acclamation. His remaining back-fringe of grey hair drooped limply to his shoulders, blending in with his beard. His shirt needed laundering, and judging by what they saw, he probably spoke with a snuffle. Arbuk, using his authority, walked over and called him to the table. He looked reluctant at first, but when Arbuk mentioned Erons, his stride increased and he released a smile.

"Ralph, I would like you to meet some friends of mine. They have come from afar just to have some drinks at your bar, but we do have some questions to ask of you."

Alana wanted to get straight to the point, but Philip gestured his hand and she quieted.

"There is no ostentation here," Baygorn said, "no false show." Ralph seemed inordinately pleased with what Baygorn had said. "We do—that's all of us, know that you know of, or rather have met, a very important gentleman in the last couple of hours."

Ralph's sparse grey beard twitched to the grimaces of his face on hearing Baygorn's words. But before he could say anything, Philip butted into the conversation.

"You know, I consider truth to be one of the strongest bonds between people; no matter the consequences. I understand you enjoy the same republican blessings we do where we come from; I am strongly in favour of continued peace and friendship between our generals."

Ralph began to tremble.

Lexia unmistakably noticed the look of fear written all over his face.

Philip continued. "I don't think there is anyone in the Periphery who has so near to his heart the ideal of peace, as I have. I can truthfully say that, since I succeeded my illustrious father to the leadership of the state where I come from, the reign of peace has never been broken. Perhaps I shouldn't say it," he coughed gently, "but I have been told that my people, my fellow citizens rather, know me as Flambers, the All-Knowing."

On hearing the name Flambers, Ralph broke down and cried. "How did you know?"

Ramaan broke in. "The other man who was with you blew his head off. We just followed the trail he left behind." Arbuk called somebody on his communicator, and a few minutes later, two heavily clad officers strolled into the bar and took Ralph away. As Ralph disappeared through the doorway, Arbuk congratulated Baygorn and Philip on their subtle way of calling his bluff. An hour later, Arbuk received the confession through his communicator.

The two of them had met one night as the unsuspecting Donial came into the bar for a drink and looking for a bit of action. The two of them started talking, and Donial duly found it with the new owner. Turns out the bartender had placed blanks into Donial's firearm, while he himself stood two metres away and pulled the trigger. Donial thought it had been a team effort and that his gun had killed the general. The bartender put the blame on Donial, leaving no trace of his presence. In the beginning, the pub owner had promised him the world for his participation; but instead, it led an innocent man to his death.

On their way back to the hotel, Arbuk invited them to a succulent dinner. It was his way of thanking them. "I'll pick you up at seven, be ready."

In the hotel reception, after a hot bath and some refreshments, a flashing sign caught Philip's attention. "It makes cents not to spend your erons. Arkos seemed almost too human. The majority of the inhabitants spoke a reasonable level of English; well, more like an old Frenchman with high school knowledge of English suddenly appearing here on the street. Lexia was making clear advancements with the Lep language and had tried explaining its vocabulary and verb structure whenever Philip had the time.

Leading out of the reception area, the bar Lexia previously noticed had a working jukebox playing soft squeaky music. A painting called *Territory One* decorated a false door against the wall, while two elegant Victorian-style functioning gas lamps fixed just above the painting offered an eerie sublime light and enhanced its beautiful scheme of colours.

At seven, Arbuk came in to excuse himself. Head office had contacted him, requesting the official death report on their desk by morning.

"I am so sorry, please forgive me," he said. "It's urgent. If I don't write it now, I'll have problems. I'll have to work on it the whole night! Tomorrow, as soon as I've dropped it off at the office, I'll come pick you up."

Arbuk ran out the front door, giving no one time to say a word. Philip thought it was a relief, and decided to get an early night for a change. Tomorrow they were going to visit one of the manufacturing plants.

Like the Peblinus, the Bods used tellurium for their semi-conductive manufacturing needs, but here they mixed it with germanium, silicon, corilium, and a variety of other elements to obtain perfect conducting results.

Ramaan was the first one to get up as the tiny bell on his wristwatch woke him from a deep sleep. For a few moments he was disoriented, unable to remember where he was. He sat up on his bed and rubbed his eyes. The thirty-one-hour-day of

Retolox was the closest thing they had encountered that resembled normality since their arrival here in the system. It drove their watches mad. Surviving on these planets was eternal jet lag. They endured the time differences most of the time on these infernal government-rationed stay-awake tabs. Terron headquarters called them Perma-Eye. The worst part was they tasted of lemon, and Ramaan hated lemon.

They ate breakfast in the lobby at six, a red-bean-and-sausage something. On one wall of the dining room, a wide variety of glass-encased poems from twentieth-century poets jutted out like inverted portholes. Philip could make out DH Lawrence and Allen Ginsberg. *What a lovely way to memorialise them,* he thought, *so elegant and so romantic.*

Their punctual red-eyed guide-cum-chauffeur strolled in through the front entrance moments later. "Good morning, ready to go? There's a long day waiting for us."

Out in the morning briskness and way in the distance, Ramaan caught sight of a long, white, unmarked veil on the horizon unnoticed by him the night before. It only became visible from the parking area in the light of the morning.

Arbuk noticed Ramaan's captivation. "That's the radiation shield. It separates the tellurium plant from the city, working as a radiation sponge absorbing any unwanted rads. It is made of the same plastic material you found on the outer planets. It is five hundred metres high and almost three kilometres long. The majority of the excess radiation is absorbed by the force field above it."

The roads were curvy and lined with trees resembling cypress. A well-kept, beautifully nurtured deep-green bush hugged the base of each tree placed about ten metres apart. They reminded Ramaan a bit of Hollywood Boulevard. The condition of the road was excellent all the way to the entrance. Philip and Ramaan were excited about seeing a working tellurium plant for the first time from the inside.

The tellurium plant's two huge funnels reached up far into the morning sky. White, waving fingers billowed from their extremes, spewing unwanted hot air and residues from below, finally dissipating on the force field.

"What process do you use for the extraction?" asked Ramaan.

"Volcanic. Although there's no activity close by, we bored directly into a fissure in the crust of the planet. It is the first time we've done this. You see, our mounting need for tellurium sometimes involves risk; and this time, and I will admit it, was dangerous.

"The mine where I'm taking you has two levels. The first level is the access tunnel. It goes down twenty kilometres all the way to a city. It is from this city where we tap directly into the lower lithosphere. Wow, the problems we had. No one had any idea that the temperatures of Retolox could reach such high levels." Arbuk's demonstrating hands flew about in all directions.

"The access tunnel in some sections reaches 200 degrees. Cooling is our main concern. The temperature and liquidity of the magma killed many of our first engineers as well. No one knew what they were up against until it was too late. They thought it would be the same temperature like on other planets. Of the few whom have seen it, they say the magma leaves the rifts and vertical fumaroles a whitish-blue."

Philip told Arbuk about the close encounter on Phot with a metallic life form that burrows down into the magma and surfaces coated with tellurium.

13. Inner Mine

"The Blagorian. They were so named after their discoverer, Richard Blagorian, a hundred years ago. The idiot was later eaten by one when he tried communicating with them. They can be real pests sometimes. They exist on all these planets in the system. It is a forgotten process by us here on Retolox. We haven't used the Blagorian method for decades. I presume you came across some in our underground bunkers then?"

"Yes, we have met," replied Alana bitterly.

"Then you know what they are capable of. The method we use is safer. We found the Blagorian too temperamental. They occasionally turned on us without reason. Many years ago, we dissected one. They were a mystery, a real enigma. We wanted to find out what made it tick, to discover the secret of how and why it burrowed, and how the tellurium became attached to its body. Two years later, we made a breakthrough.

"Thanks to our investigation and research, we now use the same method and manner that the Blagorian uses. We have successfully imitated them. It is like having the Blagorian there to do the work for us, but at the same time, he has taken the day off. We consequently call our tellurium separator the Hafnium Resonator. Down in the secondary levels our Hafnium Resonator goes to work and separates the tellurium from the other unwanted molten elements."

Ramaan tapped Philip on the shoulder and pointed towards the nearing veil.

Lexia looked out the window. They all did. The veil they'd seen earlier from the hotel had broadened and now filled the windscreen on all sides. According to Arbuk, their objective was on the other side of the large wall through a single entrance-exit point ten metres square, allowing access to only one vehicle at a time. The road led towards the tiny squared aperture in amongst the infinite white backdrop. Philip watched it grow. It grew until an amber yellow light much like a traffic light stopped them. A sign on the outside in a variety of languages told them to close the windows.

When the yellow light turned green, an entrance-sized thick glass door controlled by hydraulic arms opened and revealed the interior. The inside was automatic and washed the car in foam as they came to a standstill. The water stopped, and Arbuk drove them to the other waiting glass door that immediately opened as they neared. The process was painfully slow. The hissing hydraulics finally allowed them to continue with their journey. A rough-looking filing cabinet-sized security guard ogled the vehicle as they drove past. Alana waved at him, but his gaze continued eating through Philip. *God, am I his type?* he thought. Was that a smile he saw? Philip quickly turned and looked forward just in time to see a bridge. They passed under the walkway, noticing people scuttling everywhere in between neatly parked vehicles. Here, there was order.

Arbuk interrupted Philip's thoughts. "That is our fire department. They can extinguish any inferno, or so they claim. Doesn't matter if it's chemical, fuel, or volcanic, it's all the same to them."

Just outside the fire station entrance, Philip saw a parked, jet-propelled fire engine. A sign decorated both doors: "If you light the flame, putting out is our game" was written in big yellow, hand-painted letters. Two fire engines were ready for immediate deployment, complete with staff standing close by, wearing red or green outfits.

"The red ones are the firefighters; well trained too," added Arbuk. "The green are their assistants. Look, there's the entrance door." The door Arbuk referred to was between two huge rocks, a sliding door that split down the middle, probably measuring twenty metres. A multitude of vehicles entered and exited the work area through the two giant doors. Bods were scurrying everywhere.

"That is where the shaft begins," said Arbuk. "At any time there are 10,000 workers down there. We have on-site geologists and doctors that practically live down there. At the base of the shaft, in the extraction site and underground city, there are another six thousand workers, along with chemists and a scientific department. The lower-level teams only come up for air once every six months." To the extreme left and right of the entrance, an independent round orifice worked without interrupting the flow of the shaft. Arbuk explained it was an express train service, to and from the base.

"If need be, we could evacuate the workers to the top in two hours. They have been prepared and well trained. Unfortunately, the radiation workers on the lower levels are the ones in real danger. They are constantly exposed to excessive levels of alpha and beta radiations and can, at best, perform two years down there. Their families are handsomely rewarded and compensated, but every year we lose many good workers."

"Don't you have machines to do the work for you?" asked Baygorn with a concerned look.

"Yes, but they don't want to put their lives in the hands of a machine. Truth is, we had some problems with machines a few years back. One of them malfunctioned and several hundred workers were killed. Since then, only Bods work down there. If a machine fails, from whom do we claim? That is what they say. In a way, they're right."

The plant was a fully contained, self-supporting city completely isolated from Arkos with the exception of the entrance where they had driven in earlier. A chemist, a dentist, even a public relations office, two pubs, a hospital and a restaurant, it was all there. "On this side of the veil, the workers don't pay for anything. Everything is at their disposal, whenever they want. Even medication and treatment are free."

Arbuk led them towards a museum dedicated to those who had died in the mine. Philip was in awe at the number of plaques. Motes of dust drifted lazily in a bright shaft of sunlight that pierced one of the mullioned windows. The thin, red second hand of the wall clock swept soundlessly around the dial. Towards the back of the museum, a dimly illuminated set-aside section was dedicated to their ancient history.

"When we excavated the mine, we found these skeletons almost five kilometres down. An ancient civilisation lived here long before us. They are called the Dontrian. It means Masters of the Universe in the Spician language. They were a strange society of people who dwelled here tens of thousands of years before us. We know very little about them and often get bone samples to study from Traxon, one of our other mining colonies nearer to Mintaka."

Their vehicle waited for them just outside the shaft entrance. People were rushing out through the side door seals from the train exit into the morning shadows. Philip felt a breeze against his cheeks as they zipped past. The vehicle came with extra padding to protect them against whatever classes of radiation they were likely to encounter. Thick laminium windows offered a grey oblique view, hardly worth the effort. The doors also were much heavier than normal and made a profound clang on closing.

There was a weighty, subsonic racket as Arbuk pressed one of three buttons on the vehicle dashboard console. The ground rumbled, shook and, like two gigantic hands, the plastic doors slowly slid apart, revealing the inclined mine shaft. Downwards was a mind-boggling pinprick, an artist's depiction of an infinite hell. Steam gushed outwards. Five or six Bods came with it. Arbuk started the vehicle and drove on through the entrance. Bods were everywhere in constant movement. They drove about a hundred metres inside and stopped on a red line.

Arbuk turned and faced Philip. "Welcome to the police search barrier." Seconds later, a laser scanner fizzled on and ran up and down, invisibly dissecting the vehicle. It hummed faintly before dissipating. The moment it switched off, the doors started closing behind them. Philip felt sealed on the insides of this mind-boggling excavation. A sudden rush of anxiety struck him.

Arbuk said the descent to the second door would take half an hour. They looked through their small round porthole windows, but Arbuk was driving too fast for them to see anything of interest, so they steered their attention to the front. The shaft descended at a twenty-degree incline. From the driver's aspect, workers were harmoniously busy in all directions, mounting, dismounting, packing and unpacking. Many more vehicles of similar design to their own were parked here and there. Boxes were everywhere. The ceiling strip lights the Bods used in the mine were identical to the ones they had seen on Braan in the hangar. Ten minutes later, they pulled up in front of another two doors.

"Welcome to inner protection," said Arbuk, slowing down. "There's another at the base of the shaft called base protection. These doors close on any minimal alarm and can only be opened from surface control or from this control panel here." Arbuk pressed the second green button on his console, and the vehicle continued to move on. Humming ventilators were sucking out unwanted heat towards the surface.

"The heat generated here is relayed to the surface; we use it to power these ventilators." As he spoke, the vehicle's dashboard air conditioner automatically lit up and clicked on. The console thermometer read 40 degrees. From that point onwards, there wasn't much to see. It became monotonous; even the lighting felt like it had grown dimmer. The tunnel seemed endless. It accentuated their apprehension. Philip felt a bit claustrophobic and then a ping in his left ear became a pain. Seemingly unnoticed, he winced.

Arbuk steered his head with regretful eyes. "Not long now, almost there." Finally, as the protection doors appeared through the smoky murk, Arbuk pressed the third green button on his console, and the doors began to lethargically separate. A Bod worker squeezed through the gap towards the vehicle. Three more ran towards the already-filling surface train. A waft of ferrous chlorite drifted through the vent. Baygorn commented on its sharp odour.

"Get back, go back to the surface!" The worker was terror-stricken. His trousers steaming, reams of sweat dripped from his brow.

Arbuk braked, opened the door, and asked him what had happened.

"One of the ermithium trucks is going to catch fire. We'll be fried down here if it explodes!" The worker ran towards the surface train while another pushed a button. The train immediately shot off like a bullet. Philip got out the vehicle and immediately felt the incredible rise in temperature. *It must be 50 degrees down here,* he thought. *How can anyone work in this heat?* Adjusting himself and rolling up his sleeves, Philip ran past fleeing workers and entered the open cavern. The cause of the commotion was a small rivulet of extremely liquefied lava. It had broken through from an artificial fumarole placed there to relieve the digging site of any build-ups of pressure and gas. The safety valve had failed.

The rivulet ate into the soil, leisurely advancing towards a stationary truck loaded with its valuable cargo. The sound it made was almost deafening.

The fire chief's voice broke over Arbuk's communicator. "This is Fire Chief Short, what's going on down there?"

Philip took the communicator from Arbuk's hands. Down here in the hell of Retolox were geologists, medical teams, electricians, plumbers, and even a dentist. He didn't see a single firefighter anywhere.

"A small stream of lava is advancing towards one of the ermithium trucks."

The chief cursed and Philip imagined spit hurtling out the speaker.

"Use the green extinguishers. They're mounted on the far wall!" he shouted.

The green extinguishers were on the other side of the advancing rivulet, and the heat went beyond tremendous. Multitudes of workers were scrabbling for the exit. Some of them bumped into Ramaan and Baygorn, almost knocking them down. They were even fighting amongst themselves, contending for their place on the express train. It zoomed off and more Bods waited for the next. A couple of workers were trapped on the other side of the rivulet and unable to move. They were on their knees, filled with exhaustion.

Through the piercingly white glare, one of them looked at Philip with urgent hope. Ramaan shouted and pointed towards a green bottle that hung next to them and then at his own feet. The noise was deafening as the rivulet lethargically devoured the surface. Over the brightness and racket of hissing crackle, the terrified Bod unhinged the extinguisher and threw it over the rivulet, making a thump as it landed close to Philip's feet. Quickly he picked it up.

"Careful, Philip, that stuff'll fry you in a second!"

Arbuk's comforting words came at the right time. Heat hit him like needles, thousands of them, and then his clothes began to steam. He was over two metres away from the heat source.

Using the long nozzle extinguisher, Philip pointed it directly at the lava stream and pulled the trigger. A harsh, yellow steam like smoky mustard hissed out. The flow stopped dead a mere six metres from the ermithium truck.

"Good job!" shouted Arbuk above the noise. "Now you can cool it any way you want."

Finding outlets of fresh water, Baygorn and Ramaan opened them. The cavern filled with steam as the water flowed on the floor and reached the molten river. The rivulet lost its whitish texture and cooled to a reddish-yellow. The danger was over. Two brave workers passed Philip by with a smile.

Arbuk walked to Philip. "You're quite the brave one. No one would have done what you just did. Thanks for your invaluable help!"

A clean-up crew arrived to finish dousing the danger. Behind them, a big man arrived dressed in a heavy-duty firefighter's outfit. "Where is he?" he hollered.

Arbuk's hand swung in Philip's direction. "It's the fire chief," whispered Arbuk. "Careful, he's a shrew."

The robust man proudly walked over and faced Philip.

"Apparently five workers were killed when the rivulet burst out and escaped. It must have splattered a bubble or something, a build-up of pressure, maybe, but it could have been worse, much worse."

Lucid eyes drilled Philip's conscience for a respectable answer. Philip's fury gave him the reaction he was seeking. "There was only one extinguisher. Not only should there have been more, they should've been situated all over the place. Trained firefighters should be down here alongside workers, not up on the surface twenty kilometres away!"

The chief gave a shrug and lowered his posture. "We've never had problems down here. Because of today's episode, things are going to change. Thanks for your courage and honesty." The fire chief broke eye contact, gave a grunt and toddled off.

Arbuk adjusted the air intensity and sighed with relief. "Don't worry about him, he'll sort it out. Hey, while we're down here I'd like to show you where the tellurium comes from."

"What, another fumarole?"

Arbuk brushed aside Ramaan's remark, following him back into the mine shaft towards a small roughly made opening in the wall. Arbuk went ahead. "We finished it six months ago. During that time, it has produced ten times more tellurium than we expected."

Lights came from within a long cavern beginning as a man-sized chiselled hole in the wall. Alana peeked in. On the other side, it went beyond her imagination. It was well lit with some humming, throbbing ventilators maintaining the cavern at a steady 35 degrees. The entire area, bathed in a silver-white luminescence from hundreds of suspended lights, revealed its immensity. Arbuk said that in some areas the roof reached two hundred metres high. It was a world within a world. Here and there, an active fumarole breathed superheated yellow smoke. Some sulphurous columns almost touched the roof.

"Found anything else of interest apart from tellurium; anything unusual?" put in Philip.

"A month ago, not far from here, we unearthed three of the skeletons I told you about. They were definitely Dontrian, according to the bone structure, but unlike any specimens we'd found before. We carbon dated them without success. We estimate that they were older than 14,000 years. Astounding, don't you think? The curious thing was that each hand only had four fingers. First time we'd seen it. Up till now, all of the discovered remains were either too battered or too charred. These were in excellent condition. Come, I'll introduce you, they are still here."

Philip and the others walked with him to the retrieval site about fifty metres away. Five closed, neatly stacked crates awaited collection by a scientific team. Arbuk leaned over, grabbed a crowbar off of the top crate and opened one of the lids. Philip's first impression of these ancient mine dwellers was that the cranial structure was larger than normal, and the rest of the body seemed more or less humanoid, having two arms and two legs. It was humanoid—with the exception of the eye socket. It was one single, gaping, centrally placed hole that once had the ability to see, just above the nose. "Who are you? What could you see?"

Baygorn studied them with immense interest. "Seven unilateral ribs. Fascinating."

"Was anything else buried with them?" asked Philip.

"Only bones and dust." Their teeth indicated they were meat-eaters, and the length of the foot revealed they could also run at great speeds.

Ramaan sent the data to the pod to see whether the brains on Terron could shed any light on this ancient race.

Farther into the cavern, they came across a newly excavated short passageway.

"What's this? This wasn't here before. It's not on the map." Dumbfounded, Arbuk toyed with the irregularly placed, flimsy plastic tape between two posts, apparently put there with the hope of preventing entry.

On the wall above a post, writing grabbed Lexia's attention: a handwritten message in what could have been chalk. 'Pligro di mort.' "Hey, it's a warning, it means danger of death!" On further inspection, they noticed it had been written dozens of times all along the length of the wall, all the way to the back. Arbuk broke through the barrier tape. Philip and the others followed. The ten-metre walkway was an entrance ending at a wall. Hanging on the far wall, a round, centrally placed object the size of a plate captured still further attention.

Ramaan was the first to reach the back wall. "Fascinating. What's this? What's all this scribbling? What do you make of it, Lexia?" They neared a bit more. Ancient writing curved around the rim of the plate.

"It's a tellurium plaque," said Arbuk as Lexia moved to have a look.

She leaned forward. "'All beware who discover me,' or something like that. No wait, it says, 'Beware all those who open me.' Beware of what? What's behind this wall?'"

Philip turned and stared at Arbuk. "It's the curse of the Magnopod." Arbuk, flustered, took an agitated step backwards.

"I should have known." His agitation changed to embarrassment. "How stupid of me. Beyond this rock wall is more tellurium than you can imagine. It can buy cities, it can buy spaceships. The Magnopod sealed it eons ago to prevent us, or our predecessors, from going in there. Unfortunately, it appears someone has stumbled upon it." Arbuk came forward again. "It will kill all of us, even if we even think of taking it! The temptation of any man's wish is only metres away. Magnopods go back hundreds of millennia. It was probably these guys who killed the Dontrian all those thousands of years ago."

Baygorn coughed. "Doubt it, Arbuk. If that were true, you wouldn't have had bones to study. I think your Dontrian died from natural causes." Baygorn's uncalming words didn't ease the tense air. "We met them on Phot. They can mind-read."

Philip leaned forward. "It looks awfully easy to take off. Don't sneeze, anyone, whatever you do. Maybe it's there to prevent them from leaving. Maybe it's a sensor."

Arbuk's haunted glance came back with a tinge of torment chiselled over his face, bringing out the texture of his whitened profile. His nervous hand pointed. "If this thing is removed or accidentally falls off, I can't imagine what would happen."

Philip added salt to the wound. "I wouldn't be surprised if they already knew we we're here and standing outside talking about them."

Speechless, Arbuk pushed past and made his way back to the entrance. Philip and Ramaan looked around at the immense substructure one more time and hastily joined him before returning to the surface. On all levels, although they were uneasy, Bod workers were once again slogging away as before as if nothing had happened, but news down in the mine travelled fast. Back on the surface, however, Arbuk's colour had rejuvenated somewhat. They had returned just in time for lunch. Arbuk walked to the mine kitchen mumbling. "After all that commotion, I'm starving. There's chicken, or if you want, today's speciality is mandenar. It's very tasty. I recommend it."

Without enquiring what it was, curiosity ruled over the stomach and they requested mandenar. The attendant arrived with six plates of a goulash-something, except the meat strands weren't meat. They were, after Lexia's inquisitiveness, sliced tree roots. The sauce was delicious. When the time came to receive the second plate, the alarm wailed.

Arbuk pressed Talk on his portable communicator and went pale again. "What? I don't believe it, we were just there! One of the workers has discovered the seal to the Magnopod lair. He yanked off the plaque. What a shambles. He must have followed us down there." Arbuk's tone was angry. "Bods were scuttling out of the mine like ants from a nest."

"I have an advantage," said Philip. "I know what that Magnopod can do. I know what they are capable of. They've reached into my mind before; I'll let them do it again."

"Yes, but this is not Phot. Maybe this Magnopod isn't in a good mood," said Alana with concern.

"True, but I'm the only chance those people have. If I don't go down there, those workers won't stand a chance."

14. The Magnopod

An official ran out from an office. Philip cut his path. "Where's the worker now?"

"Cellblock 6. We caught him when he came out of the mine."

"Is the insignia safe?"

"It's under lock and key in the adjoining cell."

"Good, get it for me. Quickly! I'll return it to the Magnopod before it's too late." The official dashed off and returned moments afterwards carrying the metallic tablet. Sweat ran down his brow and neck.

Philip looked at him and hastily grabbed the plaque out of his hands before turning to the others. "I have to do this alone—it would be suicide if you came with me."

Philip walked towards the vehicle, placed the plaque on the passenger seat, turned on the communicator and upped the volume, only to hear shouting and screaming. There were dozens of vociferating whimpers with an odd, occasional clinking and clunking, all appearing at the same time as one simultaneous scramble.

The workers were trying to escape from the lower levels, but the immense door was preventing their flight. There was no system override down there. Once the state of emergency had been declared, it would remain shut. Frantically, they bashed and banged the door from the inside, hoping that someone would hear their plight. But their fearful screams for help only bounced back into and down the shaft whence they had come.

From the vehicle, Philip pressed the first green button to open the surface doors. Bods poured outwards in search of cover. An overly filled express train arrived at the same time. Fortunately, these trains didn't have restrictions, so workers could climb in and out, even during alarm status.

The surface was in chaos. The police scanner had automatically switched itself off during the commotion and gone into standby mode. Philip began his descent armed only with a motion tracker and prayed it was all that he would need to find his way.

As he arrived at the second level a half-hour later, he pressed the green button to open the suite of doors. They clanked with a heavy thud and rolled open. Then he felt it: a sudden lonesomeness. He felt as if someone had swooped up all the living people and that he was the last man left in this hell. Even the radio was quiet. Everyone had simply vanished, and he had only the droning of ventilators to accompany him for the rest of his descent. *Maybe they are hiding somewhere*, thought Philip. Maybe they have already escaped. Unmoved boxes were stacked and machines were still chugging and churning. He trembled. There was still nothing coming from the radio, only hiss. During the eerie descent into the semi-darkness, it was his self-discipline that allowed him to chase away the lingering fears. After the doors had opened, he began to think about how he would communicate with the intelligence roaming below. Would it be in the same amicable manner as before?

For a further three kilometres, now close to the inner containment doors, he hadn't seen a stir, not a single living soul, and not a sound representing desperateness or flight.

Moroseness became the new tenant of the mine. Stillness governed the mine shaft with a continual hypnotic hum from the hungry ventilators. Philip became restless and impatient during the last of the descent, and his fears intensified, thinking of the first time he had encountered these beings on Phot.

"Oh God, maybe Alana was right. Maybe this Magnopod is different," he said out loud. He trembled at the thought of seeing one again, still remembering the time it killed a man right in front of his eyes.

As the third-level doors slid open, the same deathly stillness clogged the atmosphere. Bereavement had served justice here, all right. Apart from the constant hum, a perpetual, faint hiss of escaping steam and the dripping of distant water from a sidewall echoed through the base. No Bod workers worked at their chores. No maintenance crews came to greet him as he motored on into the reddened cavern. There was only a stronger, more asphyxiating, hotter air as he proceeded.

Farther down, some well-hidden survivors who had managed to hide in sporadically placed vehicles popped their heads up behind vehicle windows at the sound of Philip's engine as he drove past. He placed a vertical finger to his lips to warn them.

Fifty metres farther down, he winced as he started to see it. The same horror he'd seen on Phot, only this time it was everywhere. Workers, or rather what was left of them, filled the panorama. Bodies over rocks, getting in or out of vehicles, in the middle of eating, taking off boots, groups of bodies They were everywhere. Lifeless sacks of fully dressed skin. One was still trying to kneel down to do up his shoelaces. Some still had an expression of fear on their boneless faces.

Philip switched his tracker to motion sensing. Finally noticing the base wall, he swerved around a couple of bodies, turned off the engine, and got out. He was deep beneath the city. The thick air was rife with acrid chemicals and sulphur. The side tunnels were illuminated red and orange. Philip could see that a long time ago some architects had drilled field-lined pits into the molten mantle of the planet. They were bottomless shafts that served as hungry mouths for industrial waste.

The smell, let alone the sight, almost made him vomit. Heaps of dead Bod miners were incapable of extracting anything else, save song and prayer from their waiting families on the surface. A lucky few had gone home for supper this night.

The entrance to the surface train, too, had been a scene of slaughter. Fifty or more frantically escaping remains lay over the safety railing. The train was still waiting for someone to lift the handle to send them to safety. The red pulsating roof light hadn't turned green. Turning away from the shaft, Philip walked towards the entrance of the tellurium mine. Nearing the jagged opening, apprehension clouded his vision. He stopped, placed his hand over his eyes, rubbed them and continued.

"I haven't come here to steal your tellurium or harm your kind. I am here to return what was stolen from you." The words left his mouth in a clear tone. High above and faintly in the rocks, his voice echoed and came back. A long way off, he made out a crack sound, like a twig would make when stepped on. Then a blip emerged on his tracker. A pain griped his bowels as déjà vu repeated itself by ramming into his subconscious. Then came the voice, the same harsh voice like the one he'd heard on Phot. It was clear and abrupt, and he was tremendously scared, knowing what these things could do to him. Still, his defiant side erupted and burst outwards.

"We know who you are. Welcome to our lair."

Philip slowly inched towards the dig site he'd visited earlier. There, in front of him, the thing slithered like a half-nutshell moving from side to side, silently scrutinising his thoughts.

"Do not be scared, human. We will not hurt you. We know why you have come to this system. In return for your gallantry, I offer you the knowledge you seek." The Magnopod slid backwards slightly and left a package on the floor. It was a large cardboard box.

"With this gift," he said telepathically, "we will watch you closer, listen to your thoughts and observe your kind with more enthusiasm."

"But these people didn't mean you harm," said Philip in a desperate tone, thinking of the bodies not far behind. "There was no reason to exterminate them!" With eyes shut, his head placed between his open hands, he now gave them a clear line of communication.

"They have to learn by their mistakes," said the Magnopod. "They have knowingly destroyed thousands of our eggs on various planets in this system with their thieving habits! We have endured their simplicities far too long. You are the first people to approach us with a pure heart in all the timeless aeons we have been here. We are proud of your valiant efforts and honesty. I must leave you now. Put the inscription back where it was when you first saw it, and I will cause them no more harm. You have my word. If you ever need us, call us like you did moments ago. We are in your debt."

The Magnopod hastened away. Philip, with great difficulty, lifted the plaque to chest height and slotted it back into position. Slowly, his mind returned. He knelt down, picked up the heavy box and left the cavern. This time it would be for good.

On the way back to the vehicle, Philip didn't look down, and as he later described, he didn't even breathe. He just couldn't make himself look at hundreds of expressionless Bod workers, of which most of them did not know why this had happened.

Going up, he drove slowly and opened the window, taking in clean gulps of cooler air while searching for someone alive. Workers had quietly hidden themselves behind crates and stacks of boxes. Heads appeared, noticing that Philip was still alive after his encounter with the Thing. They started following the vehicle. More Bods emerged out of nowhere, and by the time he'd reached the surface almost an hour later, hundreds of petrified souls ran out and disappeared to their homes.

Arbuk and Alana reached Philip first. "How'd it go?"

"Actually, it went very well. Very well indeed. The Magnopod said that we were the first race to ever approach them in the countless centuries they have been down there."

Philip steered his head at Arbuk. "They won't cause you any more harm. The Dontrian managed to live in harmony with them; why don't you do the same? Don't enter their lair, and most certainly don't steal their tellurium eggs! Close the areas. Find a way to secure and protect it. Spread the word, tell those workers, educate them! If you want, I will tell them."

Arbuk looked strangely at Philip, but he understood every word.

Baygorn broke the atmosphere. "And the box?"

"It's the knowledge that we seek. It is a reward for my gallantry and honesty. The Magnopod left it on the floor before he slid away."

Baygorn gently took it out of Philip's hands and tenderly broke the seal. Inside were schematics and formulas. Baygorn and Lexia went through the contents carefully. Philip looked back towards the mine entrance and telepathically thanked the Magnopod for his gift. He was sure he was heard.

The next day they would be moving on to Vlox, the most violent planet in the system. Their last views of Arkos city and the Bod race, gone super-intelligent and super-crazy, were spent in front of a drab-looking bar called Smiley's Tavern.

"Hey, I knew a Smiley's Tavern in Brooklyn," said Ramaan with a widening smile. "I once won a hundred bucks in a drinking contest there. Speaking of which, what about these Erons? I heard they accept Erons in taverns."

Alana perked herself up. "Silly man, let's go mingle and have a chat, find out what they know. You never know, it could be interesting." An assortment of wind mobiles was parked outside. Some were similar to theirs. Opening a heavy wooden door, they sat down at a square table. It could only accommodate four, so they squeezed in the best they could. Alana looked around and called the waiter.

"Excuse me," she said sweetly, "I would like to buy those two over there a drink. What are they drinking?"

The barman's eyes widened. "Arcian yellow wine."

Alana smiled. "Give them a round and charge it to me. Here." Alana peeled off some Erons. "Think you can do that for me?"

"Done," said the waiter, quickly moving towards the bar. Less than a minute later, the two approached Alana to thank her for the drinks.

"Why don't you pull up a chair and sit with us?" said Philip. "My friend here overheard you talking about a war. Please enlighten us."

One of them took a sip and leaned forward. "We were talking about the war between the Blagorian and the Peblinus. The Blagorian have served the Peblinus for too long a time. There is speculation that they will soon rise out of the darkness and avenge their slavery. They say that the new communities on Ganus will suffer greatly because, under the tranquillity of the Ganusian landscape, hides millions of Blagorian. The Bods know this. They have sent them there to die! I say the Peblinus deserves whatever comes to them."

Philip listened to what the Bod had to say. "What you say is true, but you are talking about innocent lives. Two billion lives, if I am not mistaken, and which are already suffering against the Platnios and the rebellion of their man-eating tentacles."

"It won't be anything compared to this," added the Bod. "The Blagorian are faster and stronger. They will rise up with all their power against the Peblinus suppressor. Do you think they know the difference between guilty and innocent? We feel it's going to happen very soon."

"Most of the Peblinus have stopped their barbaric method of extraction," Philip said, "Things should be different."

The Bod could only smile. "Old wounds stay old wounds, I'm afraid."

"How long have you two been living around here?" asked Alana.

"Twelve years. Before that we lived in the city of Boros on the other side of Retolox. In this place we only exist because of the poor supplies sent to the encampments of the workers."

It turned out that the Bod they were speaking to was a worker in the same mine they had visited earlier.

"The Bods exploit us, like the Peblinus exploit the galaxy."

"What is happening here is normal," said Ramaan. "It's the rich man, poor man syndrome that exists in every part of the galaxy."

Philip decided not to touch on the topic of what happened this afternoon in the mine, as the Bod might become overly curious and do something stupid. Instead, they drank up, said goodbye and returned to the vehicle.

Outside the tavern, they looked up and down the streets and into the metropolis of Arkos. Well-illuminated streets lit by cylindrical lamps on the ends of long poles dotted here and there lightened the drab, forgotten part of Arkos, the uninviting part.

The real situation of the city became evident, as the illuminating capacity of the lamps not only lit the streets; it revealed the occasional Bod lowlife stalking the dark side roads, looking for an encounter of their own. Not even Arbuk came to say goodbye.

In the distance, a tall chimney billowing white smoke was the last thing they saw as they entered their pod and departed. Comfortably inside, Ramaan breathed a sigh of relief before taking off.

From the outer atmosphere and watching the lake diminish to a tiny dot, Philip briefed them on the next phase of the journey.

"It's not going to be a joy ride. Vlox is a violent place. It habitually receives abnormal amounts of radiation from Mintaka due to its primordial, almost non-existent atmosphere. In addition, if that's not enough, Sentrywatcher has plotted more than 20,000 active volcanoes on the parched landscape. We're to land on the morning side, which gives us twenty-nine hours to do our research and get out. The only thing down there is carbon and sulphur dioxide. It's high on the scale, too."

Philip was right: Vlox was dead. As its blackened orb crept nearer and onto the viewer, Sentrywatcher had a better opportunity to dissect it and search where they couldn't see. Information began rolling onto the screen when suddenly a red line appeared on the results.

"That's impossible! There can't possibly be life down there." Alana studied the red line meticulously. "Maybe it's just an accumulation of gasses on the surface," she said.

Ramaan rubbed his chin, shook his head and sighed as *Excelsior* shuddered and rumbled when it entered the outer atmosphere.

Alana leaned forward. "Anyway, what's wrong with gasses?" she snapped.

They looked at her and at one another as the *Excelsior* attained orbit. They climbed into the pod as Sentrywatcher fed all the information onto their C-12 devices.

"Remember, the suits restrict the line of vision, so be alert at all times. If we do encounter whatever it is, the unrecognisable spectrum tells us that much, it will definitely be different from anything we have seen so far." Alana flicked a switch and the countdown began.

Phot was heaven in comparison to this. Volcanic residues reached into the upper thermosphere, and they were forced to use Sentrywatcher to guide them down through the haze and murkiness. After a bumpy entry into the atmosphere, they landed two hours later.

Alana drove the terrain vehicle outside while the others put on their protective clothing. Ramaan began the routine scanning procedure. "It is primeval, definitely an unfriendly world."

The results, however, also revealed a large quantity of classified Earth-based elements: carbon, silicon, magnesium—
"Ahh, there you are. There is definitely gas on the visible spectrum moving between the rocks. Its composition is argon and neon. Maybe it's a surface wind or an electrostatic charge

that excites the particles." It made sense until suddenly Ramaan's analysis was interrupted. A silence befell the cabin.

"Our gaseous host seems to have picked up our scent. It's proceeding towards us. Wait, it has stopped!" Ramaan had an odd inflection in his voice.

Stationary, it paused and seemingly watched them from a distance, waiting for a movement.

"Probably just as curious as we are." Ramaan's tone made Philip bend closer to the scanner. At six hundred metres, it began to move again. It cautiously circled the vehicle and slowly came nearer before it stopped about a hundred metres away.

Outside, Mintaka was as big as a grape half a metre from the face. The suffocating heat without the suit would have been unbearable, not to mention the absence of breathable air. Cautiously advancing towards their strange host, they encountered randomly placed cubed objects. Each of the cubes measured exactly two metres by two metres. There were forty of them, each comprised of a different, chemically pure element. Some were unfamiliar to their analysing equipment.

Alana scanned the object moving erratically, now only fifty metres from them, when suddenly a giant whack hit the vehicle on the side. Seeing the threat, the chain gun mounted on the roof automatically activated and started rattling off rounds towards their aggressor. The blip on the screen remained and continued moving in its erratic path, rapidly dodging bullets in and out where it could within the fifty-metre radius.

Ramaan asked Sentrywatcher if she could shed more light on their ambiguous host. The form changed shape from a deranged mass to round.

"What on earth is it?" Sentrywatcher knew as much as they did.

"Alana, turn off the chain gun for a moment," said Philip. Immediately the blip came directly towards the vehicle and gave it another whack on the side. One of the spotlights fell to the ground in pieces.

"Let's get a better look at you." Alana toyed with the life scanner adjustment. "Not only is it gaseous, it fluctuates in density. That's why the chain gun had no effect."

Alana activated the photon laser, and the blip disappeared after one solitary blast as if it had never existed.

Ramaan searched for more entities that might be hiding in and around the hillsides. After finding none, they climbed out of the vehicle and set out on foot towards the cubes. Each cube was smooth, and the top was covered in volcanic ash and pumiceous residue, often producing a triangular-hat effect. As the results came back from Sentrywatcher, it revealed one of their compositions to be pure molismolum. The one next to it was iron. Information emitted from their C-12s as the puzzle slowly unfolded.

"This is a live Periodic Table; all of the elements are in their pure state." Baygorn tried scratching the surface of one of the blocks with a knife without making a mark. Of the forty cubes, only twenty-eight were recognisable. It was clear proof that a vastly superior intelligence had made this somewhere else in the universe. It forced a rethinking of the place of Homo sapiens in the overall scheme of the cosmos. It was apparent that other elements existed, fabricated in the great stellar cataclysms of the heavens. Undefeated, Baygorn took out a drill and broke a diamond-tipped bit on an unidentified block.

"What are they? What are they doing here? What was that thing back there?" he asked, but no one answered. Maybe it was a curious life form. About a hundred metres from the cubes, they came across a pile of cylindrical objects scattered on the ground. These were much smaller, exactly ten centimetres long and ten centimetres in circumference.

Baygorn lifted one up with difficulty, and as he did so, one of the bigger cubes started moving.

Sentrywatcher quickly analysed the chemistry of both cube and cylinder. It took seconds for the results to appear. Both were identical. Then what was the connection? What dominating force had valued the cylinder over the cube?

"The cylinders must be a driving mechanism." Ramaan transmitted the available data to Sentrywatcher and requested a one-kilometre aerial photograph of the area. It took less than a minute for the results. Previously unnoticed, on the far side of the cubes were forty holes. Each was two metres square. They were square. They presumed the holes were for the cubes, and the cylinders were to help put them there.

"But which one goes where?" asked Lexia.

"Let's try atomic weight, just like the Periodic Table," Philip said before returning to the pod to run a full spectroscopic analysis on each cube. Returning to the cylinders, they dragged each cube into its respective hole. The task took them almost two hours, but the moment each cube reached the correct destination in the proper position, the cylinder became useless.

As the last cube thumped itself down, a fascinating atmospheric reaction began to occur. Blue spheres of lapping flame ran towards the sky. Ozone scales went off the meter. Red and green flashes coming from some of the cubes followed a lurching yellow spark that reached up out of sight. The cubes were producing a frighteningly powerful chemical reaction. Within minutes, oxygen started becoming part of the empty atmosphere. They were witnessing the making of life.

At that precise moment, Alana picked up another life form similar to the one they had seen earlier. This time it wasn't evasive and it didn't change shape. It was slow, desultorily pausing every now and then in plain view of them. It seemed timid.

Instinctively, Alana switched the ion rifle to manual. It was waiting. All she could see was a hazy patch. They waited, just as it waited. For five minutes, it never moved an inch and neither did they.

"Switch off the ion laser. I think it knows it's active," said Philip.

Alana pressed a button on a remote control. The moment the laser LED faded, the gaseous object began floating towards them.

Alana scanned it once more. "This, whatever it is, has traces of carbon. I'm getting carbon! When we landed, there was no sign of carbon. It's increasing in mass at the same ratio as the oxygen level. Look carefully; there's a ghostly form behind that haze and it's walking."

Gaping at it, the five of them made out legs, arms, and a head. Its reanimating form was humanoid. It stopped and lingered three metres from them.

Suddenly Lexia thrust her hands towards her head. "Wait! It's trying to communicate. It knows I will understand it. It has chosen me."

The ghostly form moved a bit nearer.

"I am sorry I don't understand; you are talking too softly." Lexia concentrated harder and closed her eyes. "Yes, I can make out a couple of words now. Can you speak just a little louder? Wait, yes." She repeated his words: "He who helps us can leave this world with the forty elements of life. You have helped us regain our strength and we bid you welcome. I am a Sintor, and you may proceed with your business here." Gasping, Lexia broke connection and thrust her hands downwards.

Baygorn moved forward and faced the Sintor. "We come from planet Earth in search of the truths of our past. Our search has led us to these eight worlds that circle the giant sun we call Mintaka."

The hazy form of the Sintor made a gesture. It was faint, but they could now all hear him. "Our knowledge, shall be your knowledge." As the hushed words faded to a pause, the Sintor walked into the void towards a hill.

Behind them, the forty cubes emitted an electric radiance. The once-dead sky was now alive with all conceivable colours. Each cube produced its own separate chemical reaction due to their individual proximity. A variety of blues, powerful reds and a yellow tongue impressively lapped, sounding like a constant Van Der Graaf Generator. They backed away and walked towards the hill where the Sintor had gone. The breathtaking results of this reaction were already at 3 percent oxygen.

15. The Sintor

The Sintor had wide shoulders and a voluminous cranium, obviously signifying a higher intelligence. It was at least twice the normal size. To the Sintor, he was the normal one and Philip and the others were underdeveloped, weirdly dressed, and ugly. The Sintor's leathery mouth began to part.

"You restored this planet back to what it once was. Thieves have come and gone in the past. They had no intention of solving the puzzle. Our phantom, the protector of the cubes that you encountered on your landing here, was there to scare you away, but your insistence and instinct got the better of you." The Sintor had transformed himself into a true alien being, and they were hearing him loud and clear.

"We appear this way due to the oxygen level you created. Our carbon-silicon body structure cannot survive without oxygen." The mouth was permanently open and situated right in the centre of the large cranium. He had three eyes. One was in the centre above the mouth. The other two were on the sides of the face area, more or less at the height of the human cheekbone. All of them were staring at Philip.

"Where do you come from?" asked Philip.

"We come from what you call the Crab Nebula. A neighbouring red giant star called Vega C destroyed our world when it imploded. There was nothing we could have done to prevent it," he said. "A piece of the dead star drifted across space and hit our planet, instantly killing everything that remained." The Sintor glanced downwards in reproach. "And you? Have you found what you came for?"

"Yes, but our computer has informed us of a strange anomaly close by that's causing radio interference. We want to go and take a look at it. There are 20,000 active volcanoes on this planet, and I am sure they produce irregular radio patterns from time to time. Call it curiosity."

"Our spaceship is on the other side of this embankment. Now that we have almost restored ourselves back to normal, I must continue with the repairs. Thanks to you, in a short while we will begin our departure to the planetary system of Deneb, one of our other homes, four thousand light-years away."

They followed the Sintor towards the side of the hill, where a slim and very long spacecraft had crashed into the rock. As they neared, a door on the side of the craft opened where another Sintor handed Philip a disc.

"Here, this is for you. It has star maps and details of our technology. Please, come inside our ship."

Philip gave the disc to Ramaan. Ramaan thought the disc was adaptable to the computer he found on Haradan.

The Sintor said they'd crash-landed here more than one thousand years before. The site was a timeless lava hill. "It was mechanical failure," he said. "Only when it was too late did we discover that the frail atmosphere of this planet impeded our repairs. Our kind arrived soon after the crash with the cubes, but they perished trying to allocate them into their positions before the atmospheric reconstruction process could begin. There are only nine of us left."

Inside the spaceship, Philip was sure he was looking at the most advanced technology yet seen by them. Visual touch screens and lit panels portrayed their language. In the cabin sat two more of this fascinating race. They were communicating between themselves in a higher pitch. One of their hands depressed what looked like a blink-synchronizer. The one nearest to the control panel had one eye on the visitors whilst nattering to his crewmate. Miniscule lights came on and quickly flicked off. The Sintor explained that the spacecraft was now repaired and ready for departure.

"I've given you the understanding of space travel on the disc," said the Sintor. "Go well, go safe and remember the future is but a second away. Maybe we'll meet again; you never know." He moved back inside and the door closed.

Philip turned away in the direction of the waiting vehicle and watched the slender ship silently soar and disappear with a dazzling burst. The forty cubes in the distance continued to spew forth rivers of colours, unlimited power that was slowly transforming a dead planet's vile atmosphere. The level of oxygen had already reached 10 percent in only five hours.

Alana reported that the output from the cubes was auto-regulating itself and adapting to the changes in the environment. She pointed the scanner away from the cubes towards the hillside. "There's nothing, not even bacteria. Only us!"

The five of them stared towards the horizon. One thing Philip noticed was the absence of small rocks. It was either mountain or completely flat dust, with shadows produced only by irregular wisps of sulphurous smoke from nearby volcanoes. From Philip's imagination spurted a rockless, Martian landscape with that red tinge. Vlox was barren, all right.

From where they stood, seven active volcano cones wreaked havoc. Two of the closest produced rivers of lava that crawled towards a distant mountain. They climbed into the vehicle and drove in the direction of the radio anomaly. Four kilometres away, between two volcanoes, two prominent, and at first glimpse unnatural, hills manifested themselves out of nowhere.

Ramaan took a reading. "We're close, it's around here somewhere," said Ramaan, holding the C-12 at chest level. Its fizzling speaker announced their proximity whilst a bright green arrow indicated the direction of the contamination. As they neared, Lexia thought, *This must be what it felt like to have been brainwashed, to have one's memory painted over with false memories air-brushed on the moment.* Her past suddenly seemed like a fogbound landscape of an eerie luminescent face of a cloud-shrouded moon sneaking through an opening in the blackness, like a face behind a curtain.

She could not see back through the years with the same clarity she had enjoyed an hour ago, and she could not trust the reality of what she did see.

Philip's first impression of it was a shimmering, multi-coloured peacock feather about the size of a tennis court, suspended in mid-air between two hills. Apart from that, it went beyond description. They simply stared and watched it glimmer, gyrate, and hover one metre above the ground.

They stayed in the safety of the vehicle for five minutes, speculating and unable to leave. Finally, they opened the door, stepped out and approached it. Its circular form hummed and buzzed like a harmonizing, high-voltage fence. The way its multitude of colours intertwined throughout the spectrum and beyond while altering the colours of the hills fascinated them. Ten metres away, a powerful numbness anaesthetized their muscles. It painfully raised the hairs. Without succumbing to its obvious and unknown power, they retracted themselves from the strange force field to a safe distance and returned to their vehicle.

Ramaan had accumulated enough information to send to Terron. "Hey, what's this? When did these arrive?" They had messages. "That is odd!" Ramaan pressed the Correspondence icon on the C-12.

"Where on earth have you been? We were so worried. God, we thought we'd lost you. We've been trying to reach you for two days!"

"We're okay, Jim. Don't panic. We've come across something very significant on Vlox. I'll send you the details as soon as we get back to the pod." They sat there, stared and gasped at one another. Two days had ticked by in the blink of an eye.

Jim told them the Bod freighter bound for Andromeda had exploded. "We intercepted a radio broadcast of Bod origin. They said it was a malfunction. All lives were lost." Jim clicked off without dismissal.

They returned to study the anomaly. "You know, this could be a natural phenomenon," said Baygorn, looking up. "It's just dangling there. What do you think it is?" The aberration perpetually changed shape and colour all throughout the visible spectrum. It was continuously buzzing, producing a barely perceptible low-frequency drone which intensified as they approached.

"It could be a link to another world or another galaxy." Taking the last photographs and video, they backed away, turned towards the vehicle, got in and drove back to the pod.

With their investigations completed, Baygorn looked out one last time at this arid land through the porthole of the pod. There far away, was the first wisp of a cloud. It was the first of many to come, and he wondered what type of life Vlox would produce as a result of the new world they had created.

The night side of Traxon was a steady 40 degrees. It evaded further obliteration by maintaining the same face away from Mintaka. Perpetual darkness here came in the form of a motionless, non-rotating rock. Entering the atmosphere, the darkness browned. At first, it was an obscure brick-brown, then tinging slightly orange, with silver wisps partially broken by a ring of yellow fire on the horizon as Mintaka attempted to break through. It looked fabulous and frightening at the same time.

Directly below them through the murk there were lights from an irregular-shaped city. Sentrywatcher had identified a bacterium that had accustomed itself to the day side's 100-degree surface.

Sentrywatcher identified a thriving nocturnal forest living in the arid safety of the darkness. There was no water, yet the forest seemed to be everywhere, almost completely covering the dark side. Sentrywatcher revealed it was incessantly winding its way and relentlessly inching itself towards the city, groping for free space. It wanted it all.

It was so vigorous that Sentrywatcher had calculated growth rates exceeding fifty centimetres per hour. As they lowered still more, a great fire was in command on the horizon, decimating the march of the burgeoning arboretum. The forest had endeavoured to devour another part of the landscape; a part it never had. As the jungle was reduced to dust and consumed by Bod fire, it avidly regenerated itself and edged its way as before, feeding on its own ashes.

They lowered and prepared themselves for the landing. It was a mining encampment, and the front doors immediately began to unhinge as the pod gently settled on the patio. Four Bods greeted them in a well-lit area.

"Hello, and welcome to Traxon. My name is Saramor."

They shook hands. Saramor's hands were old, well-worked and heavily veined. "Nice to be here. It isn't a very friendly place, though. We heard you lost the Andromeda freighter."

Sporadic gunfire rattled off in the distance. "Don't worry about that, that's my men fighting the forest. Please come inside, we have air conditioning. Andromeda freighter. Yes, the coolant distribution failed and the ion-drive overheated. We lost all aboard; a real tragedy," he said. "The accident occurred because of inconsistent alloys. It was a chemical imbalance. We replaced it with ermithium and the rudimentary tests have already come back positive. The new inter-galactic freighter will carry another five hundred Bods to the Andromeda region. It will begin the journey before the end of the month."

Inside the building it was fresh and well lit. He offered Philip refreshments before continuing.

"Traxon is imperceptibly rotating at two metres per year. As Mintaka engulfs two metres, she spits back two scorched ones. About a year ago, a spacecraft crash-landed here directly on the day-night barrier. The occupants must have died immediately, or so we think. If the crash did not kill them, they were cooked. A couple of days later, we sent out a search-and-rescue. The remains didn't resemble anything we had seen before. It was vegetative, quite odd, really. What was left didn't have arms, they appeared more like branches. Within days, this blasted forest started appearing and spreading out. Whatever was on that spacecraft, it must have blended in with the hot side's bacteria and started waging war on us. I am sure you detected it on your way down. Damn shrubbery keeps more than half my men busy. They are continually destroying it and preventing it from entering the complex. If they didn't, it would overtake us in days."

Baygorn asked, "What was this spacecraft like, the one that crash landed?"

"Half-moon, or maybe like a half-circle. Why?"

The words made Ramaan and Philip turn towards each other.

"How many plant things did you find out there?" asked Alana.

"We only found two. The spacecraft was small. Do you know who they might have been?" Saramor plainly had questions.

Baygorn and Alana slid their fingers onto Philip's shoulder. "You thinking what I'm thinking? Do you think they might have been scouts?" asked Baygorn, directing his whisper towards Ramaan.

"I don't know, but I don't like it one bit. Damn things are starting to show up everywhere."

Denying the benign inquisitiveness of Saramor, Philip rapidly changed the subject. "What brings you to such a paradise? What are you mining?"

"Ermithium."

At least it's not tellurium, thought Philip. "What method are you using to extract it?"

"We use Blagorian."

"Isn't that dangerous?"

"There's always a substantial risk with them. If you want to see the mine later, you'll fully understand."

"Intriguing. We'd be delighted. We are familiar with the Blagorian. How do you find them?"

"Amenable, a bit moody, but we haven't had problems so far. This mine is important because it is the only location on the planet where ermithium exists in these quantities. Our scientists are the most qualified in the system, so we were given the order to manufacture the ion-dispersion drive for the new freighter. In our plastics plant we interblend the two elements, ermithium and chromium, in their pure powdered state, with a poly-chloride, and develop them into whatever shape we want."

Philip and the others followed Saramor through a door and down a flight of steps. At the end of a short corridor he opened an entranceway leading to a laboratory.

"Ermithium is non-magnetic, twenty times tougher than your vanadium steel on Earth. We know about it because of our frequent visits to your planet. It's as light as aluminum, too. Its uses are infinite."

Saramor showed them how imaginary plastic shapes could evolve into a thought-provoked reality. Before their eyes, he explained the process and showed them plastic bearings, clamps and the most intricate mechanical and electronic parts. Farther into the complex, they entered a submerged chamber. Against the wall were three large tanks containing the components they needed for the fabrication of plastic parts.

"They're mixed in varying proportions, exposed to high temperatures under pressure, and out comes our plastic shape."

191

Philip's attention wandered around the cavern. "What are those doors?" he asked, pointing to the other side to much smaller mine-access doors that were three metres high.

"Down there is the deepest mine in this system."

"How deep?" enquired Alana, ferreting around.

"It goes down almost thirty kilometres."

She stopped. "Incredible. Can we take a peek at it?"

"I did say I would show it to you. I'll prepare the transport we'll need." His hand pressed a button on the console to the left of the door. There was a low frequency rattle-groan before the door slowly opened. A wave of heat lurched towards them and hit them in the face. Philip's eyes blinked a tear. A slight whiff of acridity followed close behind. They winced. Black powder was everywhere, filling the floor even though a robotic machine was constantly cleaning. Like on Retolox, it was a live representation of infinity.

"It goes all the way down to the upper asthenosphere." The shaft was smaller and thinner than what they had seen before.

"If an emergency happens down there, how do people get out?" asked Lexia, noticing no emergency vehicles or exits.

"They use standard vehicles to and from the base. No reason to worry."

Philip said, "You were going to explain: Is there no other method you can use?"

Saramor sighed. "We are forced to use the Blagorian because the magma here is too hot. Hafnium Resonators malfunction at these temperatures. We've tried before, believe me. We've tried everything."

A worker arrived with the vehicle and parked it. As the worker climbed out and handed Saramor the opening device, an alarm began to wail, making a three-tone stutter. An array of flashing roof lights ran down to hell itself. Bods began to run in all directions, dropping whatever they had in their hands as they passed by the vehicle.

Saramor grabbed one of the fleeing workers. "What's going on? Why the alarm?"

"It's a Blagorian riot; they've gone mad down there! They're slaughtering anything! It's horrible. I was talking to Pete on the radio when he suddenly began shrieking. Background voices only had time to say, 'aargh' and 'Blagorian' before they were silenced." The worker ran off.

Saramor told them where the armoury was. When they returned, Alana and Ramaan hurriedly set up GF rifles on the entrance to the mine. The fifty Bods who ran to the surface scuttled to their safety, but the remaining workers below were still in danger. Only the humming of ventilators rose from the depths of the mine.

A minute later, Alana's motion tracker gave a beep. Red numbers began filling part of the screen and revealed quantity, velocity, and distance.

"Five kilometres, eighty targets and rising fast. Damn, I never thought these things could move so fast!"

"If these Blagorian escape to the surface—" Philip stopped himself mid-sentence.

When the Blagorian reached two kilometres, the GF rifles began firing their deadly cargo. The confrontation lasted less than a minute.

"Why do they stir up like that? What makes them so volatile?" asked Baygorn.

Saramor explained as the vehicle sped off. "Underneath that liquid-armoured metallic surface, they appear to have common sense; there is a neuron-network in there somewhere. The Blagorian don't only work for us, they perform amongst themselves, behaving in a way we still can't fathom. We have been studying them for years, compensating their unpaid employment with time off every now and then. We release them back into their subterranean refuge so they can mingle between themselves. Up until now, they have been happy with this relationship between our two species. The Blagorian differentiate between large varieties of objects, but cannot tell the difference between the Peblinus and us. We are the slave drivers known as the Peblinus to them, and sometimes just our presence aggravates them. Most of all, if they are subjected to the elevated magma temperatures in existence here and then combine them with their prehistoric sentiments, they are likely to go a bit wild."

Michael Gilwood

They set off on their way. Only a couple of seconds into the shaft, Philip caught sight of a handheld drilling machine laying against the wall. Next to it, a couple of beckoning crates seized his attention. "Retolox" was engraved in tilted, black ink.

"What's in those?"

"Artefacts. They are the remains of an ancient civilisation that flourished here thousands of years before us. We have been uncovering them for decades. These specimens are probably the finest we've found to date. A scientific team from Retolox will arrive soon to collect them for study."

"Could you let my science officer take a look?" Philip's eyes met Saramor's.

"Of course, better before the science team arrives. Once they get their hands on it, it's bye-bye, baby."

Alana looked at him, wondering where he could have heard such a phrase. Saramor drove them closer to the crates and brought the vehicle to a halt. Baygorn jumped out and began to make speculative remarks. Philip heard the word "Dontrian" a couple of times. As Baygorn, Lexia, and Philip opened the crates, Ramaan and Alana set up the next line of defence.

16. Bones

The artefacts were mechanical paraphernalia. A rock close by had fallen on top of them, making them broken and of no use. The two skeletons, however, were in perfect condition.

Baygorn began to analyse them with a palm-sized lector. "Definitely the same as the ones we saw on Retolox. They've been here too, then." He patiently waited for the carbon scan to complete its work with a bleep. "Two thousand years old," he said, placing one of the bones back into position. "It seems the nearer we get to Mintaka—" Baygorn abruptly stopped. "The closer we get to Mintaka, the younger the remains." There was a definite crescendo in his voice. "Hey, you never know, on Rindor they might even be alive to greet us!"

They climbed back into the vehicle. Farther down, a couple of people had hidden themselves anywhere they could. Fear had ripened down here with a definite tinge of burnt sulphur. The illumination was dimmer. Shadows raced along the wall from the vehicle lights. Ahead, some of the main shaft lights weren't working. It provoked an eerie infinity in the mine shaft. They continued downwards. Every now and then they stopped so that Alana and Ramaan could place two GF rifles close to the wall.

Ten kilometres from the base, Alana received another blip on her proximity scanner.

"Hasn't anyone tried to communicate with them?" asked Philip.

"Many years ago, we performed a wide variety of tests on the Blagorian. It appears our metallic friends are deaf, but they do react to movement and light. Vibrations seem to attract them as well."

"There has to be a way to communicate," Philip said.

The next wave was a small one. Alana said there were nine. Still, they advanced with all the speed they could muster. It all seemed too easy. More crates dotted the shaft with pockets of hidden survivors behind them. Heads bounced up every now and then when they heard the engines nearing.

Saramor shouted over the vehicle megaphone, "Stay where you are. We'll send help in a short while to pick you up!"

They popped back down again into their personal gloom.

Down and down they went, farther into the abysmal mine until finally, at almost thirty-one kilometres, they reached the base.

Thumping ventilators worked every hundred metres or so. A tremendous dry heat slapped Philip in the face, numbing it, the moment he climbed out of the vehicle.

Saramor explained that if the ventilators stopped working for just a second, they would be carbonised.

Philip caressed his eyes. Suddenly, Lexia shrieked and Philip, still rubbing his eyes, followed her glance.

Everywhere on the floor towards the back section and close to an entrance lay human parts. Maybe Saramor was right and they couldn't communicate with them, but something clearly had to be done. Atrocities like that shouldn't go unnoticed or even unpunished. Chewed arms, smashed legs, half-eaten heads, it was all here.

Philip's stomach gave a heave and he turned away.

After reaching the conclusion that there was nothing they could do, Alana and Ramaan set up the last defence wall. The intention of communicating with them had dwindled.

They entered a large doorway, and once more, the sight was sickening. Hundreds of bodies, mounds of them, were stacked up like warehouse boxes.

A voice entered Philip's head. It was the same husky low-pitched voice he'd heard on Phot. His head began to throb as the voice lucidly modulated into his brain. His hands rose. It was unmistakable. The others, like before, were too busy staring at the spectacle. They didn't hear a thing.

"Human, do not enter. It's a trap! I told you we would be watching over you. The Blagorian need to escape, and the only obstacle in their way is you."

The tone and meaning of the Magnopod's voice alerted Philip. He spun around and faced everyone. "Alana, rig up the last of the GF rifles at the entrance. We have to leave now!"

"Philip, what-what's up? You've gone white," Alana said.

Everyone jolted at his sudden spasm. He felt a cold sweat cloud his brow. Touching Alana on the shoulder, he said with authoritative tone, "Don't ask; back to the vehicle. Now!" He was trembling as the words left his mouth.

Quickly arriving once more at the base entrance, Alana and Ramaan placed the last ten GF rifles. They ran to the vehicle, started the engine and shot off towards the surface. That was when it happened. Ramaan's foot was flat on the accelerator and racing up only five kilometres from the base when Alana released a shriek. Ramaan looked at his scanner.

"Jesus! What the hell is that?" The screen was white.

Alana stared at Philip in shock. "Oh sweet God, how did you know? That area we just left, it's alive. It's crawling down there, there are hundreds of them. Can't this thing go any faster?"

The enormous gathering of metallic life made its way past the recently placed GF rifles, destroying them as it went with hardly any casualties.

At the next base, they weren't so lucky. The scampering river of silvery Blagorian lost hundreds. The Bods, too: The survivors they'd seen in the shaft on the way down had almost certainly died. The gathering continued upwards. At the third barrier, hundreds more were vaporised, but this didn't stop them from trying to reach their goal, the surface.

Jumping out of the vehicle, Alana peered down at her scanner. The LED read just under four hundred moving objects. A wind blew between their feet; adrenalin rushed and tweaked their reflexes. They could make out something moving down there, something far off and very fast.

At the exit doors, an anxious, fully charged and hungry shield in front of a human barrier waited for them to come into range. It was a futile attempt for the Blagorian and was all over before they reached a hundred metres—all except for one tiny ball of morphing life. It changed shape, becoming a rock, then a boot.

They left it untouched on purpose; Baygorn wanted to study it. It measured four centimetres in diameter. *What harm could this little fella do?* he thought. It squirmed and twisted, looking for a way behind them. It stopped for a few seconds and then in a last dash of hope, it leaped forward with all its speed before one of the GF rifles spotted it.

As it disappeared, Baygorn sneaked off to study the remains of the Dontrian. "These bones are fascinating. I would love to know more about them, to meet them."

"Baygorn, you never know; on Rindor you may have that chance," said Philip with his own looming, unanswered questions going through his mind.

As a precaution, they left the surface barrier active. Forty-six survivors had crawled out from behind the crates and were being helped by others.

Finally, they prepared to make their way on to the last stop in the system, the wondrous planet of Rindor.

17. Rindor

Blink. They were 10,000 kilometres away when the first pulsation drew their attention to the control panel. Sentrywatcher was warning them with a flickering, yellow blink.

Blink. There it was again. Rindor was watching them just as they were watching it with Simcolators and Spectrum Analysers. Invisible eyes roamed and searched their spacecraft. They could feel it like an itch. It dissected them, each one of them, and their technology. Someone was curious about their presence. From their distance, Rindor with its vast cities looked peaceful: a vast river globe almost the size of Jupiter—no turbulence or gas, just varied vegetation and dense forests.

Hynede, one of Rindor's four moons orbiting from 90,000 kilometres, constantly touched the surface and donated well-needed, persistent shadow from the fierce Mintaka only seventy million kilometres away. The other three moons, Rioll, Miobin and Izarno, orbiting on their slow-moving and lifeless trajectories, showed them how uninteresting they were through Sentrywatcher's viewer.

Apart from Hynede, a greenish-yellow protective layer covered the entire planet, offering life and tranquillity to the inhabitants below. This stratum, one hundred kilometres above the surface, stretched itself like an eggshell to the fledgling. It was indeed successful isolation from the inferno just above their heads.

Alana was sure there was a superbly intelligent culture flourishing below the artificial atmosphere. Luckily, while in their own particular universe, they were unaware of the dangers elsewhere in the solar system. They were occupied only with what was at hand. From closer viewing, the beckoning face of Rindor exuded harmony like nothing they'd seen so far, so they decided to study this inspirational world from a closer distance and prepared to break away from the *Excelsior*.

Alana flicked a switch and pressed a button on the transmitter. She seemed anxious and looked towards Philip for a response. Philip gave none.

"This is the orbiting spacecraft *Excelsior* from Earth requesting permission to land for scientific purposes."

Silence, and then a hiss exited the transmitter for less than ten seconds. "Permission granted," said a voice at the other end of the speaker. "We are the Shelot and bid you welcome to our planet. Our shift-assistance beam will guide you down."

Suddenly they felt alarm. What were they doing? "This entity who calls himself a Shelot does not appear in our databases. There's no record of them," said Lexia with a worried tone.

The *Excelsior* creaked and groaned as solar heat from Mintaka made a correction to the hull. They hurriedly glared at the scanner looking for clues, for anything. Only blips were revealed. From up there, they didn't see anything out of the ordinary. Everything seemed peaceful.

"The only way we're going to get down there is if he guides us down." The tone was hard. Philip also noticed the renewed reluctance on Alana's face; he knew she would have preferred to take them down herself.

They entered the pod and readied for separation. There was a vague thump as the Shelot took control. The outer hull of the *Excelsior* had reached 200 degrees, giving off sporadic expansion groans. Meanwhile, the surface of Rindor only registered a temperature of 35, a permanent summer. Their unknown host waited for them.

It took two hours to reach the outer crust of the barrier. It was a greenish, eerie haze, and it seemed to move like slime. A piece of barrier peeled away from beneath the pod and disappeared. In full control of the Shelot's tractor beam, a wing of living force field branched out and reanimated directly on top of them, encapsulating them and closing the fissure above. On contact with the planet's inner atmosphere, the outer hull began to smoke wildly as the immense temperatures of their protective shell battled in vain against the cooler interior. It gradually dissipated as the lower atmosphere of Rindor quelled the fierce Mintakan temperatures on their exterior.

With care, their mysterious host vigilantly guided them towards their undisclosed landing site. They drifted, feeling powerless, as their waning altitude revealed panoramic splendours and landscapes. Constructions and tall hexagonal structures slowly came into view. Other buildings, revealing themselves as tiny hazy points far in the distance, later became prominent shapes as they approached. Wispy white clouds brushed and wiped them as they passed through.

Between many of the structures, thick vegetation and a vast green carpet covered the spectacular panorama. Philip saw a farm on this marvellous place, with miniscule inhabitants the size of ants. As they ventured lower on their final approach, winding roads exhibited strange vehicles wandering nonchalantly on their paths. Three or four huge wooden buildings loomed up. More indiscernible shapes moved around. Their sun of enormous dimensions filtered an eerie whitish light through the barrier. It was a fluorescent white, certainly not the typical sunshine they longed for and were used to.

They floated towards a heavily guarded complex. Ants became human figures. Lower and lower they went, gaping in awe at their surroundings. Vegetation and buildings were everywhere. The Shelot race ambled around unperturbed by their arrival. Some carried objects. Some were talking, holding hands, not phased by the pod's appearance.

The pod set down onto a round platform. Four brawny armed security guards stood grinning as Phillip and his crew stepped into the hot, oxygen-rich atmosphere. It felt good and it smelt like heaven.

Accompanying their euphoria was a sudden and intense fizzling sound. The security guards turned purple as a bright, powerful cobalt force field separated them and encircled the pod.

The Shelot, to whom they had spoken with while in orbit, stepped onto the platform. "Hello again, I bid you welcome to Rindor. Apologies for the little inconvenience." He moved his arm to acknowledge the guards. "Now tell me, what is the purpose of your visit to Rindor?"

Phillip moved to the front. "Greetings. We have come from Earth to explore the eight planets of this system, its cultures and inhabitants. We are a scientific crew of five and request permission to explore your world, so we may relay its wonders to our people."

The man adjusted the distance between them and moved equally forward. "Intruders have come before you. They tried to take our world from us. Needless to say, they failed. We are peace lovers, but know how to deal with problems if they occur. Our way of life is unchanged for thousands of years. If you want to visit our world, you must leave your exploratory apparatus on your small craft. Once you have accomplished this, please feel free to stay as long as you wish. Learn our way and enjoy."

It is a little price to pay, Philip thought. Yet, he felt the urge to ask him how he dealt with intruders, but he didn't say a word. The force field fizzled as it dissipated.

As they stepped off the platform passing the four guards, the energy shield re-emerged behind them and produced its deadly crackle once more. The Shelot greeted them formally by putting out his hand. It had only four fingers. Baygorn stood back.

Alana's face brightened. "Then it's true!" she said, "We found remnants of your kind on other planets."

Philip stared at the Shelot. Something wasn't right. Something was out of place. The man ignored Philip's curiosity with a smile, making him relax.

"My name is Obnar. Tens of thousands of years ago, our people lived in this quiet, peaceful system on a variety of planets until the others came. Many other forms of life that pillaged and raped us of our knowledge. We slowly migrated here. Five hundred years ago, we set ourselves behind this impenetrable protective force field and have had no trouble from outsiders since then. Our only allies in the system are the Magnopods. We live well together, and it was they who told us about your eventual appearance."

Somewhere in his mind, Philip could make a connection between the two.

Obnar proceeded to tell them stories. Some they already knew; the scrounging for metals, the disarray of human values, the unnecessary slaughter. Obnar explained the Peblinus and their atrocities.

Philip assured him that the Peblinus was a self-destroying nation, and it was only a question of time before the Platnios completed their task.

"Not true," Obnar countered. "The Peblinus are not only here, they have various settlements scattered over the galaxy. Altair has one. Rigel is the biggest. With recent findings they've also stretched into Alnilam and Alnitak."

"Alnilam, that's where another one of our research teams is," interrupted Lexia. "Maybe they had similar problems."

"It's possible. Out of curiosity, how many more expeditions of yours are out there?" asked Obnar with interest.

"One. Captain Branigan is in charge. He's probably deep into the system of Alnilam by now."

Obnar had a perturbed look. "I am afraid I have bad news. I shall be the one to inform you. We continually monitor outside activities with intex reception frequencies, not forgetting your ancient digital radio signals. It came to our attention a few weeks ago that your Captain Branigan was killed by an unknown force on Telus-Three, the sixth planet of that system."

"What! But, but our superiors on Terron haven't told us a thing!" Philip said with a jolt.

"And they won't. They would've kept it quiet because there is no time for bodge-ups caused by personal feelings in space. It's too expensive. They want results, nothing more."

God, it couldn't be true. Phillip's lifelong friend gone forever. It just couldn't be true. Both Lexia and Alana came to stand near Philip. He placed his head between his hands.

Obnar stepped away and left Philip in his private hell for a minute. Then he said, "Come, Philip, I'll show you around. Then we can eat something, you are probably hungry. The meal is being prepared as we speak."

Philip managed to thank Obnar for his hospitality as a tear emerged. At that precise moment, he made himself a promise: He would find out what happened to Mike and his crew.

As Philip's thoughts briefly returned to his academy days, Obnar led them towards a large central building and through a door. Philip rubbed his eyes one last time and forced thoughts of Mike to one side; he had to, he would get to him later.

Michael Gilwood

On the inside of the building, Shelots were coming out of somewhere or disappearing into somewhere else. Like the Bods or Peblinus, they resembled the human in every respect.

Philip studied them toddling about and only knowing this seemingly wonderful, yet forlorn planet.

"That is true," said Obnar.

Philip looked at him sideways. "What?"

"Don't be alarmed, I can read your thoughts," he said. "I've been trained in the art of mind-sucking. I will know if your intentions here are hostile even before you know it. I can assure you, if we had any doubt, you wouldn't be walking by my side. The Magnopod gave us a good impression of your kind when you approached it. They said you were helpful and honest. We like that trait in our guests."

"Have you received many visitors in the past?" asked Philip.

"Yes, many have come. The Peblinus came a year ago on one of their stealing stints. We sent them on their way without any harm coming to them."

"One other thing," said Philip, "you do know, of course, that we are direct descendants of the Bods and indirectly have them to thank for our being here today."

"Yes, but I can see the New Bod, or as you call yourselves Humans, have evolved into a far more intelligent and sensitive being. I have been studying and examining different races throughout these systems for decades. The machine is a development of the tool. The Bods are simple tools. This rock I hold in my hand can also be a tool. Man made the tool and later he made the machine. It's a simple process. The history of man is the history of tools into machines, ever-increasing in their complexity. You are the result, the Homo superior, the Homo Bod."

Philip smiled at the remark. "Tell me, why do you think the Blagorian flare up like they do and kill hundreds of Peblinus and Bods?"

"Like the Magnopod, these beings existed long before us. They were happy living in their subterranean boroughs, thriving on the heat emanating from the planet's core. Of course, that was until the Peblinus arrived. We never intended on disturbing

204

them for any reason. When we first met the Blagorian, they never attacked us. We co-existed. They probably attacked you because of your resemblance to the Peblinus. As for the poor Platnios, they are nothing more than an ambitious experiment gone wrong. Their only objective in their simple existence is to kill Peblinus or whatever gets in their way, preventing their evolutionary development. The Platnios are spreading fast within these three systems, and it's only a question of time before they exterminate the Peblinus. If they found out about Rigel's immense Peblinus population, they would have a field day. They'd be extinct within a week."

He continued. "The sordid story began a hundred years ago. The Peblinus genetically experimented with plant life with the intention of creating a genetic slave by incorporating their own DNA into the formula. The Peblinus by nature are lazy; minimum labour with maximum results, that was the key. The experiment failed horribly and generated a deformed, Peblinus-thinking, shape-changing plant with extra sensory perception and a hunger for flesh. There is a darker side to all this, I must add—"

Philip's heart pounded with jackhammer ferocity. *Goddamn Peblinus. Goddamn Platnios*, he thought.

"The Platnios have already begun changing into their next phase, a super-quick species of intelligent, ravenous animal. It's this new evolutionary breed, I fear, that might have killed your Captain Branigan on Telus-Three. The Platnios come equipped with an accelerated evolvement gene. As each day passes, six years of their evolutionary process ticks by. The Peblinus not only modified the gene pool, they added two nucleotide bases."

Philip carefully absorbed Obnar's words and returned his thoughts to the Peblinus. What the hell had they unleashed? A sepulchral silence loomed as Philip and Obnar exchanged dreary glances.

Baygorn interpreted their depression. "Who are the Sintor?"

"Wonderful people, truly gifted. They have spent thousands of years running and hiding from wars. Clever, don't you think? They use a time-jump portal, an infinite nerve network of interlinking doorways joining every planet in the galaxy, most of them hidden. They use them to escape, running away from the pain and suffering inflicted by their adversaries. We also heard about the help you offered them when you freed them from their imprisonment on Vlox. It seems wherever you go, you preserve life and help the deserving." His words faded as he disappeared behind a door.

Obnar briefly popped his head back around the door. "Why don't you stay with us for a few days? Strongly consider, when you do return to Terron, that you leave the data you have collected in this system here with me. Such knowledge will be dangerous for your kind." Obnar waited for a response. Philip didn't give him one.

"Of course, when you are ready, intellectually speaking, I will hand it back without hesitation."

"That's definitely not acceptable. We didn't come all this way to return empty-handed. The meanings of our visits and the civilizations we meet will be for all to share."

"Yes, but in the end, it will not be you that decides the fate of the data you carry, it's your superiors. They know, as always, what is best for it and where to use it. They will be the downfall of an upcoming civilisation like yours. Look, I can't stop you from leaving here with the data. I can only warn you. If you decide to use it against us one day, you'll be infinitely sorry."

"Well, thanks for the warning." Philip's cynical reply made him look away.

"Tell me, Obnar, without intelligence, how is a race supposed to evolve? How are they supposed to grow, intellectually speaking, of course? Our only motive here is to gain knowledge, not use it against you or anyone. We have absolutely no intention—!" Philip held his tongue.

"Then if that's your promise, use it well," said Obnar, turning his head towards someone beckoning in the hallway. "Come, dinner's ready."

They walked through a large door, down a long passageway, and into a small dimly lit dining hall. Three muscular waiters clad in red stood back, holding candles in the amorous atmosphere. The laid wooden table was long, chest-high and ample for ten.

Before they sat, Obnar snapped his fingers. The waiters placed the candles on the table and disappeared through a door, only to reappear seconds later. One carried a large jug and something Philip didn't recognise. The other two carried steaming bowls on brass trays, and as they brushed past, Philip noticed intricate, inlaid detailing in the trays.

"Sit where you please," Obnar waved at the table.

Ramaan sat between Lexia and Baygorn, opposite Alana. Philip was at one end facing Obnar, watching him nod to the waiters as they moved nearer with their first dish.

It looked like tomato soup. The waiter, a tall and extremely handsome character, caught the attention of Alana. She giggled occasionally. He slowly and methodically approached their table with the bowl.

Philip caught sight of Alana looking at bulges and muscles before she averted her sight to one side and gasped. Philip had never seen her so wonderingly popeyed.

"Excellent," uttered Philip, looking at Obnar. "What is it?"

"It comes from the zamoran plant. We use its leaves and fruit to produce the succulent soup you are eating."

Alana had two servings. Ten minutes later, as plates disappeared into the kitchen, the same three waiters appeared, wheeling trolleys. The drifting whiff of garlic emanated from what looked like a leg of lamb. Philip peered at it as they passed by.

Obnar noticed his interest. "This is a delicacy served only to hierarchy," said Obnar. "It's plog, a rare and almost extinct species of animal only found on Rindor. It has been basted and adorned with a sauce we call boranda. It has an after-smell that the ladies here adore."

They drank Shelotian wine called Evermet. They laughed, cried and shared their most intimate visions with their host.

As Obnar waved his hands about explaining something to Alana, Philip gazed at him and felt there was something out of place. Without turning his head and as if he knew Philip was watching, their eyes sharply met.

"Come, I want to show you where you'll be resting for the evening. Tomorrow is a long day."

He led them up a stone stairwell to their five individual sleeping quarters. The magnificently polished stone balustrade felt cold under Philip's hand.

Alana's eyes searched for the waiter still lingering below. On the wall all the way to the top, well-fastened, eye-height poignant paintings depicting strife and destruction hung. Ramaan paused. One of them caught Philip's attention. Obnar tapped him on the shoulder.

"Do you like it?"

"No! My God, it's horrible, not in the least." Philip couldn't believe what he'd just heard and exchanged glances.

"You know," said Obnar, "it's fascinating how you can have a painting of a Blagorian eating someone on the wall. Your taste in paintings is just as good as your taste in words!"

Philip and Ramaan looked sternly at Obnar's grin before continuing upwards to the landing.

Their rooms were archaic and pretty. A king-sized wooden four-poster bed placed over a shaggy carpet largely ornamented the centre, while two wall-sized wooden cupboards hugged each side. A large iron chandelier affixed to the ceiling with dangling crystalline paraphernalia illuminated the room. Behind the bed, a black wooden-framed mirror stared back at the onlooker.

"Oh, one last thing," said Obnar. "If you want to leave the premises at night, it is permitted, but you'll need special permission slips when you return. The guards around here ask a lot of questions at night. Here are your authorization cards, if you need them." Obnar turned and made his way for the steps.

They prepared their rooms and met shortly afterwards in the hallway. Their escape into the ten-hour night of Rindor was most exhilarating. Young thoughts crept in and they loved it.

"Where shall we go first?"

18. Enchantment

The evening was warm. Humidity here didn't stand a chance. In fact, it felt like one of many summer evenings Philip enjoyed in Kenya looking at Kilimanjaro in the distance. There he found he could forget the qualms and hiccups of the space academy and the suffering he endured after his parents' accident.

Here it was easy for Philip to forget where he was. Just looking around made him feel at home. All the attention and the fuss of being noticed and the looks people exuded as they walked past reminded him of where he really was. It even helped to sooth the soreness of losing Mike. Baygorn and Lexia greeted many of them by raising their clenched left hand to their nose. Obnar had explained the gesture in detail. The curiosity of the Shelot equalled the crew's.

The cultural difference reminded Philip of the first time he went to South Africa. They were the same, yet they weren't. Philip had a sense that something was up. Was it their attire maybe, their voices as they spoke; was it the way they walked?

They are just being inquisitive, thought Philip. They had heard about the landing, and here they were awaiting the arrival with anticipation lining the streets like the Tour de France. Importance returned to their souls. The Shelot women smiled and giggled as they neared. They were obviously eager to find out what makes these travellers tick. Regulation, however, prevented the crew from doing this kind of research. Although thinking about it, five single, completely able people on an alien planet does tend to raise the eyebrows a bit. Farther down the street, a group of Shelots ushered them into their home. The crew looked at one another and curiously followed them in.

The house was semi-detached and very neatly decorated. Around a table, three women and two men sat with bottles and glasses. They raised them in a jolly manner. Two women sat on the floor and got up the moment they entered.

"Would you like some of our wine?" one of them said. Her English was perfect.

"Best thing we've heard all day. What is it?" The wine colour was a dark green like freshly squeezed chlorophyll.

"Estoril Green, but, if you prefer the Purple or the Black, we have all three."

"No, no, Green is fine, thanks," said Alana, fascinated by the colour.

The woman placed five glasses on the table and poured the liquid. Eyes drilled into them, they could feel it. Curious people peeked through the windows from the outside to see what was going on. Occasionally Philip heard a scrape along the glass to get their attention.

They went into a living room and sat down on sofas. One of the men moved forward and asked them about their home planet and where they came from. As they intently sat there listening and asking more questions, Philip and the others drank more wine. This time it was the Black.

Some laughing came from the street. Ramaan was doing the explaining and for the first time, Philip heard him stumble. A woman moved closer with another bottle. Baygorn took it out of her hands.

"Would you like to try some of our Shelovin?" It was yellow and from where Philip was sitting, it had a nasty, strong appearance. Feeling the effects, Baygorn was also beginning to drift into the nether. The three women were ravishingly dressed in a fine semi-transparent material. They wore a most adorable perfume, making the pores of Philip's nose stand up and salute. Every now and then, he caught a glimpse of a shaven area and his tongue did a leap. He did not know if it was his imagination or the wine. Maybe it was both.

Alana seemed particularly excited as one of the male figures assumed a sybaritic reclining pose and reached to serve her more Shelovin. He was a handsome man. Philip estimated him to be thirty. He showed interest in Alana. The evidence was clearly visible, as bathrobes do not come with bulges on the front. Before temptation could get its irreversible grasp on them, Philip stood up and said it was time to leave.

Alana was as close to hitting him as she ever was. "Now wait just a minute!" Alana jumped up. "What's all this? What do you mean, Philip?" Her tone was harsh.

"Alana, you know the regulations, no physical contact with other races, under no circumstances, remember?" Philip grabbed Alana by the shoulder.

"Yes, we're fully aware of the regulations, but no one has to know about this. We haven't had any physical contact for more than six years!"

"You think I don't know that? However, I was there when you signed the celibacy contract at headquarters. I saw all of you sign the contract. I was witness. Come on, pull yourself together. It's time to go."

Lexia and Ramaan superciliously raised from their comfortable positions and returned a brief look to their hosts. The Shelotian women sighed in disbelief. Baygorn, too, had begun to feel the effects of the Shelovin.

Signing the contract at the time seemed like a good idea. It was the only way for them to get into space; if only they hadn't. Now they thought about hacking their loyalty with a scalpel. With their blood, they had signed the celibacy contract stating that each one of them would entirely respect their profession down to the last letter.

It had worked well, and none of them had ever had any problem regarding this fact. But as all contracts do, it went much further. Clause 37b read: "No physical contact with any form of life other than your own." Clause 37c read: "The ethical status of the human shall be upheld, and will be obeyed and respected at all times."

Outside the house, quiet and infuriated, they stared upwards into the night. The force fields intertwined, while callous yellow fingers slowly waved through the distant, pulsating phosphorescence.

It was a warning to possible intruders while keeping the immense heat from Mintaka at bay. Returning their attention to Rindor, Shelots were on every street, in every alley, even peering through windows, smiling or waving. Braver ones approached them and shook hands just to find out what they felt like. One of the female workers walked to Baygorn, stuck her nose on his neck behind the ear and sniffed, making his hairs stand up. The reception was adorable and they loved it.

Early the next morning, there was a knock at the door as Philip was brushing his teeth. "Come in, it's open."

Obnar strolled into the room with his hand outstretched. "Hope you slept well. I just wish to say that you are probably the most honourable person I've met in my years. Last night without you knowing, we were watching you. We are tremendously grateful for your loyalty to both your kind and ours. Come, I've something to show you."

"Let me clean up first, I'll see you downstairs in ten minutes." Philip continued getting ready after Obnar left. Putting a brush into a cup mounted on the wall, he scanned the bathroom for toilet paper, noticing there was none. *Odd*, he thought. A red light flashed on the wall where there should typically be a toilet roll. It seemed to flash quicker the nearer he got. Philip lowered his trousers, finished the normalities of nature and wondered what the button was for. Apart from perfumes on a shelf, it was the only appropriate wonder in sight, so it could have only been what he thought it to be. He pressed it.

Flicker-flicker-flicker.

Something behind the wall whirred, and then a long, rotating brush arm filled with a bubbly violet-smelling soap appeared from the side of the lavatory. It spun with ever-increasing speed as it approached his rear section. He felt paralysed. The plastic limb pulsated and throbbed. It seemed almost alive, excited, as the revolving brush rubbed and washed. Philip almost jumped up vertically. A squirt of water and drying fan completed the work.

Downstairs the others were grinning. Ramaan whispered, "Used the crapper yet?" They laughed loudly and the others came over, with the exception of Alana, who didn't say a word.

"Good morning." Obnar was in a jovial mood. "I thought you might be interested in seeing our city's power source."

"We've already discussed it. We are curious, though," replied Philip as Obnar's pointing hand led them towards an awaiting vehicle. The driver was stubbing a cigarette and immediately opened the doors as they neared.

Mintaka had begun to rise above the horizon, and the fresh morning air had already reached 30 degrees. They immediately drove off in an easterly direction. Minutes later, they reached a highway. Vehicles of all shapes and sizes zipped past in every direction. A little farther down, the driver increased speed to two hundred kilometres per hour until he reached a clump of trees hiding a turn-off sign, where the driver slowed and turned left.

Far off, two tiny figures were ploughing a field near a wooden cabin. To their right, the sheer side of a cliff dropped off two or three hundred metres, while to their left, a towering wall of red sandstone almost touched the clouds. In front of them and away on the horizon, two large triangular buildings dominated the middle of a field. The driver turned down another road and drove directly towards them. He parked alongside a metallic ladder.

"We're here," said Obnar, beckoning them to get out. Obnar walked towards the side of the building.

"Surrounding Rindor are eighty energy accumulators like this one. They store the power coming directly from Mintaka and re-use it. We call them Stonium Cells. The building over there on the horizon is the energy reflector. I'll show you one later." They followed his hand. Obnar continued, "It continually points upwards and generates the steady green force field surrounding the planet. Alongside each accumulator and energy reflector are two backup Stonium Cells. If the shield or part of the shield goes inoperative for just a second, Mintaka would fry the surface of Rindor with temperatures of 200 degrees. Mintaka's radiation is perpetual, with sufficient power for our force shield and the city. To put it into technical language, the accumulators store seventy trillion watts per second. We know the energy from the star will never diminish, so our force field will always be operational. We have learnt to control it from down here in every way. As you can see, our star is of immense importance to us."

"Well, we can also see your star from Earth. It is one of the principal stars in the constellation of Orion. Our astronomers have been studying it for centuries." Philip told him about the probe Earth sent in 2080 to study their solar system and discover new planetary systems. "It was the information received by the probe that caused us to come out here."

Obnar listened attentively and lowered his head. "Here we have the means to synthetically produce almost any material. As for our medical needs, we are the best equipped in the galaxy. Our life expectancy is on average two hundred years."

"What about a governing body? Do you have a president or prime minister?" asked Ramaan.

"No, our political structure is simpler than that. Instead of one person governing, the responsibilities are broken into four categories. Our exterior governor controls all external relations to Rindor, everything from the shield outwards. He and his ambassadors constantly monitor alien transmissions emanating from other systems. That is, of course, how I knew about your captain, Mike Branigan. They also send exploratory teams to other planets, much like the reason you are here.

"The Defence Governor maintains and assures that the molecular force field, accumulators, and defence mechanisms are always functional. You'll see them test-firing the defence beams twice a day at set times. The Defence Governor, with his nine hundred maintenance crews, is always on full alert and can act at any time.

"The Internal Governor watches over the well-being and health of the people here, giving them whatever they require. He is in charge of medical, agricultural, social welfare, housing, and entertainment.

"The Works and Education Governor, that's me, assigns the proper task to the proper Shelot and educates them in the universal Shelot way that has been with us for thousands of years. The people here work hard for their good life," he added. "It's not always a bed of roses, we know this, but everyone here is well trained and deserves the best. Between us all, we see to it that they get it. The population on Rindor is currently 800 million. Money does not exist; we exchange commodities for labour. Labour is measured in digits. As the digits increase, so does one's capabilities."

"Has anyone or anything ever tried attacking your installation in the past?" asked Philip.

"On various occasions the Peblinus or the Platnios have tried to get through the barrier. Our defence mechanism is superb, it obliterates them easily. As you know, energy reflectors are scattered all over Rindor."

"Any chance we can see one from a little closer? You did say you'd show us."

"It will be my pleasure," replied Obnar with a smile, beckoning once more to the vehicle.

From a distance, the finger-shaped obelisk didn't seem so spectacular. From closer inspection, it filled the windscreen.

"It must be four hundred metres at least." Ramaan gaped upwards. A yellow light flashed on the extreme end. Obnar explained that the yellow light was the communication link between towers. Three burly-looking guards hung around outside. Obnar waved them to one side and pressed a control panel, opening a door. The lift took them to the tenth floor, where an enormous panel flickered with all assortments of electronic life. The operating personnel trembled at the sight of Obnar, so they nervously fumbled to one side when he entered.

"From here we control the intensity and the direction of the therelium beam." Obnar walked to the control panel and started fiddling with the two keyboards. Sequencing information appeared on one of the monitors. "All energy reflector control towers are the same."

Ramaan raised an ear. "Therelium: The Magnopods described its uses in great detail in the box they left us."

"I know, you've also got a small block of it on your ship beyond the shield. Like I told you, use your knowledge well."

During their trip from the hotel, Obnar told them he was going to take them to the agricultural section in the afternoon to see their breathtakingly beautiful gardens.

At about 12:00, they stopped in front of a cafeteria close to the plantation. Their lunch was a curious fishy bean mixture. Lexia stopped as two small, scrumptious-looking pieces of broiled fish, delicately sitting on a bed of variegated leaves, were placed upon the table. She inhaled and pulled it closer. Accompanying it was a yucky peach-tasting fruit juice. Baygorn left most of his.

Obnar stood up. "Is everyone ready to go to the plantation?"

Lexia stood beside him. "Where do your fish come from?"

"There's an artificial lake in Argowan three hundred kilometres from here: 20,000 breeding tanks. It's a bit of a rough journey, but if you want, we can take a drive over there to see it. When we're done at the plantations, I want to show you our zoo." They wondered what he might have stashed away in there. An alien zoo sounded most intriguing.

As the vehicle sped away, Obnar continued. "Sixty thousand species from all over the galaxy, all neatly placed in their little dens and cells. It is quite comfy, but of course some of them aren't so little anymore." A couple of minutes later, they arrived at the gates of the plantation.

On their right, through a fence, hundreds of people were working in a field full of bushes and trees lined up like soldiers. It stretched for miles. From their proximity, Baygorn pointed out apple trees, grapevines and what Baygorn thought was an olive tree. They turned their attention to the left towards a drab-looking office block and security department. The gates opened and they moved through them.

Sitting next to the driver, Obnar's excited voice changed in pitch a bit, and his hands began pointing at two gigantic warehouse buildings.

"The one on the left is sifting and storage. The other is dedicated to research and development on the upper floors. The lower level is the disinfestations department." The gates closed and Obnar's excitement continued.

"You know, we've had tremendous problems with the seed tick lately. Some of our workers have fallen ill, and the disinfestations division has been working overtime, eliminating unwanted insects and parasites. It's a never-ending process. We have ninety different cultivatable areas, each producing a species of plant. Of course each area comes complete with its species of parasite, so we have to make sure it is thoroughly cleaned before someone stuffs it in their mouth."

The moment the vehicle came to a standstill in the parking area, Obnar got out and led them towards a line of frail shrubs. "The soup you ate last night comes from this zamoran bush." Baygorn broke off a branch and sniffed it.

"Some of our plants and foliage you might be familiar with."

Obnar gave them a detailed layout of the agricultural estate. In every direction, workers picked and packed. Some of them stopped awhile and stared at them with curiosity, just as they, in turn, wondered about them. In a side area, Obnar told them they were growing potatoes. A basket full of onions lay on a table.

"And this?" Philip picked it up and sniffed it.

"Antilovo," said Obnar, "it's very spicy and adds flavour to almost anything."

"Smells a bit like dill." Philip put it back and Obnar began to explain the research they were doing.

"We've been studying these plants for centuries; some of them we use for medicinal purposes. We have made so much progress with integrating the formulas into our medicine that hardly anyone falls ill. Before I forget, tomorrow I want to show you our medical facilities. You'll be surprised at what we can do."

"Coming from you, nothing will surprise us."

"Why, thank you, Philip."

Fascinated, on the ground floor they watched the process of disinfestation. An ultra-fast blue laser scanned each seed flowing off the moving bed towards the enhancer.

"This terminal is continuously scanning for parasites and deformed ovules. If it does come across an over-adventurous bug or deformity, the laser installed above the conveyor belt destroys it. The healthy seeds then continue on their journey to the washer and finally reach the enhancer, where they are sprayed for storage."

They followed him to the storage. The noise was deafening.

"The enhancer enshrouds the millions of seeds with a chemical product we call Sporotin. As they bob about after having survived the laser scan and washer, we spray them as they come off the belt before going towards their final destination for packing and distribution points after drying. We manufacture the Sporotin in the research section. It creates twenty years of shelf life without losing either texture or flavour. We like to keep our labour here as manual as possible, giving opportunities to the Shelots for continued work."

Obnar was shouting, so they went back outside. "That's much better. Let's go and see the zoo. It's a lot quieter there."

Agreeing, they set off in the direction of Mintaka as a hillside swallowed its monstrous orb. They thrust forward, reaching a shadow of a vertical cliff, which bathed the interior of the vehicle in a red reflective hue. To the left, the un-barricaded road disappeared, becoming a vertical scary drop hundreds of metres to certain doom. Outside their red cage, the other hillsides had transformed themselves into a golden-brown tinge, revealing an eerie, uninviting shimmer. The afternoon air was hot and cloudless.

Obnar reached into a side compartment and produced seven pairs of sun-filters. "Put these on; you'll need them for the midday glare. Without it you'll toast your eyes." They resembled two giant fly eyes almost completely covering the face. The driver steered towards another towering cliff offering its shadow. Philip noticed the road was gently beginning to decline. They were heading towards a densely forested valley. They turned into a side road and passed fields where workers with machines were digging. The driver took another side road, and they began spiralling cautiously towards the floor of the valley.

Close to the basin, sparse, beautifying patches of flaming brush lit up the embankments. Bright yellow flowers dangled at frail stem ends. Curving and eventually reaching the basin floor, the air became cool, so the driver flicked on a heating device. There in the distance, four buildings took charge of the horizon. Four uniquely different architectural representations were built for a large variety of life.

"There it is! Wonderful, isn't it? What do you think?" Obnar was excited.

The road came to an abrupt end at a fence that surrounded the entire zoo. A blinking orange-eyed, red skull-and-crossbones above the entrance certainly attracted everyone's attention. Signposts dotted the entrance in a variety of languages.

Positively, no food allowed and no drinking on the premises.
Food and drinks provided in certain areas under observation.
No photographic equipment allowed.
Video recordings of the animals are available from Reception.
You do NOT watch us. WE watch you.
Under NO circumstances feed the animals—RISK OF DEATH.

As off-putting as it all seemed, they had in front of them the beginning of a bizarre and most intriguing collection of land and sea animals from all over the galaxy.

Obnar opened the gate and they followed him. Nearing the installation at the end of the pathway, there was another sign: "Welcome to our cosmic pride."

The path then split into four sections, with each heading towards its particular building. Detailed grass-embedded maps also described what lurked inside each installation.

Obnar stared at the map and they followed his pointing hand to a small square, neatly tucked in between two of the four installations. "That's the lab where I reconstruct universal evolution. I often come here when I have free time."

Walking down the first path, the augmenting sounds of animals and bird chirpings drifted through the air and reminded Baygorn of a jungle in Borneo on a hot summer's day. It was a mixture of the strangest and certainly the most bizarre cries they had ever heard. A lot of them were unrecognisable.

The path Obnar had beckoned them to take was to the small and medium land animal and insect section. Excitement surged through their bodies as they approached the complex.

Obnar's hand began bobbing about again. "The flying species are over there." It was a four-storey, wire mesh-enshrouded cage much like a lampshade.

"One of our finest flying species that we captured on Capella-F managed to escape three years ago. The thing ate through the wall of its cell and flew off, headed directly for the city, and killed fifty-seven people in one afternoon. It was a real tragedy. The cage you see was donated and installed shortly afterwards by the people of the city to prevent any further incidents. It was the most poisonous specimen in our collection, and it was a shame to put it down."

Obnar pointed in the other direction. The aquatic building was a transparent multi-floored aquarium. From where they were standing, they could see dozens of marine species were swimming about in their transparent homes. Exhilarated, they felt the urgency to see all of it.

"Larger land animals are housed over there." Once more, they followed him. Continuing their walk, a beastly looking Platnios lurched towards them from behind its cage. It made a crash as tentacle met metal. Obnar came between the cage and Philip. "Don't worry. You are quite safe. Each cage has been double-reinforced, calculating the maximum strength of each species."

Obnar turned and faced the Platnios. "This is what I fear might have killed your Captain Branigan in the Alnilam system. They have evolved into a perfect killing machine. This specimen we encountered last month on one of our routine inspections on Telus-Four. We were lucky to find it alone."

They edged past and went in. It was similar to a three-floored mini-coliseum. Attendants roamed everywhere. The centre section, subdivided into a variety of crawling animals, buzzed with observers. A guide, without recognising Obnar, walked up and offered his services. Obnar brushed him to one side and walked towards a stairwell and elevator connecting each floor. Security was tight, with two armed guards around the entrance to the lift. Another two roamed the stairs, and on closer inspection, Philip noticed they were mingling everywhere.

Potentially dangerous creatures were on the move in the zoo, and though none so far had shown active hostility, a good guide would take no chances. As an extra safeguard, Ramaan noticed there was always an observer up on the higher levels watching with a scope. From this vantage point, the whole interior of the zoo could be easily watched over, and customers could be kept under regular observation. In this way, it was hoped to eliminate any possibility of danger.

They walked up the stairs to the first floor. "You know, Telus-Two has some of the strangest forms of life; well, certainly the most diverse in the galaxy. Here is a talking snake named by the locals, a snarhan. It was a real discovery. Over millions of years, they have evolved in their hunting skills and abilities so much that they can talk you to sleep before they kill you."

"Talking snakes that kill? Obnar, you're joking!" Ramaan laughed.

"On the contrary, they seem so sweet and harmless. Just look at those cute eyes and those eyelashes. Snarhan squiggle up by your side all nice and friendly and begin conversing with you in a soft tone of voice. Once you've fallen asleep, they expand themselves into a giant killing mechanism and eat you alive." They looked at the snakes worming their three-metre frames past the glass. Watching, watching.

Obnar grew excited. "This is the spider section." He pointed to various aquariums with name tags stuck on them.

Lexia looked around, glancing only for a moment at each of the bizarre creatures staring at her. Then she leaned her head back and noticed the green dome of a ceiling far above her head. Some kind of thin, flexible ribbing could be seen in isolated spots, but it was covered over by a thick green canopy on the outside.

"The ceiling is mostly vines and similar plants, along with the harmless indigenous insect life that harvest the useful fruits and flowers," Lexia heard Obnar say beside her. "It is a complete living ecosystem that has the additional advantage of being an excellent covering for the building and keeping us cool in here."

Baygorn edged nearer. "What in God's name is a Romalov stick spider?" His befuddled look accompanied his hand running through his thick hair. The spider moved about in its habitat and seemed to sense that Baygorn was near. It jumped onto the glass. Baygorn retreated a bit.

Obnar gave a smile and watched Baygorn's reaction.

"It's a spider that jumps on the back of its prey and sticks its large fangs into skin, if it can find any. If it's successful, the spider immediately proceeds to inject venom to render the victim's nervous system useless. This process continues while it sucks its victim dry. These spiders come from the planet Romalov in the Vega system. This is but one of two hundred specimens of spider. Of course, they are not all as deadly as this example here."

Obnar continued to unravel the strange wonders for them. In mid-afternoon they entered the second building. At the entrance in a cage, a Peblinus sat chewing his nails and glancing at the ceiling.

"What the dickens is this doing here?" Philip asked angrily. "This is no animal, it is humanoid!" Obnar told Philip the Peblinus attacked some of his crew while they were looking for a specimen of beetle on Ganus.

"Don't worry, we look after him well. He has been with us now for more than ten years." The Peblinus wasn't bothered with their presence.

Later that afternoon they continued to study all forms of life in the buildings, from the most normal to the most bizarre and abnormal. Obnar answered their questions with enthusiasm.

Lexia moved closer. "Obnar, what can you tell us about the Gorinos? Who are they, and where do they come from?"

Obnar's face soured and the smile disappeared. "Where'd you hear that name from?"

Obnar's stabbing remark didn't affect Lexia. She moved closer. "On a couple of planets in the system. Why the fuss?"

Obnar steered his head away from Lexia, sighed and looked down. "Problematic, that's what they are." His head came up again and he looked in Philip's direction. "It's been that way for as long as I can remember. They tap our radio transmissions. They introduce viruses into our operating systems. They frequently bombard our defences with something new every time. Once they managed to disable part of the shield, and it killed dozens of people. Don't you see, they are worse than the Platnios. Don't mention that name again!"

Lexia took a step back and apologised, realising she'd touched a nerve.

Alana moved closer to Lexia. "Don't worry," Alana said, "probably just needs his bed. It's late in the afternoon. Anyway, I'm sick and bloody tired of spiders and snakes." She looked at Philip with a grin.

"Still friends?" asked Philip.

"Of course, you silly."

Philip returned a smile.

✧✧✧

On that note, they returned to the central palace, parked the vehicle, and enjoyed the late afternoon temperature before for dinner. A scrumptious aroma drifted through the front entrance.

They were ushered into the dining room. Before sitting, Obnar asked Philip if he would reconsider leaving tomorrow without their weaponry schematics. Philip looked at him and sensed fear in his words. *What was his problem?*

Obnar averted eye contact.

"Obnar, it's our duty and responsibility, and might I add, intention, to leave tomorrow with the data. You only have to know that our purposes are peaceful. You have my word."

Agitation filled Obnar's face despite Philip's response. *The mind is a labyrinth of unanswerable nightmares*, thought Philip.

As they finally sat down at the dinner table, Obnar asked a most absurd question. "Does anyone remember earlier in the zoo two cells farther down from the Peblinus? There was an open cubicle."

They sat there, blankly looking at each other, trying to visualise the vacant booth. They had all seen so much that day, that no one was able to recall it.

"No," was Ramaan's simple reply.

Obnar placed his hands on his hips. "I have a cubicle reserved for a human example for my study purposes. I will make sure he or she receives the best treatment. It will be just like good old home." He paused a bit, watching their reactions as a cat observes a bird. "And of course," he paused again, "your friends can visit whenever they please." They looked at each other. There was a brief silence in the dining room.

Ramaan bit his lip. He thought it might have been a bad joke. "Will you provide the transport for us to come and visit from Earth?"

Before Obnar had time to reply, Ramaan saw his intention and interrupted his parting lips with a stern face. "Now you listen here, it's not in our way to lock up human beings in cages where we come from, or Peblinus for that matter!"

"I have studied your culture," Obnar said quickly. "But may I remind you? This isn't Earth." Another minute of silence gripped the dining table.

Ramaan, now defeated, sat down, so Alana, wearing a smirk, stood up in his place. "Can we leave the cage during the night and return in the morning? I could not help but notice many places of relaxation and enjoyment here. I'd hate to miss it all."

Obnar actually thought she meant what she asked. Once more, before he had time to answer, Alana's smirk changed to a loud laugh.

Obnar, now feeling awkward and uncomfortable, changed his tone. "Well! I don't think the whole night would be possible. We could let you out for say, two hours, but it would have to be under the supervision of one of our guards."

By this time, both Alana and Ramaan erupted with laughter. Philip, too, was at the point of exploding when suddenly, Obnar banged his fist on the table top. Plates fell to the floor and broke.

"Enough!" he shouted. "Enough of this pathetic human behaviour. My choice has been made. The rest of you are to leave immediately and return to your antiquated starship beyond the barrier."

Ramaan got up out of his chair. Philip stopped him. "Look, Obnar, we're not going to leave without one of our companions, just as we will not leave without the data we have collected on our journey. You know full well we will be back for both. We will use force against you if you are persistent. In the beginning, you demonstrated devotion, now it's betrayal! All the data you think we have has already been sent to Terron. It was sent three days ago."

As Philip spoke, Obnar gave him an irritating smile. His glimmering, protruding chalk-white teeth lined a vacant grin. "Hey, I was only joking. I love to see the reactions of different species. I find you so interesting." With a thinned atmosphere lingering, the waiters moved forward and continued to put food on the table.

"I have a great admiration for your kind and your method of thinking."

Unconvinced, they finished their meal and retired alone without escort to their rooms.

"Do you think he meant it?" asked Baygorn, looking troubled towards Alana. Lexia added, "I examined him while he was making his declaration. I felt this deep hatred he has for us. It was something between fear and jealousy. On the other hand, it is possible that he has some plan up his sleeve. But not to worry, we're leaving tomorrow morning, so let's just forget the whole thing."

19. Abduction

The next morning, Ramaan and Philip got up early to start packing when suddenly it came to Philip's attention that Lexia wasn't amongst them. "Ramaan, one moment. Where's Lexia?"

Ramaan ran into Baygorn's room to wake him. Alana, half-dressed, heard the commotion and quickly opened her door.

Pulling both hands to chin height, Baygorn cracked his knuckles. "I'll rip his goddamn head off!"

They ran downstairs, only to find their friend-turned-traitor wasn't waiting for them as usual. A lanky sub-officer lingered in his place.

The officer shakily handed over a note with Philip's name scribbled on it. Philip couldn't help but notice young, agile veins full of fear. Sharing the note with the rest, they read its short contents: I will meet with you at 10:00 outside the zoo entrance.

Philip blankly looked at the others as dire thoughts swirled around their brains. Obnar's proposal was born. Philip had to come up with a plan against this absurd, cruel, and obviously insane person. But their armaments were in the pod still under guard, belligerently shimmering behind the blue force field. Guard faces turned and smirked as they entered the first impression of dawn.

"What about the Gorinos?" asked Alana. "You all saw the expression on Obnar's face when Lexia mentioned them. How could we summon them? It would appear we are quite helpless. Our comm gear's in the pod next to the weapons. I'm certainly not going to try and get past those guards. Look at the size of them!"

"Not entirely true," Philip said, placing his head between his hands. "On Retolox, the Magnopod told me if I needed help, all I had to do was to concentrate and think of them, from anywhere and at anytime, by placing my head between my hands."

Ramaan interrupted. "Didn't Obnar say he was friends with the Magnopod?"

"Yes, but I bet he lied about that, too. Just think of us, they said. I know if I can reach them, they'll come. Maybe they will send word to the Gorinos."

They arrived at the zoo early. A couple of minutes later, a guard walked towards them.

Baygorn moved forward. "Where is she? What've you done with her?"

"Come with me, please. Obnar awaits your arrival in the mammalian building."

Alana grumbled aloud. "In the mammalian building. This is getting better." She felt an urge to run over and smash his face against a rock. She stopped herself.

Silent and abiding, they made their way following the guard towards a square plaza. The shadow of morning fell across a group of people. The aromatic, clean drift of a recent daybreak didn't abate their rage.

Obnar drew nearer. Security guards surrounded him, protecting him. Obnar knew Philip and the rest were weaponless, so he intimidated them with their firearms by waving a mere five metres away.

"Don't worry, humans. She's quite safe with us. She's safer with me than she ever was with you."

"So I see. You damn coward. Give her back this instant!" shouted Ramaan, directing his rage towards the guards as well.

"No reason for concern. No harm will come to her, I promise. I will see to it personally."

Phillip walked closer. "You will not treat us this way. We are not animals. We didn't come all this way for you to hold one of us prisoner. You bloody well give her back right now, you insincere—" Philip stopped himself. "If she's not here, standing in front of us in ten seconds—"

"Ten seconds, or what? You stupid human!" The words came out of his mouth with spit. Obnar felt safe and superior behind his armed barrier.

Philip's thoughts returned to Shar.

"You offer such idle intimidation. Don't you dare threaten me! I will not listen to anything you have to say. I am tired of your worthless human words. I have endured more of you than I have expected. I only wanted a sample to study. Now I have it! You are excess baggage. Do I make myself clear? Excess baggage, and I want you off Rindor as soon as possible!"

As Obnar flicked a finger, Philip thought drastically of Lexia's safety and moved forward. One of the guards raised the weapon.

Philip thought quickly. "Obnar, if you think we can only communicate with radio devices, you are mistaken. I have already spoken with someone. That someone I am sure is listening to this conversation. With him, I don't need transmitters; I only have to think about him."

"And who might that be?"

Philip loved watching Obnar's internal suffering with his verbal payback. "The Gorinos already know about our dilemma."

Obnar's face twinged at hearing the word. All of them saw it. They noticed the two-second lapse he took to reply.

"Gha, you can't fool me. You can't call anyone from down here. You are in-com-mun-i-ca-do!"

"Not true," said Philip. "When we left the Magnopod lair on Retolox, he told me they are in our debt. If one day we would ever need their help, from anywhere, all I had to do was to think of him, concentrate on him."

"You wouldn't dare. You stupid human. You wouldn't dare!" he shouted, hands frantically waving in the air. Obnar's Mr Hyde-self erupted forth, outwards, in a burst of frenzy. He convulsed. "I've waited long for this sample: so many years! Her intelligence is astounding." He edged closer. Two guards followed.

"Did you know she's a migwim?"

"What the hell are you talking about?" grunted Ramaan.

"She has the ability to teleport simultaneous, multiple thought patterns in five different dimensions! We call them migwims. She doesn't know it yet. I am going to exercise and focus her intellect. She can control her alpheta waves to such an extent; it is like nothing I have ever seen. People like Lexia are scarce, and I was secretly observing her when you arrived." Obnar returned to his Dr Jekyll, ecstatic self.

"Her intellectual quotient far outweighs yours or mine. Her mental capacity is unlimited. She's such a fascinating specimen that I have to keep her, so just let things be as they're supposed to be," said Obnar, retracting himself backward.

Alana raised a hand, hitting the air. "She's not a specimen, you damn clown. She's a human being, a scientist, migwim or not! Desist, stop. You'll be sorry. We're not going to stand here and let you take one of us hostage by pretending she's a specimen for your bloody zoo like an animal!"

Initiating deep concentration as the Magnopod had shown him, once again, Philip placed his head between his hands.

Obnar brushed him to one side. "If you don't behave, I will put you all alongside your companion, but I only need her. The four of you are wasted space!" Obnar backed off with his security guards still pointing their trembling firearms with untrue aim. Inconsistent expressions looked the other way as if they knew something. Something was definitely out of place. Defeated, Philip and his crew returned to their rooms in the head palace and waited. They felt powerless and meaningless.

Day became night. Philip was still painstakingly concentrating his thoughts on his friends. "I don't think this is working!"

Ramaan's haggard face reflected his frustration. "Patience, Philip, these things need time. I'm sure the Magnopod got your message the moment you began with deep concentration. Surely there must be something else we can do to save Lexia while we wait."

"What about the other officers?" asked Baygorn.

"They could convince Obnar to stop what he was doing. Speaking of which, has anyone seen the other officers? Where are they?" No one knew the answer. Frustrated, Baygorn continued, "Then what about the townsfolk? Investigate a bit; you know, create a bit of unrest. It's another option. Let's knock on doors and get some answers."

Baygorn was bursting with abhorrence as he scuttled into the hot Rindor night. They needed help and needed it fast.

Their presence aroused those around them, and as before, the night people approached in search of adventure and pleasure. One came over.

Philip put his hands on her shoulders. "Our companion is being held captive in the zoo."

The charming face turned to concern.

"We need your help!"

"We know how you feel," the woman said. "We have had one of ours held captive there for many years. We are unable to set her free. This whole planet is one big zoo; I suppose Obnar didn't show you the others."

"What others?"

A Shelotian woman gave a shrill laugh. "I suppose he only showed you the one specimen. He would. Poor blighter has had so many experiments done on him, there's not much left. The poor brainless thing can't even think anymore. He just sits there staring at the ceiling, biting his nails."

Ramaan and Baygorn exchanged glances.

"Obnar's got a hidden laboratory behind the Peblinus; a door he calls his evolution lab. Forty specimens like you and I are caged where he frequently runs his sick experiments."

"God, we had no idea."

"I thought so. What I'm saying is, once you are here, there's no escape—you can't get away. The Bods have been captive for more than a hundred years. Obnar is really a Peblinus officer in disguise. We have been slaves to him ever since he arrived."

"And the other officers he told us about?"

"What are you talking about? There are no other officers here on Rindor, only Obnar. He's mad, but we cannot tell him to his face. He would have us exterminated like the valiant souls who have tried before."

"Then who are the Shelots?" asked Philip.

"No such thing. It's an invented name he fabricated to lure innocent victims like you into his domain."

Philip asked her if she would be able to survive without Obnar. She laughed again. "Don't even try it; you won't get close to him now."

"I am not talking about us," said Philip. "What if the Gorinos found out that a Peblinus gone mad was down here and had taken over the planet? You never know, they might come even quicker."

"The Gorinos, now that's a name I haven't heard in a while. They were the ones who built this place 10,000 years ago. When

Obnar showed up, he somehow managed to convert all this into his personal paradise and kept them out. Since then, of course, the Gorinos have tried to reclaim it, but he continues destroying them with the defence turrets."

"At least we know why he almost had a nervous breakdown when we mentioned them. Then we'll have to disable that laser turret first; it'll make it easier for the Gorinos. I only know of the one turret in this sector. Those three security guards are probably still there."

"Oh don't worry about them, they're Bod like us. Most of the workers here are Bod."

"Thank you very much, you've been a great help."

They ran to a vehicle and drove off to the defence turret they had visited previously. Philip was at best only reasonable at linguistics and the Lep dialect. Their primary language that Lexia had taught him would finally come in handy. Outside, the three bored security guards waited for something to do. Philip and Baygorn walked directly up to them.

"Podeno mirata rectil otra arriba matargo?"

Baygorn looked at Philip. "I just asked them if we could take another look around upstairs"

The reply followed immediately afterwards. "Sai, vodeno subor arriba margona negoco."

"What did he say?" asked Baygorn.

"He said yes, we can proceed with our business upstairs."

"Grabanasta" said Philip, which means, "Thank you," in Lep. As the word left his lips, the guards gave a hearty laugh.

Ramaan walked over and whispered in his ear. "Philip, it's Gracimasta; you just told them to go and take a bath."

Philip grinned as they brushed past the still-smirking guards and entered as before. In the control booth, both Ramaan and Baygorn frantically searched for a control switch to the turret. As soon as they found it, Ramaan switched it off, disabling it.

"We have to switch this thing off for good," said Ramaan, now searching for other, more sensitive sections. As he was doing so, Baygorn's right boot discovered two control circuits under the main panel. It lowered, smashing numerous printed circuit boards. Pieces clinked on the floor.

Michael Gilwood

"Good. Now the Gorinos will be able to land without danger." That was when it happened. The biggest and most massive spacecraft ever imagined appeared just outside the barrier.

"That has to be them!" said Philip, tapping Ramaan on the shoulder. "That was damn quick."

Rushing back to ground level, they saw that the three guards had already disappeared. Philip and his crew headed to the main council building with all the speed they could muster. Nearing the city, a slim craft droned almost silently through the barrier and directed itself towards the pod's location. Lower and lower it went, making a slight thump as metal touched down alongside the pod. The security force field had been switched off. Four magnificently dressed men stepped out into the hot, fresh air as Philip pulled up alongside the pod.

"We are the Gorinos," said one of them in a baritone voice, "We received an urgent message from the Magnopod. How may we be of service?"

The four dark-complexioned, athletically built men were armed to the hilt. Their dark armour, complementing and almost completely covering their powerful bodies, enhanced their effect. On each of them, an incessantly moving throat gun irritatingly watched. It persistently aimed at anything that moved. It waited for instructions from the Gorinos as a tiny wire disappeared from it into the Gorinos' headgear. It bobbed from left to right, following any movement as if it possessed a life of its own. Each of them had two rifles quietly placed at their sides.

Philip moved forward and introduced the others. "Thank you for responding to my message," he said. "We come from Earth. We have travelled to this system for exploratory reasons and deactivated one of the laser turrets, enabling your safe landing here. It has come to our attention that this was once your planet. It was stolen from you by the Peblinus, the governing body that now rules here." Philip could not see the face, but he did sense the tension.

"Oh really," stammered another with his rich, clear voice. "Then it was he who fired on us the last time we tried to land here."

"Where is this governing body now?" asked another.

232

"Probably in his headquarters," Philip said, pointing towards a small building. Two Gorinos scorched the ground and disappeared.

"My other dilemma is that our companion is being held captive. We need to set her free before any harm can come to her. Others, too, are being held captive."

"That will be done," said the head Gorinos, looking at the remaining guard. The guard climbed into their landing vehicle and set off, knowing exactly where to go.

"We have been observing your race for thousands of years," said the Gorinos. "We have an immense interest in you. You show great courage. Like the Magnopod, we are in your debt for returning our planet to us. Return with your woman, who is being released. Go in peace, and we will meet up again one day."

Obnar came out of his quarters, dragged by the two Gorinos warriors. "I'll send word, human, to the empire of the Peblinus to rise up against you. Your escape from this part of the galaxy won't be easy!" yelled Obnar.

"Take him away," shouted the head Gorinos. "Get him out of my sight!"

The third Gorinos returned with some of the prisoners.

"I've left the dangerous animals in their cages, for now," he said.

Baygorn ran towards Lexia and gave her a long hug. "Nice to see your face again. Hey, did you know you're a migwim?"

"What are you talking about?" She returned the hug. "It's nice to be out of there. It stank like hell. What's all this talk about a migwim?"

"Something Obnar said, forget it. Are you okay?"

"Of course I am, silly. I knew you would come. Obnar took off one of his fingers to simulate the appearance of the Dontrian. He told me while I was in the cage."

Philip, overhearing what Lexia said, "Of course. How could I have been so ignorant? The Dontrian only have one eye. Obnar had two."

Philip took hold of the Gorinos' hand and shook it firmly. "Thank you, if there is anything we can do to help in the future, it would be an honour."

"What's your name?" Philip asked, looking directly into his visor.

"My name is Gradonga, warrior leader and troop coordinator."

"Gradonga, can you tell us who the Dontrian are?"

"You mean the Slordian people, the four-digit ones. It was rumoured they moved out of this system over 10,000 years ago. We have never seen them. Though, we sometimes see their craft roaming through the depths of space."

Gradonga climbed into his craft with the others. It silently lifted and disappeared through the barrier.

Philip bid farewell to the wonderful inhabitants of Rindor and promised them to return one day.

On-board the *Excelsior*, Alana prepared the engines to take them on their long journey to Terron.

20. The New Earth

It took the *Excelsior* four weeks to reach Terron from Rindor. As it slowly appeared on their viewer, Alana reduced speed to one-tenth of light. Comments echoed throughout the *Excelsior*.

"My God. Man could not have made that in only two and a half years." Nevertheless, he had. As man built, more freighters came; then another, and another. It was an ongoing, rapidly expanding, harmonious human culture, procuring their future and safety in the orbit of this once-dead and barren planet.

From space, undoubtedly, Terron was an Earth city. Its architectural design told any space traveller that humans lived there. Brilliantly illuminated buildings, surface vehicles, abundant life; what more could you want? Alana looked at the diversity of antenna dishes. These were clearly visible, one fore and one aft, as were several omni-antennas and one large directional dish, aimed steadily in the direction of Earth. Alana wondered what instructions were going down the beam.

Terron was a global human signature revealing triumph and success, having surmounted difficulties of the past. There again, man was renowned to conquer difficult times; history was full of it.

Two hundred and forty-seven engineers had dedicated their lives to the making of Terron: the first buildings, the atmosphere regeneration process, the communications towers. All had made their claim and left their mark. By deleting the problems one at a time, Terron was where it was today, a fully functional human space city, every bit as capable as its mother Earth was.

They clambered out of the pod with magnetic boots onto a preliminary undercover landing deck and asked the way to the head office. A screen directed them towards a long hallway. Philip could see that Terron had suffered damages from raids by the Platnios. He recognized the signs. Philip wondered if the Platnios would ever reach Earth, and thought of what that would

Michael Gilwood

look like if they did. Lexia had recovered from her cage incident, although at times Baygorn laughed about it, saying she had become a bit cagey.

After decontamination, Philip walked towards the interrogation offices. Jim, already knowing this, joined him. Eagerness turned to sorrow when he firmly took Philip's hand.

"Philip, oh Philip, it's wonderful to see you all again after such a long time. I'm sorry to have to inform you of this. We lost contact with Mike on Telus-Three a couple of weeks ago."

"Yes, Jim, thanks. We already know. Wonderful to see you, too."

Jim continued, "We fear him dead. While they were making a forced landing, he was shouting. 'They are everywhere.' That was when the radio died. We've not heard a word since. It's possible they were attacked by the same species of plants that attacked us a few weeks ago, some kind of mutated spider plant. You mention them in your report. You call them Platnios."

"Yes sir, that's them."

A well-dressed, white-clad scientist came over and tapped Philip on the shoulder. "Captain Wakefield, we're waiting for you. Can you come with me, please?"

"Go on, Philip, the council members are waiting for you. I'll see you in two days. Good luck in there."

Twelve specialists sitting at a long table waited with unopened files in front of them. Each one, trained in a particular field of science, began to ask detailed questions concerning their findings, while others extracted the information and samples they had collected for study. Never before had they seen such an accumulation of data or such a vast amount of information. The crew spent two full days with blood tests, brain scans, psychiatric examinations, psychological evaluations, and answering questions; giving them all the satisfactory answers that the scientists required.

Jim walked into the examination room after the interrogation. "Philip, why don't the five of you go to the Alnilam system and finish what Mike started? After what you did in the Mintaka system, you are the best candidates for the job. Anyway, he's your best friend. We want you to go down there, beginning on

236

the tenth planet. Find out whatever it was that he was after. Find him if you can, and bring him home."

"Don't worry, sir. If Mike's down there, we'll find him."

Jim handed Philip the information Mike had accumulated before his disappearance.

"It's all we have. The *Renaissance* hasn't been transmitting anything. Mike forgot to switch on the auto-vigilance circuitry."

"I doubt it, Jim. Mike wouldn't have forgotten; he obviously couldn't."

Philip knew him better than anyone else, they had been boyhood friends. All ten of them had trained together, fought together, passed the exam side by side. Indeed, it was a sad moment for them to think of what atrocity had occurred to Mike and his crew.

"So we only have details of the tenth planet?" Philip asked.

"That's right. Before the *Renaissance* stopped communicating, we managed to get patchy data from Telus-Three. After Pleniton, Mike apparently went directly to Telus-Three, which can only mean he found something. The other eight planets remain a mystery. That's your job, I think. Oh, and another thing. The *Renaissance* is still in orbit above Telus-Three. I want you to programme her to return to Terron the moment you arrive."

"Consider it done, sir."

"And remember, be careful. We don't know what's out there, what happened to the crew of the *Renaissance*, or if they're dead. Whatever it is, it's extremely dangerous. And oh, what the hell, take care of yourselves, okay?"

"Don't worry, Commander, we will." Philip shook hands and walked into the corridor. Alana and Baygorn were reviewing the latest maps, charts, and surface specifications that they had received before Mike's disappearance. Alnilam suffered frequent surface eruptions and forced them to upgrade their radiation shields. Not only the *Excelsior*, the pod, the vehicle, and their thermal suits would have to come with an extra layer of padding to ensure their safety.

Looking at the charts, Baygorn said that Alnilam was ninety light-years away. Alana estimated it would take them two months before they could reach the first of its ten gigantic planets.

Ramaan was in another laboratory reviewing data concerning the new radio equipment they were installing on the *Excelsior*. "We call it Encoded Super Digital Transmission, or ESDT." The technical engineer smiled. "If an enemy is listening, ESDT makes it extremely difficult for them to understand any of our little chats we have from time to time. Our radio transmissions travel at speeds greater than that of light. As you know, the "c" in our physics equations became history as the highest velocity attainable fifty years ago."

Ramaan was intrigued. "Babble-blah, sounds perfect. We'll keep you informed on its performance." The technical engineer shook Ramaan's hand and left the laboratory.

During their two-day meeting, Jim gave the *Excelsior* top priority and had more than three hundred scientists tweaking her up. Terron's 55,000 men and women were top-quality, scientifically trained personnel from Earth. More than 200,000 still waited for their transfer papers. It was the dream of every young scientist to become part of this interstellar conurbation floating upon the breast of the planet below. Nights and days fled across the continuously altering face, but in the passageways of Terron, it was always day and darkness never came. There was no moisture in the thin artificial air, and the city knew neither heat nor cold. Terron was a universe in itself. Men had built cities before, but never a city such as this. Some had lasted for centuries, some for millennia, before time had swept away their names. However, Terron alone had challenged the monstrosities, defending itself and all it sheltered against the onslaught of beings, the ravages of decay and the corruption of rust. Since the city had been built, the oceans of Earth were slowly rising, and the deserts had finally encompassed all the globe. The city did not care; Terron would protect the children of its makers, bearing them and their treasures safely down the stream of time. They had forgotten much of their home world, but they did not realise it.

They were as perfectly fitted to their environment as it was to them, for both had been designed together. To them, Terron was all that existed, all that they needed, all that they could imagine. It mattered to them that man had once possessed the stars. Yet sometimes the ancient myths and history rose up to haunt them. They stirred uneasily as they remembered the legends of the past when Terron was young; a mere three years before, before it drew its lifeblood from the commerce of a bustling Cornopea, a planet five hundred kilometres below. They did not wish to bring back the old days, for they were content in their eternal daytime. The glories of history belonged to the past and could remain there, for they remembered how history had met its end. At the thought of the invaders, the chill of space itself came seeping into their bones. Then they would turn once more to the life and warmth of the city, to the long golden age awaiting whose beginning was still fresh, not lost, and whose end was yet more distant.

Other men were dreaming of such an age, but they alone had to achieve it. Still on their home world, they were living in the same cities, walking the same miraculously unchanging streets, while more than one thousand light-years away hope waited.

Terron's artificially generated oxygen originated from a similar generator Philip had installed on the *Excelsior*. The Pseudator, or Pseudonon Generator, invented in 2049 by Professor Claude Hopkins, converted any helium atom into pure oxygen simply by bombarding them with trilium, a radioactive component discovered in 2030.

A field engineer entered the room. "In two years, the atmosphere of Cornopea below us has risen by 3 percent."

Philip told him about the forty cubes that reconverted an entire atmosphere in a matter of hours.

The thin face turned to a smile. "By George! How's that possible?" The word "possible" appeared as small globules of expectorate. "Sorry about that. How do they work?"

"It's a chemical reaction caused by forty metallic elements placed into their order of atomic weight. You should have seen the fireworks display!" Philip's hands waved about, reanimating the fiery yellows and oranges.

"We came with cylindrical samples if you want to see them."

Without finishing, the engineer vanished through the door. Philip saw all this information was good for humankind. Although Terron was an Earth city, there was nothing new about it, except for the information they supplied. At least it would keep them busy for a while. Philip could do nothing more than explain to knowledge-hungry scientists the wonders they'd encountered in the Mintaka system.

As the day to leave approached, engineers and scientists walked with them, explaining the modifications to the *Excelsior*.

"Your protective clothing has also undergone changes," said an engineer. He was a tall, skeletal man. His skewed tie and unbuttoned shirt revealed that he had had little sleep. "I don't know how you could have seen through those old visors. These have 160-degree line of sight. Much better, don't you think?"

At four in the afternoon, their arduous voyage towards Pleniton began. Terron was the only place that had retained the twenty-four-hour barrier as the base line for time. It was synchronised with Earth. Philip and Alana perused the charts.

"Three light-years from Pleniton, our journey will take us through a small asteroid belt known as Riley's Asteroid Belt. Its founder, Lieutenant Bill Riley, who had accompanied Mike on the voyage, was the tactical and navigation officer on the *Renaissance*. He is also presumed dead until our arrival can prove otherwise."

Terron disappeared off the radar. Alana excitedly scanned the new controls. "It's like the dashboard of a new vehicle!"

Ramaan was evaluating the new ESDT transmitter when Jim's face appeared on the square screen.

"Hello, Philip, I suppose you are now well on your way to Pleniton. On the main console, there's a small red button. Have you pressed it yet?"

"No, sir."

"Go on, give it a bash. During your stay, we upgraded the motors on the *Excelsior*. I decided not to tell you until you were far enough away from us in case the thing blew up." There was a pause. "Only joking. Go on, what are you waiting for?"

Alana lifted an eyebrow, leaned forward and pressed the button. Slow-moving stars through the window ports created trails and became blurs. The declining frequency of Jim's voice transformed itself into a low grumble. A faint click from inside the console sounded and the automatic frequency corrector came into operation, allowing them to continue with their conversation.

"With your modified engines you are now travelling two hundred AUs per second, instead of the five you were travelling before. You'll reach Pleniton in two days. Sorry, I must go now. Keep me updated, and good luck on Pleniton." Jim's stressed face faded and the receiver switched off.

While the *Excelsior* was dodging the passing asteroid belt, they rested and prepared themselves both physically and mentally for what lay ahead.

An hour after initialising the gradual slowing process, they entered orbit. Pleniton's surface details began rolling up Sentrywatcher's displays. Reams and reams of information oozed out, including atmospheric composition, geological and geographical structures, life forms and any possible radio transmissions. Pleniton's sordid yellow colour and minus 60-degree surface temperature was as uninviting as its distance was from Alnilam. It was a frozen world. Below was quiet, a little too quiet. Philip listened intently as Ramaan gave him the finer details.

"Carbon, chromium, magnesium, sodium and iron, with the usual trace elements," he said. "Radiation levels are well within the safety limits. There's 9 percent oxygen. I have argon, high amounts of nitrogen and some methane crystals. It's prehistoric. I hope those blips aren't unreceptive," added Ramaan, looking at some pixilation in an extremely tall cylindrical funnel.

Lexia moved closer to examine the screen. "Maybe it's a different type of hostile," she said. The funnel was situated in the middle of nothing. Fauna didn't exist. Pleniton was a rounded rock with a funnel that reached forty kilometres into the stratosphere.

The enormous funnel was visible even when they were more than four hundred kilometres from the surface. Sentrywatcher zoomed in and revealed incandescent lights coming from its interior. There was life down there, Bod life. Minuscule human figures scurried about through thousands of minute windows. Life had found a way to exist on this isolated rock; but there again, life would always find a way. A gentle wisp of smoke emerged from the top of the funnel and dissipated, producing frozen rain that fell back from whence it came.

The preparation of the pod was easy. The engineers on Terron had done most of the work for them. Alana started the countdown, flicking a switch ten seconds later. The search for clues as to Mike's whereabouts had begun. Their detectors alerted them to two other life forms hungrily scurrying about the planet's infertile surface.

Alana increased the scan intensity and looked into the display. "Not only is one of them reptilian, it has an oily substance flowing through it instead of blood, which would obviously freeze at that temperature. The other is metamorphic, and it's extremely fast. I clocked one moving at over fifty kilometres per hour."

"And the funnel, are you sure they are Bod?" asked Philip.

"Not only am I sure, there are a lot of them." Alana transmitted a welcome call on all frequencies, but the radio remained silent.

"Let me try," said Lexia, picking up the microphone. "If they're Bod, they'll definitely respond." Click…"Nosotii retis pazoba vandio. I told them we come in peace."

The hiss transformed itself into a voice. The reply came in English. "Hello, Humans, we've been expecting you. Welcome to our domain. Land your travelling means on the two-hundredth level of the funnel below. I have set up an exterior, pre-heated landing pad for you. Watch for the green light."

The pod broke through the upper stratosphere and descended towards the ever-broadening funnel. About a quarter of the way up, a green light flickered on and off.

Placing the coordinates into Sentrywatcher and switching from manual to auto, they gaped down and saw the immensity of the funnel. The pod headed directly to where their hosts were waiting. On the landing bay, the pod made a serene thud as metal met surface. Bods came to greet them as soon as they'd settled themselves down.

"It's a miracle you didn't land yourselves down there. The reptilian life here is fearsome. We call them the Mordon. They spit acid that they generate in their stomachs. Welcome to Orb City. My name is Darinko, one of ten executives here." They shook hands and introduced themselves.

"Would you like to eat something before we show you to your living quarters for the duration of your stay? Here, there are no Platnios or Peblinus to worry about, only Mordon, Hemerus and the cold." Darinko was a charming man.

"We accept your hospitality, thank you."

Alana moved closer. "Darinko, you mentioned Hemerus. Are they those fast, shapeless things we picked up in orbit?"

"Yes, that's them. The Hemerus have always been here. We think they originated from what you call Telus-Two. Hemerus are shape-changers. They can imitate a boulder, a cliff face; even turn themselves into a donga. Their amoebic cell structure is fascinating and deadly. But, of course, they have to survive like the rest of us, and occasionally one of us falls prey to its simulation."

They walked along the landing pad and headed for the entrance to the funnel. Their first impression of the interior of the gigantic funnel-shaped city from the two-hundredth level made their mouths gape. This floor, like all the others, was a wide platform surrounding the inner perimeter of the funnel.

21. Evolution

Word quickly spread through Orb City informing its inhabitants of their landing. Curious, the Bods walked to Philip and the others, occasionally brushing past, ogling their evolutionary differences as inquisitive eyes culminated in a furious nattering. On every floor, a long, gentle curving line of square alcoves that could have been living quarters had Bods scampering about their interiors, busily transacting their livelihoods. Each room, although small, contained four or more Bods. Darinko told Philip that two thousand such rooms were on each floor. Through novice eyes, Orb City was a mind-boggling artist's impression of a science fiction shopping centre. The brightly lit space in the centre, scaffolding structures, lights; so many lights. The interior space was so large that it stretched away towards a hazy infinity.

The exception was that this shopping mall had no window displays, and there was nothing for sale. In each of the nearest anterooms, gatherings of Bods worked in front of terminals. Hands wafted the air, controlling small holo-displays. Technology had left a footprint, even on this void planet.

A mantle air-conditioning system in the nerve centre kept the interior temperature at a steady 20 degrees. Philip detected a faint smell of ozone in the air. It was the unmistakable signature of working electronics while being accompanied by a constant and distant drone of mechanics.

To their right, a transparent safety barrier extended itself upwards to the next floor. Philip walked to it and peered downwards. Comprehending the vastness of the largest construction ever made, he pulled back to reality with a jerk.

Darinko laughed at his pale face. Orb City had striking similarities to the funnels they had encountered on Braan. This one was thousands of times bigger, and to withstand the immense weight, it had been constructed of pure ermithium plastic.

"You get used to it when you have been here forever," said Darinko.

"Each family here has their individual responsibility. Some manufacture, some cook, some teach, some heal. Each one of us looks after each other with his or her own speciality. On the 700th level, we have our engineers. They listen and observe."

Darinko explained that they had intercepted transmissions from Retolox, and more recently from Terron. "We've been hearing about your progress in the Mintaka system and have been tracking you ever since. We knew you'd come sooner or later."

Their resting quarters were at the other end of the funnel, almost a kilometre from the pod. "Make yourselves comfortable. I'll collect you in about an hour after you've eaten."

Their alcove's two small windows revealed an astonishing external representation of the planet's surface and surroundings. This striking and arid beauty was about to give birth to a spectacular sunrise. The first streaks of a distant Alnilam began filtering above the bumpy horizon. Philip could make out hills, while fluctuating, undulating tendrils of browned coherent solar light, intent on breaking the still-black morning sky, carved magenta shadows and cut out mountain shapes.

A Bod servant came into their room with breakfast. Behind him, a robot languidly followed behind carrying a red liquid aperitif on a tray. Alongside, five oval trays of bean sausages and an artificial vegetable actually looked quite appetising.

Baygorn got Philip's attention with a whispery undertone. "Hey, this guy's identical to the ones we saw on Braan."

"Yeah, but this is no harvester."

The robot, sensing their talking about him, turned its stepper-motorised head in their direction with an abrupt whirr.

The red aperitif they drank had an apple taste and left a slight peppery after-burn. Ramaan found it very refreshing.

Their room had two beds and a single toilet area with a bath. There were clean towels and, on a basin, a heavier-than-normal hard green soap that briefly smelt of mint. It provoked Philip's imagination, and so, glancing at his surroundings, he closed his mind. Their environment was Earth once again. The Bods had left behind so many trademarks for them to utilise, and they, like good citizens, had used them in every respect.

Later, Darinko popped his head around the corner to see if they had finished. He entered and sat on the edge of a vacant bed and began discussing their past.

"We started arriving here 20,000 years ago. As always, first came the explorers. They were followed shortly afterwards by more, many more. It's much like your Terron. You send scientists to build the city, explore any resources, find the riches, the basics, and then come the civilians when all is safe. Orb City was created primarily as a research and development community; but because of the shortage of supplies, especially weapons and medicines, we found ourselves, instead of researching and developing for other Bods, we were researching survival, our own survival." Darinko transmitted a charisma that made Philip feel quite comfortable.

"When Orb City was in its initial stages, a multitude of other settlements were going up in other regions of the galaxy. Some of those outposts are located in the Mintaka system. Descendants of the same architect who designed this funnel later designed the vertical columns you saw on Braan."

Baygorn's face turned crimson as Alnilam entered the window aperture. The pathetic amount of radiation it donated did, however, reveal some activity far below on Pleniton's surface. It wasn't much, but it was enough for him to see what was going on. He beckoned Ramaan and Philip to the window. The ground moved. It was alive. Something squirmed under the sand down there. Darinko moved closer.

"You say they spit acid at their prey?" asked Alana worriedly. Her heart gave a brief thump.

"Not just any acid: molecular acid. Damn stuff eats almost anything. It pre-digests their victims and converts them into a sticky slime; easier to consume. Anyway, enough of that. Tell me, what is the purpose of your visit to Pleniton?"

"We're an exploratory, scientific team. Like Mintaka, we are here to investigate these ten planets and find out what happened to one of our earlier teams. It appears they've gone missing." Philip paused. "We seek the possibility of fusing our two species back into what we once were. After all, Darinko, we are in fact one and the same. Are we not?"

"Yes, it's true. Before you, another explorer came. He called himself Captain Branigan. He came with the same pretext you do, but had no idea about the connection between our two species. You, on the other hand, come with a better introduction."

Ramaan noticed Philip's face cringe before quickly regaining his usual composure.

On that note, Darinko insisted on showing them around his domain. "In our vertical island, two million Bods perform their daily duties. We have one hundred continuously functioning elevators serving the seven hundred floors. Orb City's heating comes from the upper mantle of Pleniton. We tapped into it when we arrived. While the inside is a constant 20 degrees, the outside is a hairy 60 below, if the wind isn't blowing."

They walked to a window. Darinko pointed to a hill. "Over there in the distance, we have teams continuously collecting minerals."

"How do you get past the Mordon?" asked Lexia.

"A simple force field rigged onto the vehicle's undercarriage prevents anything from sticking to it."

"Have you ever lost anyone out there?" asked Philip.

"Not to the Mordon, but they are constantly attacking our vehicles. Luckily, we constructed Orb City before the Mordon arrived. The base of Orb City is impenetrable, even to them. The Hemerus are more passive; that is, of course, when they are not hungry. The Hemerus' stomach is adapted to anything. They even eat the Mordon when all else fails."

"Could we try the effectiveness of our weapons against them?" asked Ramaan.

"Go ahead; be my guest. Follow me to the ground floor." They entered an elevator, passing the medical research levels. Bods clad in white were running in all directions.

"What are they so excited about?" enquired Lexia.

"We're working on a cure for Dilatsus disease. We've been working around the clock for months. We get it from being here too long, lose as many as twenty per week."

Baygorn's ears tweaked. "Get me a sample of it, I'll give it to my virometer and see what it comes up with." Darinko gave a nod and pressed a button on the lift panel.

They walked to one of the labs while Baygorn eagerly went to the pod. He returned carrying a metallic box under his arm. A medic placed a single blotch of infected blood onto the recipient dish, and the virometer excitedly lit up with a click.

Ten seconds later, the display screen provided an antidote possibility, and a viable sample appeared in a tiny test tube.

"Inject them with this," said Baygorn, handing over the test tube.

The befuddled medical officer asked, "We've been working on a cure for Dilatsus for almost a year. How can you come up with a solution so quickly?"

Baygorn smiled as he motioned to the virometer. "Here, you can have this one."

Philip saw him briefly explain to the medical officer the workings of the virometer and type some simple instructions on a handheld digital notepad.

✧✧✧

The devastating drop in temperature soon became obvious long before they neared ground level.

On the fifth floor, the elevator automatically stopped, and they followed Darinko into a changing room. "No one goes below this point without protection. Down there, you die in minutes."

The changing room smelt like a changing room. Taking it in turn, they stood on a circle indicated by Darinko, where a laser scanner zipped up and down their bodies. Minutes later, after some whirring and a clunk, a hatch opened on the adjacent wall. Darinko reached inside and handed out the thermal suits. "Put these on top of your clothes."

Alana and Ramaan approached the front entrance, where a security guard was passing the morning the best he could in a centrally heated cubicle.

Noticing their interest, Darinko said, "He examines the vehicles as they pass through and come back, assuring nothing has attached itself to the underneath. Our scanners don't work at these temperatures, so everything has to be manual."

Alana and Ramaan went outside into the bitter, dim morning and placed two blue-ray rifles close to the entrance, pointing in different directions. Within minutes, one fired its lethal dosage. They returned with a thin layer of greyish ice on their visors.

Even through the thermal protection, Philip could feel the bitter wrath of cold. Directing his vision away from Alana and Ramaan and back to the funnel, the obviousness of the Bod's advancement became evident. One area in particular was construction. Another was certainly space travel. Humanity could definitely learn a lot from them.

Darinko turned and faced Philip and the others. "As the base of the funnel is made of pure ermithium and completely resilient to their acid, we focus on mining ermithium. The only location where we extract it is in the Argus mine twenty kilometres away. One of our teams is out there at the moment. It took us ten years to construct Orb City. We lost more than five thousand workers during its construction. But luckily, like I mentioned previously, we finished before the Mordon arrived, or that figure would have been much higher."

Several security guards appeared on the scene and asked them to explain how the blue-ray rifle worked. Alana disappeared with them. Suddenly without warning, an urgent message, sounding more like a scream, shot over their communication system. The security guard almost dropped the rifle.

"What the devil is happening?" A few seconds later, another voice more or less said the same thing before it, too, faded.

Darinko was listening. "My goodness, that was Tarly's voice. He must've run into a problem!"

Tarly finally collapsed into the powerful embrace of an unknown thing that began to drag him backwards towards a hole in the ground. He twisted, kicked, struck out with his fists, to no effect. He was held tightly and dragged deeper into the hole. In the backsplash of light coming through the hole, then in the rapidly dimming beam of his discarded flashlight, Tarly saw a bit of the thing that had him in its grasp, but not much.

Fragments looming out of the shadows, then vanishing into darkness again. Tarly saw just enough to make his bowels and bladder loosen. It was lizard-like, but not a lizard. Insect-like, but not an insect. It whaled and mewled and snarled. It snapped and tore at his thermal suit as it pulled him along. It had cavernous jaws, and its teeth were a double row of razor-edged spikes. It had claws and it was huge, and its eyes were smoky-red with elongated pupils as black as the bottom of a grave. It had scales of skin, and two horns, thrusting from its brow above its eyes, curving out and up, as sharply pointed as daggers. A snout redder than a nose, a snout that oozed snot. A forked tongue that flickered in-and-out, in-and-out across its fangs. There was something that looked like the stinger on a wasp, or maybe a pincer at the back end.

It dragged Tarly farther into the hole. Tarly clawed at the rocks, desperately seeking something to grab onto, but he only succeeded abrading away the fingers and palms of his gloves. He felt the cool underground air on his hands.

It dragged him into the tunnel of darkness. Then it stopped and held him tightly before tearing at his suit. It cracked his helmet. It pried at his Plexiglass faceplate. It was after him as if he were a delicious morsel of nutmeat in a hard shell.

His hold on sanity was tenuous at best, but he struggled to keep his wits about him; he tried to understand. At first, it seemed to him that this was a prehistoric creature, something millions of years old that had dropped through a time warp and out in front of him. But that was crazy. The beast tore away most of his decontamination suit. It was on him now, pressing hard, a cold and disgustingly slick thing that seemed to pulse and somehow to change when it touched him. Tarly, gasping and weeping, suddenly remembered an illustration in an old catechism text. A drawing of a demon. That was what this was. Like the drawing. Yes, exactly like it. The horns. The dark, forked tongue. The red eyes. A demon risen from hell. And then he thought, *No, no; that's crazy, too!* And all the while that those thoughts raced through his mind, the ravenous creature stripped him and pulled his helmet almost completely apart.

In the unrelieved darkness, he sensed its snout pressing through the halves of the broken helmet, towards his face, sniffing. He felt its tongue fluttering against his mouth and nose.

He smelled a vague but repugnant odour, like nothing he had ever smelled before. The beast gouged at his belly and thighs, and then he felt a strange and brutally painful fire eating into him; acid fire.

He writhed, twisted, bucked and strained, all to no avail. Tarly heard himself cry out in terror and pain and confusion: "It's the Devil, it's the Devil!" He realized he had been shouting and screaming things almost continuously from the moment he had been dragged down the hole. Now, unable to speak as the flameless fire burned his lungs to ash and churned into his throat, he prayed in a silent singsong chant, warding off fear and death, and the terrible feeling of smallness and worthlessness that had come over him. Tarly had screamed excruciatingly, but nobody had heard him. Nobody had heard his last, explosive gasps before death had taken him—only the Hemerus.

Darinko was silent for a long while. Then he explained the comparison of the Hemerus and a small morphing spider he'd read about from Telus-Two that made all of them shudder.

"Now that's what I call a clever engineer. The brylodoor spider. It makes a deep, tubular nest in the ground with a hinged lid at the top. The lid blends in so perfectly with the surroundings that whatever wanders across it is totally unaware of the danger below, until it's too late. They are instantly dropped into the opening, dragged down and devoured. One instant, the prey was dying, and the next instant it was gone, as if it had never been.

"That is also how the Hemerus kill their prey. Things are clever, and it appears they're hungry."

Lexia gave a shiver and a worried look toward Baygorn. "We have to get out there, the extractors are in trouble. Without us they don't stand a chance!" Alana came running back after hearing all the commotion. Baygorn, taking notice of Darinko's concern, immediately returned to the 200th floor. The pod drifted down soon after and landed directly in front of the entrance and the two searching blue-rays.

"Alana, you drive!" Philip shouted as Baygorn drove the vehicle out the pod. Darinko jumped in right behind Philip.

Alana accelerated in the direction of Darinko's pointing hand.

"They should be in more or less the same area, so it shouldn't be difficult to rescue them, but I may need more of your rifles." "Blue-ray rifles. Don't worry, you'll get as many as we can spare," shouted Alana behind her thermal suit.

By the time they'd reached the extraction crew, Philip immediately diagnosed what had happened to the miners. Large holes about two metres in diameter were scattered in all directions. The vehicle skidded and dodged.

"They must've been hungry. First time they've flared up like this. Oh no, we've lost a lot of men!"

As they pulled up to the mine, Ramaan leapt out and placed two blue-rays near to the entrance.

"They attacked us for no reason at all! Never seen them like this before," said one of the miners. "Who are these people?"

"They are here to help."

Alana placed blue-rays on the vacant land, scattering them as far apart as possible. Philip caught a glimpse of a Hemerus squirming in the distance. A leg with a boot was sticking out of its grotesque mouth.

The Hemerus measured more than four metres long. The pike face and split tail menacingly swished from side to side, moving as a surgeon's scalpel would through the terrain. A blue-ray fired.

"Bring everyone as close as possible between these two rifles. They'll be safe!" yelled Alana.

The seven survivors huddled together as Darinko started one of their vehicles. "Come on, get in!" he shouted and ushered them into the vehicle. The workers clambered as quickly as they could into the back section and disappeared in the direction of Orb City.

Dispassionately breaking away from the calamity while thinking about Mike, Philip stared towards Orb City. It was a most magnificent funnel. It towered well into the lower stratosphere. Dwarfed methane clouds reached only the lower sections. The speeding vehicle in the distance brought Philip back to his senses as he thought of them reaching safety.

"Don't worry about them now, the medical staff will take care of them when they arrive," said Darinko, noticing Philip's interest in Orb. A smile was discernible through his visor.

252

Philip turned and faced Orb City. "You know, it's astounding that you constructed that in only ten years." Philip's creased expression, barely noticeable through the thermal suit, made Darinko smile once more.

"We could've done it in less time if this place was a bit more hospitable. It is cold. It has horrible beasts roaming about; not to mention they're always hungry. Once the base and first floors were up, it went easier. In that first year, our losses became our drive and strength to continue."

Darinko's handheld radio suddenly erupted with the voice of the security guard at the entrance of Orb City. "They are here, all okay." Darinko's sigh of relief was broken in two.

Alana walked over holding her C-12. "I have movement. Two thousand metres, over there!"

Philip followed Alana's hand past a small hill. "Let's go take a look before going back."

When they reached the source of the life-sign, it was nothing more than a hole in the ground about two metres in diameter. Strange markings and scrapings led up to it. Bones of all types scorched the surface. One of them shattered as Ramaan's boot walked over it.

They stood back while Alana continued her scan. "Twenty metres deep. Careful, mind your step. You don't want to fall down there."

From the outside, it was ominously quiet. Too quiet. It was quieter than a graveyard in a forgotten village on a Sunday night in winter. Not even a breeze.

"Must be a Mordon nest. I didn't think they'd be like this," said Alana with concern, while fixating on her C-12.

Ramaan sporadically placed six rifles around the perimeter of the hole. Alana threw down a smoke grenade. The silence broke as reverberating rumblings shook the ground. Firstly, it was a distant shuffle, then a catatonic cry—many louder and louder cries. The more agile ones appeared first. On the surface, they saw Darinko and lurched with lightning, slithering speed towards him. The blue-rays fired. Then the longer, heavier, worm-like Mordon lurched outwards in vast numbers. The blue-rays fired again.

Even in his life-threatening situation, Darinko seemed unperturbed, somewhat distracted by the horizon. His back was only metres away from the dead Mordon.

"Any more movement, Alana? Anything else?" The voice rang with perplexity. Darinko placed fear on his words.

"Nothing," she replied. "Absolutely nothing."

Unconvinced, Darinko turned and faced Philip. "They must be watching us. I can feel it. They have been close by; so odd. Where there are Mordon, there are Hemerus. They normally make patterns on the surface. Where are they? Only that one at the encampment site since you've been here? Got to be lots more."

"They're probably curious," Philip said.

"Gha, they're not the curious type, not their style. The Hemerus abode goes far beneath our feet. One of our scouts found one a couple of months ago. It wasn't too far from here, either. He mentioned something about a vertical vent. Needless to say, the scout entered with jet boots. So stupid. I spoke to him myself. I remember he said, 'It's almost two hundred metres deep!' At the base, he reported the walls were coated with a sticky secretion. He repeated the words 'animal remains' two or three times. He also said that, leading off from the one base chamber, were many other vertical vents up to the surface in all directions. That was when the radio died. I never saw him again. They capture their prey coming up from these underground caverns. There are hundreds of them, so if I were you, I'd stay away from the sand and keep to the rocks. They have to be around here somewhere."

Alana nervously examined her C-12. "Wait, what's that? Jeez, out of nowhere. There's one right under our feet!" Alana's alarming, sudden distress bounced them onto the rocks with a jerk. Alana and Ramaan drew their weapons. "I tell you, there was something!" she said. "There's nothing out here except for fear and disorientation."

Philip turned towards Darinko. "Darinko, what was Captain Branigan after? Did he mention anything before he left?"

"No, he just asked about the same things you did, knowledge and—"

That was when they saw Darinko for the last time. Something dashed out right in front of Philip, two metres from his face. It jumped up and out of the sand like a huge, hungry flyswatter. He imagined the wind stirring as it devoured Darinko. It was something big and tremendously fast. Not even their blue-rays had time to react. Philip could not move, he froze, he had lost control over his body.

Ramaan was shouting at Philip to get back into the vehicle.

At first, he didn't hear Ramaan. Philip remained in a stasis and in shock until Alana came over and whacked him across the visor. "Philip, for God's sake, we have to get out of here. Come on!"

They ran back to the armoured vehicle and drove like the blazes to Orb City. Once inside, Ramaan and Philip confronted the assigned committee and told them their story of the death of Darinko.

The committee thanked them for their honesty and help. "This incident will not change relations between us. Feel free to return at any time. Thank you for all you have done." The man who had spoken walked over. Philip shook hands with the man, who had introduced himself as Brern.

The *Excelsior* was more than just a modern spacecraft; it was the crew's salvation and safety. This time, however, it had been a relief to smell that familiar, slightly lemony whiff of artificial oxygen as they took off their headgear. The five of them were there for each other and yet, sometimes they felt alone, even when someone sat next to them. It is a different kind of lonely when you face death from so close and then return home to no one. They were beginning to experience what psychologists call forced isolation. If they were present, they would have said, "You brought it upon yourself; you enrolled. It was you who signed on the dotted line."

Baygorn came over with a syringe and jabbed Philip in the arm. "This should relax you a bit. See you in about an hour."

Out here in this diverse hell, their way of life affected them in many different ways, especially this current voyage. It's not fun watching your host become a planetary meal. During their travels, they'd learnt that anything was possible; they kept all possibilities open.

At reduced velocity, their voyage to Telus-Six would take five days, and it would give them time to digest what had happened on Pleniton.

Henry Telus, the manufacturer and designer of the Charon telescope, discovered six of the ten planets circling Alnilam and dryly named them after himself. Their high albedo increased their visibility from Earth, but the other four, until recently, had remained invisible. Telus-Six was the second-smallest planet in that system.

The routine and protocol Philip applied on the *Excelsior* during the journey hadn't changed in the slightest. Apart from surveying, analysing and planetary study, they conducted all their imperative daily chores, which of course to five scientists could be very boring. Nevertheless, they loved it. It was their way of life; it had to be, out here in the middle of nowhere. Each one of them took his or her turn to cook and clean along the journey. There were no exceptions, there just couldn't be.

They conducted maintenance checks regularly in each of the sections as they, too, had responsibilities apart from duties. It was this break, this interruption between planetary examinations, which saved them from going crazy. The *Excelsior* was a large spacecraft and housed a vast engineering and maintenance department.

Bio-created food supplies were grown in the hydroponics centre on one side of the *Excelsior*. Their two holding decks were full of spare parts, weapons and automated robotics. They kept nothing under lock and key; they had no reason to. To the back of one of them, a reserved space for medicines and drugs under Baygorn's supervision came complete with a spare electron microscope. They had the medical provisions to treat virtually any Earth-known ailment, and, from the first day, Baygorn received full responsibility of their health during the journey. They frequently underwent checks and examinations, both physical and psychological.

The voice of Alana broke everyone's attention. "Thirty thousand kilometres. I'm cutting the main engines."

"It's really hostile," Ramaan said, looking at the results of Telus-Six inching on the viewer.

"It's always hostile," answered Lexia, following his eyes.

"What do you expect with 2 percent oxygen, a whiff of methane, a speck of argon, way too much nitrogen, and a lot of carbon dioxide crystals?" She couldn't disguise her panic, and Baygorn couldn't argue with her. Her alarm told them she was scared.

Each planet was different. They never spoke about their fears. Just as they never knew what was on the surface, of course, that was until Sentrywatcher had completed her scan, which could take some time. None of them enjoyed speculating. They were too scientific, maybe a little too unimaginative, and always following the dotted lines. Most certainly, they were still too new to all this to summarise and make any assumptions without scientific proof.

22. Transmission

Telus-Six crammed the viewer, accompanied by a faint, eerie radio transmission coming through the speaker. Sentrywatcher immediately began hacking it to pieces to find its origin and determine its contents. There was a clause in their contract which clearly stated that if they came across any signal or transmission coming from the surface of the planets, it had to be investigated. It was Priority One, especially if it was an urgent call for help. Of course if this transmission was malignant, there would be no knowing it until it was too late. It was possible that Mike went to investigate it before coming to Telus-Six. Mike was always the curious, dotted-line follower, the obedient one. With this pretext, the *Excelsior's* crew ignored it and sceptically examined its contents. The signal was a series of blips, with digital jargon that Sentrywatcher hurriedly deciphered into an SOS.

"Could it be a warning and not an SOS?"

Alana, re-checking the source, confirmed its origin was definitely Telus-Three.

Ramaan transmitted a reply in the same form of blips requesting to know what the urgency was. No reply came. It was only the same repeating, uninterrupted, pulsating whine.

Alana prepared them for their descent. She had no intention of making the same mistake that Mike had. This meant that under the circumstances they had broken their first rule. They had motive.

Emerging from the blips, from within the massive data stream, Sentrywatcher suggested that there could be a binary or digital content buried within the alien transmission. Ramaan excitedly inserted another extraction routine into the signal to search for binary, trinary, octal and hexadecimal imbedded content. It seemed to be fragmentary maths on a base-sixteen model, and masses of data contained the higher-base layer. The de-coding seemed impossible, so they left it to Sentrywatcher to continue the analysis.

The pod disconnected from the *Excelsior*. Telus-Six was a cold, light-blue world. A bright bluish luminous cage enshrouded the planet, while trapped, charged magnetospheric particles caused a magnificent display of violent colour. Two sets of faint planetary rings surrounded the planet. Solar particles barely able to penetrate the atmosphere gave the surface below a ghostly brown and yellow appearance.

The radar beeped. On the horizon eighty kilometres from their present position, a strange, dark object emerged silently out of nowhere. It was much bigger than the *Excelsior*. From their distance, it was a dim, shimmering green light and could've easily been another star.

Alana steered their pod towards it, but the object mysteriously disappeared away from them into the blackness. Whoever it was, it seemed to be curious about who they were and what they were doing. It stayed its new distance of two hundred kilometres, and as they shifted position, it compensated for the difference. Sentrywatcher had no information on what it was or where it came from. Its unfamiliar design floated in the void and occasionally scanned them. Letting its interest follow them, they broke the chase and headed for Telus-Six.

The wind outside the pod was sour and tinged with a whiff of chlorine. Alana registered many varieties of unintelligent life on the scanner. One of them was subterranean, so they climbed into the vehicle and made their way towards it. The nocturnal landscape was full of scattered, odd vegetation in round patches resembling long-haired moss that crept under rocks and onto cliffs. As far as they could see on this hill-less landscape, the vegetation patches were the only source of oxygen.

One of the other forms of life Sentrywatcher had informed them of resembled a small moth. Ramaan was frantically photographing one as it swirled and swooped about the vehicle. A low whine emanated from its flapping wings.

Five minutes later, Alana pulled alongside the subterranean site. Getting out, Baygorn noticed that the low whistle continued.

Michael Gilwood

One of the moths had gotten a wing caught on a foothold on the roof. Baygorn carefully dislodged it and held it up to his visor. "It's mostly bone and hard muscle; suppose they have to be to survive in this place. Hairy little critter, though. Damn strong too." It squirmed between his fingers, so he let it flutter off to do whatever they do.

Walking to the cavity, Lexia pointed the scanner down towards the depths. Many strange prints and markings led up to the hole.

"Interesting, they look like hamster-rats; Hamrats. I'm not picking up anything else, nothing else down there."

The entrance was grubby. Their protective suits came with nasal samplers that automatically warmed cold air, allowing ambient odours to enter. A wafting smell of rotting meat floated out, making Alana twist her suited body away. Excrement was everywhere. Alana placed three blue-rays around the perimeter and set them on Stun before throwing down a smoke grenade into the interior of the hole.

Like the Mordon had reacted, frantic Hamrats produced a profound, almost deafening squeak. There was havoc below. The sounds of chaotic, rushing, pounding feet became more and more audible.

A loud crack made Lexia check her C-12 and confirm, "Should be coming up any moment now. Trying to escape—Jeez, look at them scamper!"

A second later, dozens of cat-sized, long-haired, toothy rodents jumped for safety like popcorn out of the popper.

Philip and the others stood back while the attenuated blue-rays did their job.

"They'll be dozing for a while," said Baygorn, bending down with a xenon torch to pick one up. "It's got a rat face." Baygorn's obscured face couldn't hold back his amusement and astonishment. "It's heavy, probably weighs five kilograms, maybe more." The long fur in a wide variety of colours, along with four stubby feet, lay limp as Baygorn placed the fascinating creature back where he'd found it. In the span of only a minute, more than a hundred rodents dotted the surface.

When their sensors detected no more movement, the crew clamped on magnetic jet boots, and descended into the pit with

260

xenon lamps and hand pistols. It was a six-metre vertical vent leading in both directions at the base. The still-smoking expended gas cylinder lay dormant. They squeezed themselves towards an opening. It was a large den with smaller, messier dens to one side. Small- and medium-sized bones lay scattered, and an intense urine smell drifted in the air. A bleep sounded from Lexia's scanner. Two motionless Hamrats out of the smoke's way had snuggled into one of the smaller dens.

A distant snivelling aroused their curiosity. They edged their way into the den. In the corner, the female of the species was giving birth. Five little furry things the size of thumbs lay next to her. As another plopped out, the mother, showing all her teeth, lurched frantically forwards to protect them from this gigantic vertical enemy. A metre away, she suddenly stopped, became timid and backed away when it saw Alana's drawn pistol.

"Did you see that? She knows what this is, she recognised my weapon." The second one did the same. It rushed over after hearing the rumpus, and when it saw Alana's pistol, it stopped dead in its tracks, then walked to the female's side to protect her. White teeth made an unthreatening, subtle hint as Baygorn bent down to stroke it.

"Must be the male," he said. The little ones squeaked like tiny guinea pigs, sensing the parents close by.

Back in the passageway, farther into the lair, they came across another bigger opening in the ground.

Ramaan pointed his scanner into the blackness. "Almost twenty metres straight down!"

To one side of the hole, built into rock and probably natural, a gigantic cavern bathed itself in their curious xenon light. Redirecting their lamps downwards, they turned on their jet packs and went in. Loose stones dislodged by their boots fell into the hole and made a dry echo as rocks clanked and clinked. The sight at the bottom was disgusting. It was as off-putting as a morgue on a busy day and smelt like a rotting corpse. The cavern stretched for hundreds of metres and was full of skeletons as far as their lights could reach.

Baygorn and Lexia turned up their oxygen supply. Baygorn commented on the discarded human bones. A light flashed on

Alana's scanner. "There's something else down here with us!" Philip turned and stared at her.

"There's movement and no, I didn't imagine it!" she said, still looking at the scanner. A distant scrabbling noise caught Baygorn's attention.

Ramaan flinched in his suit. "That's no damn Hamrat. Let's get out of here! Whatever that is, I prefer we confront it on the surface. These little Hamrats were the welcome face. They couldn't be responsible for all this carnage."

They quickly turned on their jet packs and left the hole.

Outside and rapidly un-strapping their jet packs, Lexia augmented the scan area while Alana set up additional blue-rays. They were prominent auras, fuzzy images reminding her of a three-footed ape. She focused the scan. Big, round eyes dominated the upper half of the cranium, while two short, extremely hairy arms joined to the middle of the body, culminating in a big mouth under the eyes. They omitted a low bark. All this was packaged on three squat legs.

"I bet they run like the wind," commented Lexia.

From their vehicle, Alana placed the new physical pattern of the ape-creatures onto the firing sequence of the blue-ray. Alana set them to Vaporise to unleash their full power. The thousands of skeletons they'd found earlier in the cavern had proven that these creatures were dangerous. Alana monitored their movements. They appeared to be running unwittingly towards a remote and unseen exit. Scant minutes later, the blue-ray began firing its deadly inferno towards them in the distance, so they fled back into the vertical vent whence they'd come.

Doubling back to their end, stones started shooting out of the Hamrats' hole. One of them hit Alana on the arm. The apes were throwing rocks at the blue-ray tripods in an attempt to dislocate those fire-breathing machines. They, too, like the Hamrats, knew the danger, but as penitence, the rifles dealt with them in a savage manner.

"There's still movement in the lower levels. They seem to be more tranquil," said Alana.

Philip wondered what the apes' next move could be, and how they evolved on this dead world, along with their rodent friends.

The rodents might have been food for the apes. If this were true, then where did the rodents come from? Questions became speculation.

Possibly, every now and then an innocent space traveller would encounter this animal dwelling, becoming an instant meal.

"Still doesn't tell us where they might've come from. Where was God when this place was made?"

Alana and Baygorn drove to the other exit hole and mounted another two blue-rays on the surface. The C-12 erupted with her voice. "This one is really deep. Jesus, what's down there?"

Two smoke grenades disappeared down the deep opening. Seconds later, the ground began to tremble, culminating in the oddest, most haunting ululation. *No earthly animal makes that kind of noise*, thought Baygorn.

Far below them, pandemonium reigned. Less than a minute later, apes, dozens of them, rushed out from both exits, scrabbling in fear, escaping this foggy, unfamiliar enemy. Reaching the surface became their only goal. When the scanners on both sides revealed that only a few remained, Baygorn came to collect Philip, and they ventured below once more.

Lexia brought up the question of food. "Without suitable vegetation, what could the Hamrats possibly eat to sustain themselves?" No one answered. They were almost certain that the apes ate the rodents. The skeletons they discovered in the vast open cavern told them that. But what about these little fellers? What did they eat?

At the bottom, Baygorn stopped in his tracks. "Of course. It must be a rotary evolvement. It can only be. The one animal eats the other to survive, and in order for the second one to survive, it eats the excrement of the first." It sounded vile, but the beauty of survival often has its ugly side.

Ramaan punched a couple of commands on his remote and set their rifles on the surface to Stun. What they had done here today was more than enough.

The remaining few apes were cowering and trembling in one of their coves with a look of terror on their odd faces. They had miniature bodies, less than a metre tall. The lower sections of the area did not contain any other form of life, except for a strange beetle like a cockroach that waddled about in its never-ending search for scraps.

Farther down the passage, something out of place caught their attention. Lexia noticed it first. "What's that on the wall?" It resembled a white medicine cabinet. Alana treaded her way to it. It had no markings, but it was clearly locked.

"No ape or rodent could've possibly made this," remarked Philip. Ramaan fired his pistol at the lock. Inside, a single square box with two lumpy, round protrusions jutted out from the smooth surface. It was extremely light, weighing about the same as a box of matches. On closer examination, the two large protrusions were buttons.

Philip pressed one and the box immediately jerked to life, producing a loud hiss. Unexpected and astounded, he jumped. The noise was louder than he'd anticipated. Fascinated, he let go and pressed the other button. The hiss ceased. Between the two knobs, a tiny hole that could have been a microphone made him press the second button once more and speak close to the apparatus.

"Is there anyone there?" Philip began to feel silly at his action, but still wondered if anyone was listening. No reply came.

Ramaan gathered the communicator and quietly placed it in his bag. *Who was at the other end of the communicator?* Baygorn thought. Who had been listening? Nevertheless, and most important, why was it down in the ape den?

Three hours later in the safety of the *Excelsior*, Alana saw no sign of the ominous black alien spaceship that had been following them. It had mysteriously vanished. The good news was that Sentrywatcher had deciphered the interplanetary signal from Telus-Three by the time they'd docked.

Telus-Five was on the other side of Alnilam, which meant that they had ample time to decrypt and study the video information they'd retrieved from Telus-Three. Its intriguing contents could do nothing but produce frustrating, unanswered questions, making Philip and the others feel incapable and insignificant.

What little they had seen so far, the system of Alnilam was a savage and cruel universe. Mike should have gone to Mintaka.

Philip's guilty conscience stabbed at him. *I should have gone to Alnilam*, thought Philip. But there again, that was the overwhelming power of a coin. They'd tossed for it, heads for Mintaka, tails for Alnilam. Mike lost.

Sentrywatcher suddenly bleeped. Alana swivelled on her chair and entered a command on the console. Before their eyes, visions of unknown races, both normal and bizarre, flickered on the screen. Accompanying them were snippets of languages, images of strife, war, constructions, and civilizations. Out of the fifty examples, they were only able to recognize the Magnopods, Blagorian, Gorinos and the Sintor. The transmission, a brutal compilation of life and death, formed an intergalactic history of anguish and grieving that, between them all, had created this galaxy. It could have been possible that this broadcast had been transmitting for decades, even centuries. It was a vision of what lay ahead for those with enough stomach and intelligence to face if they ventured forward and beyond.

Philip's thoughts returned to Pleniton. It was the closest he'd come to death. It haunted him, thinking the amoebic monster could have grabbed any one of them. His thoughts transpired into lucid words. "Thank the stars it seized Darinko. We should be so grateful to him. It was over in less than a second. Poor bastard." Baygorn stared. Philip turned to the others. "I couldn't imagine being on this ship with one of you missing."

Ramaan began testing the communicator they found in the apes' lair. It was lightweight. Who could have made it? Ramaan hooked it into the analyser. The transmitting frequency was 33 terahertz. It wasn't the frequency that astounded him, it was its amplitude. Nothing on Earth could assimilate a transmitter this powerful, let alone at this frequency. Ten thousand watts of pure energy coming from a tiny, 60-gram box.

"It's just a box of tubes and bits of metal." Ramaan scratched his head. "The Bods aren't even close to developing something this advanced. Metal tubes instead of the usual wires, with optical cable fusing the circuits. It is an exceptionally high-level design. How could it produce so much power?"

Baygorn walked over. "Maybe as these apes evolve, the first one with enough common sense would open the white case on the wall. Maybe he'd smash it. Who knows? Break the lock somehow and press the transmit button out of curiosity. He'd be compensated in some way. What do you think?" Suddenly, the communicator came to life.

"Liggwa agaa revolus machin baa?" The voice stopped suddenly.

Ramaan almost dropped the box on the floor. "Who in the name of Crom was that?"

Lexia was as bewildered as the rest of them. "It's not like any language I've ever heard before," she said nervously, transmitting a reply the best she could. There was no response, yet he or it was definitely listening. Lexia tried in various languages, but still no reply came. The signal emanating from Telus-Three continued in the same eerie undisturbed manner, and their alien visitor had reappeared on the horizon.

23. Visitor

The curious craft began to follow the *Excelsior* from a safe distance as it proceeded towards Telus-Five, now only 200 million kilometres away. Whoever they were, they seemed to know the capability of the *Excelsior*. The alien craft maintained a distance of five thousand kilometres. It never approached, yet it showed curiosity about their presence, as Alana detected sporadic scan signals emanating from them. They felt the urgency to know more about the *Excelsior*, just as it did about them. Yet Philip suspected that they probably already knew everything there was to know about it.

The next day, as Telus-Five crept onto the viewer, nothing new had occurred. No more sounds had come out of the alien communicator, and their ominous visitor had mysteriously backed off again. The eighth planet was the first of the inhabited worlds. Alana scanned five varieties of life on the surface. Like Venus, this giant red planet of mostly iron composition was spinning in reverse to all other planets in the system.

Alana typed in some commands.

"Recognise anything down there?" asked Ramaan, sneaking closer.

"Well, we have Bod, Peblinus, and a long-beaked flying bird. You should see the teeth on those things, they could be scavengers. I'm still working on the other two."

They circled the planet, doing a meticulous surface scan before putting themselves relatively close to the nearest Bod sector. Twelve percent oxygen appeared on a digital readout.

At first sight, the Bod settlement seemed dilapidated. Large chunks of odds and sods, and once-useful machinery lay in ruins. A dispirited sofa and comfy chair lay for dead. Tables, tin cans, a monitor, and a deceased engine block, too, formed part of the sandy terrain.

They cautiously neared the settlement and saw something peeping out through a long horizontal slit in what appeared to be an old wartime shelter. There were shapes shuffling around inside; lots of shapes, but no one ventured outside to greet them.

"If they are Bod as I know them to be, then they should already know who we are. What the blazes are they afraid of?"

Lexia's frustrated tone made Philip look to the side. Joined to the left of the shelter, shaped and disguised like a gigantic rock, a garage with heavy plastic doors slowly and silently began to swing open. From the inside and kneeling low, a Bod frantically and silently waved his hands about and signalled for them to enter.

Inside, they were met by a friendly face with an outstretched hand.

"Welcome, sorry for the hesitation back there. Blaradah! It's so nice to see new faces around here." He smiled. "I'm Blard. You're the first visitors in over a year."

Imperceptibly, the doors closed with a distant hiss.

Philip interrupted Blard's enthusiasm. "What's with all that mess outside?"

Bod's curious eyes scrutinized and watched him as he spoke. "That's the Flaboxian. They've been making our lives a misery lately."

Ramaan quickly rechecked his scanner. "There's nothing."

Philip steered from Ramaan's words back to Blard. "Then, you mean those flying birds? You call them Flaboxian? Impossible, an avian can't do that much damage. They are too small."

"No," said Blard holding back a laugh, "Flaboxian are a metamorphosed equivalent of the Platnios. They started showing up a short while ago. Appears the Peblinus have been experimenting again by unleashing yet another disdainful weapon of plant design. The Flaboxian are the subterranean version of the Platnios. That's probably why you didn't pick them up on your scanner. The things are considerably more intelligent and stronger. Move at a much quicker pace as well," explained Blard. "Appears they've found a new means of breeding, too. Our communications with Telus-Four have confirmed some frightening stories."

Philip raised his hands. "Whoa, wait a minute. What do you mean?"

"Warehouses, bunkers, any storage place that we leave behind. We build them, they use them. These things can even bury themselves underneath the sand, surprising their enemies when the bombs go off. They are better protected and out of harm's way."

Ramaan's slice-of-lemon grin and Baygorn's cough made Philip raise a hand to his face. *What had the Peblinus unleashed this time?* he thought. A bad situation was becoming worse.

"This facility has existed for decades," said Blard. "When the Peblinus arrived a year ago, that's when all our problems started. You see, they don't come and fight their own battles, they send in their genetic fleet of weirdoes every other day. This last year has been a tremendous struggle for us. Our operation has had to eventually move itself underground."

Philip explained some of their experiences with the Platnios. He also said, "Short-sightedness, that's what it is. The Peblinus are rapidly putting themselves on the extinction list. It's so obvious; it's just a question of time."

Bod workers watched them as the news spread of their arrival. Bods liberated their inner fears as they ventured into the lower tunnelling section, feeling secure just at the sight of them. Power engulfed. It made Philip feel like a god. Everywhere was a smile or a turning face.

They gained access to one of the side buildings via the well-lit, recently built underground tunnels. A receptionist was sitting at a desk, busy monitoring local Peblinus radio frequencies. Ramaan patted him on the back. The receptionist removed his headphone set and placed it on the table. Ramaan showed him the communicator that he'd found on Telus-Six.

Ogling eyes fixated at the square box. "Where on Bellatrix did you find that?" he asked.

"Telus-Six," responded Ramaan.

"This is a dream come true!" The man jumped out of his chair. "It's Dontrian technology."

"Is that so?" Ramaan said. "We found it stashed in an ape burrow. Why do you think it was there?"

"I haven't the faintest idea. I can only say Dontrian technology is the finest in the universe. This communicator is an excellent example. It can lie there or anywhere for tens of thousands of years without ever running out of power. The components don't run down and wear out like ours; somehow, they keep up to standards with the time barrier. With your permission I would like to analyse it."

Ramaan shook his head. "No way, this one comes back with us intact when we leave."

"I promise you," said the receptionist, "I only want to analyse the chemistry, not the insides; I won't damage it." Ramaan released his hold.

He grabbed it out of Ramaan's hands and, before Ramaan changed his mind, ran to an ion-spectra analyser against the wall. As they watched, he placed the Dontrian communicator underneath a small flap and pressed a button. The analyser lit up with dozens of chemical formulas on a screen. He brushed off dust that had accumulated, obscuring some of the numbers. They sat anxiously awaiting the results. A minute ticked by.

"Yes, just as I thought. It's germilium," he said, barely able to contain his excitement. "It's probably the rarest element this side of the galaxy. Germilium has only been found on the systems of Edasich 9 and Capella. It is a highly prized and sought-after element. How much do you want for it?"

"It's not for sale," said Ramaan, snatching the box from him. "Thanks for the info, though."

Philip moved closer. "Another thing, Blard, we have picked up an anonymous radio signal coming from Telus-Three. I think my good friend is down there and may be in trouble."

"What, on Telus-Three? You've got to be joking. Your good friend probably stumbled on the signal like you did and got lured to his death. That damn signal has been playing non-stop for decades. I wouldn't go there, if I were you. They'll be waiting."

"Good," put in Philip, "we've a few scores to settle. Oh, another thing, there's been a spacecraft following us from Telus-Six. They seem to be interested in what we were doing down there in their ape burrow."

"That, my friend, could only have been the Dontrian. Did it look something like this?" The receptionist quickly drew a rough sketch.

"Yeah, that's the one," Philip said.

"Hmm, don't try anything with them. They watch and learn. They're the all-seeing, the all-knowing, and until now, they have never caused us or anyone any harm."

"But who are they? Nobody knew anything about them in the Mintaka System."

"They originate from Asmidiske, on the outer regions of Puppis, nine hundred light-years away. We often refer to them as the Slordian people. Slorda is one of the giant planets circling Asmidiske. The Dontrian developed themselves into an ultra-intelligent race dozens of millennia ago and constantly search the galaxy for other forms of life, intelligent or otherwise, peacefully transmitting their way. We know quite a bit about them, but nobody has ever seen them that I know of. Their physical appearance remains a mystery."

Farther down the hallway, Blard showed them his molismolum production. As he explained the possibilities of molismolum and iron blending, they moved closer to the computer.

"By simply pressing a few buttons on this computer—" He never had time to finish the sentence. The radio receptionist ran in, out of breath.

"Blard, sir, I've lost complete contact with the Peblinus bases. They might be up to something. They're never this quiet! The transmissions have stopped, all of them. It's the scariest thing."

Alana, taking a sudden interest, walked to Blard. "Tell us more about these Flaboxian."

The receptionist walked to a wall cupboard and took out some photographs. "Here. One of our scouting parties took these a few days ago on their routine recon inspections of Peblinus territory. These others were taken about six months ago."

The Flaboxian structure was similar to that of the Platnios; it was obvious at a simple glance. The superb, unimaginative Peblinus mind didn't delve too far into the unknown. Their slimmer design enabled a more rapid, slithering movement. The mouth area was bigger, proportioning longer, sharper teeth.

Baygorn could only presume they came equipped with a larger brain because modified, shorter roots revealed a steadier, more accurate movement.

Without wasting time, Ramaan and Alana programmed ten blue-rays to the specifications provided and began placing them on tripods outside on the arid landscape.

Philip asked Blard how the Bods defended themselves against these horrors. He rushed out and returned a few minutes later carrying a selection of weapons.

"We have GF rifles and the standard-issue ion-plasma rifles."

"Well, at least here you've got something; you only had basic ion weapons on Pleniton."

"That's because nobody ever goes there. Pleniton is a forgotten world. It's just an outlandish, frozen, R&D nightmare. They need weapons with built-in heaters. Here, where things start warming up a bit, our application forms are filled out with more importance."

Alana walked in and closed the door. "They're ready. In position."

"How many Flaboxian are there?" enquired Philip, frowning.

"Not many, most of them are on Telus-Four and -Three. At most, about five hundred."

Like Philip and his crew, the 10,000 Bods living in the complex were not adapted to war conditions of any kind. Even though the last years' familiarity had given them first-hand experience in survival, it wasn't quite their customary occupation. They were mostly labourers and scientists trying to do a good day's work and nothing more. Endurance had become the new first Bod law, the first commandment. It began those scant few months ago as the first Flaboxian crawled out from somewhere, and since then have made their continual appearance.

A year later, as the Flaboxian approached the complex once more, no one really knew their real skills and abilities. The Bods were tactically void of any knowledge of their adversary. To Philip and the others, this was all new; but it seemed that the Flaboxian knew the weak points of the Bods. They knew when and how to strike. Due to the lack of shared information, their blue-rays could only deal with about two hundred on the first attack.

Alana noticed that sometimes they could dodge the rays emitted from their rifles with perfect precision.

The battle with the Flaboxian lasted well into the afternoon. As the last Flaboxian fell to its dusty death, Philip thought of the extra-sensory perception they possessed. *Would others come and assist?*

When Blard told Philip that the nearest Peblinus operation was twenty kilometres from them, Alana started the vehicle.

Telus-Five's water was artificial. On the outskirts of the Bod settlement while leaving for the Peblinus complex, they noticed the concave agua-genie, a slanted metallic panel like a spoon continuously facing Alnilam. Six vertical tubes ran the full length of its nearly four-metre height before disappearing into an already full plastic collection trough.

When the complex came in sight, Lexia peered down at her scanner and told Philip the Peblinus complex was deserted. Nothing moved, not a single living soul registered on their motion detectors. It was a ghost town.

Cautiously, they drove to the front entrance. The gate was leaning, battered and heavily scratched. Drawing nearer, there was the horror of it all: hundreds of mangled, decapitated, dismembered bodies; some half-eaten.

Baygorn jumped out of the vehicle. "Look, no bones, no goddamn bones. They've taken everything!"

It had been a massacre. How did they get in? Philip wondered. Blard had told them a solid three-metre electrified metallic fence encircled the complex. Obviously, someone had switched it off by mistake, or there was a power failure.

The yanked-off single door leading into the development was low enough for them to tread over and enter. "This happened recently," said Baygorn, looking at tattered remains. He sighed. "Damn it, such a waste. Such a stupid waste!"

The inner perimeter of the square had offices whose doors had been ripped off, too. More scattered remains lay in front. In a futile attempt, the Peblinus had tried to hide as a last resort.

Like a desert of rubbish, mechanical and electronic parts lay everywhere. Just like the Bod complex, the Peblinus complex itself had suffered immense structural damage.

Ramaan grabbed the attention of Philip. Towards the back of the patio, an unharmed, intact office stood out from the rest. The

Flaboxian had tried in vain to gain entrance, because the windows were armoured and double thick.

They walked to examine the large office. Machines and chemical bottles lined the walls. It was a laboratory. Philip called Baygorn to come have a look. Ramaan forced the lock.

Death was the new inhabitant of the development. Apart from an occasional gust of wind, not a single sound reverberated through its once-lively passageways. The Flaboxian had initiated their strike against their creators, and it was obvious they were not going to back down easily. The Flaboxian were vermin, mistakenly created by a misguided race. Greed ruled the simple mind as this nation of plants, barely a century old, wanted the galaxy, the universe.

Philip knew they would destroy anything that got in their way. Their own personality and behaviour resembled their creators. They were a disturbance upsetting the balance of intellectual, interstellar evolution. The Peblinus had given birth to and unleashed a monster. But there again, the Peblinus were by now renowned and infamous for their inability to think. They did what they thought to be right. They stole whatever and wherever they could, but in the end, it would prove to be more expensive than they could ever imagine.

The Peblinus were suffering more than anyone in this war. The guilty few, who had initiated this plan of mass beneficial genetic slavery all those years ago, obviously had no idea that the Platnios would later turn on them. There was nothing anyone could do to prevent it, because their metamorphosis was changing with each passing day.

The planet had another four settlements of Peblinus, and they were sure that each one of them was as dead as this one. They were a dying race headed for extinction. Philip had to do the only humane thing possible; to save what remained.

The leftovers of the complex revealed nothing of interest except for the lab. As they began to filter through the rubble, their C-12s began to sound. It was an urgent message from Sentrywatcher on the emergency channel. The mysterious space vehicle that had been tailing them was trying to contact them on Channel 80, the emergency frequency.

"Let's do it from down here." Ramaan returned to the vehicle and hooked up the portable antenna while mumbling something about why were the Peblinus manipulating plants, and not flesh and bone, as the connectors clicked into place.

Baygorn overheard him. "Plant life grows quicker. Their genetic manipulability is uncomplicated and straightforward. Obviously the Peblinus needed results, and the faster they got them, the better."

Baygorn's task at hand was to discover their method. The microscope they found inside the lab, especially equipped for the job, handled most of the gruesome tasks, whereas bad luck had done the rest. If they had planned everything with precision from the beginning, it might have been quite different.

As soon as Ramaan had rigged the portable antenna and the last cables clicked into place, they set themselves in front of the visor display, ready to get their first glimpse of the Dontrian. Ramaan pressed the transmit button on the emergency frequency and waited. The visor immediately came to life.

24. Dontrian

Simultaneous thoughts of admiration and horror dominated any words that would have normally been an introduction. They were awestruck. Everything about the man on the screen was different. He had a larger cranial cavity, smaller shoulder dimensions, and one single, complex embedded motionless eye that scrutinised their every thought, their every word and movement. He had no ears.

They were Dontrian, all right. Baygorn recognized the filled skeletons he'd seen on other planets.

The Dontrian greeted them, raising his four-fingered hand in compliance. A tiny vertical aperture for the mouth began uttering their first audible impressions from this superbly cultured nation.

"Greetings to those who come from Earth. I bid you welcome. We have been following you since your departure from Pleniton and entry into this region of the star system that you call Alnilam.

"We come here only as observers and need your assistance in an important matter. There is a situation on Telus-Four and -Three. The Platnios and Flaboxian have begun to obliterate most other forms of life.

"We have an outpost on Telus-Three that is insufficiently armed. We cannot get word to them. I fear their receiver may be broken. As we speak, I am sending across the information you will need. It is vital to the survival of this outpost. If we cannot reach them, they will most certainly be destroyed!"

The image flicked off and blank faces did nothing but stare for a few seconds.

"Let's have a look at what they sent." Alana pushed a button on her communicator. The received images were in tremendous detail regarding every living thing on both planets.

"So nice. What are they doing out here without weapons? How can they call themselves Dontrian, if they can't even protect their own kind?" blurted Lexia cynically.

Philip couldn't answer her, yet it did seem odd. His previous imaginings of the Dontrian seemed to fizzle away and die.

Baygorn continued his search for information in the genetics lab. He searched cupboards and drawers. Everything was unfastened and overturned for inspection, sometimes by applying force. All information they could possibly dig up concerning the Platnios and Flaboxian behaviour, even the microscope, went with them.

"Did you find anything?" asked Blard sharply as Philip stepped out of the vehicle.

"For a start, you won't be having any more problems with the Peblinus. They've all been killed by the Flaboxian."

"What!" Blard's worry was genuine.

"The Dontrian have sent us details of an eruption of Platnios and Flaboxian on Telus-Four and -Three."

Philip quickly returned to talk to the receptionist, who was intent on overhearing the conversation. "And you, what do you know about germilium?"

"Well!" he exclaimed. "The stuff's flawless. Germilium won't produce compounds. It has to do with its high melting temperature. Its semi-conductivity surpasses even light tubes. It's the ultimate element," he said excitedly.

"Imagine what we could do with this technology. Think of the possibilities," whispered Baygorn, turning around and facing Philip.

Looking at the detailed surface map of Telus-Four, they localised two neighbouring Bod settlements. Alana could contact them from the *Excelsior*. The receptionist had given her the correct frequencies to use. Telus-Four was only a day's journey.

✧✧✧

"This is the *Excelsior* calling the Bod community on Telus-Four. Are you receiving me?"

Without hesitation the radio erupted to life with an excited voice. "Hello Humans, we're waiting for you. We've been expecting you. How long till you land?" Radio crackle.

"In ten hours. Arrange for an urgent meeting with your superiors and troops the moment we land."

"I'll get to it right away." The radio clicked off.

The Siberian-blue surface of Telus-Four and its numinous surface temperature of two degrees explained what waited for them in more words than any scan could. It was expecting them, this vast, watery world the size of Mars that was pitted with decarnated islands. Certain perils waited with its dangers—some of which they knew.

They followed the Bod signal and landed the pod directly in front of the Bod community. The moment the pod touched down, an official impatiently trotted towards them with six soldiers following a pace or two behind.

"Thanks for coming, and welcome to Telus-Four. My name is Floyd. The other planets have been informing us of your progress through the system. Come inside."

Philip walked in and introduced the others. "Tell us, Floyd, what's been going on around here?"

"To begin with, the Flaboxian have destroyed three settlements of Peblinus, and are now putting all the pressure they can on us. They are persistent, all right; they have been attacking us at regular intervals. The second Bod community, not too far from here, has received minimal damage. The Flaboxian are continually trying to gain access to both our settlements. They come in vast numbers. I know we cannot hold them off indefinitely."

"How many are there? How many have you killed?"

"Well," said Floyd, "five hundred per day, but it's nothing. There's more than 100,000 out there, scattered about in huge groups; more and more with each passing day. Our scouting teams recently informed us that the Peblinus didn't kill any of them. We think they must have attacked them at night, so we've had extra surveillance scouting during the hours of darkness." Floyd offered them some refreshments.

"Our second outpost has annihilated about four thousand of them. They appear to be holding out pretty well under the circumstances. They are going to need our help and fast, because the next batch of Flaboxian comes off the production line later today. If we don't get to the outpost soon, they won't survive much longer."

"Production line? What are you talking about?"asked Ramaan.

Floyd turned. "The Flaboxian have created two regeneration stations in the vacant Peblinus laboratory hangars. It seems they no longer need their queen to reproduce. Not only are the Flaboxian getting smarter, they're getting faster. It's changing daily; no one knows how."

Philip was sure he blinked his eyes one thousand times, as this was indeed bad news. "Floyd, you obviously haven't heard. The Platnios come equipped with a rapid-evolvement gene. These things aren't just evolving, they're climbing the ladder so fast that by the end of the year they'll be sending their progeny to school to attend maths classes."

"B-but how is that possible?" asked Floyd.

"Oh it's possible, believe me. They knew we were destroying their nests, sneaky swine. Must've found another way to breed. They're slaughtering their creators, utilising the laboratories that gave birth to them while using their genetic architects as food and building material. These things really do have Peblinus blood pumping through their veins!"

Philip huffed. "This regeneration process: how often?"

"Twice a day at set times, about 12,000 at a time."

"Damn, this is serious, very serious," Philip said.

"That's not all," added Floyd. "The new ones go directly to Telus-Three. Another thing, the last ones we clocked at nine kilometres per hour."

By this time Philip was almost speechless. "Anything else you'd like to add? Damn it, this goes beyond comprehension."

Alana pushed into the conversation. "I could send two Tritium bombs to the hatcheries."

"Not enough," broke in Floyd. "The walls of the regenerators have the same enhanced resins that we use. They'll deflect the heat generated by your bombs."

Philip's eye did a wink. "Then we wait till they come out. They have to open up sooner or later. The moment they do, Alana can launch two Tritium devices and detonate them inside."

Alana's cynical look soured. "That's absurd. Philip, don't you think you're cutting it a bit fine?"

Ignoring the comment, Philip asked, "When's the next batch due?"

"In an hour." That was all the information Philip needed. He looked towards his crew. They knew him; they understood and could read his thoughts. They'd spent more than a decade together. Without further word, Philip and the others ran out, leaving Floyd in a stupor with questions of his own.

Alana started the engine, looked at Philip, gave a frown and drove to the location Floyd had pointed out on the map. It was true. Indeed, this hunter wanted to keep close to both Bod encampments. Scattered Flaboxian guards strategically encircled the two hangars of mass production.

Alana stopped the vehicle a kilometre from the gigantic sliding doors and parked in a ditch out of sight. Alana and Ramaan began setting up the two launch pads while Philip placed a couple of short-range blue-rays around their new temporary installation. Lexia and Baygorn waited in the safety of the protected vehicle. Alana programmed the computer to launch both Tritium warheads the moment the outer hangar doors began to open. They crouched low and peeked over the rim.

It was obvious the Flaboxian were not expecting any trouble. The guards were few in number, but they seemed anxious about something. They were nervous and jumpy looking.

As the hour ticked by, both hangar doors slowly, almost unnoticeably, began to slide apart. Seconds later, a sea of barking, neonate Flaboxian playfully streamed out towards the awaiting spaceships on the other side of the hill. The Tritium warheads launched automatically. Eight seconds later, both warheads silently detonated with total blue-white flash. An unstoppable wave of heat erupting from the fusion instantly incinerated everything in and around the hangars. The barking stopped. Silence. A deadness spawned from hell itself.

Philip had felt the tremendous heat through his suit and imagined for just a brief instant that another sun had appeared.

A minute later, Alana looked at her scanner and gave Philip a diagnostic. "There's still a lot of interference from the explosion. Nothing moving, if that's what you want know."

Enthusiastically, Philip popped his head up above the rim and stared in the direction of the hangars. The sand was black, one giant ink stain of fused, crackly sand. Carbonised remains of

Flaboxian were blowing everywhere, provoking a strange ozone odour.

Alana, armed with renewed stamina, drove the vehicle out from the protected ditch.

Ten minutes later, they neared the second Bod complex. Two Bods, lurking near the front entrance with GF rifles, had obviously had seen the incredibly bright flash of light from the explosion.

Alana stopped the vehicle. Ramaan jumped out and walked up to them. "Hi there, any idea where they go after they come out of the hangars?"

The Bod raised an eyebrow and silently studied Ramaan's words. Finally, he spoke. "Over the hill. It's the same place every time."

The Bod's vague answer annoyed Ramaan, forcibly making him pry for more answers, "And the guards; where are they?"

The Bod seemed confused by Ramaan's presence and questioning. He curled his face sideways with a strange grin.

Lexia began to feel uncomfortable. Philip said, "We're going to rig up a defence barrier around your perimeter wall. It will secure your safety and ours while we're here."

Philip's comforting words didn't make the Bod change his aspect. He continued glaring with off-centred bewilderment. His left eyebrow fluttered out of line to the rest of his face. Seconds passed before he answered with a stutter. "Tha—that's kind of y-you."

Alnilam was beginning to set itself picturesquely on the horizon, concluding the day. By the time Baygorn, Lexia, and Philip had reached the centre of the complex, Ramaan and Alana had already placed twenty blue-rays along the perimeter wall.

Baygorn commented on the Bod's eccentric behaviour. "Could be fatigue, I've seen it many times. But wait, come to think of it, Bods normally introduce themselves. This guy has hardly said a word."

"Leave the poor man alone," intervened Lexia, "Like you said, it's probably fatigue. Remember, they've had a rough couple of days."

"And we haven't? Anyway, I still think it's odd. Guess I'm just used to good manners."

25. Metamorphosis

They entered the darkening laboratory, immediately noticing an abundance of laminium experiments strewn on work surfaces. Dust and pieces of rock spewed over from scratched, dirty tabletops, falling uncaringly onto the floor. Crinkled papers and bent folders governed the floor in heaps. Their still un-introduced host robotically went on and showed them the rock samples they had extracted earlier that day.

Philip noticed the date tag plainly showing four days before. Ninety-six hours before. As Philip mentally compared the date with his spoken words, the Bod suddenly and abruptly placed both hands onto his head and jaggedly backed away from them. A high-pitched, ear-piercing scream that would have made the hairs of a bear stand up abruptly left his lips.

Here in the lugubrious shadows and the approaching darkness of the laboratory, Gahm and Bobby once more sprang to their minds. They then realised that this Bod colony was lifeless. It had died four days ago when the Flaboxian regiment had changed, transmuting themselves into this likeable Bod race during the day and decided to pay a visit.

The Platnio-oxian could perform this metamorphosis with any culture. It was the same as Haradan. They must've entered during the day in their human form, made acquaintances with the tired and worn-out settlement. By then, it was too late. When nighttime had arrived three or four days ago, they transformed themselves back into their Flaboxian likeness and killed everyone there. It was too easy. It was the way the Flaboxian liked it, and it started making sense. By this time, the Bod in front of them began to change. They watched his body slothfully remodel itself into a fully grown Flaboxian war machine. Alana vaporised it before it had completed the cycle.

Outside in the camp, nothing had changed since their descent into the lab, as there was still too much light. They used these last few minutes to their advantage. They picked up some belongings, left the settlement and left the perimeter wall of blue-rays active and armed to kill.

At the other colony, an anxious Floyd awaited their return.

"We could feel the heat from here. How's the other colony holding out? Did you manage to talk to Brandton?"

"So that was his name. He never told us his name. To answer your question, Floyd, I am afraid to say, they are all dead. They were killed three or four nights ago by a disguised Flaboxian battalion. They must've mutated and entered the encampment in the form of Bods." Floyd didn't seem convinced, so Philip handed him some of their belongings to prove his story.

"Floyd, we've seen this happen before. The most important thing now is to destroy those two spacecraft on the other side of that hill before they take off and warn the others. Believe me, they will come."

They climbed into the vehicle and made their way towards the hill with a lightning dash. Reaching a tall dune, they stopped, climbed out and peeped over the top. Two spacecraft well in the distance, two or three kilometres away on a sandy plain, still waited for the new Flaboxian to arrive. The sporadically placed Flaboxian guards were nervous and on edge.

Ramaan had to get the exact location. They ducked back down. If the guards saw them, they wouldn't stand a chance. Ramaan reached into his side bag, extracted a heli-spy, switched it on and released it into the air, while Alana prepared two mini launch pads. Once Ramaan knew the exact coordinates of the two craft, he would feed them from his heli-spy into the launch pads.

The heli-spies also gave Ramaan a 360-degree view of the terrain. He looked down at the screen. "Ah-ha, that's better, you little—"

Philip peered at the monitor with the typical melon-shaped craft together with hundreds of anxious, waiting soldiers just in front. Ramaan quickly extracted the information from the heli-spy and fed it into the launch pads.

Without a second to lose, Alana and Baygorn sent the two missiles on their way. Alana said it would take twelve seconds for the missiles to reach the targets three kilometres away. There were two brilliant, yellow-white flashes. The spacecrafts' inhabitants died seconds after, culminating in an orangey fizzle.

Death no longer was the unwanted visitor disguised as the Flaboxian or Platnios. The reanimated landscape of Telus-Four, now quiet and tranquil, had regained the natural stillness it once had. It became just another planet in the system of Alnilam.

The only remaining Flaboxian on Telus-Four were pretending to be their human foes in the second Bod complex under guard by their blue-rays. Returning to the encampment, Floyd was ecstatic when he heard their story of the two spacecraft disappearing in an orangey fanfare.

"That's fantastic! Come, I've something to show you," he said, grabbing Philip's arm. "It's payback time. These Peblinus chaps are in for a bit of a shock. We've also been experimenting with gene splicing. I think our methods are a bit more advanced than theirs, though."

They lowered themselves into a large subterranean room where the already well-underway operation had produced sixty small, icky sacks the size of a fist.

"Those are the remainders; we sent the other forty to Telus-Three a few weeks ago. They should be coming back any time with the results. Maybe they can help shed light on them."

Each egg was lying on a separate thermo-tray behind an isolated heavy door with a rounded window. Two guards patrolled the exterior.

"Unlike the Peblinus, we've taken their experiment this time and introduced both Bod and Peblinus DNA, altering Chromosome Number Three. The results are going to be spectacular. I can't wait to finally see them on the battlefield. Isn't it exciting? We are going to mingle them in with the Flaboxian. Ours will be stronger and a lot more intelligent, of course. Naturally, they will be under our control."

"You say you sent forty to Telus-Three?" Baygorn wore a worried look.

"Yeah, the growth from bacteria to egg stage was so rapid, it only took six days—I was so thrilled, I nearly cried. I'll show you some of the matured ones later."

With raised eyebrows, Baygorn looked at the others. "Floyd, I don't know who is worse. What are you going to call them? Peblods, Bodloxian?"

Floyd gave a laugh. "Don't worry, my friends." He smiled. "You've really got nothing to worry about; the experiment is well controlled."

They followed him up a ramp.

"The first eggs started appearing from the soup two weeks ago, and by golly do they grow." Floyd reached into one of the trays with unprotected hands and lifted up one of the bright-yellow soft eggs the size of a blown-up balloon. It was lightly speckled with brown spots and gave Philip the shivers. It looked venomous. Surrounding each egg was the green, sticky soup that smelt like ammonia, and had what looked like dead flies floating in it.

"No, we are not going to call them Peblods or the other thing. Before you, my friends, is the beginning of the Bodan. Imagine the worst of the Flaboxian mixed with the worst of the Bod and Peblinus. These three wrongs will make it right," said Floyd ecstatically. "You'll see."

"Where did you learn that? Christ, this is biochemistry, not mathematics. Things in biochemistry go wrong just as they do in nature."

"Like I said, don't panic. From our vantage point, we will control them and they will think like us. They will eradicate the Flaboxian, and we will be the victor."

Alana stepped in. "And what if they don't? What if they interbreed with the Flaboxian, what then? Imagine an overly intelligent, Lep- and Peblinus-speaking intergalactic metamorphic weed that eats people."

Ramaan laughed.

Floyd wasn't amused. "Not entirely true, the batch we sent comes with a built-in destruct mechanism. It's there if something goes wrong."

"Then destroy them all. My God, in case you haven't noticed, Telus-Three's our next stop. I'll be damned if we're going to go down there with a frying pan as well," added Baygorn teasingly.

"What's a frying pan?" enquired Floyd.

"Drop it, will you!" snapped Baygorn, "Where's this remote destruct mechanism of yours?"

"On the wall by the window." Floyd's hand pointed to a relatively small, square box.

"How long do they live after it's activated?" pried Baygorn.

"Ten minutes," commented Floyd, unhurriedly getting out of his chair. "Are you sure you want me to do this?" he asked.

Simultaneously Baygorn, Lexia, and Ramaan shouted, "Yes, now!"

He lifted the flap of the control panel and revealed a pulsating red light. He turned and looked at them one more time before pressing the button. The light went off. He closed the box and returned to his chair. "That's it," he said, "The process is irreversible. I couldn't stop it even if I tried."

Philip then told him to destroy the sixty dormant eggs on trays.

As he walked to them, brushing the security guards to one side, the eggs began moving around, sensing his nearness, twitching. Something alive inside each tennis ball-sized sack made Ramaan comment on fingers. Floyd pushed a red switch. The movement stopped instantly.

"And the forty you sent to Telus-Three?" Philip's enquiring grin made Floyd reach for the communicator.

"Floyd calling Ghabi station, are you there?" A friendly voice came on the speaker.

"Hey Floydie, how ya doing? Some of your eggie things started waking up a few moments ago. Some died; I count at least twenty here. Handsome little critters they are."

"Listen to me, Ghabi. I've five real good friends here that have probably saved us from a big fix. They are due to arrive on Telus-Three in two days. Whatever happens, I want you to destroy the eggs. Get rid of them. Leave the live specimens; they'll know what to do when they get there."

"Must be those humans. I've been hearing all about them. Don't worry, Floyd, I'll make sure no one touches them. They'll be all right."

Before they left Telus-Four, Alana gave Floyd and his elite squad twenty blue-ray rifles. She explained the programming and mounting procedures. "Leave them active at all times. Don't trust anyone who wanders into the camp from the outside. Except for you, there's no one out there!" She somehow knew that what she'd said wouldn't sink in, so from her remote station she programmed the twenty blue-rays around the perimeter of the second encampment to shoot for Bod or Flaboxian. Within ten minutes, every living thing in the second camp had died. She returned them back to their neutral position.

"Well, Floyd, I believe our task here is complete. We'll contact you from Telus-Three."

"Thank you for your help and for what you've done for us," said Floyd. "We are forever in your debt."

"Now, don't start getting melodramatic on me," Philip said as he waved goodbye to one of the good guys.

26. Renaissance

As they made the final preparations to orbit Telus-Three, the unceasing transmission emanating from its surface gained in amplitude. Everything about it was eerie. Through the speaker, it sounded like a cat being strangled in an echo chamber. The random pitch drifting and low frequency modulation dwindled into a hissing silence every five minutes. The five-minute interval of hissing silence contained dense multi-layered data pockets of video, data, and audio into which were crammed ninety terabytes of information. Why did Mike come here instead of following orders? He knew he had to investigate the planets in their order. *It wasn't his style,* thought Philip, listening to the transmission for the umpteenth time. It just didn't make sense. Maybe he'd interpreted something hidden in the signal that Ramaan hadn't figured out yet and came straight here.

Apart from the thousands of images, the person or people sending the transmission needed help, Philip was sure of that part. It was in all intents and purposes an SOS, but there was no mention of why. The more Ramaan tried to untangle it, the more baffled he became.

"Even stranger," added Lexia, "I cannot pinpoint the exact location of the signal." Lexia had recreated a similar code and prepared a blip transmission destined for the unknown area. It simply read: "What is your emergency?"

The instant Lexia transmitted it, the signal from Telus-Three ceased. Galactic static and hiss broke over the speaker with the odd occasional radiation murmur-gurgle from Alnilam. Less than a minute later, the radio broke its own silence and a voice came hurtling through the speaker. "Is that you, Humans? We are the Peblinus. We could be destroyed at any moment by Flaboxian. We not last vely long."

Ramaan grabbed the microphone. "We have some urgent business to take care of first, we'll be there tomorrow. Hold out for as long as you can, you hear?"

"I cannot guarantee that," said the voice as Sentrywatcher's radar detected a stationary object with a flickering orange light on the horizon.

Philip rushed to the screen. "Look, there she is. Oh Mike, where are you?" Philip studied the radar as Lexia moved closer and tenderly touched his arm. Mike's ship came up as an oval blip flickering in yellow.

Anxiously, he moved towards Alana in a hopeful tone. "Any life signs?"

Alana pressed a couple of switches. "Nothing. Not a goddamn thing." Alana looked up. "Sorry, Captain; I know you'd like to hear something different. I just wish I could say it."

Philip relaxed and placed his hand on her shoulder. "I know, Alana, thanks. I have to face this thing." He shrugged and squinted once more at the enlarged visual image of the *Renaissance* still one thousand kilometres away. It was a mirror image of his own *Excelsior*, a replica, cold and quiet, covered in a yellow hue caused by atmospheric radiation and bitter cold.

"There's more, Philip. A month in space with life support deactivated also means it is gently heading on a collision course for the planet. It wouldn't take long for Telus-Three to pull the *Renaissance* towards certain destruction."

Alana quickly calculated that it had already lost eighty kilometres since Mike's disappearance.

"She could probably withstand only another two weeks of orbital deterioration, at best, before it's too late. That gravity's getting too strong. Good thing we came when we did."

Although the beckoning planet yanked, pulled and tugged at the *Renaissance*, it seemed to float motionless at its near-nine hundred kilometre height.

Ramaan fired a secondary retro rocket to pull them gently alongside. Lexia and Baygorn made the final preparations to join up and board her. There was a soft magnetic clunk as the two spacecraft met.

Ramaan opened the outer hatch. A rush of stale air breached through onto the *Excelsior* with a faint hiss. Philip inserted a diagnostic cable from the *Excelsior* into an identical slot on the *Renaissance*.

"Okay, let's do another scan."

Ramaan, carrying a portable device, peered at the screen. "The on-board computer seems to be online and working okay. The interior compartments have ample oxygen, sufficient for life support. There's also lots of stored data for retrieval, but there is definitely no one on-board, Philip. Mike and his crew are undeniably not there."

"All right then, let's open her up."

Baygorn opened a bag of spanners and selected one. "I once rescued seventy oxygen-starved passengers from the *Defiance* with this spanner when it was orbiting Naiad, Neptune's smallest moon. At first, the insurance company tried blaming it on a small rock that had pierced the outer hull, producing a hole one millimetre in diameter. Most of the oxygen had leaked out by the time I reached them. What they didn't know is that the Adams ring is not comprised of the substance they found in the tiny rock sample, so sabotage came into the limelight."

"You must have been proud of yourself, rescuing all those people."

Baygorn's face strained as he turned the spanner. "I was. The fault was later diagnosed as being caused by a simple short-circuit. Apparently, an air filter exploded and a housing nut acted like a bullet, rupturing the hull. It was the insurance company who'd come up with the rock story," said Baygorn, giving the final twist.

The inner door opened and gave way with a long, fusty hiss. The smell was strong and somewhat metallic. The interior light was subdued with a bluish tinge. Philip's eyes adjusted. A constant, low-frequency humming reached out from beyond the passageway. It came from the ever-weakening trajectory stabilizers battling to keep them in orbit. Everything at first glance seemed intact and unharmed without evidence of foul play. There was no sign of activity and nothing moved. There were only lights blinking in the distance on a control panel. It seemed like a still-life painting.

Philip went straight to Mike's cabin to look at his log entries and computer readouts. Before leaving Earth during one of his silly moments, Philip had played hide-and-seek with Mike and his crew on this very ship. They weren't always those hard-figured, sour-faced, unsympathetic captains everyone grew timid at the sight of.

Where are you hiding now, my friend? Philip thought. One of his pods was missing, so wherever it was, Mike would be, too.

Ramaan came to give Philip a hand with the computer. "Let's see what we've got here." Ramaan flicked a switch.

"Just the last ones concern us; Terron can sift through the others when the *Renaissance* gets there." A synthetic voice announced the message.

"Captain's log 841-2100." Mike's handsome, stern face came on the screen.

"The composition of a strong distress signal originating from Telus-Three has veered us from our original path and brought us here. After several unsuccessful attempts at the decoding of its content, we had to come and see it for ourselves. Not only is it an emergency beacon with a message, its modulation, frequency and amplitude go far beyond our technological capabilities." -End-of-message.

"The others are mostly Pleniton and the funnel," said Ramaan, switching off the computer.

"I was right, it was the transmission that lured him down there." Philip retrieved the data Mike had captured before his disappearance and muddled it together with the data the Dontrian had given him. They needed as much information as possible before landing in the middle of the battle zone.

Lexia and Alana had programmed the *Renaissance* for its journey back to Terron, which would take almost two weeks. The main engines taking her to light speed would only fire when she was well out of the orbit of Telus-Three.

"That's it." Lexia joined Philip and Ramaan in Mike's cabin. "The *Renaissance* begins her countdown in ten hours."

Alana, walking in a minute later, commented on the spotless surfaces. "Hey, has anyone noticed the cleanliness of this place? It's been a couple of weeks, but the floor's so clean we could eat off it!"

Philip stopped thinking about the transmission and looked at Alana, hardly understanding what she'd said. Subconsciously, he looked at the floor. One thing about space, the longer you leave a room, a fine layer of dust always accumulates, like on Earth. Dust does exist in the profane depths of space. In the cargo bay, Baygorn discovered sprinklings of it, but only in that sector of the *Renaissance*. The rest of the ship was completely clean. Someone or something had come aboard during Mike's absence.

"Ramaan, look: As absurd as it sounds, Alana's got a point." Philip ran a finger over Mike's tabletop.

"See, Lexia. Run another scan, tell me something. Whoever or whatever they were, there's no sign of them. They must've come and gone."

The *Renaissance* had all the modern luxuries that Philip shared on the *Excelsior*. Mike had exactly the same weapons they did, and he knew how to use them as well as Philip and his crew. They also went to the Military Academy together, which meant they had the same tactical experience. Even the dried-up tea expender in the passageway was still hot and undisturbed between the office rooms.

Ramaan tapped Philip on the shoulder. "Whatever the reason is for their leaving," Ramaan said, "there's nothing broken. It's all here as it was, as it should be." Their expending machines only served a variety of teas and not other delicious beverages. During the trip, they had often made remarks about their tea-bag faces, or tea-leaves for brains.

Leaving Mike's cabin and strolling into the passageway, Alana pointed out a beetle the size of a grape sitting on top of Baygorn's helmet he'd left on the rack. Its carapace had a beautiful metallic sheen; in fact, she would almost have been prepared to swear that it was metal. That was an interesting idea. Could it be robotic and not an animal? She stared at the beetle intently with this thought in mind, analysing the best she could the details of its anatomy. Where it should have had a mouth was a collection of manipulators that reminded Alana strongly of the multi-purpose knives that are a delight of all red-blooded boys. There were pincers, probes, files and something that looked like a drill. But none of this was decisive without closer inspection. It sat there staring and rubbing its long antennae before scuttling off in the other direction.

"How'd that little critter get on-board?" Lexia's question directed itself at Alana, but she had no answer.

"We haven't yet seen Mike's laboratory," Philip said, changing direction. Mike's round laboratory, like their own, contained four tables, all covered with jars and specimens. Two beetles lay cut open and dissected beneath the microscope viewer.

"This must have happened just before he left," commented Philip. Ramaan came and reviewed the medical logs. Once more Mike's face came onto the viewer.

"We've come across a cloud of space insects that entered our venting system, so we've had to go down to Telus-Three with what we can to escape from this menace. They are venomous beetles. Shorda and Sheppard have been bitten and have fallen ill. My virometer cannot come up with a medical solution. I, too, may succumb to these small creatures if we don't get off the *Renaissance* as soon as possible." *Mike never backed down or worried about anything*, thought Philip, but he could plainly see Mike was perturbed.

The log continued: "They seem to react only to extreme heat. We cannot fire on them because of their size and their number is too great! The space cloud took us completely by surprise. It passed directly on top of us 40,000 kilometres above Telus-Three. According to Sentrywatcher, the space cloud contains eight billion beetles."

After hearing the log, they stared at one another. "So Mike left in a hurry to get away from these little creatures. It's time we went back to the *Excelsior*. There's not much we can do from here unless we want to end up like Mike." Without further word, they set off for the *Excelsior*.

Alana walked to the Sentrywatcher console and made a proximity scan. "I got them. There they are; little freaks. We didn't see them cuz we were more interested in the *Renaissance* and the planet below; didn't think anything would be above us. Who said beetles don't have strategy? Really clever."

Alana was programming one of the Tritium bombs. "Someone told me they like heat. I got a nice self-guiding atomic cocktail for them. I hope they like it. As you know, tritium in the vacuum of space is gonna cover a much bigger area." Alana switched off the panel, remotely placed the Tritium bomb into the manual launch pad and gyrated the joystick before selecting the densest area of beetles. She looked at Sentrywatcher's statistics of the cloud. "That looks like a nice clump." Her left hand reached down and pressed the ignition. Eight minutes later, a supernova sunburst of white-blue flash shone through the portholes. The menacing cloud disappeared in an instant.

Philip walked to the communications console. "We've located the *Renaissance*, Jim."

"Excellent news. How is she?"

"Perfect condition, but there was an infestation of venomous beetles aboard. Looks like Mike had to leave in a hurry. We are going down to Telus-Three to find him. The *Renaissance* will reach you in about two weeks. Take good care and watch out for beetles when you open her. Over and out."

Alana disengaged the *Excelsior* from the *Renaissance* and put some distance between them before they turned their sights once more towards the planet below.

The extreme climate of rain and snowstorms revealed that the surface of Telus-Three was as un-welcoming to the space traveller as it was to the sturdy land-dweller already living there. After performing the protocol regulations, Alana disengaged the pod from the *Excelsior*.

During the descent, Ramaan and Baygorn analysed the accumulated data once more, and an hour later, they came up with the ultimate plan to save all concerned. Alana would land them in a boggy section situated quite close to the Bod encampment. The three were in a tight V with the Platnios right in the middle. The farthest were the Dontrian, all nicely snuggled-up in their antisocial base in the south. They would be more difficult to reach, so Philip would go and see them last.

On the other hand, the Peblinus always liked to stick as close as possible to the Bod. It was in their nature, and their reasoning was that they didn't like to be left out of anything.

27. The Plot

Nearing the surface, their radar confirmed that the Flaboxian and Platnios had concentrated themselves in the middle of the three outposts at equal distances, just as the hunter always likes to stick close to the prey. Only in this case, there were millions of them against Philip, the Bods, the Peblinus, and the Dontrian. They were a pitiful few in comparison, and well outnumbered. Philip made a guess of a thousand to one. Then what were they waiting for? They could take them all in a day, wipe the ground with them. The differences between them were their technologies. Their weapons would be the deciding factor in this war, not forgetting their advanced brain. Of course, Philip was referring to his crew, and the Bods or Peblinus.

They'd initially hoped the Dontrian would've been the deciding factor; the much-needed crowbar. But they were still a mystery, and their first and last conversation could only but make them wonder if they were going to be of any help at all. The hunter was armed with voraciousness and a hunger that went beyond the limits of comprehension. It came bundled together with an equally incomprehensible number.

They had two hundred blue-rays at their disposition, having taken the stock from the *Renaissance*. Their objective was to place a formidable wall around each encampment before provoking the Platnios into an attack.

"Remember, we have to do this quietly. Any sound can trigger off their alarm, then it's all over!" exclaimed Philip.

While Alana inconspicuously drove to Ghabi station, taking the longest possible route so they wouldn't set off the alarm, Ramaan noticed four Flaboxian battle craft settle in the distance. Alana had to stop the vehicle, so as to not to be seen.

"Look at them. They are coming from all over the place." From a distance, even before pulling up in front of the Bod complex, they were instantly recognised. As Alana steadily slowed the vehicle to a halt, a flow of comments leapt through the air.

"Look, it's the Humans!" one of them joyfully commented as he walked over with four others.

Philip instructed him, "We're going place blue-ray rifles around your complex. How many of you are available to operate them?"

"We have less than five hundred good shooters. Last week, we lost eighty of our best shooters in an unexplainable gas explosion close to the Peblinus sector."

"They will be enough." Philip explained his simple plan. "With sixty blue-rays strategically placed around your encampment, you should have sufficient protection."

Alana and Ramaan disappeared with a couple of Bod helpers.

"One important point: From this time onwards, do not to use your radios. The Flaboxian could be listening to your conversations. Another ten elite, the best of you, will each receive another blue-ray to use as a manually operated weapon. The Dontrian and Peblinus bases are going to get the same treatment. We have to rid ourselves of this genetic plant before it's too late!"

Philip stomped off and returned to the vehicle to collect Alana and Ramaan.

Twenty kilometres to the east, on their arrival at the Peblinus base and laboratory compound, the outer doors automatically began to open. As Alana drove inside, a waiting group of white-clad scientists approached their vehicle.

One of them immediately began to speak, even before they had time to climb out. "We don't know where they come from," he said. "These new creatures, they're our Platnios and they're not. They're hollible, they just came out of nowhere!" Arms were furiously flying about in all directions like he was a monstrosity from the deep about to attack. "You gotta believe me!"

"All right, calm down. What are you trying to say?" asked Philip.

"I'm talking about this new Platnios. They seemed to have created themselves and no one knows how. One day they just appeared and attacked us completely by surprise."

"But you must've known about the accelerated-evolvement gene? Your Platnios were genetically engineered with it. As each day passes, six years of their evolutionary process ticks by," said Baygorn.

"We're engineers; we know nothing about this gene, this—this genetic determinant. The Peblinus must've researched it on another planet."

Philip could see the reply was genuine. He could also see that things were getting worse as the grim picture got grimmer. The fingers that had stigmatised Telus-Three suddenly stopped pointing. *Then where do they come from? Who was responsible?* Philip thought.

Ramaan and Alana mounted the blue-rays along the perimeter wall, as there was nothing more they could do at this stage. Looking at these Peblinus, their aspect, their morale, it was evident they had suffered a great deal. Their worn-out and tired behaviour made it evidently clear.

Driving away from the Peblinus, full of divine wonder, Alana swivelled the vehicle south. So far, their plan had been a success. During the drive and thinking of what lay ahead, Philip compared his anxiety to his initial NASA assessment hearing eleven years before.

Ever had that feeling when you are about to meet the big boss of a large corporation? The interview of a lifetime that would not only guarantee a fat paycheck, it would come with a sporty vehicle, and status that boosted the lowest of morale. Philip was one of seven hundred fit and intelligent enough to qualify for this command position. One day it dwindled down to five. He was one of them. That day he was to meet the executive chairman and vice president of NASA. It was to be a five-hour interview. Philip sat on a chair with a glass of water and answered questions shot at him from six different directions. It was the hardest interview of his life, but he answered every one of them, putting him where he was today, in the thralls of meeting the Dontrian. Philip felt now, like he did back then. Blinking, Philip smiled and returned to face the front of the vehicle.

Their aerial infrared revealed they could reach the Dontrian encampment by going twenty kilometres farther east before going south. Various Flaboxian scouts had dug themselves in along the route, evading visual scanners. From there, they would have to move in a southwesterly direction ten kilometres, and then due south. Dense clouds formed and it began to drizzle.

The Dontrian encampment was round and built like a garrison with a blue laser grid preventing them from entering. Drops of slow, steady rain fizzled, vaporising on the laser shield. They stood outside the force field on the desert landscape one metre away. Philip could feel the hairs on his body standing up. On the other side of the grid, a slow-moving creature came towards them.

"Hurangh largmat em sturnyap?" he asked.

Philip could see that despite his appearance, he was just a young man. "I am sorry, we don't understand you. Do you understand me?"

The Dontrian twiddled with something on his shoulder. The device gave a click. "Who are you, what is it you want from us?"

Philip moved away slightly from the grid. "Your superiors have contacted us. They seemed worried, they can't reach you. They say your receiver is down, maybe broken. They want us to help."

"Oh, you must be the Humans," the Dontrian said. The face produced what Philip thought to be a smile. "We have been expecting you."

With a simple gesture of his wrist, the force shield fizzled off and dissipated. Alana drove their vehicle inside. Philip couldn't help but notice they were doing everything in slow motion.

"I know this disturbs you," said the young Dontrian. "Where we come from speed is not of great importance. We have the ability to move faster if need be. Our technology moves fast, not us."

"You might have exceptional technology, but your superiors feel that you are inadequately armed. They say you won't be able to defend yourselves against the threat of Flaboxian twenty kilometres from here. The Flaboxian could arrive at any moment. We have come to help. With your permission, we will install sixty of our special rifles along your perimeter wall. They will give you more protection."

"Be my guest," said the young Dontrian.

"We will use the remaining five blue-rays just in case."

The entire Dontrian complex housed three hundred of their species. Four spherical guardhouses floated ten metres above

Michael Gilwood

the sandy terrain. Within each transparent, drifting, globular complex, two Dontrian patiently waited for the Platnios. Occasionally, the Dontrian eyeballed them as well. Philip could feel it; his sixth-sense thingy always warned him. Philip asked the young Dontrian why he hadn't responded to their high command's urgent request.

"That wasn't high command, it was my father. I refused to speak with him because he thinks I cannot take care of myself. We know about the mutant threat. My well-trained staff and I can take care of it. Oh! I must apologise. I haven't introduced myself; I am Gor Betican, the first son of Lord Betican of the Capella System. We are honoured to have you here as our guests."

As Gor spoke, Philip studied him, from his extraordinary orange apparel to strange looks. It didn't intimidate him in the least. Philip actually began to feel comfortable around him.

"Thank you, Gor. I would like to tell your father via your communicating device that you are in one piece. And then I would like to discuss our plan of attack together with your forces against the Platnios."

"Please, go ahead," said Gor, showing him where the elaborate transmitter was and how to use it.

"Hello, Lord Betican, this is the human. We spoke earlier."

Lord Betican replied, "I see you've reached my son in good health and timing. Protect him well and you'll be rewarded well. We have been studying the enemy for you from our vantage point up here. They are breeding extremely fast. They add 10,000 to their forces every hour. It appears they are waiting to gain enough in number to attack. If they move, I will notify you."

"Thank you for all your help, Lord Betican," said Philip, placing the communicator back on the table.

While Philip was speaking to Lord Betican, the others were installing the remaining blue-rays along the perimeter wall.

"That's the last of them," said Ramaan.

"How many tritium warheads and launch pads are there?" asked Philip.

"Five," responded Ramaan.

Philip pressed Talk on the transmitter. "Lord Betican, can you give us the exact location of the Flaboxian?"

"There are two main forces. One is exactly 21.8 kilometres from you. It is due north, 312 degrees. The other is more active. It is based at between 20.6 and 22.5 kilometres, at north 316 degrees."

With this information, Alana programmed the five warheads to explode simultaneously, loaded them onto their launch pads and sent them towards their targets.

There was a distant flash and a blinding scorch as an enormous wave of light contained the message of triumph and glory.

The radio erupted with the voice of Lord Betican. "Your aiming was perfect! Your antiquated weapons appear to have completely devastated the Platnios, but various subterranean Flaboxian battalions have come to the surface and are directing themselves towards the complex of my son as we speak. Protect him well and we will meet up sooner than you think. And by the way, Philip, refrain from calling me Lord Betican. Please call me Alixus."

"You should be honoured," said Gor. "I can think of only three people who can call him by that name. We are two of them."

With regenerated esteem and lesser concern, Philip broke radio silence and communicated the results to the Bod and Peblinus complexes, advising them to be on maximum alert.

Unperturbed by the danger, Gor started explaining to Philip and Lexia a little about the Dontrian race. Philip, in turn, explained that they had seen evidence of their kind in the Mintaka system some months before. "How long have you been based on Telus-Three?"

"Three months," said Gor.

"During that time, have you seen a man dressed like myself who came here ten weeks before? His name is Captain Branigan."

"No," said Gor, "but when this is all over, I will personally help you find him."

From their raised position on a slight hill in the Dontrian complex, Philip had an all-round view of four kilometres. Alana and Ramaan had placed eight blue-ray rifles in higher, tactical regions to be on the safe side. Over flat areas, the firing distance of the blue-ray could reach up to five kilometres and the remaining fifty, now strategically placed outside the wall of the complex, had the perfect view. They were ready for them, ready to serve proverbial justice on the dinner plate and feed it to them.

Ramaan walked over and asked Gor about germilium.

"It is the fourteenth element in our table of elements," he said. "It has the same weight as what you call lithium. On our planet, we have 209 elements. Germilium is freely available, and we use it in anything electronic or mechanical. Its melting point of 7,000 degrees and ideal semi-conductivity makes it the perfect element. It is also immune to all types of radiation in existence and has the equivalent strength of what you call tungsten. The abundance of this element is also protected by us. I am sure Alixus would love to share its secrets with you."

Suddenly, the radio splattered out the voice of Alixus. "They're ten kilometres from your position!"

All Dontrian were on full alert. When the first wave arrived, they were immediately vaporized, even before they could reach three kilometres. The second wave changed aspect by donning a human form. Alana pressed a few buttons on her display pad, and they received the same treatment. Philip could hear their barking even from that distance. Wave after wave they advanced, and wave after wave they died. Then there was a silence as the blue-rays cooled.

A minute later, they continued without firing a single shot. What were the Flaboxian up to? Suddenly, out on the horizon, one of the blue-rays seemed to throw itself into the air by invisible hands. Another two followed. They didn't see anything; where were they? Two more blue-rays flung themselves, high into the air.

Alana frantically looked around at the barren panorama with her infrared and saw nothing. The visible advancing, sidewinder-slide of footprints made by the invisible advancing stalker made it obvious of the diminishing distance between them. Philip could hear them barking, but they were not to be seen anywhere.

"I don't see anything!" Alana said with concern. "I'm switching to ultraviolet!" Alana tapped in a command. "Ah, there you are."

Alana's toothy smile looked down at their bluish forms on the scanner. Two of the faster ones were turning up blue-rays.

"Switch to ultraviolet, they've changed composition!" shouted Alana, firing manually at the oncoming barking wall. They all died.

Philip quickly lifted his radio. "Leave that one. I'm going take it back with us to study."

The four guard towers dislocated themselves and floated off to destroy any vagrants. As Ramaan placed a hardened glass case around the Flaboxian captive and readied it for transport back to the pod, Gor walked over.

"My father was right to have sent you." Gor grabbed his communicating device.

"Hello, Father." The language briefly changed back to their own.

From Philip's distance of three metres, he could clearly hear Alixus' raised voice through the speaker. He had no idea what they were saying, but judging by the expression on Gor's face, it told him everything he needed to know.

"My father wants to speak with you." A quick outstretched hand passed over the mouthpiece.

"Thank you. You have achieved what I asked of you. I am entering the atmosphere of this world called Telus-Three in our antiquated transport. We will be arriving shortly."

Five minutes later, the unbelievably sophisticated Dontrian spacecraft floated down and landed directly in front of them. It looked like a flying Lamborghini: a pointed golden-brown and white streamlined dream. Closer and closer she came before coming to a halt without lifting a single speck of dust into the air. She measured about thirty metres front to back and hovered ten centimetres above the arid landscape. She was a futuristic machine full of imaginings, yet Alixus had called it antiquated. He stepped out into the now rainless, cool daytime air, followed by two guards. The three of them went directly towards Gor. Philip could hear them speaking in their dialect.

Gor approached them and said, "Thank you, again, my friends, for what you have done. I have to go now." Alixus waved his hand and Gor disappeared.

He stopped where he was without a movement, then sharply turned and looked at Philip. "I never thought I would someday stand on a planet outside our own system while rescuing my son, thanking your kind of the certain atrocities that would have befallen him. I cannot think of sufficient words to explain my thoughts to you, but thank you will have to suffice," he said. "Thank you for what you did for me, and especially how you did it. We watched you from up there; we observed your every move and listened to your every word spoken. Your respect for life eludes us."

Then he took Philip's hand very firmly and shook it. It felt like it was in a vice. He shook all of the Humans' hands.

"I've prepared two things for you, Philip," he said with a faint smile.

"One of them is right here in front of you. I give to you my spacecraft. It has more than everything you would need for the remainder of your journey onward towards Alnilam and eventual trip back to what you call Terron. The second will be waiting for you there in Terron on your arrival. The necessary parties have already been notified." He moved closer. "I will leave you my personal guard Xhor to assist you in finding your friend, the one you call Captain Branigan. He will also explain to you how the landing craft works. Until another moment then." Alixus, with a movement of his wrist, made himself and the rest of his landing party, along with the entire encampment of Dontrian, disappear, leaving Philip and his crew alone with Xhor to find Mike.

The source of the radio signal emanated from where the Flaboxian had come from. It had begun its cycle again. From down here Alana could pinpoint its source easier. They stepped into the Dontrian landing craft. It seemed disrespectful to call it just a landing craft. It was an artefact of prime composition. The control bridge had horizontal and vertical touch pads placed in a semicircle under the observation window. Ramaan, agape, bobbed his head up and around.

"Where's the radio device?" asked Lexia excitedly.

"What weapons does this baby have?" Alana swung around and faced Xhor.

"And the steering, I don't see how it's possible to steer her. Have to steer before you can fire anything, Alana." Ramaan rubbed the back of his neck.

Xhor, noticing their frustrations, smiled in his Dontrian way, moved closer and began to explain in impressive detail how the unimaginable Dontrian craft functioned. They watched and listened. In the middle of the main console which, to Philip's eye, was more a skylighted chamber housing gross and subtle instruments that came with mnemonic amplifiers, were tactility sensitisers and alpha-wave response trainers. He could only guess at what he saw. It was all misty, even the other stuff to which he had no idea. No similarity came to mind.

"It's like flying a bird," commented Xhor. "No bumps, just gliding up and down, left to right. It functions with alpha and beta waves. It reacts to you, the person in charge." What a feeling it would be to be in command of this remarkable navigational instrument of alien design and steer it with mere thought power! It was inconceivable to think that such craftsmanship existed, but here they were inside, observing and learning to use a tacton-thought-powered extraterrestrial vehicle.

"We have deactivated some of the features to prevent future problems," Xhor said, putting a hand onto a touch panel. The tacton vehicle gently lifted without sway and moved towards where the Flaboxian were first spotted. During the trip, Xhor explained the manner in which their thought patterns motivated the tacton vehicle.

At the flattened detonation site, thousands of obsidian burn marks, death blemishes, painted the charred panorama. Disorderly remnants of melted Flaboxian spacecraft and ashes of Platnios and Flaboxian covered the terrain in all directions as far as the eye could see. It was a spooky crematorium.

In the middle of the Telus-Three sitting in a deep, well-protected ditch, they arrived at a single, dirty-looking shed with a long antenna mast bent alongside it. The top had disintegrated. Next to the shed was a parabolic dish.

"Now I know why we could never pinpoint the radio source, look at this hut's location!" said Alana. As Xhor opened the door to the shed, a single Platnios crawled out. It was terror-stricken.

With the speed of a true expert, Xhor quickly moved his hand and the beast disappeared. Lexia looked at him in disbelief. Inside the shed, the transmitter of unknown design was operational. Two magenta lights flicked on and off. Alongside it, a small solar converter provided the power. A single wire ran its course to a computer similar to the one Ramaan had found on Haradan.

"This must be its disk drive. The thing's probably been running forever." Ramaan unplugged it and placed it in his side bag. The transmitter blipped quiet.

Lexia whispered something to Alana, so she moved alongside Xhor.

"Xhor, how do you do that movement with your wrist? You know, that twisty-flick thing you did when the Flaboxian came out of the door."

His smile returned. "It's a technique we are born with, we call it Shamuula."

Lexia, deafened by perplexity and her anxiety to discover more, asked Xhor about the tacton radio device. "How could we reach our home base on Terron from here?"

"You put your left hand on this touch pad and think of the frequency you want. The computer does the rest."

"Go on, Lexia, give it a try," prompted Philip.

Lexia laughed then began thinking of the frequency, two point, four, seven, nine terra-cycles.

The dimly illuminated control panel adjusted itself. A faint bleep emitted from the panel, and the familiar face of the commander showed up in a 3D holographic image.

He was having lunch. "Damn. Where in the dark devil are you calling from?" he asked.

"From the insides of a Dontrian tacton vehicle, sir," they all said in harmony. There was no delay in their transmission.

"Listen here, you guys. We're starting to receive visitors. The Bods are here waiting to see you, and the Peblinus high council is here as well. They won't tell me anything till you arrive. Do you know what's going on?"

"Afraid not, sir; you know as much as we do. Keep them occupied till we get back in a couple of weeks. We've found the source of the radio signal here, but there's still no sign of Mike. I'll let you know the moment we find him. Over and out," said Philip.

Philip began wondering about the pod's homing beacon. Why hadn't he heard it from orbit? Why hadn't Mike activated it before he went missing? This, of course, was a question Philip already knew the answer to: Something must've gone terribly wrong. Philip didn't know what to expect when they found him or the pod. He began bluffing himself. If he was dead, Philip didn't want to see it.

"If you do not know where your friend's space pod is, think of him, think of his landing craft. Put your left hand here and the tacton vehicle will go to it."

Dazed and intrigued, Philip did exactly that. Ever so gently, the Dontrian tacton craft lifted and made off towards the west. They travelled for ten minutes at about fifty kilometres an hour.

As the tacton began reducing speed and eventually stopped, there, lying among rocks, was the debris of the pod. The five badly decomposed bodies lay strewn and broken on the landscape.

Xhor moved himself closer to the bodies and withdrew what resembled a small metallic tube about a foot long. Moving the tube upwards over his head, then from left to right, it formed a blue wavy barrier between the five dead compatriots and themselves.

28. Rebirth

"We have another technique," he explained. "We call it Bradamaar. You would call it limited space-time displacement." Xhor pressed hard on the one end of the tube, and the bluish bubble-shaped shield turned red. At precisely that moment, things within the shield began moving about like in a fast-motion film, as if he was rewinding that particular piece of universe. A twig moved. A missing finger reappeared, a helmet that wasn't there appeared out of nowhere. There was a C-12; it wasn't there a moment ago. The five bodies began to fill out like the long-dead Count Dracula receiving fresh blood a century later. Dislocated bones went into place, muscles formed; skin appeared, an eye popped back in; and then clothes pulled themselves up and over the bodies, dressing them like an invisible mother.

They were witnessing a miracle. A marvellous sensation began creeping through Philip's body. His heart pumped harder as he watched in awe as the five bodies reanimated themselves back into their once-human form.

The process took twenty minutes. Xhor banged the other side of the tube, and the red shield turned blue once more before it fizzled away. He walked to the bodies. Philip watched as each of them made a groan and awkwardly got up. Shorda and Sheppard were still lying there, unable to move. At first, Mike didn't know who they were. He was dazed and unfocused. Riley sat up next in the same manner. Then Chax stumbled to his feet. Shorda and Sheppard, who had been stung by the space beetles, were unable to move. They lay there groaning. Xhor knelt down between them and gave them each an injection below their ears. Two minutes later, they, too, wobbled uneasily to their feet.

Death no longer lay in front of them. It was as it had been, they were together again and they were reunited. Mike and his crew were murmuring and groaning. They placed Mike and the others onto the tacton vehicle and shot off towards their awaiting pod.

It was Sheppard who spoke first. "Agh, where am I?" His whispery voice exuded pain.

"Hello, Sheppard, old friend," said Philip. "Do you know who I am?"

The eyes squinted. "Hello, Philip. Tell me where I am. My God, my head hurts."

"You're safe, you all are. You're going back to Terron."

Xhor told Baygorn his reaction was perfectly normal. The microhealing would take some weeks before they were fully themselves again.

When they reached the pod, Xhor told them it was time to depart. He gave Philip a small, square, transparent container with a single blue button.

"If at any time you need us, place your left forefinger on this blue surface and think of us. We will come to you wherever you are." He disappeared in the same manner Alixus had.

They clambered into the pod and shot off to the waiting encampments of the Bods and Peblinus. When they reached the Bod encampment, Ramaan asked about the hatched eggs that Floyd had sent from Telus-Four. A Bod, hearing his words, rushed off to a laboratory and reappeared a few seconds later.

"There's no sign of them anywhere. They've—they've disappeared! We were so concerned about the arrival of these Flaboxian things I didn't even think about them. Damn." The Bod was furious.

"We're still waiting for the bad guys. Where are they?" The Bod directed a head movement at Philip.

"Not today, my friend," Philip said as Mike got up and walked behind him.

"Let me help you with that, Philip," Mike said, clearing his throat and holding his head.

Philip dropped one of the newly collected blue-rays and placed his hands on Mike's shoulders.

"Damn, you're a sight for sore eyes! Welcome back, old friend."

Mike gave off a lemon-slice smile. Slowly the five of them regained full consciousness and started murmuring. Ramaan and Lexia were repacking the blue-rays into the back compartment of the pod, when both Mike and Sheppard started to help. Phillip's crew didn't stop them; instead, they looked at the five of them and began to laugh.

The best thing Philip could do now was to put Mike and his crew into the *Renaissance* and send them back to Terron where they could rest. Leaving Ramaan and Lexia with the tacton craft, Philip set off in the pod in the direction of the *Renaissance*.

The *Renaissance* was still orbiting Telus-Three, waiting for the signal from her own Sentrywatcher to enable the main engines. He still had one hour; plenty of time to board her again and place them in their quarters before returning to the *Excelsior*. Baygorn went with him. He was the only one who knew how to open the outer hatches of the *Renaissance* without losing patience. Philip explained the situation to Mike and his crew as he, Alana and Baygorn entered the *Renaissance* for the last time.

"Now you rest, you hear? We'll see you shortly on Terron in good health. Sentrywatcher will look after you." Mike mumbled something. To this day, Philip doesn't know what it was.

Ramaan and Lexia were already on-board the *Excelsior* when Philip arrived. "How's Mike?" enquired Lexia.

"Still groggy," said Philip. "It's better for them to be on Terron amongst friends. They'll have the best medical treatment there, and they'll regain full consciousness and health."

Philip contacted Terron and informed them about the arrival of Mike and his crew aboard the *Renaissance*.

Jim said that it was the best news he had heard in a long time. "Oh, another thing, Philip, I have more of your friends here. They call themselves Magnopods. We've been mind-chatting all morning. They give me the best references of you and your crew. They're looking forward to seeing you again."

What on earth was going on? thought Philip. *Why was everyone meeting in Terron?*

Alana and Ramaan completed the final tweaking of the controls and set course for Fornax. During the journey, Philip was thinking about the safety of Terron. There were so many new species; yet, with this cross-culture mix literally on their doorstep and now under one roof, Philip knew and felt that Terron would be safer than it had ever been.

Fornax was the smallest of the Alnilam worlds. Ramaan gazed at its dull-blue volcanic sphere creeping onto the scanner. Their nearness to Alnilam was beginning to show, as the white star of class B0 was now full on their visors. The surface composition of Fornax, mainly carbon and iron, made it invisible to the detecting methods used by the Charon telescope years before. It had completely missed this barren, tough world. Sentrywatcher revealed only one form of life: Peblinus.

"What on earth could they possibly want down there?" commented Ramaan.

"Well, to start with, there are 40,000 of them, very active, too," replied Alana. This time they put their weaponry on the tacton vehicle and readied it for the landing.

Ramaan moved closer. "The *Excelsior* has already recognised the tacton as one of ours. We can open and close hatches on the *Excelsior* from the console. We have the same control we have in the pod! This thing is amazing; there are no heat shields like on our pod," added Ramaan, rubbing his hand over the outer hull before closing the hatch. "The tacton has an automatic heat-correcting mechanism." Ramaan placed his right hand on a touch pad, opened the *Excelsior's* external hatch and released them directly over hell. "Going down!"

The ride without turbulence, bump or sway took fourteen minutes to reach the surface.

Ramaan uttered loudly, "The pod would have taken over an hour. What a ride, so smooth." He lifted himself from the Dontrian seat and climbed out with an ear-to-ear smile. Ramaan thought about reverse engineering and how the pod would be, using Dontrian technology and some of their own. There again, maybe the Dontrian wouldn't mind parting with some schematics, as Ramaan couldn't possibly deface such a wondrous gem.

Fornax was another mine. The population, however, had heard nothing about Philip's arrival and immediately ran towards them with weapons.

"What's all this? Now wait a minute. Hold it!" Philip shouted, moving to the front. "What's this, what's going on? We come in peace. Look, I don't know what stories you've been hearing, or where you might've heard them. Ask us if you want the facts. Now, if you don't mind putting down your weapons, we are not the bad guys here." The Peblinus lowered the weapon.

"What's going on here? What is this place? What are you mining?"

The Peblinus answered, "Tellurium."

"My God, it seems wherever we go, all you do is mine tellurium," said Philip, noticing that one of the others was still pointing his weapon towards them. He quickly lowered it after Ramaan's drilling look made him feel stupid.

"We've been asked by the Rigelian Council to make six fuel pipelines and eight ion dispersion valves for two spacecraft. We got the order from Telus-Two two months ago. It's a strict deadline, the spacecraft are almost finished."

"Two spacecraft? Don't you have enough in your arsenal already?" Philip pried.

"These are different, they're gigantic cargo freighters. Some of us are going to move to the Antares system to start over."

"Move? But why?" asked Philip.

"Our lives in these parts are very difficult. We want to move on and begin afresh."

"Oh come on, it can't be all that bad."

"Wrong. There will never be peace between the Human and the Peblinus!" said another guard, suddenly raising his basic weapon.

Philip kept the others behind him. He was not afraid. "We can help you resolve your political issues and your search for peace. I can also assure you, you won't find it in the Antares system."

"But Shar's officials told us that Humans kill and destroy the Peblinus wherever they go."

"It seems you have been out of touch with what is going on. I take it you believed them? You really, honestly believed them? That was almost a year ago. We are on a peaceful, research mission. We're not here to harm anyone unless we are provoked," added Philip.

Philip began explaining the story of Shar. He then told them about their Platnios. "Here they are called Flaboxian. There's a mass meeting on Terron, our home base. It appears you're all invited." The Peblinus relaxed. Philip continued, "If we all lived in harmony as one gigantic being in this infinitesimal piece of the galaxy, you wouldn't need your two spacecraft. There would be no need to run away." The guard finally holstered his weapon and led them towards their mining operation.

The typical inclined Peblinus design went down towards the edge of the planet's asthenosphere. The exterior was bustling with life. The Peblinus workers seemed fatigued and were in some way glad to see them. Obviously, some rumours had made their way across the gulf of space. Their head guard had a deadline to meet, and the workers had to comply with his orders. The Peblinus were working hard to fulfil their two-month deadline.

Making friends here would be easy. Wherever Philip went, the stirred emotions became more and more evident. Their presence enhanced morale, even amongst the Peblinus.

After asking around, Ramaan discovered that the mine, with its thirty-five kilometre depth, had 12,000 permanently based men in the mine at all levels. At the bottom of this, they were about to open another entrance, to continue down twenty kilometres. Apparently, the hotter they extracted the tellurium, the purer it became.

The mine was the deepest known facility in the system, and they were here to witness the opening gala. The shaft extended all the way towards the beginning of hell itself. The walls were ovens of over 400 degrees. Familiar gigantic funnels on the horizon spewed forth vapour and unwanted heat from the depths. Vehicles were coming and going all the time, and all were extremely busy. The second section was due to open shortly, and one of the Peblinus workers explained its development.

"We began the second shaft a little over three months ago. Our mechanical worm drilled a parallel tunnel to the same dimensions you already see here on the surface. When the two tunnels connected at the base thirty-five kilometres down, we made the first-base level. As soon as we'd finished the first base, we proceeded deeper, only this time, we went down at 25 degrees. Any more inclination and our transport would have become ineffective, especially if they are loaded with material. Air circulation at this depth also proved to be a real challenge, as the oxygen became volatile and explosive, so we had to install special ventilators. They even said when the worm drill left the new mine shaft and directed itself to the surface, it was bright orange. The thing took over a month to cool down."

The Peblinus worker dismissed himself and waddled off once again towards the mine shaft and out of sight. In the distance Mount Sheldon was erupting.

Ramaan and Baygorn clenched their noses. The air was heavy, laden with sulphur dioxide, making Lexia's nose hurt when she breathed. "How do you manage to breath with all this sulphur in the air?" she asked a passing worker.

"We're accustomed to it. We don't smell it anymore." He, too, disappeared towards the mine shaft.

Mount Sheldon proposed no threat to them. From their distance, she was nothing more than a distant cone abruptly lit by sporadic fire and flames. The lookout posts reported that remote rivers of lava were pouring in the other direction.

They retreated inside one of the compounds and ate before attending the opening ceremony, which was due to begin in a short while. Two hundred affiliated workers had gathered outside the complex, laxly scrutinizing six long tables filled with food and beverages. Peblinus workers anxiously stared down at sandwiches and canapés. Alana saw one reach down, grabbing two before stuffing them into his pocket.

The head guard walked over and pompously took his place, making rude comments to whoever came into firing distance. "They push us too far. I lost my best friend down there."
The whole area became deceptively silent. The ceremonial area was well illuminated and had big spot lamps efficiently doing their jobs.

From her perspective, many had died due to exhaustion. Lexia told Philip that two Peblinus had died due to heat burns used by insufficient security in the lower levels only three days before.

At precisely that moment, the ground started to shake and rumble. One of the wall lamps suspended by a metallic bar fell to the ground, as well as an overly tired Peblinus began swaying to compensate for the change in ground direction. As quickly as it had started, it stopped and all continued as before.

Philip asked one of the passing workers if this happened frequently, and he said, "That's the first one in over two years. The only rumblings you hear around here are the stomachs of the workers."

The head guard continued sitting on his throne issuing orders. *All he needs is a whip*, thought Alana.

29. Threat

One of the lookout posts shouted down. "Sir, sir, there's something on the horizon! It's coming directly towards us." One of the guards got up from his chair and rushed up the metallic ladder that flanked the lookout post and grabbed the pair of binoculars the worker was holding. The guard began rattling off words, hardly making any sense.

Lexia said, "I think he's saying something about a gigantic river of lava coming towards us."

Ramaan pushed past some workers and climbed the ladder to take a look. "Shit, it's a big one, four metres high at least. It's coming straight for us!" Ramaan jumped off the platform without using the ladder and ran towards Philip.

"A secondary side vent must have been dislodged by the tremor earlier. It's coming straight this way. The pressure below must've forced up the magma." The only thing they could do was to get into their tacton vehicle and use the on-board weapons to divert the wall of certain death to another direction.

Ramaan and Lexia were by now fairly well trained in their tacton vehicle and showed Philip briefly how the weapons console worked. As the tacton lifted into the heavens, Ramaan saw the immensity of the threat the wall of lava heading directly for the Peblinus mining community.

"Look at it," said Baygorn. "Damn, it must be hundreds of metres wide!" The brilliance of the blue-white lava flow was as blinding as it was unstoppable. The only advantage of the situation was that the wall, being in this overly liquid state, could easily be diverted by perforating a ten- or more metres-deep ditch with their on-board weapons system.

Philip fired the laser cannon by placing his left hand on the weapons console. Firing lasers by thinking took a bit of getting used to, but once he got the hang of it, the laser fire became an extension of his left hand. It became an extension of his mind.

He could even adjust the potency of the beam by using his own alpha-beta wave patterns. Philip felt like a god.

His lasers dug a two-kilometre ditch as far away from the complex as possible and forced the oncoming lava in another direction. When the first section of lava discovered the channel, it automatically rerouted itself to the new bearing. The tacton infrared scanner indicated that the lava had a temperature of over 3,000 degrees and would have incinerated anything with the slightest touch. The complex was safe for the moment, but they stayed in the air to be sure there was no further threat.

Alana landed them an hour later. All Peblinus, including the guards, came to thank them for saving them. They also told them that they had just received word that a major conference was about to start in Alnitak. "It's on all radio frequencies," they said. "Listen."

Philip placed his ear to their radio receiver and heard the news. Philip walked to the tacton vehicle and contacted the commander to find out what the dickens was going on.

"Philip, I have someone here that wants to say hello."

"Hello, do you remember me?" It was the Sintor. "We got wind of this big social get-together, bash thing and decided we couldn't miss it for anything. When will you be returning?"

"In the next couple of days. We look forward to seeing you again. Hope everything is to your liking. Are you being treated well?"

"Splendidly, thank you."

"That's good, I am glad. Can you put me back with my commander, please?"

When Jim came back on speaker, Philip asked him if an outpost probe had detected the *Renaissance*. Jim told him that the *Renaissance* had already been spotted by an outer-region reconnaissance scout and was due to be picked up shortly by the salvage team. "He'll be here before you."

The radio went silent and Philip smiled. As he turned around, a group of Peblinus, including two head guards, had gathered up behind him. One of them walked up to him. "If you hadn't been here, I'd hate to think what would have happened. On behalf of all of us, I'd like to express our gratitude."

"Why don't you lighten up a bit on the workers?" said Philip. "They are good and decent people. Now, about those freighters. You've obviously heard about the meeting, and we are waiting for further orders, waiting to see what happens. In the meantime, feed these people and give them some time off; they need it. We are going to Terron right away before going to Telus-Two."

Ramaan set course for the *Excelsior*. "All right, let's go find out what's happening on Terron," said Alana, peering through the tacton console. Sentrywatcher acknowledged and the tacton lifted gently into the air.

In a matter of two years, after their departure from Earth, the TGC engine had been made obsolete and redundant. "Advancement"; that was what they'd called it. With their new motors, the ones that Jim had installed on the *Excelsior* during their last visit, the immense journey of almost one hundred light-years to Terron would take them a little over four days. The human race was advancing as it had never done before, and their improvements were astoundingly evident. Slow-moving stars became streaks of light as Alana once again pressed the eager red button.

The *Excelsior* automatically began to reduce speed as they drew nearer to the system of Alnitak. At 600,000 kilometres per second, Alana steered them towards the last planet, known astronomically as Cornopea. Terron was in a fixed orbit five hundred miles above, like a monstrous space platform. Strands grew as they got closer, becoming hallways and links to other portions of Terron. Dozens of antennae of all shapes and sizes covered a control centre attached to Terron with a walkway. More than 40,000 scientists of every category worked and relied upon the integrity of the others as Terron grew and grew.

Cornopea was an iron world. It provided the supplies of metals and alloys they used in the construction of Terron. Jim had constructed a refinery on the surface, and freighters were continuously coming and going, offloading supplies, enlarging the interminable and formidable ever-growing Terron.

The refinery called Messina was coexistent. It was also self-sustaining, a blossoming city constructed under a thermal protective metallic structure allowing easy access by the freighters. In the centre, the landing bay had neatly parked vehicles in their allocated sections. They saw the Sintor craft and a replica of what the Dontrian had left them on Telus-Three: a Gorinos craft, a Bod transport, two Peblinus vehicles, and three others they couldn't recognise.

"Hello, Jim, requesting permission to land."

"Nice to hear your voice. Welcome back, Phil. Permission granted," said Jim's chirpy voice.

Leaving the *Excelsior* in orbit, they made their descent towards Terron in the tacton and settled her down next to the Dontrian vehicle.

Climbing out, they walked into the bay area where a warm reception waited, complete with a red carpet lying across the floor. Twenty armed, fully dressed guards, ten per side, lowered their weapons as they passed by. The two at the end escorted them from the entrance hatch into the main corridor.

"This can't be for us," exclaimed Baygorn, looking at what was going on. "Just look at this place. In the few weeks we've been away. I mean, just look at all this new stuff. Not even the landing bay was here on our last visit last month. How do they do it so fast?" The escort led them directly to the central committee room where everyone was anxiously waiting.

The escort then guided them to an elongated table laden with exotic flowers and notepads and jars of refreshments. Inscribed name tags hugged tops of elegant marble tables. Each of them sat down at their allocated place and waited for the presentation.

Jim entered the room with four Bods. Walking behind them was Lord Betican and his son. Jim was the highest-ranking official on Terron and he made all the decisions, but on this one occasion, he was on a live video conference call direct from Earth. Someone wanted a say in the matter.

As Alixus and Gor sat down, Mike and his crew were wheeled in through the main door and sat alongside their table. Everyone was there, from the Sintor, Gorinos and five Peblinus. Two Magnopods squirmed in and slithered to their places. A numbing silence took control of the conference room as the remainder of the High Commission took their places.

Jim abruptly stood up. "May we have your attention, please?" He rang a small bell on the side of the table. "Sorry to have made you wait; I think that I speak for everyone present." As he terminated his short introduction, ten guards brought the captured Flaboxian into the meeting area, safely placed behind its glass protective barrier. They put it in the far corner for everyone to see.

It was nothing more than a rebellious, belligerent genetic failure whose only objective was to get out of its glass cage and destroy anything in its way. Its inadequate pincers were unable to break the armoured glass, so instead, it just sat there exhausted and staring at everyone with invisible eyes.

Just then, a scientific investigator strolled in and immediately started placing information on the laser projector. It was part of their accumulation of many months of hard work, revealing the truths of their distant and not-so-distant past to everyone present.

Mike gaped in awe at the spectacle when he saw what was before him. "My God, I had no idea!"

Jim continued with his speech. "It has been brought to our attention that on planets in both the Mintaka and Alnilam systems, all nations present here today, with the exception of the Dontrian, Gorinos and the Sintor, have caused harm or even death to others by their own greed." He paused.

"Before you, you'll find the reports that were given to me by the *Excelsior* crew. They have given us their findings and beliefs down to the last detail. Each of you present has a copy of the report in your respective language." Jim nodded and looked out the door.

"Just as important, our scientific workers have been analysing the Blagorian. They reassure us, if we leave them in peace, there will be no further incidents."

As Jim finished, a scientist roamed into the briefing room with a Blagorian slithering and squishing about behind him. Nonchalantly, it jumped up onto a vacant platform and flattened itself like bread dough. Silence quelled the conference room as eyes of all shapes studied the metallic ball the size of a deflated football only metres away. Some were trembling.

The conference room was broken into four sections. The ten of them situated at the back side-by-side, sat at a long table. Jim and his self-nominated brigade of seven were facing Philip and his crew. In each corner, two security personnel looked straight ahead like the Buckingham Palace guards, each carrying a blue-ray pointing upwards.

Above them and above Jim, ten monitors mounted on the wall were filled with anxious faces. Eagerness paid strict attention to what was going on. One of the faces Philip recognised. Bernt Sullivan was the man responsible for his being here. During Phillip's absence, they'd made him deputy general at NASA.

To Philip's left, the Magnopods appeared relaxed on a pedestal. Next to them were two Gorinos dressed in tight-fitting, sinister, dark garments. Their throat guns lay flaccid and pointed downwards. The Peblinus High Council sat there, all flustered and nervous with the presence of the Blagorian. Philip could feel the tension between them. To his right the Bods and the Sintor were talking together, catching up on lost times, while the Dontrian did nothing except scrutinize everyone present in the room. Xhor was amongst them.

30. Treaty

Between the laughter and silence, Jim's voice once again erupted. "There is an excellent possibility we can coexist in harmony as one singular being under a one-government rule. As we have experienced in the past, even in nature, there will be conflicts. It would be normal during the melding process.

To begin with, the protocols have been written; we will allow all races present here today to coalesce. We will watch and study them. Call it a giant cooking pot of cultures, if you will. This commencement begins here on Terron and three planets from the Mintaka system. The chosen destinies will be Rindor, Ganus and Haradan. We feel it would be adequately suitable for this purpose. Once we have found a suitable planet in the Alnilam system, families will begin settling there, too. Three hundred families or Terron-farmers have already been selected and await immediate placement during the forthcoming month." Jim took a long sip of water.

"We will finally return to what I firmly believe we were many tens of thousands of years ago. The Dontrian, Bods, Gorinos and the Peblinus have decided to travel to Earth at their earliest convenience to assist in public relations. This will culminate, ladies and gentlemen, in what will possibly be the most important and beneficial act of science since the beginning of time as we know it. I believe four of the Sintor will be accompanying them." The ten figures on the monitors expressed their approval.

"After their arrival on Earth, they will select adequate candidates to travel with them to their respective worlds for an inter-cultural swap. Two ambassadors will remain on Earth. This has turned out to be a most exciting time for us all." Jim looked towards the tabletop.

"After long discussions with the others present today, it is in all our best interests to form the United Interstellar Federation of Planets, the UIFP. The nations present will nominate two governors and two ambassadors."

Jim stood and looked in Philip's direction. "This, of course, ladies and gentlemen, wouldn't have been possible without the valiant efforts of the ten men and women who sit before you."

At that moment, all eyes focussed upon Philip and Mike and their crews.

"Secondly, due to the absolute and complete success of Mission Outbreak, it is my pleasure to announce that Captain Philip Wakefield and Captain Michael Branigan and their teams be awarded with the correct military ranks due to them. Let it be known and for the record, Captain Wakefield and Captain Branigan be given the rank of colonel. Their team members, without exception, have been designated as of this moment, the rank of captain. Please come forward and collect your medals."

Philip helped Mike hobble to the front. Jim gave Philip a smile. "Good to see you, Philip." They shook hands. "This couldn't have happened to a better man," he whispered eagerly.

After the presentation of rank, Jim cleared his throat. "Now, where were we? Especially you, Colonel Wakefield, it was you, without your knowledge, who actually summoned this meeting. All of us present today wish to offer our gratitude."

Everyone who had arms then rose and clapped. The ten figures on the monitors back on Earth, too, showed their gratitude. Mike, standing by Philip's side, clapped, too. Seeing that made Philip feel good. He had so much admiration for the man, and he was glad to see him alive and well again.

"Not only have you summoned this meeting, in return you have revealed our ancestry. Our past has come full circle. We on Terron believe that there is a common denominator between all our species. Maybe hundreds of thousands of years ago we were one. I will inform you that we are working hard at finding out what our common roots are. No disrespect intended to our Flaboxian friend here." The Flaboxian sensed Jim was talking about it and began a futile struggle against the armoured glass.

Jim looked at the struggling creature. "This is the result of unguided research," said Jim, tapping the cage with a cane.

The Peblinus looked in the other direction.

"This type of research could lead to our eventual destruction. This specimen is going to be dissected and analysed." He stared directly at the Flaboxian. "We're going to suck you dry and find out what makes you tick."

The Flaboxian went berserk.

"Unification and symbiosis, that's the key issue here. We will not tolerate violence of any category or under any circumstance. Any one singular act of immoral intimidation resulting in the harm of another shall mean the breach of this contract. The effects and ripples could be disastrous for all those present. The necessary documents have been drawn up and prepared."

Jim turned his head. "They just await your signature, Philip."

Philip bent towards Jim, gave him a hug, and shook hands.

"This is a big day for all of us, my friend." Philip signed the twenty-six documents.

"To each one of us, from today, we have a responsibility and a duty to fulfil. Speaking of duty and apart from being captains, I would like to offer to the crew of the *Renaissance* the Medal of Honour. Please come over and receive them. If you are not capable, our staff will help you." Mike's crew slowly hobbled towards Jim's table.

Mike, standing beside Philip, broke in as his crew claimed their awards. "There is a part of the story you don't know." He paused a few seconds. "We followed orders and investigated a signal that emanated from the surface of Telus-Three. As we approached orbit, space beetles attacked our spacecraft, the *Renaissance*, so we fled to Telus-Three. As we were about to land, our engines were clogged with these beetles and it became inoperative. We crash-landed! We had all lost our lives. We were dead!" There was silence in the conference room as he breathed in deeply.

"Philip later came with the Dontrian technology and restored us back to life." Everyone again stood up and clapped. Mike returned to his chair.

At that point, a scientist came into the meeting room carrying the computer they had salvaged on Telus-Three. Jim hooked it onto the display screen for all to see. The video snippets that followed brought a new light onto the situation. Of the fifty alien species, only thirty were recognizable. Not even the Dontrian knew some of them. The meeting hall came alive with gossip.

"Quiet, please. It has come to my attention that a Bod freighter carrying five hundred scientists is en route for the Andromeda sector. Apparently, it has already passed Mirach. We have concluded they are going to have problems, serious problems when they arrive. They are heading into completely uncharted territory, and judging by what we have just seen on this video feed, some of these species don't look friendly.

"The Bods have already given us the schematics of this engine. We are working hard at producing a similar vehicle ready for use in the next couple of months. With any luck, our spacecraft will intercept and cut off the Bod freighter before its arrival and before it's too late. The rescue team will be heavily armed, so the sooner we leave, the sooner we can intercept the Bod freighter and save them. With the technology and data handed to us by the *Excelsior* crew, we're at the beginning of a new epoch. A doorway before unthinkable has already been opened for our careful passing. A recovery craft is already en route to Phot to recover the information in the subterranean library they discovered. We have also selected and designated twenty families who will, with immediate effect, depart for the unoccupied city of Sporna. There, they will live and prosper. These families of diverse categories will have a permanent video link to Terron and sufficient supplies necessary for the duration of their five-year stay and, of course, they will be fully armed. There they will search for Haak survivors. In times of war there are always survivors hiding somewhere."

Philip never found out where the video came from. Instead, he sceptically reviewed its contents time and time again. Why were video images mixed in with an SOS? Maybe it was a warning after all, a subtle warning of what was out there. He also never gave the book he'd found in the subterranean bunker to the committee. Instead, he placed it on his shelf in his new living quarters on Terron. He looked upon it every now and then, sharing it with the rest. They glimpsed at ungodly pages, reliving the most incredible voyage into the unknown.

Before him, Jim had the treaties waiting his signature. It was a procurement of peace. Everyone in the meeting room came forward, putting pen to historical paper.

And so began this little slice of history, this reign of strengthening humanity. The United Interstellar Federation of Planets was formed this 11th day of April, 2103.

They'd leave Telus-Two and the other planets for another day.

Addendum

Just as there have always been conflicting beliefs concerning ancient constructions (the who's and the when's), the real archaeological discovery is still believed to be out there somewhere waiting for man to find. Historical evidence also confirms that over the past 10,000 years, we have been quietly visited many times. The author believes they have been amongst, mingling, and observing us since the beginning of recorded time.

The author himself also confesses to have been witness to three sightings on two continents. "No Earthly vehicle could produce what I just saw," he said early one October morning at 2:10. It was a blue, circular light carrying a gentle hum that suddenly stopped before turning at a 90-degree angle. What could it have been? Where did it come from?

It would seem that we are nearing the time for contact. Welcome to the evolution.

Dear Reader,
If you enjoyed this book, please tell your friends,
and write a review on GoodReads.com and Amazon.
Thank you, Michael

www.ingramcontent.com/pod-product-compliance
Lightning Source LLC
Chambersburg PA
CBHW070537260626
47161CB00002B/422

*9 7 8 1 9 4 7 6 4 6 0 7 0 *